ALSO BY THE AUTHOR

Whitegirl

My Notorious Life

A NOVEL

KATE MANNING

SCRIBNER

New York London Toronto Sydney New Delhi

Scribner
A Division of Simon & Schuster, Inc.
1230 Avenue of the Americas
New York, NY 10020

First Scribner hardcover edition September 2013

SCRIBNER and design are registered trademarks of The Gale Group, Inc.,
used under license by Simon & Schuster, Inc., the publisher of this work.

For information about special discounts for bulk purchases,
please contact Simon & Schuster Special Sales at 1-866-506-1949 or
business@simonandschuster.com.

The Simon & Schuster Speakers Bureau can bring authors to your
live event. For more information or to book an event contact the
Simon & Schuster Speakers Bureau at 1-866-248-3049 or
visit our website at www.simonspeakers.com.

Manufactured in the United States of America

1   3   5   7   9   10   8   6   4   2

Library of Congress Control Number: 2012031031

ISBN 978-1-4516-9806-0
ISBN 978-1-4516-9808-4 (ebook)

For my children,
Carey, Oliver, and Eliza
And my husband,
Carey

Note

*T*he following memoir was discovered in a bank vault belonging to my great-great-grandmother Ann, upon her death, in 1925, at the age of seventy-eight. The account was written over many years, in a barely decipherable hand, in the pages of seven leatherbound diaries, a pattern of forget-me-nots adorning the corners of the paper. Some light corrections had been made, evidently by Ann's husband, my great-great grandfather, with some words blacked out. Errors of grammar, punctuation, and usage were, however, left intact. Pasted in were newspaper clippings, correspondence between Ann and a respected New York City charity, and letters from Ann's sister, her lawyer, and others.

Perhaps due to its controversial nature, this material was hidden by the family for almost a century, mysteriously ending up in a hatbox in the attic of my father's house, where I stumbled on it last year, after his death. My siblings and I were most astonished to discover that our family had such a scandalous American character among our forebears. "Madame" had not been mentioned in the stories handed down to us by our parents and grandparents, who include doctors, bankers, academics, barristers, and politicians. In spite of sharp disagreement in the family over certain matters described here, in the interests of future scholars and historians—and to correct the public record—I have decided to make this account public without further comment.

—Teresa Smithhurst-O'Rourke, PhD
Trinity College, Dublin

Chapter One

Confession

*I*t was me who found her. April 1, 1880. The date is engraved on my story same as it is on the headstone, so cold and solid there under the pines. What happened that morning hurts me to this day, enrages me still, though many years have passed.

The time was just before dawn. She was there in the tub. It had claw feet, gold faucets. Marble was everywhere in that room, so magnificent. A French carpet. A pair of velvet settees, a dressing table, candelabra, powders and pomades, all deluxe. I knew something was wrong right away. When I knocked I knew. There was not no noise of bathing, just that slow drip. That plink of water landing on water, so dreadful. I went in and there she was. A scarf of red across her shoulders, down her chest. The water was red and cold with all her life leaked out. A bloodbath.

My hands were trembling. Terrible sounds strangled in my throat, quiet so as not to wake the house. My little daughter and my husband were fast asleep. The maid was not yet up.

Mother of God she was dead. I collapsed down at the vanity reeling and keening. I couldn't look but I had to. The scene was reflected so clearly in the mirror, and strange, how it was serene, almost. She seemed at rest. The way her hair fell you did not see the red cut. You saw the profile of the nose, the chin. She was a bather in a painting, so peaceful, but I hated her for what she done to herself. Even after how I cared for her so long. She would be my undoing now, too, not just her own. Who would believe a suicide? They would say I killed her. They would write me again in the headlines, as Murderess. Hag of Misery. She-devil. How they'd lick their chops. They'd come for me with their shackles and their oakum and their lies, then put me away for good unless by some conjurer's snap I could get her poor corpse out of the water and away down the stairs and out to Fifth Avenue to disappear. It was the very morning of my Trial. I was due in court in three hours.

What could I do? What would happen to me now? If I could change places with her. The thought came to me. If only it was me dead there in the water.

I imagined it, picking up the knife.

My troubles would end. I'd not be a grief to anyone. If only I was dead. These ideas raced now through the panic. I looked again in the mirror at her reflection over my shoulder and seen all of a sudden how it wasn't a bad resemblance. Our age was close enough. That black hair. And it was the mirror, that morning, the way we were doubled in it, that shown me the way to my escape.

Fast, I took the rings off my fingers. The gems from my ears. I put them on her. Her skin was wet and cold as fish, a shock to the touch. The diamonds sparkled on her delicate dead hands, on the collops of her lobes.

Why? I asked her, silent as I worked. But I knew why. Why was not the mystery.

There was not no choice. They would come for me. I ran now. I packed a bag. A reticule filled with cash. He helped me with it and kissed me good-bye, both of us afraid.

—Hurry, he said. —You got no time to waste.

My throat closed with panic and sadness. But I left him to it, my husband, to carry it off, to say it was me dead in the bath. He'd know what to do. He took the risk of it. He knew people. He had connections of influence. They'd believe him. He said we'd find each other later. There was no choice but to trust him. She was dead and the traps would be knocking any minute. There wasn't no other way. I went out the back door in a hat and veil, which was nothing special at our address. Ladies was always coming and going in their veils and disguises, the curtains of their victorias drawn. Half of them would have worn mustaches or pup tents, anything not to be recognized departing from my notorious parlor. I went east across Fifty

Second Street on foot, as it would not be advisable to use the driver. My carriage was well known as myself in all parts of town. I got on the omnibus down the Avenue, and from there I was off to the railyards, to book a ticket.

Meanwhile at the so-called Halls of Justice downtown, my enemies was coiled snakes lying in wait. How eager they was to see me in the dock at last. How disappointed, how outraged they would be, to receive a telegram from my lawyer with the news. The case was a bust. Stop. The accused was dead. Stop. Madame DeBeausacq a suicide. At first they scoffed and pshawed under their preposterous hairy mustaches. It was somebody's idea of a joke, they said. They noted the date: April 1. They were sure that soon I would show up so they could smite me with their sanctimony and their outrage. But I did not show up, and soon half them toads had a new theory. That I was murdered, that a Tammany hoodlum snuffed me out to hush me up, to kill my society secrets along with me. Whatever they thought, the b*****ds was stunned out of what wits they had, which was not many. In the end, they celebrated. They bragged. They got me, was their feeling. Finally they got me. They said I would take my secrets to the grave.

They should be so lucky. The grave under the white pines at Sleepy Hollow has its own secrets. She died to keep hers safe. But I'm d****d if I'll keep mine. Here they are, written out from the beginning, from the time of my early life and up till now.

As for them c**ks***ers, I have just one thing to say: APRIL FOOL.

BOOK ONE

Ax of Kindness

Chapter Two

For Bread Alone

*I*n the year 1860, when the Western Great Plain of America was the home of the buffalo roaming, the cobbled hard pavement of New York City was the roofless and only domicile of thirty-five thousand children. In our hideous number we scraps was cast outdoors or lost by our parents, we was orphans and half orphans and runaways, the miserable offspring of Irish and Germans, Italians and Russians, servants and slaves, Magdalenes and miscreants, all the unwashed poor huddled slubs who landed yearning and unlucky on the Battery with nothing to own but our muscles and teeth, the hunger of our bellies. Our Fathers and Mothers produced labor and sweat and disease and babies that would've been better off never born. The infant ones, small as a drop of dew on a cabbage leaf, was left wrapped in newspaper and still bloody on the doorsteps of churches, in the aisles of dry goods stores. Others among us was not older than two, just wee toddlers with the skulls still soft when they was thrust Friendless upon the paving stones of Broadway. These kids dressed in bits and pickings. They begged what they ate or filched it. Many never had known a shoe. The girls started out young to sell themselves and the boys turned to thuggery. Half the babies dropped at the foundling hospital died before they had a birthday. The rest of the so-called street Arabs was lucky if they lived to twenty.

Me and my sister Dutch and my brother Joe was nearly permanent among this sorry crowd, but by the mossy skin of our teeth we got turned from that path by a stranger who came upon us and exchanged our uncertain fate for another, equally uncertain.

The day in question I was not more than twelve years of age. Turned up nose, raggedy dress, button boots full of holes and painful in the toe, dark black hair I was vain of pulled back, but no ribbon. And my father's eyes, the color of the Irish sea, he always said, blue as waves. I was two heads taller than a barstool. My legs was sticks, my ribs a ladder. I was not no beauty like Dutch, but I managed with what I got. And That Day we three got our whole new proposition. It walked right up and introduced itself.

Hello there, wayfarers.

We stood in the doorway of the bakery. If you stayed there long enough, you could get maybe a roll that was old, maybe the heels they would give you of the loaves. We were not particular. We would eat crumbs they swept out for the birds. We was worse than birds, we was desperate as rats. That day the smell was like a torture, of the bread baking, them cakes and the pies and them chocolate éclairs like all of your dreams coming up your nose and turning to water in your mouth. We Muldoons had not eaten since yesterday. It was February or maybe March, but no matter the date, we were frozen, no mittens, no hats, us girls without no woolies under our skirts, just britches full of moth bites. We had baby Joe warm in our arms, heavy as beer in a half keg. Dutch had my muffler I gave her, she was so cold. We wrapped it around my head and her head both, and there we stood looking like that two-headed calf I saw once in Madison Square. Two heads, four legs, one body. Two heads is better than one, but we children should've been smarter that day and seen what was coming.

A customer started in the door. This big fat guy with big fat neck rolls over the collar of his coat, like a meat scarf.

Dutch said, —Mister? with those blue eyes she has, such jewelry in her face, sparkling sadlike eyes.

The Meat Neck Gent said, —Go home to your Ma.

Dutch said back, —We ain't got no Ma.

—Yeah yeah yeah, he said. —I heard that before, now beat it.

—Please mister, I said. —We ain't. It's the truth. (Though it wasn't exactly.)

—Just one a them rolls or a bannock of bread.

And the guy said, —Beat it, again. He was a miserable cockroach in fine boots, but he was not the one who ruined us, that was the kindness of strangers.

So we started to cry very quiet now, me and Dutch, because we had not had food since yesterday noon, standing there the whole morning with pain like teeth in our guts. The scarf around our head was frozen solid with our tears and snuffle.

Along at last came another customer, quite fancy. This one had the type of a beard that straps under the chin, and a clump of hair left stranded in the center of his bald dome that we saw when he removed his tall hat, like a rainbarrel on his head.

With the tears fresh in our eyes, we said, —Hey Mister.

—Why hello there, wayfarers.

Right away he got down low, peering hard at us like we were interesting, and asked in the voice of an angel, —Why you poor children! Why are you here in the cold? Don't cry, sweet innocents. Come inside and warm yourselves.

—Nossir, I said, —we ain't allowed. They tell us scram and kick us.

—That's an outrage, he said. —You'll freeze to death.

Picking baby Joe out of our arms and handling him, he marched us into the warm smell of the shop. We were hemorrhaging in the mouth practically with want. You could eat the air in the place, so thick with bread and warmth that it stang our cheeks.

—Out out out out, cried the bakery hag when she saw us. The dough of her body was trembling with fury. —Out! I told you.

—These children shall have three rolls of that white bread there, and tea with milk, said the Gentleman, and he slapped down his money bright on the counter.

The dark scowl of the miserable proprietress smoked over at us in fumes. But she swallowed her bile when she seen the Gentleman's copper and fetched us tea. It scalded our tongues but did nothing to damage the softness of her bread or the crunch of its golden crust. It made no sense to have such a hard woman with such soft bread. We were fainting and trying not to wolf it down like beasts. The Gentleman watched us eat the same as if we were a free show.

—There now, he said, his voice a low burr in his throat, —there you are, children.

Dutch threw her arms around his neck. —Oh thank you kind Gentleman, she said. Her sweetness was like payment to him, you could see by his smile. Even with the grime on her face, Dutch was a pretty child. No one could resist her blarney and her charm, and though she was only seven years of age, she knew this well.

When we were done with the first bread, he says, —Are yiz still hungry?

Wait. Let me get his voice right. In fact, he said it all beautiful, with elocution: —Do you jolly young wayfarers still have an appetite?

And we said, —Yessir.

It was our lucky day then, for he bought us another round of penny rolls and fed us under the glare of the bakery woman's eyes.

—Children, where are your parents? the Gentleman said.

—Please mister, our father art in heaven, said Dutch. It was the wish to be proper was why she mangled her vocabulary with a prayer. Our father was not our Father Who Art in Heaven, though he was dead. Perhaps he was in hell, what with the one sin we knew of him, which was his death two years before, from drunkenness and falling off a scaffold while carrying a hod of bricks, leaving Mam with us girls and Joe, his infant son. It was just after Joe's arrival and our Da was celebrating with his lunch bucket and a drop, for he did like his drop, Mam said, coming home every night, so dusty and singing Toura loura loo, a stick of licorice in his pockets if we was lucky and a blast of whiskey in our faces if we wasn't. —Fill me the growler, there's a good girl, Axie, he says to me nightly, and I'm off like a shot for the shebeen downstairs and back in a flash without spilling. Then Da would raise the bucket in a toast and sing out, —You're a Muldoon, dontcha forget it girls. Descended from the Kings of Lurg. The daughters and sons of Galway.

—The Kings of Lurg did not have nothing over your father, Mam said in her grief when he fell. —He was a grand hard worker, and more's the pity for there will be no payday now he's gone to God.

After he was gone to God we was gone ourselves, away over to Cherry Street to live with our father's sister Aunt Nance Duffy, while Mam went out to work as a laundress to a Chinaman.

—Where is your mother then? the Gentleman asked.

—She got an injury, I says. —She can't get out of her bed for three days.

—And where do you live? he asks us. —Have you warmth and shelter?

—Truth, says I, —it's the food we miss.

—My name is Mr. Brace. He put out his hand, which I inspected, lacking the manners to shake it. It was clean and soft as something newborn. —Who might you be?

—Axie Muldoon. And these here is my brother Joe and sister Dutchie.

—A pleasure to make your acquaintance.

He did not look like it was a pleasure exactly, and stared like he was a police trap in brass buttons, frisking us in the face to find out our secrets. He was a big gaunt man, with pale eyes dug back in his face, an overhung forehead, jutting jaw, nose long as a vegetable, and big flanges of nostrils. There were hairs in them that I could see from down low where I was. Like any child I was disgusted by the hairs, but hoping to extend his philanthropy just a few pennies longer, I said, —Thanks mister for the bread.

—Certainly, my dear. Still you must know that man does not live for bread alone, but lives by every word that proceedeth out of the mouth of the Lord.

We gazed up at him without no idea of what he was going on about.

—I should like you to have bread, said he quite gently, —yes, but more than bread. I should like you three children to come along with me.

It seemed he was going to give us cakes and ale and possibly a handful of silver, so I was all for it. He picked up our Joe and took Dutch by her hand, which she surrendered, trusting as if he was Our Lord the shepherd and she was the sheep. Not knowing we were marching off to our Fate, we all trooped out together. I was last, which was to my advantage because on the way out I gave a loud raspberry to the bakery lady. Very satisfying it was, too, and you should have seen her face, the cow. Full of her baking, we followed the Gentleman down the street.

—I would like to bring this bread to your Mother, he says. —Where do you live?

He had a parcel with the telltale shape of fat loaves under the brown paper, so despite Mam's instructions never to truck with strangers, there was no choice but to lead him home. For bread alone, I done it.

We walked at a brisk trot around onto Catherine Street, past Henry and Madison, Monroe and Hamilton, names of our nation's heroes and presidents, though at that time I had no knowledge of presidents nor nations. Just these streets, with their shanty wood buildings, their flashmen and hucksters, their carts and piles of ash overflowing the bins. The horse mess was rank under your shoes and the smell of it a bad taste up your nose. We stepped over bones and oyster shells, through the tight crowds of people, across the frozen urine slush and past the women selling rags and their cold hard bread twisted in rings. We dodged a dog with a ladder of ribs like mine, only she had pups you could tell from the teats. Soon I would be old enough, Mam said, for pups of my own, but I must remain virtuous and not be grown before my time.

At last we came to Cherry Street, where no cherry bloomed in six lifetimes. Along we went to number 128, around the mess of little boys, Michael, Sean, and Francis, pitching pennies, only instead of pennies they used pebbles. They scampered back away from the Gentleman like roaches before a light, but he only smiled. —Hello boys, he said to their stony faces. We passed the hop house, where through the doorway I seen our uncle's brother Kevin Duffy alongside Bernice his wife, drinking theirselves stupid, and then picked our way along the bone alley over the trash, with our feet mucked up past the laces in wet ooze, to the rear tenement where we had our rooms. The wash above was hung so it blotted out the dollop of sky between the buildings. Sheets and knickers flapped off the fire escapes, the lines crossing the airshaft in a piecework ceiling of laundry. The women with their red knuckles stood scrubbing it on boards and clipping it up. It had to dry before it froze.

—It is so dark, said the Gentleman when he started up our stairs. I saw the wrinkle of his toffee nose as the smells choked him in the nostrils, the cabbage cooking and the p*** in the vestibule, the sloppers emptied right off the stair. Mackerel heads and pigeon bones was all around rotting, and McGloon's pig rootled below amongst the peels and oyster shells. The fumes mingled with the odors of us hundredsome souls cramped in there like matches in a box, on four floors, six rooms a floor. Do the arithmetic and you will see we didn't have no space to cross ourselves. As for the smell we did not flinch, we was used to it.

—Pardon me, the Gentleman said very genteel when he banged into Missus Duggan on her way to the saloon to fill her buckets. —Pardon me.

—F*** off you, said she. —Inless youse the cops. She laughed so her dudeen pipe fell out of her mouth, and she had to feel for it on the floor and cursed us for devils. It was a danger to be there with a Gentleman like

Mr. Brace making his way through our building. Gangs of Roach Guardsmen and garroters just for the sport of it would be glad to rob him and push him down the stairs. But this Gentleman had more than bread alone for Mother, so I brung him there. I blame myself to this day.

Mrs. Gilligan's baby coughed and coughed. You could hear the bark of it as we passed the door next to ours. It was a runt with its eye stuck shut, a crust of yellow in the corners. Already once this year, the Gilligans had the white rag fluttering off their door for the undertaker, when their old baby died of bilious fever. —Is a child ill? the Gentleman asked, concerned as if sick kids was some new scandal out of the penny papers. We did not answer, for at last we had arrived at our own rooms.

—Shush, I said to the children, —because might be Mam is sleeping. They hushed while I pushed the door open. —Mind the bottles. The floor had many empties lying about. They were dead soldiers, our Uncle Kevin Duffy always said. It was dark as the inside of a dog. I couldn't find a lamp, but we could hear a man's snores.

—Who's there? asked our visitor.

—One of the Mr. Duffys, our Uncle Michael, I said. —Also our Aunt Nan is in.

—She has a baby coming, said Dutch, full of information.

—Mother says they's all sluiced drunks and stay clear of them, I explained. Duffys was no good even though Aunt Nan Duffy was a Muldoon, my dead father's sister. Without Nancy Mam said we'd be on the streets, but that Michael Duffy her husband was a sot and a rover. So for seven dollars the month, it was the eight of us in the two rooms together with the terlet in the hall for six apartments, and the pump downstairs for all the souls of number 128 Cherry Street. Daily we tripped over each other and Mam said when the baby Duffy came it would be worse. Perhaps it'd die like the Gilligans' died, though it was wrong to pray for it.

Now we guided the Gentleman past the sleeping Duffys to the back room where our mother lay on her shakedown bed. Some daylight was left coming in the windowpane, so the Gentleman could see how her cheekbones was hard plums under her skin, her brow beaded with fever.

—Mam, there's a Gentleman to see are you all right.

She stirred and opened her eyes, the gray color of smoke. —*Macushla,* she said. —It's you Axie, *mavourneen.*

Her words fell weakly around me like dust in sunlight. I loved her like I loved no one else.

—Missus . . . ? said the Gentleman.

—Muldoon, she whispered. —Mary Muldoon.

—I am Reverend Charles Brace of the Children's Aid Society. The whole mouthful came out in his Fifth Avenue voice. Chahles, he said. Suh-SIGH-ettee.

—'Tis a pleasure to make your acquaintance, Mam said, her voice Irish but proper.

—He's brung you some bread, Mam, I said.

—Brought you, she whispered, correcting my savage grammar. We children had poor mouths, she was forever telling us. And she would know, as she went to a proper classroom five years back home in Carrickfergus, while our education was only a smatter of lessons at P.S. 114.

Dutch had climbed on the bed and was laid out by our mother's feet, stroking the coverlet over her ankles. The baby was clamoring, —Mam Mam, in his pitiful way.

—Is there any water? Mr. Brace asked me.

I ran for the pail and brought it to him.

—Let me help you now, he said. He sat at her side and placed his white hands very tender beneath her shoulders to lift her. She cried out so next he raised her head only, and held the cup to her lips while she drank.

—What is your ailment? he asked, his voice gentle as the pigeon's coo.

She did not move nor say. I pulled back the cover to show him.

He gasped. There was her arm mangled and cooked, burned red with the flesh on it dried black and angry, hard white streaks under the peeled-off skin. She could not bend the elbow nor fist her fingers even a little. A blast of odor came up from under the blanket. Mr. Brace turned his face away and then made himself turn back.

—Madam, he said, his eyes emotional, —how did you come by this injury?

—I got my hand caught in the mangle with the aprons, sir. The roller press took the whole arm and burned it in the steam, so it did. Three days ago.

The accident happened where she worked at the laundry on Mott, when an apron string pulled her fingers between the hot cylinder and the rollers and cooked the whole arm while the other girls took ten minutes to get it free.

—Lord have mercy, said Mr. Brace, —I will escort you to the hospital.

—No no no.

—By the grace of God we'll save your life.

—I can't accept no charity.

—The central figure in the world of charity is Christ, he said. —It's our Lord's grace and not my own. He gives value to the poorest and most despised among us.

—'Tis sure I am despised.

—No madam. Our Lord despises not one on this earth. In His love, you will find a friend, who can make your life an offering of service, and dry your children's tears.

—If he can dry them then sure he is my friend, my mother whispered.

Mr. Brace smiled. —Then shall the splendor of heaven come to this dark and dreary den and lead you to reform as well as charity, madam, for I must tell you, your children are exposed.

—Exposed?

—Certainly, he said. —Exposed to the temptations that beset the unfortunate: sharpness, deception, roguery, fraud, vice in many forms, and offenses against the law. Not to mention starvation and disease.

—No doubt, said she, —the devil himself has his eye on 'em.

—At the very least let me take your little ones away from such influences.

—If it kills me, said my saintly mother, —you won't steal them.

—Have no fear, said Brace. —I do not propose to steal them, but to save them. Wouldn't you like our Aid Society to find them good homes in the countryside out West?

—For faith they've their home here. It's not no castle, sure, but it's ours.

—The best of all asylums for the child of unhappy fortune is the farmer's home.

—I lived in a farmer's home all me life and it's just why we emigrated.

—Madam, it is your duty to get these children away to kind Christian families in the country, where they will be better off.

—Children belong with their mothers.

—Allow me at the very least to take you to the hospital. I shall pay the expense. You have a gangrenous fever in that arm. If you don't relent, you may not last the week.

My poor injured mother was no match for the blunt elocution of the Reverend Mr. Charles Loring Brace. He plied her with stories of our doom and hers, if we did not all come along with him.

—Madam, these are the little children of Christ. Do not be among those who, by their ignorance, promote the development of a dangerous class of urchins, with depraved tendencies to crime and dissolution. It was the Lord's Work, he said, for him to take us three somewheres warm and safe, a place of hot cider and oxtail stew, new boots and green grass all around.

Soon he had her swanning and thanking him through her tears and anguish. —Oh mister, bless you for thinking of such poor souls as we are. We watched her bobbing her head and curtsying even in her agony, struggling to walk out the door, and down the stairs. —Such a fine gentleman, she said, combing her hair with the fingers of her good hand.

And he was, too, very fine, with his Christian hymns and mentions of Our Lord. I would not claim that he was not kind. He was. He meant well. I would not claim either that he did not save the lives of many orphans and poor scabs of youth such as us. He saved thousands and was famous for it. I would only say that Brace was a sorter. He thought he knew best. He plucked us up that day away from our mother, and set us down into our fate, sure as if we was kittens he'd lifted by the loose wet skin of the neck and put in a sack, and for that I do not forgive him, despite how I became a sorter of sorts, myself.

Chapter Three

Asylum

*B*ack by the bakery on Broadway and Catherine Mr. Brace had his private carriage and driver waiting in the cold. It might as well've been made of crystal, so surprised were we to see it there for us to ride in. Our mother climbed up with great effort and lay her head pale against the seat. The Gentleman helped us three into the trap to sit beside her.

Before you could say Beat It, we was trotting along, past all the mugs staring at us in their mossy jealousy. I known they were thinking, There goes a fancy cove and his toffee family. We looked down on them through the curtains and smiled like cream was in our mouth. You might say that my future fancies, what the newspapers called my FLAMBOYANCE, was born in that moment. So this is how it feels to go wheeling past the hoi polloi, me in my chariot, I thought. Nice.

But the enjoyment was tainted by worry over my Mam's fatal appearance, and the ominous kind Gentleman, with his pale eyes crinkled up at the corners, watching.

—Where are you taking us? I asked.

For an answer the carriage stopped in front of a massive stone building. Bellevue Hospital, said the words carved above the entrance.

—You little wanderers must wait here while I take your mother to see the doctor, said Our Protector.

—We'll come along, I cried. —Won't we? Mam!

—You must go with Mr. Brace, said Mam, in pain and surrender—and if he's good as his word I'll meet you again soon on Cherry Street when I'm improved.

—I'm good as my word, madam, you can trust it, says he.

—And Axie, listen, Mam said. —For the love of God promise you'll take care of our Joseph and our Dutchess. Keep them with you d'ya hear me?

—Yes I promise Mam, I says, fainthearted.

Mr. Brace helped her down, and she leaned on him into the gray building. We kept our six eyes on her to the last. It was not a ceremonious nor hysterical farewell. We did not cry nor cling to her but bit down on our fears and obeyed as she had taught us. We waited in the carriage with a warm robe over our legs, and after a time we fell asleep.

We was awoken by the noise of wheels on cobbles, and seen the carriage was off again, but our Mam was not with us. —Where is she? I accused Mr. Brace.

—The doctor must see to her injury. We're off to find you some dinner and a bed.

Dutchie clutched at me while Joe whimpered on my lap.

—Suffer the little children, said Mr. Brace, with a tender look.

—We are suffering, sure, I said. —You took our mother, you don't need to tell us.

—'Suffer the little children to come unto me,' said the Lord Jesus Christ.

—It was you that said it, I told him.

—My only motive in life is to do good for the unfortunate, dear child.

Brace was the pooka, I thought, come to haul us off to the hills, turn us to cabbages, cook us and eat us. The unfamiliar streets passed till at last we arrived very nervous at a house with a grand porch and fluted columns, its tower topped with a golden weather vane in the shape of a rooster. The snow lay around it pure and cold as froth on a draft of beer.

—What is this place? Dutch asked the Gentleman. —Is this where you live?

—This, young lady, is the Little Roses Orphan Asylum.

—We are not no orphans, I said hotly.

—Of course not, my spirited girl! His voice was honey in his throat.

—You may stay here until such time as your mother is able to take care of you.

We were taken inside, limp with traveling, and Brace introduced us to a Lady, Mrs. Reardon. The look of her was starched, her apron white and stiff, her hair pulled back severely on her small head. Plus we never seen such a rump on a human. It was its own continent, but we did not stare now, as we were stupefied to distraction by the sight of the sweeping staircase and the high ceilings, the statue of a stone child holding one stone rose there in the vestibule of the Asylum.

—These merry rascals are the Muldoon children, the Gentleman told her. —I found them half-frozen on Catherine Street.

—Poor lambs.

—The home is patently unfit, he whispered low to her. —Terrible vice and degradation. I left the Mother at Bellevue. Her prognosis is dire.

Dire he said. The word stang me with fear, but before I could ask its meaning here was Mr. Brace bidding us farewell with a wave of his leather glove hand, leaving us to the Asylum, where it was common knowledge among the children of Cherry Street that the matrons kidnapped Catholic kids to sell them into slavery.

Mrs. R. led us to a large dining room, a lordly place full of tables, every one of them with uniformed children sitting, banging their forks in a racket till somebody rang a bell and the room went quiet. All those scrubbed orphan eyes turned our way, and I seen us now as they must, unwashed and reeking of misery. We had to sit right down amongst them. —Let us give thanks, said Mrs. R.

Like one marvelous machine, the orphans folded their hands and bowed their heads. We did likewise and mumbled along with the blessing.

—Amen, said all the kids. The word was deafening.

—Where yiz come from? said one girl. She was the size of a man, nearly, with red pimples on her long face.

—Cherry Street.

—I'm called Mag. You?

—Axie Muldoon. And this is Dutchie my sister.

—Ha! said a big rough boy who known he was good-looking. —Ax and Dutch. What kind of crank names is that?

I did not say what kind. Nor how my sister was Dutchess Muldoon named by our Da like royalty and I was our dear Annie called Axie by Mam because I was forever axing so many questions. I only scowled at this big b*ll*cks. He was cocky and black-haired with a dangerous jaw that jutted out in a hard underbite.

—Ax Muldoon, he muttered. —A girl named Ax.

—You've the mug of a bulldog, I says, —so is that your name then, Bulldog?

—Name's Charlie, he says with a smirk.

—Bulldog, I says, and smiled at big Mag.

—Don't make no problems with him, she said. —Charlie's the pet and so clever he charms all the matrons. Any trouble, they marrow you good.

Dutch began to snivel at the idea of a marrowing but quieted down when she smelled dinner arriving. We was served each a bowl of soup, thick with carrots and potatoes. Chicken fat floated in golden rings on the surface. Our Joe was on my lap, and hummed while I fed him. We three was just about bamboozled into thinking there was never a better place than this Asylum, when Mrs. Reardon comes along with her arms out for Joe.

—We'll have the baby from you, she says. —He'll sleep in the nursery.

—That's our brother! He sleeps with us.

But the hag lifted him up under the arms.

I pulled his legs. She pulled back. Joe was stretched like a taffy between us, twisting himself and screeching.

—He's our brother, we cried, as I hammered her.

In a blink, two more apron ladies had a hold of me.

—She's a hellcat, cried Mrs. R. —Keep her down.

—PUGGA MAHONE, alla yiz, I said, which is Irish for Kiss My *ss.

—None of your papist curses, said Mrs. Rump who now had a grip on my hair.

I bit her.

—Dear Lord in Heaven, she screamed, my teeth in her arm.

I kicked at both them matrons and flailed, swinging. The orphans went wild with laughter and remarks, with that Bulldog Charlie the loudest, cheering. —Atta girl, Ax.

—Silence! said Reardon, ringing a bell like a mad steeple. —We do not tolerate heathen behavior here. I saw a red mark on the white meat of her forearm and I was that starved I might have gone for seconds had she not grabbed me by the ear. —Apologize!

I would not. She twisted my ear like it was a doorknob and I cried out in pain.

—I'll give you a hiding and lock you away, said she, but still got no sorry out of me. Apology or none, Mrs. R. had won the prize of Joe. She carried him off even as he wailed for us, —AxieDutch. He called us always the one name, AxieDutch. But the hard-hearted cow did not turn nor relent.

Miserable, but full of our dinner, me and Dutchie followed the mess of girls in a line up the stairs, then to a room of nothing but washbasins.

—You will scrub yourselves, girls, a matron said. She gave us a cloth for it and raved on about how we were dirty. —You are like one of the darker races.

More evidence she would soon try to sell us.

She handed us a gown to sleep in and took away our clothes, held them away with her nose wrinkled. —Infested, she said, and put them in the bin.

Next Mrs. R. sentenced us each to sleep in a cot alone.

—My sister sleeps with me, I cried, and wrangled with them again till they gave up in exhaustion. At last we two Muldoon girls clamped around each other in our narrow crib, and slept. We was each the only safe thing we knew now, in that dark Asylum.

In the morning, we and the orphans was all rousted up with Mrs. Rump banging a gong. There was nothing tender about it, not like our mother who sang low to us in her lilty voice. —Wake yourselfs, it's a new day. Up with yiz all, ya Flibbertigibbets.

The matrons now gave us blue smocks with new itchy woolies, and nice charity boots used only a little. —Thank you very much, I said to Mrs. R. —Now please we will take our brother and go find our home in Cherry Street.

Mrs. Rump pressed her lips together in a hard string across her face, as if she was tying off the neck of a sack. —You will go about your chores and not a further word.

But I had many further words for her, like Hag, Knacker and BOG-TROTTER.

—Miss Muldoon! said my tormentor. —You will stand in the corner, face to the wall, and count the bricks.

But instead of bricks I counted the hours till I was free to sit in my mother's lap, her two hands braiding my hair. When I was done counting, I wrestled Mrs. R. again for Joe, and badgered her for our return to Cherry Street.

—You're relentless, Rump said. —Child, you try my Christian soul.

Dutch did not try anyone's soul. She clung to the matrons, and they stroked her head and said what pretty hair, what pretty eyes, so I was jealous and glad when she climbed into my bed in the dark with night terrors, and in the morning she attached like a whelk to the rock of me as we was hauled to church to sing hymns till we were blue in the face. *Amazing Grace, how sweet the sound.* The sound was sweet, I will admit. *I once was lost but now am found.* But we were not found. We was lost as sheep in a wilderness. You could shave us and make a wool coat.

Chapter Four

Amputated

One late March day with old snow dirty over the grass, Mr. Brace showed up at the Asylum with a great surprise. His bulbous eyes was bright with excitement as he sat us down in the vestibule. —Good news, he said. —You Muldoons are chosen for our Western Emigration Program. He smiled expectantly.

We stared at him dumb as socks while he conned us.

—Good country families are waiting to take in friendless city children like yourselves, and give them lovely homes with a warm hearth and ample room to roam. Perhaps you might have a pony or a dog. Your jolly brother here will learn to fish and hunt, while you young ladies will learn to set a fine table, and cook a rich country meal.

Mister Brace was a ridiculous fancy talker and though we never seen a field, now we dreamed of pony-owning.

—To date, three hundred and twenty-seven orphans from this city have settled on farms out West, with new mothers and fathers, and all the trappings of a country life.

—But we don't need no other mother, I informed him. —We already got one. So let's go get her straightaways, and off we will be to the countryside.

Now his eyes got tragic and mournful. They were set deep in his head and ringed around with darkness. —There is something I must tell you, he said, very grave. —Your mother has had to have a serious operation. The nature of her injuries was so severe that the doctors were forced to remove her right arm.

—You cut her arm OFF? I roared.

Dutch shrieked. She put her hand over her mouth in horror.

—Hush now, hush, Brace said. —Had we not taken her to Bellevue when we did, she would surely have died of gangrene.

—It can't be, I cried. In my mind I saw a bloody stump off her shoulder, and my mother's chopped limb lost somewheres. The warm crook of her elbow, the freckles on the wrist, the fingers that soothed my fevers, tossed now, who knows where? It made the bone ache all along the marrow of my own wings. —You cut her arm off, I cried, —you bungstarter of a b*****d.

—Hush now, dear child, Mr. B. said, alarmed. —The doctors saved her.

Now, years later, I'll admit they did save her, but then I said, —You are a wicked man.

—I hope I am not, poor child. I must tell you, your mother was so grateful that you three were chosen for the Westward Settlement, she gave her consent right away. She asked me to tell you, take care of each other, and remember to say your prayers.

I did not cry nor let the black tar of how I hated him come from my mouth.

—Take comfort in the knowledge that our Lord was poor and suffered terrible mortifications, said Mr. B. seeing our stricken faces. —When they crucified Him, nails went right through His flesh. Yet He rose to live among us and be our Savior.

Dutch was crying now louder than ever at the mention of those nails. She climbed into the Reverend's lap and put her arms around his neck. He soothed her down and failed to notice the fury buckling the space between my eyebrows.

—Why shouldn't we have you three young rascals on the next train to the country? he asked. —Would you like that?

—Oh yes, kind Gentleman! said Dutch, a traitor already. —I can't wait to go on that train!

She did not have to wait long. They came for us not three weeks on. We were at lunch awaiting our applesauce, when here comes Mrs. Reardon trundling down the row of tables, tapping certain orphans on the shoulder.

TAP! —You're going to Illinois, she said.

She comes to Mag, and Tap! —My dear, you're on the train.

Tap! She touched Bulldog Charlie, and the boy next to him. She got to me and said the same. —You're on the train for Illinois. And Tap! —So's your sister.

—We WON'T, I cried. —We ain't no orphans.

—No argument, said she.

—What about our brother? Dutch said.

—He's going to Illinois same as you, said Mrs. Rump. Her backside continued down the line, moving as if she kept a separate animal under her skirts.

I sprang out of my seat to make my stand. —I will not go on no train without our mother. She ain't dead.

—Sit down Miss Muldoon, this instant.

Mrs. Rump was done with me.

Out in the yard later, everybody was talking about Illinois. The big boys, especially, were all for it. —In Illinois they got great gobs of butter in your mouth, three meals a day, said Charlie Bulldog. —Mushmelons lying around just there for you to pick.

At sixteen he was the oldest of us, and when he climbed up on the rain barrel in a pose, one finger in the air, all the orphans gathered round to hear him talk. His dark eyes was restless as minnows, and as he started in speaking all silvertongued about the West, it was like Mr. Brace himself had hypnotized the words into his mouth.

—Alla youse orphans can stay here and be lowlifes and rowdies, but if yiz do stay here, you'll be a beggar livin' offa charity the rest of yer natural days, mark my words. But come West, boys and girls, and you'll soon have servants to tend you, and a fella to open your mouth and put great slices of pumpkin pie right in it. Don't know about you, but I want to be SOME-BODY, and somebody sure don't live here in no Asylum. So come out to the prairie alla ya, for a happier day!

—Hip hip hooray, the orphans cheered, deluded by talk of the West.

That night the matrons gave us each a Bible and a cardboard suitcase. They handed around charity trousers for the boys, dresses for the girls. Dutch tried on her new skirt and twirled herself dizzy whilst I chewed my fingers down to the nerves.

—Sleep now, youngsters, said Mrs. R. —Tomorrow you'll be away on the train.

But I did not sleep. In the shadows of the dormitory girls pulled pillows over their faces to muffle their sobs. Dutch crawled nervous under the covers beside me and flang her leg over my hip with her long hair tangled in mine so you could not tell whose was whose. Through the night worries crawled on our skin like silverfish along the floorboards.

—Girls! girls, Mrs. R. cried, and rang the morning bell. —Today is the big day!

We lined up and she presented us to a couple called the Dix. Mr. Dix had a face like a small ball of suet and his teeth ratted out over his bottom lip. Mrs. Dix was a fine lady, young and slender, with her brown hair in enormous loops at her ears like some variety of spaniel.

—Please give Mr. and Mrs. Dix a warm welcome, said Mrs. Reardon. —They are the agents from the Children's Aid Society and will be traveling with you.

The little ones clapped and the older boys sniggered at the name Dix.

—Good morning, lads and lasses, said Mr. Dix. —We are in charge of finding you all happy new homes on the prairie, all the way beyond Chicago, Illinois.

I determined to run at the first opportunity, but swiftly in the half darkness they herded the twenty of us into wagons and sent us off, everybody waving, all of us jittery. As we neared the rail yards, motes of soot was thick in the April air, and soon we arrived at a tremendous shed of glass and steel. Beyond, the locomotives waited in the open yards. —Trains! the orphans shouted.

But to me they were not trains. They was fast snakes that swallowed up mice such as ourselves, and deposited only our bones somewheres else. The Dix marched us along into a maze of noise and baggage, all the proper people turning to stare, each one thinking, Oh look at them poor pitiful guttersnipes. It was a decent crowd to get lost in.

—Dutch, I whispered. —We will carry Joe now and run out that door to the street. We can find our way to Mam, they won't never catch us.

—But Axie, she said. —I want to go on the train.

—Train! said Joe. He was keen for it, though at two years of age he had not a clue what the f*** was a train. You never saw a nipper sweet as him.

His hair was that dark red of our dad's, the color of rusty blood. A pepper of freckles was across his nose and round cheeks, and his britches was half the time falling off his backside. He had a habit of tilting his head to the side to look at me. Axie? he said my name with his head tipped like that, and then he took my face in his two hands, the knuckles dented. He kissed my cheeks and pressed me nose to nose so the bones of his small forehead butted up against mine, like he was trying to enter into my skull. He did that now, pressing on me, and he cried, —TRAIN, with a wild look of joy on his face.

And so it was that the whims of my sister and brother prevented me from running out the door, brainwashed as they were about prairies and pie. And it must be confessed I was afraid to run, for I had heard too much now from the matrons about how we vagrant children was worse than the pagans of Golconda. If we was left alone on the streets, they said, our childish faces would soon have the long black story of shame and suffering written upon them, a future like hell before us.

They packed us at last onto a train car, me and Dutch together with Joe on our laps. —Goodbye New York, I whispered, and took Joe's little hand to show him how to blow kisses. As the train moved out of the station all us three Muldoons' kisses were feathers drifting out the window into the New York air, over the buildings to find Mam.

The train clanged and chugged, getting up steam. Everybody bounced in their seats, crowding the windows. They were boisterous and singing for an hour. Mr. Dix led us in rounds of Come Ye Sinners Poor and Needy. He loved that infernal song. *God's free bounty glorify* . . .

Soon the Dix passed out a free bounty of apples and gingerbread. We pressed the crumbs against the seat with our fingers and licked them off so as not to waste any. Dutch's pinky curled as she did it for daintiness came natural to her.

—Axie, said she, —I do like this train.

The wonder in her eyes looking out the window was in every orphan's also. At Spuyten Duyvil we crossed a trestle over the river, such a cold hard ribbon you could not believe it was wet. White sails of ships were moths drowning on the water below.

—What's that! we said, peering out pointing. —What's that? The scenery went by the windows so fast. For the first time we saw hills. We saw streams. Milk cows and beef cows and horses roamed free without fetters. Acres of trees rolled by in green walls. We never knew so many trees was possible. We grew quiet, without vocabulary for the immensity of the land, or for the distance increasing away from the patch of it we knew. What small certainty we had was dusted down now, to just our names and the contents of the satchels we carried in our childish fists. Night fell. The vast blackness out the window erased our past. It was blank as our future. We chugged through a town where the houses and stores were all lit up warm. Was there a window like that somewhere lit for us? It seemed the answer was: fat chance.

Through the long night kids was crying for their mothers. There were infants needing milk, and several others were crawlers, fast as centipedes across the floor. There was a pair of brothers with a juicy vocabulary of curses between them, they were all eff you and eff ess eff. Them two Dix was run ragged chasing down the little ones and shocked out of their drawers at the mayhem and the language. —You are vessels of blasphemy! Mr. Dix blustered. —Your speech is so vile even the farmers won't take you.

I worried, if the farmers would not take us, what then? We'd be left to roam the prairie, carcasses for the ants. Every day, to avoid such a fate, the Dix chastised us for cursing and made us to practice proper words for a servant, yes ma'am and no ma'am, please and thank you. —Now you will not be savages, they said.

—When will we be there? Dutch plagued me. —Where are we going, Axie?

—Illinois, I said, over and over. To me the place had the sound of ANNOY and ILL but that's not what I told my sister. —Every lady there has a feather hat and a coat of fur. Their dogs is poodles with haircuts like lions, their horses got ribbons in their manes.

—For real? she asked. Her eyeballs moved over the scenery outside the window. They went to the right, then back left again to reload on something new, and this motion gave her a dreamy sort of insane look as she listened to my tales.

—In Illinois you will sleep on a feather bed soft as this eyelash on your cheek. Feel, I said, and blinked my eyelid against her face. —Mam says this is the kiss of a fairy's wing.

—Mam will be in Illinois, said Dutch.

—No she will not.

At this Dutch began to cry again and it was all I could do not to join her, as just then Joe made a sick sound and threw up his dinner. The mess landed at our feet and the reek of it soaked the air. Orphans moved away, holding their noses, jeering remarks. I was left cleaning. —You big lump, Dutch, I said, —get a rag so's you can help me.

—I want Mam, she said, and put her delicate head back against the seat cushion with Joe whimpering at her side.

There I was with the two of them. One useless, the other sick. Knowing Joe, in a minute he'd be bouncing, never better. The boy was a handful. He whined and fretted. His droozle went all over us, and he could not learn to use the privy. We had to hang his drawers out the window to dry, as there was nowheres to wash them. Every minute he was insane to run off. —Get down! he said. But there was no getting down. There was only going forward on the train, the fear and the panic and the boredom.

For days we traveled, stained and weary, past the date of my thirteenth birthday and further after that. The Dix tried to pass the hours, preoccupied with did we know the Bible? Morning, noon, and night, we sang There's a Rest for the Weary. Mr. Dix moved along the aisle of the train talking about the Lord. —Let us pray!

I prayed for him to stop his effing sermons.

As Dix talked, we three mimicked his expression, top teeth over the bottom lip, like a rat, scrumping up the nose, making a rat-squeak by sucking air through the space between teeth. Charlie the Bulldog saw me do it. He laughed and tried it, teeth exposed, nose wrinkled like he had whiskers. I stuck my tongue out at him. He smirked and stuck up his middle finger so I cocked a snook at him, thumb on the nose and the fingers waggling. The two Dix was happily preaching and did not notice.

—God has smiled on you lucky children, Mr. Dix said. —You will trade the sewer gasses of the city for the fresh breezes of the countryside. Let us sing all together:

From the city's gloom to the country's bloom
Where the fragrant breezes sigh . . .
O children, dear children, happy, young, and pure—

We was not pure, but a raggedy chorus. Passengers from the other cars came to listen with a tear in their eye. —Oh the innocents, they said. Truth is, while the orphans sang, I worried, what would happen? We would be separated. Sold off and parted. They would whip us, feed us like dogs. These thoughts of loneliness came over me like steam from the grates in the street, and like the steam it held a memory of heat that turned damp on the skin, sinking through your clothes into your bones. How I wanted my Mam.

Chapter Five

Chosen

One warm day toward the end of May we were awakened to the feel of slowing. We heard the sharp metal sound of the brakes, the shush of steam. The bell clanged and there was the lurch of the stop. I put my hand out across my sister's shoulders. My brother's head was a damp weight in my lap.

—Illinois! Illinois! The conductor was calling out the name of a town. Half cooked with sleep, I didn't hear it. —Illinois!

—Children! Children! said Mrs. Dix. —Tidy yourselves. She herself was none too fresh. The spaniel-ear hairdo of hers had come loose long ago. She had a bun like a knob of potato now pinned to the back of her head. —Quickly, we must disembark.

—Oh Axie, said Dutch, —this is Illinois?

We peered out the window and saw nothing but a depot in the midst of nowhere. No buildings to speak of, just a sorry wooden rectangle with a door, a window, and a cold chimney. That was the station house. A dirt trail wandered along in front of it. That was the main street in town, called Rockford. There was not all that many rocks to speak of and beyond the one building was only: long grass. We had seen so much of the stuff out the train window, and now we come to find out we traveled all that way for more of it.

Climbing down off that train we was rusty as old people. I set Joe down, and away he ran in the direction of the grass. His fat legs showed in a pale flash below his trouser cuff. —Joe! I called. —Come back! He skipped and twirled. He didn't know to be worried about what Fate lay ahead, dumb and free as a dog. That boy Charlie chased him down and swang him up, so our Joe laughed and laughed. —Here's your brother, Charlie says, and handed him over to me. He and the rest of the Big Boys were all for going to find the plum trees and especially the cows.

—I bet money I could milk one easy, says Charlie, so cocksure and bawdy, how he described you do it, squeezing his hands in the air. He mooed like a cow and said UDDER and TEAT. Mrs. Dix put her fingers in her ears.

—Enough of that talk now, Mr. Dix said, covering the delicate ears of his wife.

The boys continued anyways, and when Charlie seen me laughing he winked at me and I felt caught, my cheeks red.

Mr. Dix rang his bell. —Children! Children! Line up.

We set off carrying the babies, marching toward the steeple, a white spear down the road. What a sorry raggle-edge group we was with our paper luggage, our shoes with no laces and our faces with no clue where this was on a map. We came to a clump of plain raw buildings that Mrs. Dix said was the town. We grumbled it did not look like no town. We passed a store. It featured a sign tacked to a porch post that read:

Arrival of ORPHANS from New York City
Thursday, May 31st
First Congregational Church
Homes on FARMS are Wanted for
CHILDREN cast FRIENDLESS upon the world
Those desiring to acquire a child please INQUIRE
of the Screening Committee.

We were notorious already. At the church, a crowd of people in country clothes stood around. They stared at us as we came up the road. We climbed the steps and they whispered and pointed, goggle-eyed.

—The New York orphans. Well I'll be, said one fella.

—The poor dears, said a woman, shaking her head like we was lepers.

Joe hid his face and Dutch clamped my hand. That showoff Charlie grinned, waving at all the country people.

Inside the church, up front, was a half circle of chairs. That was where we would be sold, no doubt. First, however, we were given coffee and biscuits. They had plum jelly, and bits of ham and butter to fatten us and dull our senses. Some of the ladies came to take the babies away, to coo at them, but I was d***ed if I would part with Joe.

—Here, let me hold him for you, says a woman smelling of licorice.

—This is my brother, says I, and clung on.

—He's a little red-haired lamb, she says, sucking a horehound drop.

As soon as the townsfolk had us well stuffed, they brought us to the front and sat us down to be inspected.

—Lookit the queer shoes on that one.

—That's a little oliveskin boy. Are you Eyetalian?

—Are you one a them New York hooligans?

—Lookit her hair.

Their eyes on us were terrible millipedes crawling. One man pulled Mr. Dix aside, asking questions. —Are they able, strong and willing? Or are these all young thieves and hoodlums?

Two big men made Bulldog Charlie stand up. —Show your arms, the bearded one ordered him. Charlie stuck his jaw out and flexed his muscles like a fighter. He grinned right at me, so I seen how he enjoyed to make me squirm. It was then I was approached by a desperate old article with raggly strings of hair circling the bald spot of his head. He paced around where I sat, with Joe on my lap. He circled Dutch.

—You are brother and sisters? he asked.

—Yes sir.

Joe began to whimper.

—Stand, said the b*****d. —Turn around.

I did.

The geezer chewed something as he made the tour of me. His lips were stained brown, his teeth dark in the cracks, and his mouth appeared like it was leaking mud.

—You're a fine young lady, said he. —So's your sister.

He was squinting, sucking his lips. —I want to see about your teeth. Open your mouth, say ahhhh.

The hinge of my jaw was rusty. —Ahh, I said barely, and at that he stuck his stinking finger in my mouth and ran it around the gums.

That SONOFAB****. I bit him, right down through the gristle to the bone.

He roared like an animal. —She's bit me!

—Axie Muldoon, what did you do? Mrs. Dix came rushing over.

—This fiend has gone and bit me! cried the old scoundrel. —That she-devil!

—Let's go Dutchie, I said, carrying Joe. —We're on the train home again.

—Calm down, Mrs. Dix said, soothing me. —We'll find you a nice home.

The church ladies milled about, inspecting us. One of them lifted pieces of Dutch's hair, while some others started gossip about me. —She's wild. Bit a matron at the orphanage, too, they say. Curses like a sailor.

It was a terrible spectacle. Mag was getting sized up by a woman with an eyeglass on a stick. People were at the windows looking in. One lady squeezed the meat of Joe's thigh. A man in farmer overalls touched his hair like it was a curiosity.

Now a dark-bearded gentleman in a waistcoat began talking to Dutch. She smiled up at him from under her lashes. —How old are you? he asked her, with kind eyes.

—Seven, Dutch replied.

—Seven? He beckoned to a petite lady with combs in her pompadour. —I'd like you to meet my wife, he told Dutch. The lady's eyes were the same sky blue miracle color as my sister's. The husband remarked on it. —Why you could be our own child!

The wife smiled. —What is your name?

—Dutch, said she, already forgetting the Muldoon.

—She appears to be just the right age, darling, said the man, as his wife sized up my sister with a faraway look on her sad face.

Joe squirmed in my lap. —Down, he said, and got himself off me. He was making his way back to the biscuits so I had to chase after him. But too late. One of the ladies had him, that same licorice-smelling one who tried to get him before.

—Get down! Joe cried, struggling and reaching for me. —AxieDutch!

—He's a sturdy little fella, said the woman, a blast of odor off her as she handed him over. —Would he like a horehound drop? Would you?

I should've had my guard up, but I was preoccupied about Dutch, left with the gentleman looking her over. Not to mention I had to find the privy. The horehound lady directed me to go outside, around the back of the church.

—I will keep an eye on your little fellow, said she.

It was my mistake to let her.

Outside, I seen the pocky farmer herding Bulldog Charlie toward a team of mules, and watched as he swung himself up onto the wagon seat. When he saw me he lifted his hat, and grinned very contagious. —So long, Ax! he says, and was gone.

So they just take us off like that, then, I thought, in a panic now, and raced back to guard my sister and Joe. But Mrs. Dix snared me and steered me over to a pinched crab of a woman. —Mrs. Hough, said Mrs. D. —I'd like you to meet Axie Muldoon.

—Axie? said Hough. —What kind of a name is that?

—The name my mother gave me.

—You can call me Mother now, she replied with a simper.

—Mrs. Hough has agreed to take you in, said Mrs. Dix. —And your sister and brother have found places too.

—I'll go with them, I said. —It's the three of us Muldoons as a package.

Mrs. D. took me aside. —Please reconsider. It's not easy to place three at once. At least you would all be here in the same town. Otherwise you'll have to travel on to the next location with the others.

The others. These were the ones not chosen. They had to get back on the train and go farther on. —You can choose to stay with Mrs. Hough, Mrs. Dix said, —or come with me on the train in the morning.

I bolted away with this news to my sister where she sat on the lap of the blue-eyed lady, and pulled her by the sleeve. —Let's get out of here. We're going back on the train.

—No, Axie, Dutch said to me, cheery as Christmas. —Mrs. Ambrose will take me home, where I will be their little daughter. The father will buy me a pony.

And then Horehound held up my brother Joe like a prize turkey, showing him off to a ruddy man with a brown mustache. —Meet your son Joe, she says to him.

—He's not your son! I shouted. —You can't have him.

—And who are you? said the ruddy man.

—That's his sister, said Horehound, frowning. —I was thinking . . . Chester—?

—I told you one is all, said her husband. —And the sister's known as a hellion.

Events were transpiring all around me, an avalanche of catastrophe. I looked from Joe to Dutch, back and forth to the adults smiling away. —No, no, no, I said. —You can't take them separate or without me. We are all three Muldoons.

—Trust me, said Mr. Dix. —There's no one here able to take the three of you.

—Let's GO, Dutchie, I said. —Mam said keep us all together.

But Dutch was ready to cry. —My new mama says I shall have a china dolly. Please Axie I ain't going back on that train one more minute.

—Then we are separated! I cried.

A look of honest surprise came on her face. —But maybe you'll get a china doll of your own! Seven years old and bribed away from me. The two Ambroses looked at us, sorrowful again, apologizing. The wife took Dutch by the hand and began whispering poison into her ear. I scowled at her and stuck out my tongue.

—Gracious! the evil kidnapper said.

I tried to drag Dutch off but was distracted by the terrible sight of Horehound heading toward the door with Joe in her arms. —Stop, I cried, torn between them, and scrambled after my brother through the crowd. —Joe Muldoon!

—Oh there you are, said Horehound. She took Joe's hand and made him wave.

—Say bye-bye, she said, in a baby voice. Joe reached his arms for me.

—Joe!

—Now, now, says Horehound, —you'll see him when we bring him to church on Sundays and you'll see him plenty.

—NO! I tried to kick her as she shrieked and pulled Joe away.

—You must do what's right for your brother, said the frazzled Mrs. Dix, while her husband held me back by the shoulders. —Say goodbye now, Axie.

—Joe, I said, panicked. I kissed his forehead, stroked the dark hair off it. He lifted his miniature hand and I grasped it.

—AxieDutch, he said, very tired. But he did not fight when the Horehounds strode out the door and off toward their wagon. I watched as he was handed up onto the bench, and they drove off waving.

—We must be going now ourselves, said that crab Mrs. Hough. —Come with Mother. I threw off her claws in a frenzy and ran back to save Dutch at least. We would get Joe back and get on the train home. But no. There my sister was with those Ambroses, holding their hands.

—Say your farewells, her pretty kidnapper said, looking guilty as the criminal she was. My sister put her arms around me now.

—Stay with me, I whispered, and hung on. They peeled her off. They held me back and led her away. She seemed deranged with confusion, glassy with fright.

—Dutch! But there she was outside already, framed in the doorway. The sunlight glinted off her black hair like a sign she was anointed, then she was gone.

In the doorway of the church I stood with my hand lifted in a stopped wave as my brother and sister was driven away by strangers. Then the crab Mrs. Hough led me toward her sorry-looking wagon though I kicked and twisted out of her grip.

—Get off me, I said, and flailed with my satchel. —I WILL NOT GO.

—Well then I will not take you, said Mrs. Hough, and huffed away.

—You've done it now, said Mrs. Dix.

—You're in a terrible predicament, said her husband. —Your only choice is to come on the train with us to the next town, and see if we can find you a placement.

—I will take the girl, said a voice in a quaver.

We looked at the emptying church, and there sitting quietly coughing in the front pew was a white-haired woman with apple cheeks and hair like spun glass on top of her head. Her name was Henrietta Temple, and she was the Reverend's wife.

—Let this young lady board with me for a time, she said to the Dixes. —If we can't find her a placement here in Rockford, she can ride back with you when you come through this way again.

It was the least miserable of my options, and so I was glad to let the Dix leave without me. They rounded up the four or five unchosen orphans, Mag among them.

—Goodbye Mag, I said. —Write to me.

—I will, she said, but I known she lied for she did not know how.

When she and the Dix was gone I went with trembly old Mrs. Temple around to a white house in back of the church with my little suitcase in hand. As we went, she was wracked by coughing so it was plain I was farmed out to a consumptive. She showed me to a narrow room by the kitchen, so deluxe with its own bed, a washstand, and white curtains in the one window, made of dotted swiss. It was all just for me.

—You can be our guest here for the time being.

—Maybe you wouldn't mind having my sister and brother here neither, I said, enthusiastic. —We'd all share the one bed, no complaints.

Mrs. Temple's eyes ducked away from me. —We can't take in every orphan that comes our way. As much as I would like to.

—Are your children grown?

Mrs. Temple looked sadly at me. —I always wanted a kitchen full of youngsters. But God had other plans for me.

I wish I'd of known Mrs. Temple during the troubles of her younger days, for I'd have prescribed her raspberry tea and black cohosh root and a regimen with egg whites, and she'd not long have remained barren. She was a kind woman. She patted my knee and gave me lemonade, but she could not take me permanent.

That night in my private room I slept alone for the first time in my born days and wrapped the Mrs. Reverend's white piqué coverlet over my raw thumb and suckled it for comfort. At thirteen years of age, I was no better than a baby, and with the knuckles of my thumb pressed against the taste of dread in my mouth, I fell asleep.

Chapter Six

My Heart Is Like Wax

*T*he next morning, Mrs. Temple put a fat book down beside me at the kitchen table. —The Book of Psalms. Start copying where you like, and fill the page. She gave me a pencil and paper. I copied the letters with great effort while Mrs. T. coughed and mended socks and didn't care that I had not more than five spotty years of school before my father lost his balance and died and we children was sent out to beg. —Read aloud, said she.

—I am poured out like water, I read, halting and bad, —and all my bones are out of joint. My heart is like wax. Yea dogs are all round about me. A company of evildoers encircle me.

—Keep going.

—Save me from the mouth of the lion, my life from the power of the dog.

—Very good.

—What is that? What happened about the dogs? The whole story excited my interest very much.

—It's a Psalm of David! she said, smiling like we were talking about sunny days. —It's about a man hunted and hounded and forced to flee into the wilderness. Copy the whole verse.

The hounded man and me had much in common, but writing him out was grim hard work and Mrs. Reverend was a stickler for me to finish. My pencil wore to a stub.

—Considering your deficiencies and deprivations, said Mrs. Temple brightly, —you are not a bad pupil.

The heat came to my face and despite her backhanded praise I was proud. —When can I see my sister Dutch and brother Joe?

—On Sunday Mrs. Trow comes to church with the boy. And your sister's family the Ambroses come regularly too.

—They are not her family. We ain't orphans.

—I see, dear, said Mrs. Temple. But she did not see. All week, she drilled me in spelling and reading. She brushed my hair and petted me, taught me fancy sewing and the words to Shall We Gather at the River. On Sunday at last she tied an enormous white ribbon in my hair with big loops like the ears of a rabbit. —Oh you do look sweet! She put her pale spongy arms around me, smelling of tea roses, and we went over to church. I skipped up the steps in a lather to see my brother and sister.

When Dutch arrived, she was a stranger in a new dress, her hair done in corkscrews. —Axie! she cried. —I miss you.

—What have they done to your hair?

—Mother curls it with a curling iron.

She might as well have taken that same hot iron to my eyeballs, calling this pretender Mother.

—I got my own room, Dutch blathered on, —and a doll with glass eyes and a music box that plays Oh My Dear Old Augustine. Last night we made ice cream!

My heart grew a green algae of jealousy.

—Sure, me and Joe would like to come along with you for dat, I said.

—For THAT you mean, said somebody, interrupting. —Not DAT.

Mrs. Ambrose had come up behind us smiling while correcting my speech.

—Dutch darling, says she, very frosty, —you found Axie Muldoon.

—Could my sister and our Joe come for ice cream? Dutch inquired her. —It ain't much trouble for you and Father.

—ISN'T much trouble, Dutch dear, said the false blue-eyed mother.

—I knew it! my sister cried. —It ain't no trouble, so yiz can come after church!

The Ambrose woman was wincing in dismay. —No, I meant ISN'T any trouble, not AIN'T. I was not suggesting . . .

But now we sisters was distracted by the sight of our own Joe across the yard aloft in the arms of the Horehound, who was showing him off. —Joe! We ran to him, but when he saw us he put his head down on the Horehound's shoulder and hid his face. I put my arms out for him, but he would not come to me and clung on to her baggy neck.

—Joe, I said. —Pat a cake. I clapped hands and sang about the Baker's Man till he peeked at me from under her bonnet strings and gave me his half-cocked smile.

—You remember Axie? said Horehound to Joe as she handed him to my arms.

As if he could forget his own sister. She was all syrup to my face, so generous to let me play with my own Joe, except now we had church to endure, and Reverend Temple began his sermon about the judgment soon to be upon us poor SINNERS.

—Let NOT those who live a life of poverty and distress FLATTER themselves that in their SORRY lot they shall escape the judgment of God. The Rev. thundered on, talking about ME. —Thus saith the Lord, although I have cast them far off and SCATTERED them, yet will I be to them as a sanctuary. O my hearer, make the Lord thy habitation.

I did not see how the Lord could be a proper habitation at all, so when church was over, I proposed to Dutch again to get me and Joe into her new home.

—But is it true you hit Mrs. Hough with your satchel? asked my sister.

—No, only with my fists and boots. I thracked the c**p out of her.

—Oh Axie, you must not curse, my mother says.

—She ain't your mam, and I'll curse when I want, and thrack that person you call your mother just like I did old crab Mrs. Hough for trying to steal me.

—My mama says you're wicked and it's best I don't think of you Axie! my sister wailed. —It's best I be their little girl alone. Every day I miss you, but they say I'm not to mention nothing of it.

—No, you are a MULDOON, never forget, descended from the Kings of Lurg.

—But what will I do? she cried, hysterical. —I am called Dutch Ambrose now.

*   *   *

The next Sunday neither the Ambroses nor the Horehounds came to church.

—Must be they've caught a summer cold, Mrs. Temple said. —Maybe next week.

But they did not come next week, nor the next. I known it was because I said AIN'T. Because I cursed. Because I hit Mrs. Hough and bit that old man. My heart was like wax, melted down into hard drops. In my little room, Mrs. Temple sat on the lip of the bed and took my raw hand all red from my nightmares troubling it.

—Axie, you must not think of them, she said, and patted my hair. Her voice was soft, but the words she spoke were hard stale crusts with no comfort.

—Why can't I stay here with you?

—I am very old, and I am not well. Best to move on. We are meant to accept and rejoice in His wisdom. The Lord works in his strange ways.

His ways were not only strange but downright perverse, as far as I could see. Still, in case there was something to it, I tried my best with the prayers. *Lord hold us young Muldoons in the palm of Your hand and carry us home to our Mam.*

That summer Mrs. Temple occupied me around the church and the kitchen when she did not have me at my letters. For hours in the garden I pulled pigweed and Spanish nettles from the squash plants. I wrote out the Psalms of David till my hand cramped and my head buzzed with the words I Am Poured Out Like Water and All My Bones Are Out of Joint. There was no one to talk to. No one who showed up to say, Oh come and be my little daughter, I will corkscrew your hair.

On a dull August day, full of self-pity, I was out by the road kicking dust, when there along walking barefoot, his pants too short by half, was a rough-looking boy. When he got up close, I seen it was Bulldog Charlie from the train.

—If it ain't the orphan girl with the mother, he said with a sneer.

—Talk about my mother I'll scratch you.

—Try it, your claws will break.

—So, you got a last name now? I heard you was Charlie Booth.

—Don't never mention the name Booth to me. It's the name of a thumb-sucking liver-hearted puke.

I hid my thumbsucked red hand behind my back as he sat down next to me on the steps. He broke a long thin branch into fractions.

—How is your placement then? I asked, frightened by how he snapped the twig.

—Finished. I nearly ripped the beard off Booth's face. Give me a chance I'll cut the lids off both his eyes.

He rubbed his right thumb across the hard calluses of his left palm, as if preparing to strangle something. —I worked Booth's plow every day till the sun went down. Yet still the b*ll*cks called me a lazy Irish b*****d. Fed me pig scraps. Woke me before sunrise to slave some more, without stop. Wake up Mick, he said, ya dirty Fenian Arab, muck the stall. Well I'd muck HIM if I had half a chance.

He threw the smithereens of twigs into the air and they fell on the dusty road. —And you, here, Miss Half Orphan. What about you?

—They make me write out psalms, I said, nervous of him.

—Psalms? Is it psalms you're complaining of? he scoffed. —Look here. Then he pulled up the back of his shirt and showed me wheals of a whip on his back, red and raw.

The sight was mortifying. Charlie didn't look at me, but only picked up a stone and threw it hard and wild at the road.

—You want a chicken sandwich? I asked after a bad minute.

He shrugged, so I brung him around to the kitchen door. Mrs. Temple was not at home. Charlie sat down at the table in his black mood and ate a sandwich without stopping. —You'll make yourself sick, the way you eat, I said.

—Not me. Who I'd make sick is Booth. I'd go after him right now. Cut out his tongue and cook his liver and mail his organs to New York.

—There's a train back there Mrs. Temple says. Paid with a ticket.

—You're joking.

—Just before Christmas.

—Then I'm on it. What about you?

—Not me. My brother and sister's here, and I've swore to look after them.

—Your sister lives in a big house outside town, he said. —Two stories and a big porch with a swing and a barn and servants. Those Ambrose set up here with their railroad swag. Plenty a room there.

—They wouldn't take three of us.

—That's 'cuz they're snoots, he said, and flipped his thumb off his nose, stood up from his chair. —Thanks for the grub, Ax. Now I'm off again. On the way out the door he cast me back a terrible wink full of fury. The screen slapped shut and he was gone.

At last in December, there was the New York train huffing steam in the hard air of Rockford. Down from the steps of the passenger car disembarked the would-be authors of my future, those two Dix. There by the depot stood me and orphan Charlie, with my champion Mrs. Reverend Henrietta Temple to see us off. She was our solitary farewell party. No last minute trumpet blast announced the appearance of my sister and brother, crying for me to stay. Nobody came to beg, Don't go. God did not scoop me up in the palm of His hand. The train huffed and snorted.

—Goodbye child, said Mrs. Temple, and pressed my head to her bosom.

There was not no home in Rockford for me, she had explained, and promised she would write me news of my siblings care of the Aid Society as soon as she could. She kissed me goodbye and I climbed onto the train. Just as I gazed my last on that dingy cowpat town, I seen a carriage stop alongside the tracks by the depot. A woman dismounted with a small girl. As the train pulled out I seen it was Mrs. Ambrose, and the girl was my sister trotting along beside her. —Dutchie, I cried.

As the train gathered speed, the two figures lifted their gloved hands to wave goodbye. My sister appeared to be smiling, her hand patting the air. Goodbye, goodbye.

—Dutchie! I ran down the aisle for the door, ready to leap.

Mrs. Dix was too fast for me, and caught my arm. —Stop now! They just wanted to wave farewell. They will write you letters, you can be sure.

Confined to my seat, I watched out the window with red eyes while the land flew backwards in waves of carpet unrolling.

Chapter Seven

A Wild Ungoverned Heart

*T*en minutes out of Rockford, Charlie the nameless orphan slid into the empty seat next to me. He punched me in the arm, just softly.

—Squeak squeak, he said. —City mice again.

—I'm not no mouse.

—We'll see about that. Why the red eyes, little missus?

I did not answer.

—Cheer up ya grannymush why don't you? We're heading back to glory, out of this godforsaken blot on the map. Ain't you glad to see the last of it?

—I'll be back, said I.

—Can't keep away from the excitements of the prairie, eh? He flicked his thumbnail off his front teeth at me, then went lurching back down the aisle of the train, cracking his spruce gum.

—Sit down there now mister, said Dix.

—No thanks, he called back. —I drather not.

Charlie was never still the whole train ride. He strolled up and down the aisles and rode between cars. He whistled and hummed. He chewed pine gum. No matter that the Dix said Sit down, please, sit down, he only leaned his seventeen years old self against the doorframe and took a piece of rope from his pocket. He began to tie knots in it, bowlines and hitches. Nooses. We were well into the next day and Ohio before he spoke to me again. He came from the back of the car, so I didn't see him till he plunked down next to me, breathless, his hair a wreck. He was windburned. Streams of tears watered the corners of his eyes.

—Where've you been?

—On the train roof, he said, his grin enormous.

—You was not.

—Was. Rode up there half an hour. It's better than flying.

—You're lyin. If you was you'd be in trouble.

—Them Dix don't give a parson's n*pple what I do. If I fell off and died they would cheer.

I tried not to laugh at the word n*pple but only failed.

—So, Charlie said, sideways at me. —Wanta? He wagged his eyebrows and pointed upwards at the roof. —You wouldn't never.

—I would so.

—You won't do it. You'd cry. You're a chicken-livered type.

I ignored him, stuck my chin out like his, even as I wished to ride the rooftops, brave as him and carefree.

—Suit yourself, says he, and made chicken noises. He swayed down the aisle, and at the end of the car, he beckoned to me. When I did not follow, he slid the door open. A blast of noise and cold came in, but none of the other passengers paid attention. The Dix were snoring.

What the H., I thought, and went after Charlie.

The platform between the cars was narrow and open to the sky. The racket of the wheels matched the churning fear in my system. Charlie grinned when he saw me, and pointed. A ladder led up to the roof. He grabbed a rung and climbed up.

—C'mon. It's easy.

At the top he threw his leg on the roof and hauled the rest of himself after. He looked down and waved me up. I grabbed the low rung and put one foot, then one hand, on the ladder. Through my knit mitten the metal bit cold into the skin. The ground underneath us raced away, a bed of blackened snow below, hard gravel and ash, the sparks off the wheels. My mouth was dry as paper. Nobody would care if I fell. I climbed till at the top rung I pushed my head above the roof line. Knives of wind cut at me, pushed back the flesh of my face.

Charlie lay on his stomach, reaching for me. —Atta girl. Grab on.

—F. yourself.

—The dirty mouth on you. I thought you was a girl but now I seen you're a hoodlum. He seemed glad of it, or even proud.

—F. and S., I said, and felt his praise as good as a pat on the back.

—Get your leg over.

I was up. I was on the roof. The train hurtled and fear froze me in the wind so I was staked there, fused to the metal, eyes streaming in the cold. Charlie grinned and called me Fraidy Cat. I could not rise farther than my knees. There was no hand hold. No foot hold. We was on all fours. Crawling. My breath was gone, stolen by the wind and sky all around. Charlie's hair stood up wild, in snakes. For a minute I believed he would push me. He laughed at me, grinning out one side of his mouth.

—It's great, ain't it? he whooped and we gazed out at the vastness passing, flat and white, glistening with snow. The glare was blinding.

—What? he says. —Are you petrified?

I was. Also thrilled. We sat up there and watched the country pass us by. It was empty of humans, not a building, not a line of smoke or sign of a crop for miles, only white with the long black track behind and ahead, the rails a silver thread.

—Ain't it swell? Charlie spit, his eyes rueful over the wasteland. —All that green fresh air. The mushmelons and the prairie sod.

—The pie and the pony. My voice was flat as his.

—All you can eat. Fresh milk and brown bread.

We watched it pass, flat and white. The train was slowing, then slowed still more. Something was wrong. Now a tomato-faced head popped up over the roof line of the train, scrags of hair whipped up in the wind. It was Dix, in a red apoplexy.

—What the devil do you two think you are doing? he cried.

—Havin' forty winks, Charlie said. —A snooze.

—Get down here this instant, Dix ordered us, and as we climbed down he lectured. —What devilment were you up to? We feared you were dead! Heathens!

Mr. Dix dragged Charlie off for a tongue-lashing, and Mrs. Dix took me by the arm and brought me to her seat. I sat red-cheeked and winded, gazing at my lap.

—Miss Muldoon, Mrs. Dix sighed, so mournful, —do you not realize that all the circumstances of life are against a friendless girl like you? You are under the worst sort of influences with a renegade boy like that. To take you on the roof of a train! This behavior can lead nowhere but to vice and degradation.

—I'm sorry, missus, I said, tracing patterns in the fog on the window glass.

She fanned herself. Little worried curls of frizz had sprang up around her hairline. —Our intention is to bring the influences of discipline and religion to bear on your wild and ungoverned heart. Will you or will you not reform your ways?

—If at all possible, I will.

—Well, if you cannot, you will be left with no choice but the streets. I must warn you there is no class in all our metropolis that combines so many elements of human misfortune as the women of the pavement. We see them in our shelters and they have no appreciation of what neatness is, or virtue. They have no discipline. If they receive a few shillings they spend it on some foolish geegaw.

Geegaw. I wished for one, whatever it was. It sounded edible, or like a jewel.

—These are cunning females who steal! or take to drinking! Worst, they become . . . Magdalenes, and live on the wages of . . . of . . . lust! I must be frank, Miss Muldoon. Half the orphans we try so desperately to rescue are the result of, ahem, sin and ruination. Is this your fate? To create more orphans?

—I would do anything to prevent an orphan, said I, ignorant of what my promise foretold but meaning every word.

—You must guard against the, ahem, chemical . . . influences of charming orphans like that one there, Charlie. What powers do you have to resist the temptations of wicked boys like him?

—I know how to write a psalm of David, I said in my defense.

—Do you? she said, softening toward me. —Do you know it by heart? Now she prompted me, quoting, —My God, my God, why hast thou forsaken me? She waited, expecting me to go on.

—But I am a worm, I said, —scorned by men, and despised by the people. All who see me mock at me.

Her face was livid with pity. —Oh dear. Poor little girl. You are not a worm.

I was relieved to hear it.

—You are not forsaken! she cried, embracing me. —Not by me, nor by our Lord, either. But you must not succumb to the influence of wild unruly boys like Charles, fathered in sin and mothered by the streets. No good will come of it.

I gave her a dutiful smile and busied myself fingering the upholstery of the seat.

—We will arrive in New York in two days' time and have made splendid arrangements for you! A lawyer and his wife are looking for a housemaid!

—I will go find my Mam.

Mrs. Dix was sorrowful. —But we have no word of her. She has left Charity Hospital. Like many of the poor, your mother was stubborn and could not see what was best for her. Last we heard, she went off with a man of her acquaintance.

With a kiss on the top of my head, and a swipe of her finger down my nose, my protector returned to her husband, who had dismissed Charlie after a long sermon. Those Dix chatted away all night about our ignorant vices and terrible lack of neatness, while I burrowed into my corner of the seat and brooded out the window hollow as a gourd.

On the morning of the last day on the train, with the fearsome Gomorrah of our city drawing near and the Dix snoring in their dreams, Bulldog Charlie slid in the seat next to me once more. My stomach tightened with nerves and danger and something else I could not name. He was wild and unruly and a man of seventeen. I was thirteen years of age only. He jigged his leg. I tucked stray pieces of hair behind my ears and tucked my childish red knuckles under my skirts. If he did anything wicked or lured me with temptations I was to scream out, as Mrs. Dix had instructed me.

—That was a gas then, wasn't it, on the roof?

—Yeah, I said.

—We'll do it again now how 'bout? Last chance.

—Not me.

—You've not got the baubles for it?

—I cannot deny I've not got the baubles.

He laughed at me while I blushed and wondered should I scream out because he said baubles and made me say it. He did not seem wicked. We said nothing while nothing passed outside the window.

—Why don't you have no mother? I asked.

He shrugged. —Legend has it, the traps found me wandering in my britches on the Battery, eating from bins, without no knowledge of how I got there. By my teeth they judged me to be three years of age.

I pictured him just bigger than Joe.

—They say all I known was my name, and the words to McGinty.

—Can you still sing it?

He waited. Then, soft in the dark of the train, he sang, so surprising, his voice half-drowned by the wheels' chuff. —Pat-trick McGinty, an Irishman of note, came in-to a fortune, so bought himself a goat.

He crooned out the verses, all the dirty ones about the goat and Mary Jane in the lane, and how that goat ate somebody's folderols, then swallowed some bank notes and kissed Nora, and was supposed to be a nanny but was found to be a bill. He had me laughing so hard I put my hand over my mouth so Mrs. Dix would not wake. I seen that Charlie liked to have me for his audience, and he sang out like a showman. —Leave the rest to Prov-i-dence and Paddy McGinty's goat.

—People threw me pennies when I sang it, says he, rather proud.

—Too bad on you but I don't have no pennies to throw.

Charlie then recounted how the police brung him to the nuns, and for eight years the Sisters of Charity spoilt him. They taught him the Our Father and the Hail Mary and the alphabet then made him read Mr. Aquinas and do the catechism. They said, Oh you're so clever with your letters, you'll be a priest!

—You're not no priest, I laughed. —Not never.

—Reason is that at thirteen years of age the Sisters threw me out. They wouldn't let me smoke. Just as well. I'm not a fella who likes to be cornered.

—How'd you manage then?

—A half-ate corncob tossed on the sidewalk makes a fine supper. Plenty of ways to get silver from the pockets of swells.

—So you're a thief? I said, wondering should I scream.

—And what are you, Miss Half Orphan? A saint?

He twirled his bit of rope very angry now, folded it three times and wrapped loops around the folds, counting them. —A noose, see? Thirteen loops for bad luck. When it slides, like this, see? He slid the coils in a slip knot. —Wham. It snaps the neck. He put the noose around my arm and pulled so it cinched the skin. —See? Snap.

—How fast do you die?

—You die slow. I seen it at the Bridge of Sighs. You twist in the wind.

We stayed quiet for a long while. Out the window the sun began to rise, pinkening the sky, and we seen thickets of houses and buildings as we closed in toward the city.

—So where are you off to in Gotham, Miss Half Orphan Muldoon?

—To find my Mam in Cherry Street, I said.

—I'll escort you then, will I?

—Don't be too sure.

—But I AM sure. Now he put the noose joking over my head and pulled like it was a necktie. It tightened up by my throat, strangely tender. I did not move nor say stop.

—You're crazy, I said quietly. —Are you?

—Half crazy. His eyes was black and shiny as hard coal.

Mrs. Dix awoke now and saw me with the noose around my neck. She came lurching over, pink in the face. Mr. Dix trailed just behind her.

—What in heaven's name is going on?

I lifted the noose off with a queer mix of tastes in my mouth, of fear, and that other disturbance without no name.

—Young sir! Mr. Dix shook his finger in Charlie's face. —Just the other day I made it quite clear that your vile habits were not to be tolerated. Are you nothing but a ruffian? Where did you get this foul skill?

—Learnt it at the Tombs, Mr. Dix, beg your pardon, sir, said Charlie, all charm.

—Come away now, Miss Muldoon, said Mr. Dix. —We'll arrive within hours.

I stood to follow, but Charlie caught my arm. —I'll escort you to Cherry Street, he said. —I can find your mother.

—You can't! said Mrs. Dix.

—H*** I can, he said. —I'll find her other arm, too.

*   *   *

Arriving at last in New York, the Dix attempted in vain to convince me to come along to my new indentured status as maid to a lawyer. Charlie was to get work as a newsboy.

—No thanks, Charlie told them. —We're off to Mrs. Muldoon's.

—If you so stubbornly refuse our offer, said Mr. Dix, —the CAS has no further obligation to you. Indeed it is the policy of the Society that our youth must learn from experience. Honest servitude offers you both a chance at redemption.

—If you won't take me to my Mam I'll go myself, I told them.

The Dix conferred alone, shaking their heads. —That girl has always been unmanageable, I heard Mr. Dix say. Tsking and tongue-clucking at my certain downfall, them Dix left us orphans with their horrified admonishments, an address for the CAS, and a fortune of two dollars pocket money each, then they disappeared into the throng of Christmas travelers and the smoke off a chestnut cart.

—We're off to Cherry Street, Charlie said. —To find your mother and her arm.

Chapter Eight

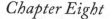

Mrs. Duffy

*T*owards evening the fast city horses of the Harlem line pulled us by omnibus through the buildings and the mad roiling traffic, past the sidewalk throngs and mess of noise. We was happy at the press of people crowding the car, the regular clopping of hoofs on cobbles. Over the crots of snow the lamplight fell golden, and the smells of hot corn off the vendors' carts mingled with whiffs of manure in the wind. The cries of the clam sellers and the catfish mongers was a ragged song of home in our ears, while above our heads the city's buildings loomed, four and five stories. Their windows was yellow cat eyes watching, ready to swallow us like we was mice. I shivered in my charity coat.

—You're cold? said Charlie.

—No.

He put his arm around my shoulders as if I was his small sister, and I did not say a word about the dangerous fact of it there or its chemical influence such as Mrs. Dix described. We got off the omnibus at Chambers Street and walked east. Charlie strode along, hands in his pockets, eyes shifting left right left. We didn't speak. After many long blocks we found our way to Cherry Street, which I seen now with new prairie-tainted eyes of shame. The squatty buildings of the neighborhood was just as Brace and Dix described, cesspools of degradation, fevernests with all manner of garbage flung out the windows. Soused old geezers stood around grumbling on the gruesome stoops. A whiskered old woman with a pipe in her teeth gave us a dead stare and held her hand out scranning for coins such as I had done. And would do again. That beggary was my fate now I knew with a hard certainty that made my palm itch for the feel of silver. Tough coves with smokes between their teeth looked ready to jump us, staring at me and Charlie like we was foreigners.

We made our way to 128 Cherry and down the muckled alley to the rear tenement. The stench when I smelt it in the stairwell was solid like a wall. I was home, with a taste of dread like chalk in my mouth. My mother waited at the top of these stairs. Did she? I feared her absence so bad I was ill of it and also trembled to face her without my sister and brother. Up we went three stories and I knocked, faint with hope.

—What is it? A man opened the door. His suspenders were at his waist and his shirt open to his hairy poitrine. He was that sot Michael Duffy. He and my Da's sister Aunt Nance must have their baby born by this time. —Who is it now?

—Axie, I says, and when he still didn't know me, I said, —Mary is my mother.

—The one arm woman?

—Yes, she lost her other.

—Just misplaced the f****r somewheres, Duffy says, laughing, and looks me over. —So ain't you a clean big girl now? I didn't recognize ya. The smell of poteen came off his breath. Charlie came out of the shadows behind me.

—And who is this great lout?

—Just Charlie, I said.

—Just Charlie looks just hungry, said Duffy. —I hope he just ain't.

—Is my mother here? She'll be glad to see me.

—We'll have a party, then, won't we? We'll raise a glass. Duffy admitted us inside now with reluctance.

Looking around in the dim I seen the place was jammed more than ever. Barrels stacked in corners, pots and chairs and baskets hung off the ceiling. Two people were sleeping on the platform up the ladder. By the tops of their heads I took them to be the Kevin Duffys.

—Mary! Michael Duffy called. —That stubborn big girl of yours is here.

Now my mother appeared from the back room like my dreams of her, surprised in the lamplight. Her dark hair was down, her dress unbuttoned too low in the front. And it was true. She had just the one arm. Another had not grown in its place, which shocked me somehow. When she saw me, her face lit and crumpled at the same time.

—Mam!

—Oh, she cried, and rushed me, making noises like a bird. —Oh, Axie. She put her single arm around me, cooing and clucking, the stump dangling in its sleeve. —I thought you were lost to me, she murmured, kissing me. —*Mavourneen machree.* She thought she would never see me again alive, she thought I was gone and lost to her, lost. I circled her waist, my head on her shoulder. Her body was thick now through the middle and it was plain all of a sudden that it was not just her arm that was missing. Her waist was gone too, now, her belly swelled. My eyes dropped down to it and she nodded her head quick and looked away with fearful eyes of shame and relief at the sight of me. We did not need no big words. Everything was said silent like that, so I known everything and nothing at the same time. I was home with her. I had not thought no further than that.

—Mam, I said, over and over. She smelled of cabbage and beer. No cologne from a Paris parfumerie ever matched her scent for heaven and I clasped her to me lost in the rush of it, her voice and embrace, till I remembered Charlie. I turned and introduced her. —Charlie this is my Mam.

—Hello Charlie. Mam smiled so he blushed. —You're a fine lad, aren't ya?

—Just a minute now, Duffy said. —Hold your horses. He was looking very frank at me, with his lip curled back off his teeth so he had the look of a fight dog. —I thought you was on the prairie, living off the fat of the land.

—There was not no fat, Charlie told him.

—Who axed you? Duffy said.

—I'm asking him, my mother says, and Duffy muttered HAG and TABBY and FEN under his breath. His little names for her.

Charlie and me now told them of our travails. Mam listened, stunned and betrayed. —The pity, she wept, and stroked my hair, murmuring her Irish endearments. —*Macushla machree.* Charlie turned his eyes away, and I thought of how nobody never said *macushla* to him nor even darling.

—And all along, for faith, I was thinking of you in clover. My mother bit her lip at the enormity of her mistake.

—We thought yiz was all cats in cream, so we did, said Duffy.

—Dutch lives in a great house, I told them, —with a swing on the porch and servants all to tend her, and she wears her hair in sausage curls, Mam.

—Does she then? she asked, with glittering eyes. —And our Joe?

I did not have the strength to tell her I didn't have the first knowledge about Joe. —He goes to church regular with the family where he stays. They feed him horehound drops and carry him around like a prize chicken.

—All I wanted was to have yiz all safe and fed. At least I've you back, Axie.

—Hold on, said Mr. Duffy. —Do you think yer all coming home to mother now?

—Ah jayz, Michael, this here's my dear daughter Axie who I pined for.

—And have you pined for this big cove here, too? Duffy pointed to Charlie.

My Aunt Bernice and Kevin Duffy now woke and peered over the edge of their sleeping loft and watched us like they was at the cockfights, lying on their stomachs with their heads propped in their hands. —He's no son of yours, Mary, said Kevin Duffy.

Charlie scuffed at the floor.

—Muldoons oughta take him in, I said, surprising myself. —He's got no last name. Charlie Muldoon's good as any.

—Not so fast, Mam said, her eyes on the floor. —I am Mrs. Duffy now.

—She's the new Mrs. Duffy, Bernice called down.

—That makes you the old Mrs. Duffy, Uncle Kevin told her, and the two of them up in their roost laughed big phlegmy cackles.

Nobody said a word about our father's sister Aunt Nance who used to be Michael Duffy's wife. Where was she? And what happened to her baby who would be my little cousin? My mother had her finger to her lips as it dawned on me Nance was gone and Mam shared her bed with the sot Michael Duffy. Now my new stepfather stared as Mam brought out half a loaf of bread from the cupboard and offered it to me and Charlie.

—Hold on there, said Duffy, eyeing the bread, his hand on her wrist.

—It's for our own Axie, so it is, said she, and petted his head. —Oh Michael, they've come a long way, so they have. And sure them Aid Society people give them a dollar. Haven't they done, Axie?

Michael Duffy's eyes flickered as I reached in my coat pocket and brought out my two coins. It gutted me to turn my money over to that man, and it turned my stomach to see how my mother stroked Duffy's head and cooed at him. But after enough of her coaxing, he lay down in the back room and his snores soon filled the place. We ate our bread and was left hungry still. My mother gave Charlie a place to sleep by the stove and put me in the back room opposite the shakedown mattress where Mr. Duffy snored. Mam lay down next to me and pulled a cover over us. All that night she slept with her only hand clasped around mine, and not even the beastly snorts and mutterings of my new stepfather could make me sorry I was returned to her.

When I woke the next morning, Mr. Duffy was gone. —I do not like him, I told her. —You never did neither. You said he was a louse.

—But he married me. Useless as I am.

—Where is our Aunt Nan? I asked. —Where's her baby she was going to have?

—She died of having it. The child along with her, Mam said. Her voice was flat and her eyes turned into the distance as she rubbed her palm over the round of her stomach. —Duffy took it hard.

—He does not like Charlie, I said.

—That fella cannot stay here. I'm sorry. We Duffys've not got the where-withal.

Nobody had no wherewithal it seemed. If Duffys had nothing to spare for Charlie, how would they spare anything for our Joseph and our Dutchie? There did not seem to be no plan to be a family of Muldoons. It was only me now. Was it?

—You've got to leave, Mam told Charlie, when he woke up. —I'm sorry for it.

—So long as I ain't wandering the cowpaths of Rockford, Illinois, I'll be grand, he said, with a bitter quirk to his mouth.

Mam gave Charlie bread and tea, and spoke kindly to him, and we all went down the stairs and through the alley to the street.

There Charlie tipped his hat. —Farewell to you Mrs. Duffy, and to you, Miss Chickenhearted Muldoon. I'll be back to check on yiz before the cherries bloom on Cherry Street. He set off with his hands in his pockets, his head flung back, watching gulls wheel in the sky. They were white chalk marks against the dark clouds.

—Don't never marry nobody poor, my mother said, watching after him.

But who else there was besides a poor fellow to marry was not in evidence.

We walked along, a porridge of slush under our feet. The wind swirled leaves and rubbish in the corners of alleys, and that was the *sheehogues* dancing, Mam said, her Irish word for fairies. She stirred up a picture of pixies in flower petals despite that it was a worse cold day than ever. It was a comfort to be near my mother. The way she went ahead briskly, her head swiveling left and right, was familiar to me. Her one sleeve wagged empty in the breeze, and with her good hand she held mine as we walked, like an announcement that I belonged to her, and she to me. But as I inspected her in the daylight, I seen my mother was washed out, draggled and old. She was Mrs. Duffy now.

—Mam, I says, —when will you go and fetch our Joe and Dutch for us?

She stopped and made me look at her. —Axie, does it look like we've a pot to p*** in? They're better off in the West, so they are.

—But I want them. We are the Muldoons. Daughters and sons of the Kings of Lurg, Da said Never forget it.

—And you haven't, and so you won't. She smiled so watery at me. —One day you'll find them again and see they're royalty of Lurg right out on the American prairie, the both of them. We'll call Dutch Queenie then and we'll call him King Joseph the Red, won't we? with his crown all jeweled. We'll sit around the old castle, sure we will, drinking sherry wine, and be glad we sent them off to gain a fortune.

She kissed me on the hair and said that was the plan, so what else could I do but picture it, the crown and the jewels and the castle, while we rummaged all that day through the cold, for money or scrap, whatever we could get. What we got was a door slammed in our face and a lump of coal heaved at our heads. We pocketed the coal and found nothing else till late in the afternoon, when my mother spied a torn sheet blown off somebody's washline, and I pried a frozen stocking from a slab of ice.

—Wool, cried Mam when she saw it. —You'll get a penny for it. She explained that the ragman would clean it and put it in a grinding mill.

—What for?

—To be woven into shoddy and mungo.

Shoddy and mungo was not a pair of minstrels but types of fabric, she said, made from such flotsam as this frozen sock, scraps and bits we might find for money. Broken down and rewoven they soon would become a soldier's uniform, some lady's dress.

—They get a new life, my mother said.

—I wish you and me could get a new life too. I'll be shoddy and you'll be mungo.

—Ah jayz, you always was a cutup, she said, and smiled at me so that if I'd have had a tail I'd have wagged it.

Through that winter, my mother expanded. She was heavy and silent, a cabbage under her dress. Every day I went out and scavenged for scraps of cloth and metal, rinds and crusts. The enterprise was next to worthless. The streets of all New York were picked clean as cadaver bones by a swarm of grubworms.

One morning, finding not a thread, I wandered thinking of Dutch warm and snug in her ringlets and Joe eating lemon drops while my own stomach withered with the hunger. After a while I arrived at Washington Square, amidst the grand houses, the private carriages and ladies strolling with their puny dogs on strings. The footman and the maids was in little caps adorned with folderols of bric-a-brac. Through the windows, I saw an old man served a glass of port on a silver tray held by a Negro woman. I saw two cats pawing a shade pull, a wrinkled lady arranging blossoms in a vase. I saw a wee child in front of a piano the size of a knacker's wagon. She sat like an angel in a red dress, plinking the keys. Her miniature patent leather boots did not reach the floor but dangled kicking time to the music. The sound jangled out faint through the panes, and Twinkle Twinkle Little Star was the tune. I stared, craving the black and white keys of the instrument, the red dress, the tune plinking away like a taste in my mouth.

—Move along there, miss, said a gentleman. —Move along.

—Move along yourself, you big ox, I said, but he had a walking stick tipped with silver raised in my direction, so I scrambled away, my head furious with plans. One day I'd have such pianos and goblets, draperies and gewgaws and gated walkways with wrought iron curlicues. For now I turned into an alley and spied a row of ash barrels set out for collection. I dug through their contents no better than a dog. There was coffee grounds and eggshell and rags greasy with stove blacking. There was the bones of a roast chicken, plus the feet, all of which I wrapped in a bit of paper for soup. Then toward the bottom was treasure: whole slices of a roast joint congealed in gravy, four or six potatoes half ate in their skins, the scrapings of plates frozen in a mash of cake and sauce, cold peas and cream. A wasted miracle from the table of some ponce. I wrapped the haul in my apron, and carried it home triumphant, launching up the stairs two at a time.

When Mam seen my findings, she set about with great excitement, slicing cabbage. She was not bad with a knife even with the one arm, and together we simmered Washington Square Hoity Toity Stew, the discarded meat stretched with cabbage and one onion cooked in a sauce of ale. The smell of it tortured us as we awaited Michael Duffy, who soon came through the door from a day hauling plaster. He grabbed my mother around her thick waist and danced her about singing Whiskey in the Jar till she shrieked and laughed and swatted at him, and I saw how he nuzzled her neck and she ducked away from him, blushing and fussing with her hair.

—You're a fine one-armed woman Mary Duffy, he said to her.

—Go on Michael, she said, her eyes bright in the firelight.

They sent me to my bed to dream of grand pianos and red shoes and someplace where my sister and brother played on ponies in fields of green, and we were the Muldoons again, only better.

In the darkness, later, I was woken by my stepfather's voice, thick with drink.

—Mrs. Duffy. I could hear the rustle of covers as he pawed through them. —Oh Mrs. Duffy.

—Shh, my mother laughed. —She'll wake.

—She won't.

They commenced to heave and roll about with sighs and explorations.

I did not understand how Mam tolerated him, or just what was the rent she paid for the roof over our heads. Whatever the arrangement, she did not fight him off, and I pulled my hard pillow over my ears to shut out their noises and whisperings. We children of Cherry Street started our schooling in such matters at an early age, no different from the farmer boys and girls of Illinois, observing the livestock. If you wonder, did this vast education influence my future choice of profession? The answer is yes it did.

Chapter Nine

A White Rag

$\mathcal{M}$y mother's child chose to be born on a day in February, so cold it froze the p*** of dogs, horses and men to a pale lemon color on the pavement. In the early morning when the Duffy brothers and my Aunt Bernie was out pursuing employment or swig, my mother called to me.

—Axie? she said, her voice peculiar.

When I got up from my bed she was standing in the middle of the cold front room. Steam rose off the water that broke and leaked out warm around her legs. While she mopped it she announced her baby would soon be born. She had gone downstairs to get Mrs. O'Reilly some time ago, but Mrs. O'Reilly had not shown herself. —Go down Axie now, Mam said, —and see why she hasn't.

Downstairs Mrs. O'Reilly was asleep in her overcoat, her fire gone out and the smell of gin strong about her so that if you had lit a match the room would kindle into flames. —Missus? I shook her, but she would not budge.

—I'll be along in a minute, she said, rasping, and opened her eyes long enough to wink one of them.

Back upstairs I gave the news to my mother, who sat heavy in her bed with her bare feet out in front of her, the heels cracked and yellow as bars of old soap.

—Well then, Mam ordered, —you'll go in the other room and stay by the stove and wait till Mrs. O'Reilly comes or your Aunt Bernice.

Years before when our Joe was born Dutch and me passed the day and night away with our Aunt Nance Duffy same as we did when Mam lost the two others. —Little lost babies, she said, —between the three live ones. But now Nance was dead and Mam only ordered me to go by the stove. —You shouldn't mind if I cry out, she said, her face pinched. —Never mind it.

—But I will mind.

—You mustn't. It's natural. It's pain to bring a child to the world. If nobody comes you're to cut the cord yourself.

—What will I cut?

She did not answer but sent me to the kitchen where I passed the time sewing a bunting. I was nervous, about the cord, the knife, that the child would die or worse, that my mother would, and how would her baby get out into the world? A fairy would bring it, she had once explained, but I heard otherwise amongst my wild associates on the street, and while I did not wish to believe humans are born the same as cows or dogs, I feared it was true. Why else was I not allowed to see it?

Soon enough, I heard her start her terrible noises. First they came soft, not worse than the moan of a mourning dove on the sill, but then high and stretched like something pierced her. I went to her. —Poor Mam, I said. She banished me back downstairs again to find Mrs. O'Reilly but the sot was out cold now and I could not roust her. Upstairs, Mam cried for a drink of water. I brought it. —Should I fetch someone? Mam? Should I? Anyone? The neighbors?

—No, she said. One of the Duffys would be here soon. I brought her tea. She would not drink. I covered her. She was trembling. Her brow was knit and sweated. She threw the cover off and gnashed her teeth and huffed her breath and yelled at me to Get Back AWAY from her, and despite her telling me Don't Be Afraid, I was afraid. She blubbered her cheeks and whickered like a draft horse and tossed her black hair to and fro on the bed and clawed her one hand of fingers at the covers. Stray syllables and curses came out of her mouth like hot coal was in her blood.

—Son of a b****, my poor mother cried.

She was up, then down, pacing across the floor while I cowered in the kitchen. Her hand was pressed to the small of her back, and she asked me, would I please push against the pain there? So while she braced herself one-handed against the doorjamb I leaned the heels of my palms hard into the bony plates of her sacrum. —There's a good girl, Axie, said she, with sweat running off her in the cold. How sorry she was, apologizing to me. —You shouldn't see none of this, so you shouldn't. Her head hung down for only a moment of respite before she arched it back on the stalk of her neck and cried out. She paced and squatted and lay down again. Long sounds like the bellows of a cow came from her throat. I stood terrified and useless, watching where she lay in her dark corner.

—Oh motherf***, I am dying, she whispered in a gasp.

—Don't die, don't die, I told her.

Why did the Duffys not come? I listened at the door for the footsteps of Bernice, hoping to hear them, but two hours passed, and my mother called to me again, her voice sharp now and ragged with no breath to spare. When I went to her she was lying with her knees drawn up by the round of her middle.

—The blanket, she said. She told me to put it over her legs, and I did. It made a tent when she bent them. —Get away now. Don't look.

I promised I wouldn't, but already I seen the coverlet beneath her was covered with dark clots of matter. Her legs was flashes of white in the dark room, smudged with swipes of blood. —Get away! she said, and I went back to the kitchen where I listened with clamped ears to my mother's noises, such cries as a banshee's keening, till after a long while there came some terrible last effort like dying, and a sudden new silence. My mother's deep breaths came shuddering and occasional. After a time, she called to me in a whisper. When I went to the corner I saw her lying spent, with her one solitary arm flung over her head, the legs straight out before her again, the tent collapsed.

—The blanket, she whispered. —Lift it but only a little.

With mortal fear that I might see my mother's naked bum, I raised a corner. There in the dimness, between her stained white knees and lying in a puddle of gore, appeared the form of my half sibling. Strings of hair were clotted on the scalp and a live rope of milky blue throbbed from the midsection, threaded with vessels and veins. It was a terrible sight to behold, my sister red and steaming in the cold air, like a coney freshly skinned.

—Lift the child up now, my mother instructed, so weak.

—But Mam.

—Do as I tell you, she said, very grim. —Mind the cord and don't pull.

And so I lifted the wee slippery creature, my hands on the warm bare skin. The blue rope hung off, pulsing and alive, and I stared at it dumbfounded to see it was attached somewhere to my mother. She now ordered me to hold the ankles in the one hand like you do a stew rabbit and pat the child on the back to start it breathing, so I done as she said, with one finger between the ankle bones, and swatted the baby's back. The pelt on it was wrinkled and white with matter. My sister coughed then and splayed her miniature fingers in the air. Her toes were small as kernels of corn.

—A wee girl, I said.

—God help her, whispered my exhausted mother. —Give her over to me now.

I placed her gingerly on Mam's middle and covered her with a piece of muslin of the type we used to strain curds. The baby cried a small mew. Mam lay there wrecked. Her dark hair was plastered to her forehead, and her eyes closed. Without opening them, she ordered me to find a bit of string or a bootlace.

We had a string left off a bread packet and she instructed me to tie the umbilicus in two places, close to the baby's little belly, then saw between the two strings with the knife. I followed her directions with as steady a hand as I could, despite the rebellions of my stomach. My mother praised me. —Good girl, Axie, there's a good girl. What would I do without you? she said, so I felt some desperate love well up in my tonsils. Her face was ghastly pale and I feared death had come into her and nested in the place where my sister had resided.

I sat on the bed. Mam rested on my shoulder, and the two of us looked down at the wee girl yawping now in the crook of my elbow. Her miniature mouth groped sideways in the air like a blind thing, yearning. She cried her small cat noise and wobbled against the stump of our mother's missing arm.

—Oh how will I nurse her? Mam said, suddenly weeping.

—Same as us others, I said.

Mam stared down at her new daughter, a raw look so helpless in her eyes.

—What shall we name her? I asked.

My mother did not reply.

—Call her Kathleen, I said. —For the song you like, Kathleen Mavourneen.

—Fine. Take her then.

I took Kathleen and cleaned her according to Mam's instructions and wrapped her again in a blanket and the bunting I sewed.

—Shh there now. I will not let you go at all, at all, little scrap, I whispered, and she looked back at me so serene. A chemist had mixed an elixir in her gaze to smite me, for I loved her very fierce already, and she loved me.

Late in the evening, Mr. Duffy came home bringing sausage and tea and a hangdog look of dread, never so surprised as to find my mother still alive and with a wornout runt of a baby asleep on her chest.

She looked at him, her face unsteady. —You have a girl, Mr. Duffy.

Kathleen fit just so with her head in the palm of his thick hand, and her scarlet feet at the bend of his arm. —Well aren't you a poorly little chipeen, he said, but with such a soft voice and a wondering look in his expression it was as if a hard bitter shell had been peeled off him. He kissed my mother and brushed the hair off her forehead.

She wrinkled her nose at the smell off him. —You devil, you're tanked.

—Can't a man have a pint when he's a new baby to celebrate? he asked, with his hand on his heart. He kissed my mother again as she tended the child and gave her a wink while she glared at him, but I saw the smile sneak up and get the better of her when he started chattering to my new sister.

—Hallo wee babby, Duffy says to Kathleen, taking her up in his arms. —Here you are at last. It's a good thing the milk is free, as we have no money for a cow. He sang her a little song about Oats Peas Beans and Barley Grow. He laughed and danced her around the place and gave out sausage for our dinner. It was a celebration, for I had a sister again. Mam did not eat. She kept her eyes shut.

—Get up now, Mam, I said.

But Mam did not want to get up. She turned her face to the wall and said she would rest.

Duffy bounced our Kathleen and jigged her up and down with a wiry bending of his knees. He held her up and showed her things like he was a carnival barker, saying Step Right Up Young Lady and See the Wonders of the World. This is a stove. Now, repeat after me, STOVE. This is the BED.

This is the CHAIR. And, young Kathleen, miss, this lump here is your SISTER, Axie Muldoon otherwise known as Madame Grand Attitude. So say Ta to her now Kathleen, can you say TA? And here is your MOTHER isn't she a beautiful bit of bloss there? He leaned over and puckered his lips at Mam and said, —Give Kathleen's father a kiss Mary Duffy. But Mam was tired on the bed, so pale. Her hair was damp and she lay sidelong with her knees bent. Duffy paid her no mind and continued his tour, saying, —This ugly cove here is your UNCLE Kevin, my brother, he's an eejit and a lowlife but his wife—your AUNTIE Bernie, now she's a lovely piece of tackle, so she is, and can hold her pint with the best of the fellas.

Aunt Bernie slapped at him, but laughing.

—CAN'T you let me rest? Mam snapped.

—What's the matter?

Mam did not say. Her eyelashes made dark half moons bordering sunken white sockets.

Bernie felt her head. —You've a fever.

Mam kept her eyes closed. I saw Duffy and Bernice exchange a bad look.

—Let her rest, Duffy said.

The baby let out a small mew.

—What's wrong with her? Mam whispered. —Give her here to me.

It took all her strength just to sit up and take the baby and shunt her to latch on and feed. Bernie helped her. Mam lay back with her eyes closed. Kathleen fretted.

—She's not right, Mam said. —She won't feed.

—Sure she will, said Duffy. —You'll make her.

—You can't make her, Mam said.

—I can, said Duffy. —She will.

He bent over Mam and tried to coax my sister. He turned her head so her mouth covered the nipple but she would not suck more than once or twice.

—Leave her, Mam said. —Leave her. She'll drink soon enough.

But she did not. The child was listless. She lay quiet on Mam's chest. Her skin had a bluish cast and her miniature monkey hand was fisted up by her face like she was fighting something. Mam did not get out of her bed all night. She turned and groaned in the dark. Duffy had the baby with him.

He held her, sitting up till dawn with his back against the wall. I stayed by Mam. I mopped her head and gave her water. The coverlet was sticky where she lay.

In the daylight, there was Duffy by the doorway, pacing with the baby in his arms. —She's not right, he said. He pulled up Kathleen's eyelid with his thumb. He leaned over and put his ear to her chest. —Open your eyes now, he said. —Open up your blue eyes, Kathleen.

My sister did not stir.

—Mam, I said.

—Whisht, said Duffy, —I can't wake her.

Neither could we wake my mother. She was hot and fevered. She lay sunk in misery, the sheets soiled and crusted, bloody beneath her. —Mam? I whispered. She shook her head with tiny shakes.

—This child is cold, Duffy said.

—Mam is hot, I said.

Duffy came to the bedside and felt Mam's head. —Bernie, he said.

My Aunt Bernice came and felt Mam's head. She looked at the baby. She and Duffy spoke in whispers.

—That's a sick baby, Bernie said.

—Mary won't feed her, Duffy said.

—She can't, Bernie snapped. —She's ill.

Duffy kicked the walls. He put the baby on Mam's breast. —Feed her, will ya? he cried. —For the love of God feed her, she'll starve.

Mam stirred and tried again weakly, but Kathleen was still. Mam leaned back against the pillow. Tears came down her cheeks.

—What now? Duffy said. —What now?

—She's gone, Mam whispered.

Duffy stood stock still. —She's not. Not another.

—She is.

—Let me have her, Duffy said. —Give her here to me.

He plucked my sister from Mam's arms. She let him take her. We three looked down at miniature Kathleen, her thin arms dangling down, just a rag baby in Duffy's hands, her features not quite formed, the nose with no bridge and the veins in her head a webbing of blue under strings of dark hair. Her fingernails were pale fish scales on the ends of matchstick fingers. Two small red patches flared on her eyelids. The dip in her skull where you could see her heart beat just yesterday now was still. Her skin was translucent and pearly as the paper shade of a lamp.

—Mam, I whispered.

Duffy did not speak. His face bent and twisted and his hands shook as he placed the baby down next to Mam on the bed. He turned and walked the room.

—Michael, Bernie said.

He pushed her away. He cursed God and picked up the coal bucket and flung it at the wall. It hit with a terrible tin crash and clattered to the floor in a powder of black dust. My mother startled so her eyelids fluttered. Duffy made a strangled sound and went out the door. We could hear him retreat down the hall, cursing and ranting. Bernie picked up the baby and wrapped her in a blanket and lay her on the foot of the bed where Mam could not see her. She found a strip of rag by the stove which she gave to me.

—Run and tie this to the door and then tie the other half out front downstairs for the undertaker to see, she whispered.

—My Mam is not well, I said. —She has a fever.

—God love her, said Bernie. —Run along now downstairs.

When I returned Bernie was kneeling beside Mam's bed, low by her knees. She was busy with some articles, a bowl and a burlap sack and a bunch of chicken feathers and pressing hard on Mam's belly.

—Shh, youngster, she said when she seen me. —Your mother has a fever is all.

My eyes did not escape the bloody rags, the bowl dark with liquid. Bernice placed them in a sack with red-stained hands and took the bowl away, scolding me.

—Your mother needs her rest now.

—What's the matter with her?

—Disorder of the bowels is all. She'll soon be well.

But she was not well. That afternoon, and all that night her breathing grew more stilted and she kept her knees curled tight to her chest. The lids of her eyes were the blue color of a new-hatched bird, and shiny. Her chills rattled the spoon in the cup of broth I gave her. She could not hold it without spilling.

—You need a doctor, for God's sake please, Bernie said to Mam.

—And who will pay for a doctor? Mam whispered. —I'm all right.

—You know that's not a normal bleeding.

I did not see blood or any mark on her, just that the color was gone from her face.

—Please Mary, Bernice said, —there's a doctor of female complaint in Chatham Square.

Mam did not resist when we pulled her upright but she could not walk. We managed her down the stairs and carried her to the curb where she sat and leaned against me with her feet in the frozen gutter while Bernie ran and borrowed a cart from the fishmonger next door. We put Mam in it and wheeled her down the crowded blocks in the cold afternoon sun, the stink of fish rising off us. The sky was a dead blue. The hard light sparkled off the mackerel scales in the cart and the flecks of mica in the paving stones and white puffs of steam blew off the hot chestnut wagons and clouded up from the horses' nostrils and our mouths as we trundled along. Mam winced and groaned as the cart bounced. I held her hand.

After only five blocks Bernie wheezed and stopped at a dingy wooden house three stories tall in the midst of the poor section of used clothing stores and pawnbrokers with their awnings and bins of rags and windows full of provender. When we helped my mother to stand, I seen blood drops blossoming darkly on the cobbles beneath her skirt. She left a trail of them as we maneuvered up the steps. I rang the bell.

—You'll be fine, so you will, Mary, Bernie said. —Axie'll stay with you. I have to go return the cart to the fishman and see to arrangements.

I stared at Bernie not comprehending.

—Stay with your mother.

By the time the door before us was opened, Bernice had scuttled away on her cockroach legs, wheeling the fishmonger's cart over the cobbles.

Chapter Ten

God's Arms

—Yes? It was a woman who answered. She wore her faded yellow gauze of hair in a topknot, all stray wisps. Her eyes were muddy green shot with red, and she blinked at us as if she had just awakened from a lovely dream.

—We are here for the female's doctor, I whispered.

The woman looked us up and down over the beak of her prominent nose. —I am no longer . . .

—My Mam's sick, I said, fierce.

She stared hard at me. Her eyes went right down through mine all the way to the fibers and bones.

I gazed up at her. —Please, I said.

She put her hand over her mouth. —Oh my, she said, like she was surprised to suddenly recognize me. —All right now, lamb. You come in.

Inside, Mam sat heavily on a bench covered in patchy velvet. There would be stains. I was worried for the furniture. Mam leaned her head back against the peeling wallpaper and closed her eyes. Her breath stuttered over her ribs.

—I don't suppose you can pay, the woman said as she left us. After a minute she came back with an old man who seemed to be a copy of her, only with a beard. They were short mild people, very white with round soft fingers. —This is Dr. Evans, said the woman.

—Let's have a look, then, the doctor said. He knelt down in front of my mother and took her wrist in his hand, checked his watch and counted.

Then he lifted one of her eyelids with his thumb. She let out a whimper, small and awful.

—Come with us now, love, said the woman to Mam, clucking her tongue.

They requested me to wait where I was and took my mother down the dark hall into a room with a smoked glass door. They emerged now and then going up and down stairs whispering, carrying bowls and blankets. It grew dark. With my cheek on the soft upholstery I fell asleep in my coat and boots.

—Child. The topknot woman, Mrs. Evans, shook my shoulder. —You cannot stay here any longer this morning. You may go down to the kitchen if you like. Mrs. Browder will give you something for breakfast.

—What about my Mam?

—She is resting.

I crept down the stairs, and there in the murk of the kitchen was a white woman servant kneading dough. Her apron divided her into two lumps, one above, one below. This was Mrs. Browder. She had flour on her hands, a smudge on her nose. She hummed a tune but stopped when she saw me.

—And who might you be, love?

—Axie Muldoon.

—Tch. You must be the child of the poor one-armed woman?

She knew my silence to mean yes.

—Poor love. Will I make you some tea? She put a kettle on the fire.

Her hair was brown, gone to gray in short, messy curls. The flesh of her face had settled into a pleasant expression that made her look as if someone had just told her a joke. —You're a good girl to be looking after your mother then aren't you? You must be all of ten years old?

—Thirteen, I said, piqued. —And I know a psalm of David.

—You're a scrawny chicken then. Short as a picket in a pintsize fence. She felt my wrists like she was considering whether I was fat enough to eat, and then in front of me she placed a mug of tea and slices of bread and butter toasted. I ate with my arms curved desperate around my plate in case she might come and snatch it away before I was done. The bread had apple butter slathered on.

Browder watched as I ate the crumbs off my finger. —That'll fatten you up, love. She gave me apple cut into slices. She gave me sweet prunes stewed in a bowl and a piece of shepherd's pie. She gave me a hard bun. When I had eaten all of it, she put me to washing up bowls. All morning I helped her in the kitchen, and did not mind, for it kept me from dwelling on the fate of my mother. Still I chewed the inside of my lip till it bled. Mrs. Browder chatted away about her son Archie who fought for the Union Army at Bull Run where three thousands of our boys died.

—But he was not killed! she said brightly. —He was only shot. Shot in the elbow by a Reb, right here in the funny bone, though it was not no joke to Archie, as they cut the whole thing off! Same as your mother!

Mrs. Browder seemed to think this was a marvelous coincidence. —They're both missing the right arm, can you believe it? They threw his in a pile six feet high! Full of legs and arms! Feet and hands! It's true! Archie said he saw it. His own arm! Lying way over there, while he was lying here.

She talked on about severed arms and soldiers' wounds while making many pats of dough, cutting butter into flour with two knives. We talked about amputees while she showed me how to roll out dough to make a chicken pie. Soon I, too, was dusted in flour.

—Look at you, she said, and brushed me off. —Poor youngster. Your poor mother.

Her expression was so full of sorrow for me now my own face crumpled under the weight of what I feared and I cried out, —Is she dead then?

—Why no, lamb. She's lucky. The doctor don't usually take them if they can't pay. But Missus Evans seen you and she always cares for a little girl.

—Why's that? Why does she?

Mrs. Browder hesitated. —She lost one, once, so she did.

—Can I see my Mam?

Mrs. Browder pointed me up the stairs. —Go on up three flights and you'll find her in the back room. Third door down. Don't wear her out.

I went up a set of plain dark stairs and found myself again at the bench where I slept. Up another staircase, this one carpeted in a faded pattern of roses. Down a corridor and up another creaky staircase, to a floor of plain rough boards, and four doors, all closed. I opened the first one. The room inside was big enough just for the one bed, where Mam lay, her face clouded and damp.

—Mam?

She opened her eyes and her smile was weak and sorry when she saw me. I sat on the lip of the mattress, and lay my head on her shoulder.

—You'll forgive me, she said. —Will you?

—You didn't do nothing wrong.

—I have. And I'll pay the price.

I did not know what she meant about the price or which was the wrong thing she did that made her sorry: sending us away on the train or marrying Mr. Duffy or losing her arm in the mangle.

—I only wanted to get you away from Cherry Street, she said. —All of you.

—We're out now, ain't we?

—I wanted you somewhere better, she whispered, so faint it was the scratch of a mouse in the walls. —Somewhere nice. Clean. The fresh air and milk in a jug. A house. Like where Dutchie is. Like Joe has. All the trimmin's.

She tried to fix a smile on me. She tried to adore me with her eyes, I seen it. But it was too much for her and in a while she dozed off. Through the window, the clatter of wagon wheels on the paving blocks floated up from the street, mixed with the cries of the costermongers and river haulers and the soft burr of my mother's snoring. I saw a pigeon land on the roof across the way. He was puffed up and rutting after a lady, pecking her. She flew off and he flew after. A spider dangled from a silver thread down the window sash. The sun made a patch of white on the wall. I rested my cheek on my mother's chest and listened to her heart. I stayed like that a long while, I do not know how long. It began to get dark.

—You'll be a good girl now, Mam said, all of a sudden, her voice from far away.

—I will.

—I know you will.

A black mold of fear grew in my lungs. Her breathing was stilted over her ribs, as if taking in air and expelling it was more taxing than it was worth. I studied her, a prayer in my mouth.

—You'll find Joe and Dutch again, she said. —Promise.

I promised.

Mrs. Browder came with soup for us, but Mam wouldn't eat it. She wouldn't sit up. In a while, Mrs. Browder brought blankets and said I should stay with my mother through the night. I bunked down on the narrow alley of floor by her bed.

In the morning Mam's breathing woke me, cracked and harsh like metal scraping. Air gurgled wet in her throat.

—Mam, don't do that.

But she did. Long spaces between each rattled breath. The rattle was an alarm to me. It wasn't like no sound I knew. Her one hand of fingers picked at the covers like she was grasping at lint, at threads, picking, picking. She dragged air into her lungs with the sound of a heavy weight dragging on gravel. I leaned away from her. —Please Mam.

She did not hear me.

—Axie, she said one time, my name only air through her lips. —You'll find them. And then after another long while, she didn't draw more breath, and made no sound.

—Mam?

Her skin was gray and tight over the bones of her face. A strand of spittle, like a white cobweb, was dried by her lips. I lay my head on her shoulder and stayed with her, whispering her name. —Please will you wake now? I said. —Please. She did not move, not even to breathe. The morning sun slanted hard daggers of light into the room. Mam was still, her eyelids blue like the sheen inside a mussel shell.

Mrs. Browder came upstairs at last.

—There you are Axie, she sang, and then stopped in her tracks. —Oh poor dear, she said, her hand over her mouth. She came to the bed, placed her hand on my mother's brow, and put her arms around me. —Ah Jesus, poor love. Poor poor lovey.

I twisted away from her. I clung on my mother. —Mam wake up. You have to wake now. I recoiled back at the cold of her. How limp her hand was and how it fell when I dropped it, like a block of wood.

Mrs. Browder murmured soft words to me. —The childbed fever. She's in God's arms now.

—Mam.

—Come along, poor love.

I went in a stupor with Mrs. Browder down the hallways of the house and we met Mrs. Evans on the landing. I hid my face in the crook of my elbow to avoid her gaze, and then I felt her arms around me.

—Shh and there now, love, Mrs. Evans said, —it's all right. Your mother asked would we keep you on here. And so we shall.

She looked at me with a terrible soft expression in her eyes, so I saw myself in them, the skin patchy with spots and the white wrists sticking out from the sleeves of my dress, an orphan.

BOOK TWO

Apprenticed

Chapter Eleven

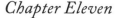

My Enemy

*U*nknown to me, My Enemy Comstock, meanwhile, was in a different order of life altogether, a fussbudget lad growing plump on pie and milk in the bosky dells and stony fields of New Canaan, Connecticut. His muttonchop whiskers was then still dormant under the skin of his smug expression as he pursued his hobby: writing in his diary about how he trapped wee soft bunnies and happy squirrels by crushing them under stones. He still had hair in those youthful days and had not yet acquired the bald pate or rotund shape of an inflated hog's bladder that was his in later life. Still, photographs of the young Tony Comstock reveal that his slack jaw and dull mean eyes were in place from the time he was in knee pants.

It has been propositioned to me by intelligent freethinkers and kind-hearted gentlefolks that no soul is pure evil and while I accept that My Enemy was a dutiful son, a doting husband, a loving papa, I can think of him only as a cabbage-hearted weevil and MONSTER for what he done to me and other good citizens too many to count.

He was just three years older than myself, and though we grew through the same times, we was worlds apart. While I was picking the ash barrels of Washington Square for scraps of gristle, My Enemy romped around his Papa's 160 acres of pasture, dawdled in the family sawmills where money grew like chestnuts on the bushes. He feasted on ice cream in the parlors of church ladies and went forth on outings to the shore at Roton Point in Norwalk, where (he told his dear diary) he chastised some sailors for looking under ladies' dresses. Even then he was a prig, with his chin weak and hands folded in his lap. Every Sunday of his boyhood My Enemy sat through four Congregationalist sermons about hellfire and damnation (so that he would know how to inflict these on me) and went to sleep each night fearing the hot breath of Satan. On weekdays he collected stamps and tried (without success) to avoid impure thoughts. He prayed and whetted the knife blades of his righteousness, all the better to smite me and the likes of me, while listening to Bible stories at the knee of his adored mother. Poor Mother Comstock! She had ten children before she died from birthing the last one. Surely she turned in her grave to see the fat poltroon her little Tony became, how he waddled along, huffing like a locomotive and bragging about how he had driven fifteen people to SUICIDE—including MYSELF, his greatest conquest—as if he had attained some esteemed heights of accomplishment.

Many years later, on the Day of our Fateful Encounter, I myself noticed his asthma and panting as he marched me, his trophy, to the courthouse. Even as we drove downtown, his wheeze was pronounced. It is still a question as to whether Mr. Comstock's heavy breathing was the result of excitement at all the smut he rounded up (to burn, he claimed), or whether it was the strain on his heart that came from carrying around so much of his own flesh.

—Madame DeBeausacq, he said, as he escorted me to jail, —I do the work of God.

—What a coincidence! I cried. —So do I!

—Yours is the devil's occupation, he said, prim as a doily. —Mine is the Lord's.

—Perhaps your God is a two-faced employer, says I, —for many's the time I have been thanked in the name of that same Lord for rescuing his poor lost lambs, which is more than you can say, I am quite sure.

—Your evil practice has come to an end, said he.

At this point, I offered him thirty thousand dollars. —Or more, I said, —if you wish.

He did not condescend to glance at me, but the bristles of his walrus mustache stood on end, while fire and brimstone came from his ears. —Madame DeBeausacq, as you call yourself, I will have you down for bribery.

I will have you down for a yellow-bellied sapsucker, you imbecile, I thought. I stared straight ahead at the liveried back of my coachman John Hatchet, listening to the hoof clop of my dappled team of grays, and adjusted the velvet cape around my shoulders with a laugh. My backbone was a ramrod, the diamonds in my earlobes sparkled in the winter sunlight, and the plumes of the ostrich feathers on my hat waved merrily in the breeze.

—The Tombs, John, and hurry, I said to my driver. —Mr. Comstock is eager to show off his prize.

It did not escape my attention that, as we traveled downtown together to meet my fate, we passed directly in front of Number 100 Chatham, the former Evans abode, with its dirty white paint and sagging roofline. It presented a dreary and unassuming façade, what our Mr. Brace might call a DREADFUL ROOKERY OF THE POOR. But I knew it once long ago as home, as the very place where I was apprenticed, and where I became the one the papers called the Notorious Madame X.

Chapter Twelve

Small Hands

*A*fter Mam died Mrs. Browder led me down to the kitchen. I sat at the table. It was nicked and gouged with hack marks of knives. I traced my finger along the grooves. Mrs. Browder put a kettle of water on the stove. I looked around blinking. Pots and pans and bunches of dried herbs hung from the low ceiling, and nailed up on walls grimed with soot was a string sack of onions, a ladle, a rug beater, a bone saw, a sieve. What would happen now? It was hard to breathe right. Mam. What would they do with her? I put my head on the table. Mrs. Browder boiled tea. I heard the clink of china and Mrs. Browder trundling down the corridor. When she came back she said, —There now, there's the cloth laid for breakfast.

She put tea leaves in a pot and poured the kettle over them.

—Now you'll see how we do here, she said. —Eight o'clock there's the breakfast for the doctor and the missus. When the patients come, Dr. Evans takes the men. Mrs. Evans helps the females, if she's in her right mind. They're quiet people. He don't say much. But her, now, you never would know to look at her what she's capable of. I seen her turn to steel. She keeps her head. I seen her with the ladies. She doesn't take too many these days but when she does you can't flap her. But God bless her. Right here in this house she's delivered mothers of four hundred babies and who knows what other afflictions. Her own two sons are grown and moved away but she had her little Celia. When she lost Celia half the life went out of her. You will scarcely hear her laugh. No you won't. And you won't never speak to her about it. If it comes up you will only say: I am sorry for your loss. You remember to say that anytime there's a loss and you don't need to say more. That's etiquette. That's manners. If you ask me that's why she took you. Why she took you in. Because you look like her. Celia.

—I am sorry for your loss, I said in a whisper.

—Bless your heart, love. Maybe she'll take a shine to you. Because that woman likes the Sanative Serum a little too much, now, between you and me. So, if you're up to it, you can be very useful. Me, I'm not up to it. My legs is bad. These stairs is too much for me. You're small but I seen yesterday you're strong. Not like the last girl. She was not up to it. She was hysterical herself, so she was. The sight of blood made her faint.

Mrs. Browder shook her head and put the tea in front of me with the boiled egg and bread and jam. —Drink that up now, sweetheart.

The smell of the egg made me faint. I put my head down on the boards of the table and closed my eyes.

—Poor lamb, said Mrs. Browder. She sat down and clasped me in. Her arms was soft and fleshy and her bosom was a pillow.

I stayed stiff with misery and mistrust.

—You lost your Mother. You've had a great blow. So it'll be normal for you to lose your appetite. That's grief, love. It's grief. And only time will heal it. She uttered her nostrums and pushed the bread at me. —Try to eat now. You're too scrawny. You need your strength. You'll see. There's no shortage of chores in this house.

I stayed with my head on the table. I did not cry. I was a plank of wood.

—Poor sparrow. Rest there and I'll be back in two shakes. Mrs. Browder went out of the kitchen banging the door and down the corridor. Another door banged and there was noises of rummaging, a crash, Mrs. Browder grunting with effort. Upstairs there were footsteps, a doorbell ringing, voices. Was it Bernie come for me? Was it Duffy? No. Would they come? I didn't care. I only wanted Muldoons, Mam with Joe and Dutchie, our Da back alive and Kathleen also, us all like a litter of cats in the bed as it was before.

Mrs. Browder returned after a long time with a bulky green canvas bag. —There we are, she said. —Your bed.

I did not see how it was a bed until she unpacked it and assembled the pieces of wood into a frame and put the canvas on it. —It's a camp cot. One of the ones the doctor uses for his patients. And it'll do you fine.

My bed? What did that mean? I would stay, Mrs. B. said. Mam had asked for them to keep me. I would sleep on a cot. It was set up along the far wall next to the ash barrel. —Lay yourself down there, now, Mrs. Browder said, —and close your eyes. Don't mind me. You must be tired, love. You've had a great loss. Lie down.

I wanted to stay in the dark harbor of my own arms.

—Poor girl. Poor orphan child. You're all alone then, aren't you? Your Mama said you've no one on the face of the earth.

I did not speak to say I had a brother and sister. How would I find them now? Despite my promise to Mam they was lost same as her, and it was only me left now, of all the Muldoons.

—Listen, Mrs. Browder said, —it's some strange things go on in the house, and I don't say it's all the Lord's work, but most of it is, and you'll be all right. Go on and lie down there.

—I don't want to.

—Don't, then. She shrugged. —You could start today. I could use you. It's a Monday and that means linen. On your feet, then.

She stood me up and handed me two metal pails with handles. I followed her through the door to a passage, past the front dining parlor, then through another door which led out under the stoop, up two steps to the street. The cold hit me and I shivered.

—We'll have to find a proper coat for you, she said. —One that fits.

I didn't talk, only followed along the packed sidewalk. I looked for Bernie in the crowd. Duffy. They didn't know about Mam. Duffy'd be glad to be rid of us so he could find a wife who didn't die. With two arms. One without no big lunk of a daughter eating all the bread. Nobody was familiar. The streets weren't. Everything was dull. Flat. At the pump, Mrs. Browder worked the handle while I held the buckets.

—There, now, she said. —That's better. Keep yourself busy. Make yourself useful. Takes your mind off trouble and sorrow. Isn't that so?

No it was not so. I followed her along back the way we came. The wet pails were heavy and dragging my arms out of the sockets, banging my shins, slopping onto my legs and freezing the skirt. In the kitchen we emptied the water into pots that Mrs. Browder heated on the stove. —Thatta girl, now, she said. She gave me her own enormous coat and sent me out and I fetched more buckets. While the linen stewed, Mrs. Browder took a lantern and showed me the dirt cellar, down seven wooden steps to a dank hole where her head touched the ceiling. A coal pile was in the back with the chute, and along the walls was a mountain of stores, barrels of beef and grain, potatoes and turnips. We filled two coal scuttles and took them upstairs to a room full of books where the doctor sat reading at a desk. He did not say a word while we raked out the ashes and put them in the scuttle and swept the hearth and laid the fire again.

—You'll rake the hearth three times a day in all the rooms if it's the cold weather, Mrs. Browder instructed very quiet, —and while you're here you'll trim the wicks and fill the lamps. You'll have to stand on a step stool to do the sconces. You're that small I'll have to feed you biscuits and butter.

We went back down. I wanted to go up. Upstairs all those flights was Mam cold in the bed. Was she? She was gone. Mrs. B. now explained how when we was at the pump the knacker came and carried Mam through the kitchen and out the back door and took her away in the mortuary wagon. She was gone.

—She's in her grave, child, Mrs. Browder said solemnly. But where that grave was, she didn't say. She gave me a black ribbon. —Tie it on your arm and don't take it off for a year.

We took the linen out from the soaking, long yellowed sheets with brown watermarks and spots of dark rusted blood set in shapes of blossoms, and scrubbed it with lye soap. The fumes burnt my eyes and my hands turned red with the sting of it. We rinsed everything and boiled it and fetched more water to rinse it then carried it out the back door to hang on the line in the yard by the lane. Later she showed me how to lay the cloth for dinner and had me pluck the feathers from a pair of chickens. —You're a strong girl, she said, approving. —You know how to work.

I did not smile but I liked her.

The doctor and his wife ate their dinner in the dining room. Me and Mrs. Browder ate in the kitchen. —Now off to your bed, young Ann, she said, after we had done the dishes. I lay down. My protectress covered me with a blanket and squatted down on her haunches, groaning with pain in her knees. I looked up at her spongy face, the creases at the corners of her eyes.

—Your Mam is in heaven now, she said. —I'll be off home to Pearl Street and back in the morning before the rooster crows.

She smoothed my hair, patted my arm, and went out into the cold. I turned over and faced the wall. A pattern of cracks made the shape of a dog's head, with a long tongue and teeth. *Save me from the wrath of the lion, my life from the power of the dog,* I prayed, and talked to Joe and Dutchie in my head. *Mam is in heaven with our Da, and Kathleen too, and you both in Illinois, and here's me with not a single Muldoon.* And I promised them, *I'll come and get you.* The lamp guttered out. In the dark I sucked a calloused thumb for comfort and abandoned myself to sleep.

Mornings, I folded my cot, then put my apron on and began my chores according to Mrs. Browder's instructions, carrying them out like I was made of pine. I did not ask for a thing, not a blanket nor a hard bun, or even no information like where was my Mother buried? How could I find my sister and brother? No one came for me, not Duffy or Bernice or any Aid Society. I did not hardly speak. In the dark of the kitchen at night I saw Mam's face. *Dutch and Joe,* she said to me. *You'll find them, Axie, won't you?* I tossed on my cot and promised her again and wept when no one heard me.

I talked silent to my sister and brother from dawn in the morning while I laid the fires and done the washing, blacked the stove with lead blacking and went on errands. To the post office. The apothecary. *Don't you worry,* I says to them, *I will find you if it takes all my born days. You are a Muldoon and don't forget it.* Meanwhile people rang the bell to fetch Dr. Evans. More rarely they fetched his wife. Certain patients, mostly females, stayed overnight. When they pulled the cord upstairs we heard a bell in the kitchen and I brought them their soup and tea. I did not speak to them or they to me. I emptied the ash from the grates, and holding my nose I fetched the sloppers up and down and dumped them stinking in the pit out back and rinsed them in the deep lead tub cursing and gagging for the smell would choke a goat. I squirreled bits of bread and apple in my pockets, hoarded nuts in a crevice of my cot, stole cake in the dark when everyone was gone from the kitchen.

—You're skin and bone, said Mrs. Browder. —Drink your milk. She fed me at every opportunity, food and information: You can tell the age of a pigeon by looking at the legs. The rattle rand is the very best piece of beef for corning. Chalk wet with hartshorn is a remedy for the sting of bees. A bullock's heart is very profitable to use as steak, and you broil it just like beef. There are usually five pounds in a heart, and it can be bought for twenty five cents.

In this way, feeding me recipes and coddling over the weeks and months, Mrs. Browder dragged me out of my stupor. —Smile now, it won't kill you, she said. —That scowl of yours will freeze that way permanent.

And it was no wonder I scowled, as she had me running up and down them infernal stairs every time the bell rang.

—You go up, my legs is old, she said.

—So's the rest of you, said I, and grinned.

—Get out ya smart aleck. She swatted with her dishcloth.

I did what she said. She didn't ask me to leave. Nor did the Evans. I cringed when I saw them, tucked my chin down to the top of my apron and pressed against the wall. Mrs. Evans only smiled at me through her watery eyes and said, —Why hello there, Annie, feeling better? The Doctor didn't seem to notice me, not much.

When the bell rang at the top parlor entrance, I answered it now in my maid's apron and cap. I thought, this is a fine job, to open the door in new shoes and a fresh apron. To me in my low class ignorance the Evans' seemed a grand house. The cabinets in the wall was full of dishes &c. Closets opened up to be full of muffs and cloaks and boots. Such bedding and wherewithal they had there: the eyeglasses and gas lamps, hatboxes and buttonhooks, corsets and mustache wax, butcher deliveries of fresh meat, and the milkman and the iceman and the coalman coming regular. The establishment appeared splendid, though I know now that even penny shopkeepers could afford a servant and 100 Chatham was only a common row house, in a dirty area of rag sellers and pawnshops, poteen houses and music halls. The threads of the parlor carpet showed through, and the treads of the stairways was worn down to splinters. A draft came in the cracked glass of the windows, and a smell of must came up from the cellar and tainted the draperies, which was gray and greasy with lampoil smuts. Outside, a riffraff of men loitered on our stoop smoking, and left behind their filthy tobacco gobs and the oily wrappers off their lunches. I gave them hard looks and cursed them for the mess they left me to clean.

I was to instruct callers to sit on the bench and wait. If Mrs. Evans was indisposed, lying on her couch upstairs with a compress on her head, I was to send the females to Lispenard Street to see Mrs. Bird or Mrs. Costello. But, if it was a man in a hurry, asking for the midwife, I was to go get my employer, even in the middle of the night. I was not never to go in the clinic, Mrs. Browder said. This was the room off the front hall with the smoked glass in the door. —Only the doctor and Mrs. Evans go in there. You do not.

I was frightened to go near, and morbid to see it, for I heard terrible suffering sounds coming from within. Vomiting. Crying. Curses. Mrs. Evans saying, —Shh love. Shush. It was the sound of babies getting born, Mrs. Browder said. —And other Necessary Pain. Necessary Pain was not an idea I comprehended, and still do not.

One morning in May, near my fourteenth birthday, Mrs. Browder made a tray of breakfast and said, —You'll take this to Adelaide in the back room. She's cast off, poor love. Her father will not have her name mentioned in his presence.

—Why not?

—Because, you thick. Mrs. Browder gave me a look.

I took the tray up to a small room on the third floor and kicked the door open so as not to spill. There I saw a girl in bed, writing a letter. She was about eighteen years of age, and enormous with child. I put the tray down on the side table.

—What are you looking at? she said.

—Nothing.

—You're right there, she said. —Precisely. Nothing. Nothing at all.

As she wiped at her tears I wanted to ask why was she nothing? For here she was with me to wait on her hand and foot. Her dressing gown had a lace collar and her day dress hanging off the hook was a dark green watered silk with an underskirt the color of celery, and when she wasn't looking I fingered it, so soft to the touch.

—Hurry with that fire, can't you? she said. She was a green sour pickle, and when she wasn't looking I flipped the end of my thumb off the tip of my nose at her. It was wrong to cock a snook like that to a girl who might die soon like my Mam, when the labor started, but I could not help it. She put on airs. I didn't like her.

Adelaide's time came, weeks later, in the middle of a morning. —Stay below stairs, Mrs. Browder said. I lugged in pails from the pump, my palms raw and my skirts wet with spills, up two flights to leave them outside the door. I did not hear Adelaide's trials and was glad because I knew she was going to die and I didn't want to pity her.

Toward evening, Mrs. Browder called for me to bring a tray of broth and bread. When I brought it upstairs there was Adelaide, a scrap of infant in her arms. She kept her eyes closed and I seen her face was pale as gravy paste. The baby let out a small bleat. Neither one was dead.

—Do you want to hold him? she asked. —His name is Vincent. She was smiling now and held Vincent toward me. I took him. His black eyes looked up at me, and even as they reminded me of my wee sister Kathleen in heaven, a smile stole over my face.

—He's nice, I said.

—His father isn't.

—Who's he?

—A codfish, she said.

I laughed.

—It's not funny. He took advantage! It was never my fault. And here I am holding the blame. The shame.

It was me holding the wee shame and I thought how mean it was, that young Vincent was called such names, innocent and small as a drop of dew on a cabbage leaf, as Mam used to say.

—Take my advice, said Adelaide. —Don't ever let a man in a room alone with you. If he says he loves you, call him a liar. They're all of them cheats and scoundrels.

—I'm sorry to hear it.

—Not as sorry as me. Don't ever trust a man who says trust me, hear?

I did hear. It was the first in a long parade of lessons, and I took Adelaide's words as my MOTTO. Because I seen she was right: Brace said trust me. Dix said trust me. Look what happened. I was abandoned no better than old socks.

Now I left Adelaide and her wee wrinkled infant to carry an armful of bloody linen down the stairs. On the landing, I nearly toppled my employer Mrs. Evans, who was on her way up, her breath shallow with effort.

—Excuse me, ma'am, I said.

—I didn't see you.

You never see me, I thought to say. I am the mouse in the baseboard. But this time she looked hard at me, and while I don't know what she saw, I noticed how shadows scalloped under her eyes in puffed sacks of skin, like water blisters. The dots of her pupils were small black seeds in the muddy green of her irises.

—You've been here some good long months now, she said. —How are you faring with us, Annie? Mrs. Browder says you are quite useful.

—She puts me to work, I said.

Mrs. Evans tucked stray hairs with a nervous motion behind her ear, and started on her way up the stairs, but I blurted my question before she got very far.

—Will Adelaide die soon? Will she?

—No, she said, startled. —Not unless the Lord has other plans.

—Mam died.

—We couldn't save your mother. We tried. It was the hemorrhage.

—What's the hemorrhage?

—Bleeding. Thanks to the stupidity of her assistant.

—What assistant?

—Impossible to say, unless you were there.

—I was there, I said, stricken, —it was me.

Now Mrs. Evans reared back. —You? No. It was someone else. A relative. A neighbor? I don't recall. You did a fine job, your mother told me. She was proud of you. She said you were a proper little midwife.

I blushed and felt my mother's praise like a touch. —Was it Bernie, then? My Aunt Bernice.

Now Mrs. Evans pinched her lips and blinked so drops of water pooled in her eyes. She was often sweaty, dew on her skin, even in the cold. —Your Bernie was only trying to help. She did what she did.

—What did she do then?

—She pulled too rough on the cord, perhaps, said Mrs. E. vaguely.

—But why?

—My, you ask a lot of questions.

—I'm told I do.

—So we must get you some answers. She took both my hands in her clammy mitts, inspecting them. —Small, she said absently, —which is an advantage.

—What advantage?

—In my profession it is. We'll see how it goes with you.

Chapter Thirteen

Bilious Pills and Liver Invigorator

How it went was several days later Mrs. Evans summoned me.
—Annie, can you say the alphabet?

—Yes ma'am.

She led me up the stairs where to my surprise she opened the door
into the forbidden clinic. Behind the smoked glass I expected more secrets
revealed, elixirs simmering, pickled parts preserved. But there was only
an examination table, a drapery curtain, and a sideboard full of sharp and
gleaming instruments that made the flesh hurt to look at them.

—These medications, Mrs. Evans said, waving her quavery hand at
a glass cabinet full of vials and colored bottles, —are to be organized by
alphabet.

I peered at them. The handwriting on the labels was spidery, reading
Bilious Pills and Liver Invigorator, Tongue Syrup and Soothing Ointment
for the Itch. There was Sanative Pills. Vermifuge. Stomach Bitters. Mrs.
Evans picked up a bottle of Calomel.

—Where does this go? she asked me, and waited till I placed it to the
left of Camphor. This pleased her and to myself I thanked Mrs. Temple and
how she tutored me.

—If not for my alphabetical classification, the doctor would be quite at
a loss. Mrs. E. looked around vaguely like it was herself at a loss, tucking at
her downy hair. —It's time you learned the system.

—I don't want to make no mistakes, I said.

—*Any* mistakes, said Mrs. Evans. —You will not make any. She instructed me how to replace the stoppers in the vials, stow them in order, and showed me a little book where the doctor kept his formulas and recipes. When she thought I was not looking, I saw her take a small vial of liquid and put it in her pocket. Her hands trembled, holding up a brown bottle stained with drippings.

—Mercuric Chloride? she quizzed me, and watched while I put it on the shelf next to Mangrove Root. —Very good, Annie, she said, in her dreamy voice, blinking. —You'll do fine.

Now in the clinic I arranged the vials on the shelf, with Aloes first, Ergot after Enema, Tansy before Tongue Syrup. Over many weeks Mrs. Evans shown me how to follow the formulas, how to tell a dram from a drop, when to use an excipient to bind the powders and when to dilute with wine or bitters, how to use the pill tile and the pill press and the scales.

—A precise dosage is important, said Mrs. Evans. There was three scruples to a dram and eight drams to the oz. One oz. of tansy would do the trick whereas two oz. would kill a woman. A dram of opium was enough to relieve suffering but a fatal dose was two drams. A drop of turpentines was a good emetic but more than that sickens. Use only ergot off the rye husk to make a powder (and remember it's not a reliable element and may cause harm). The recipes, she said, ought to be followed EXACT.

When I finished a batch of one medicine or another I bottled it and pressed the stoppers down, labeled it and left it for the doctors. I cleaned the mortar and pestle. I wiped up drops of spills and dusted residue off the countertops. When there was patients in the clinic I was to stay below stairs. If any blood was smeared on the table or the floor afterwards, I was to clean it.

—It is only blood, Mrs. Evans said. —If it's not yours it can't hurt you.

—Yes ma'am.

—There's no reason to be squeamish, no matter what you may find in the waste pail. Take it straight out back for burning.

I carried the bin outside to the pit, fascinated to look while I emptied it into the flames. One day I recognized bits of catgut suture snipped and discarded. I saw dead leeches like slices of raw liver. Another day the gauze was dirty with excrement and yellow matter, still others it was dark with blood, gouts of flesh. I saw shavings of hair and clots of substances in strings of dark elastic liquid.

—Don't look at it then, if it upsets you, said Mrs. Browder. —It's just blood.

One morning, I discovered I had blood myself and pain stitched a lining to my insides and doubled me over groaning and when it wouldn't stop I told Mrs. Browder.

—Will I die? I whispered.

She laughed. —You're only a woman now, like the rest of us. And let's hope you don't die or I'll have all them stairs to myself again.

It was nothing to worry over, she told me, and I should expect the Visitor every month now, so I should. She tore an old bedsheet, and handed me the strips. —Now you're on the rag. You'll wash these in cold water and hang them to dry, out of sight, down the cellar. And listen to me. You'll be careful, hear? Because I've seen the boys in the square watching you and that Greta your friend from next door.

—She's not my friend.

Greta was the bonded girl to Pfeiffer the shopkeeper. They were German sauerkrauts, all of them. The Pfeiffer family lived over the store, which sold notions, while Greta slept in the back of the shop. She had black hair and dimples, and though we walked to the pump and stood there morning and evening, and hung the wash out back, half the time she did not stoop herself to speak to me. Nor did I speak to her. The sauerkrauts, as Mam called them, did not like Irish nor vice versa. They stank of pickle.

—She could be your sister, Mrs. Browder said. —With that black hair.

—Not likely. Under my breath I muttered, —My sister is not no snoot with her snout in the air. I wished Dutch was here, nibbing beans with me now.

As I busied myself, Mrs. Browder gave me the hard stare. —You watch yourself around her. A girl like that is none too bright about the fellas.

—What about them?

She just raised her eyebrows. —You'll find out. But let's hope you don't.

—What does any of it have to do with the Visitor?

—You Know Perfectly Well What I Mean. And no sneaking out the kitchen door after I'm gone home to Archie at night.

After she had gone home to Archie I went out the kitchen door anyways and sat on the back step in the summer evening, eating cherries and spitting out the pits, shelling walnuts and picking out the meats. What was the danger about being out the kitchen door? I did not ask. I only polished the brass, emptied the sloppers. I swept the floorboards, the carpets, the stoop. I watched and listened, picking up scraps of information like bits of trash dropped on the street.

The best room for this endeavor was the library, where there was wood figures shaped like the bones of a hand and a framed diploma on the wall proclaiming William Evans a certified physiologist. Books went up to the ceiling. They were covered in leather, each the size of a paving stone.

One day I stood on a ladder, dusting the porcelain head called Phrenology by L. N. Fowler. It was divvied up in blue lines like a map with names for all areas of the human phiz: one for Selfish Sentiments, others for Literary Faculties, Mastoid Process, Sense of the Terrific, Blandness, Justice and Wit, &c. I was pondering the section called Desire for Liquids, when Dr. Evans cleared his throat.

—My wife tells me you read well.

—As best I can. I didn't tell him I favored Mrs. Browder's weekly copy of the *Police Gazette,* as it was full of rapes and seductions, murders and cutthroats. The doctor frightened me with his aloof manner and his silence. He had round wire glasses on a round face that he massaged while he shuffled his papers. There was a wart on his eyelid.

—I'd impose upon you, he said, —to apply my wife's alphabetizing system to this section of medical books here, by title. He pointed to a vast column behind his desk.

—Yes sir, I'll do my best.

He nodded and petted his beard, thick and white with some dark sprouts left in it. He cleared his throat again and pointed to the shelf behind him. —Many say it is not fit for a young girl to read these here. The female mind is too feeble to handle such complex ideas, and she is liable to suffer all manner of disorders—even death—if she attempts to wrestle with such books. I trust you will not attempt them.

—No sir.

—My wife has seen no need for such things.

But I knew this wasn't true for I'd seen Mrs. Evans in his library consulting the very section he said might kill me. —Stick to the lighter fare, he says.

—Thank you. I had a real reason to be grateful, for that day the doctor steered me and my feeble faculties straight to the useful information.

After that, when he was out on his rounds, I perused what he warned me against. My favorite was The Diseases of Women, by Dr. Benjamin S. Gunning. It was a fat green book with headings in gibberish such as Pruntis Pudendl, and Double Encysted Ovarian Dropsy. Here, perhaps, I could learn the secret of what killed my Mam. I drew it down and inspected it from my perch on the ladder.

The first heading was of a case entitled A Married Pregnant Female, Aged Twenty Two Years, with the Milk Leg. Milk leg. What could it be? I read how it was a horrible swelling of pregnancy occasioned by a deposit of mother's milk in the affected limb. Turning the pages, I read dumbfounded of Vicarious M*ns****tion in a Young Woman, Aged Nineteen Years, Abscess of the V*lv* in a Mother, Aged Twenty Seven, and Suppression of the M*ns*s in an Unmarried Girl, Aged Twenty Years.

All the days and months of my service at the Evans home, the library served as my schoolroom, and my head filled with lurid details of anatomy, of afflictions and the procedures to cure them, lancings and explorations and cuttings so grim that they made me cry out in my sleep. One day at last, under Hemorrhagic Fever in a Mother, Aged Thirty Two, I found what I wanted to know:

> If portions of the afterbirth be obstinately retained . . . the patient is in great danger, and sinks under disease with frequent small pulse, and burning of the hands and feet, or is carried off suddenly by an attack of profuse perspirations, putrid fever, or . . . hemorrhage.

It was what killed Mam. Was it? Hemorrhage, Mrs. Evans said. Putrid fever. Why? What could have saved her? I persisted searching through the rest of the book, and its neighbors on shelves above.

—Go along now and read, Axie, love, said Mrs. Browder. —I can live without you for a minute.

In truth, Mrs. B. was glad for a chance to nip at the bottle unobserved. She thought I didn't know, but she kept her tot of whiskey beneath the sink. While she had her drop, I climbed the ladder in the library. Another day I found a book called Advice to a Wife, where I read with alarm and fascination such items as I found on page 224:

> . . . after a confinement, the breasts are apt to become very painful and distended. If such be the case, it might be necessary . . . to have them drawn daily by a woman who is usually called either a breast-drawer, or in vulgar parlance, a suckpap. A clean, sober, respectable woman ought to be selected. Some mothers object to suckpaps; they dislike having a strange woman sucking their nipples, and well they might. My fair reader may, by using a nice little invention, dispense with a suckpap, and with ease draw her own bosoms. The name of the invention is "Maw's Breast Glass with Elastic Tube for Self Use." It is a valuable contrivance, and deserves to be extensively known.

As I read this enthralled one afternoon Mrs. Evans, my employer, caught me descending the rungs with the book open to this passage, my jaw dropped in amazement and horror. A suckpap!

—Annie?

I snapped the book shut. —Sorry Missus.

—What is it you've got there?

She took the volume from my reluctant hands and when she saw what it was, a curious smile came over her face. —Well. You must have *very* many questions now.

I blushed deeply. —I do, missus.

She looked at me expectantly. —Well?

—What is fistula? Also: what is Ovarian Dropsy?

Her pale eyebrows arched in surprise. She looked at me strangely now.
—You remind me of someone.

—Who?

—My daughter, she said, and flicked her eyes away, like they were
burned.

—I'm sorry, missus, I'm sorry for your loss.

She closed her eyes, then took something from a cabinet under the doctor's desk, a small bottle. She pocketed it and left the library.

—What did she die of, the daughter? I asked Mrs. Browder, who was
trimming shinbones for soup.

She stopped with the cleaver in her hand. —A fever, she said, finally.
—She died of choleric fever.

Now Mrs. Browder threw the bones in the pot, so water splashed up.
She pretended it had splashed in her eyes, and she wiped at them with her
apron. —It was enough to break your heart. It broke her mother's. You're
like her, just like Celia, always nosing with your questions. It's why Missus
took a shine to you.

She'd took more than a shine, it seemed, for one night soon afterwards Mrs.
Evans woke me in the dark and brung me nervous and hurrying with her
through the streets, following a man called Doggett who strode urgently
ahead, our lanterns swinging so pendulums of shadow traveled along with
us and cast our own shapes distorted against the sides of dark buildings.
When we arrived up many stairs Doggett's wife Eva was laboring on the
bed. —She has the grinding pains, the husband said, fearful. He retreated
off aways, whereas I was told to stay.

—There now, mother, said Mrs. Evans. —Annie and I have come and
all will be well. The woman appeared not to hear us but Mrs. Evans set
about making arrangements. She clipped her fingernails with a small scis-
sor and greased her right hand with a portion of lard all the while talking
calmly to me and to the patient. —Here now lie on your side easy Mrs.
Doggett, soon it will be all over, shush now dearie, you'll have another
pretty baby to love. Here's a sheet I'm tying to your bedposts, like so, and
you will pull against it with the pains if you like. And Annie come stand

here, please do, don't be nervous, and sponge her poor head. That's right, dear, that's it, push, and push very good and we'll just see here how we're getting on.

Now she put her hand beneath Mrs. Doggett's skirt. It was a mortification when she ordered me to watch and talked away in a singsong, one that I heard later, in so many lessons that I can remember it now like she was still here.

—Just now there's the crowning and it's the worst bit you're nearly there so Annie help her to raise her leg yes yes just rest it up like that don't be timid now. Why, don't tremble, Annie it's nothing to fear at all, that's right. Shush love, poor missus. I will just work here a little, very gentle, so you don't tear, love, you wouldn't want that, no. Annie see here now with the lantern, stop your quaking.

Mrs. Doggett yelled and pulled at the sheets tied to the bedposts and my teacher pulled me to look in the lamplight so I saw the horror of the parts so livid and bulging out with a patch of the child's hair visible, blood in the strands. I trembled, sure that I would see more death but instead I saw a miraculous machine.

—Hold the light, that's it, you will see how we help her to stretch the portal very gentle like this, see here Annie, the light. Now another push Mrs. Doggett very good almost done. And Annie, what we must do at this stage is place the right hand steady and firm against the fundament here below the birthplace and hold it there like this, as I do, to prevent a rupture, that's right just see how we do, firm and steady, yes, you don't want to hurry it, Annie, no no, nature has designed a good way. There's the dear little face at last, here it is, now you are through the worst of it, missus, such a lovely baby. And now, Annie, we must feel around the little neck with great care, because if the navel string is caught you would endeavor to slip it over the child's head to avoid a tragedy. We don't want anybody to strangle now, right? But that's it, here we are all clear, and a few more pushes Missus. And of course, never never pull the child from the mother but allow the forces of labor to deliver the dear baby naturally. One more push. Thanks be to God you have a little girl, Mrs. Doggett. Wonderful. That's right Annie hold her like this.

Mrs. Doggett's child was bloody in my hands, and too terribly quiet it seemed, but Mrs. Evans massaged the miniature poitrine and breathed her own breath into the little girl's lungs and turned her over and upside down until there was a wee cry. I myself did not say anything at all, for I was dumbfounded at the awful miracles I seen, and most of all at how Mrs. Doggett sat up not long afterwards smiling, and how the baby's lungs were powerful and full of air and it suckled away first thing. Alive. They both was. It appeared to me then that Mrs. Evans performed wonders. She possessed secrets and special powers. I wished to learn them for myself.

—Shall you clean her up, Annie? asked Mrs. E., handing me the wondrous live infant.

—Yes ma'am, I said, eager now, and thus began my long apprenticeship to Mrs. Evans of Chatham Street. I was fourteen years of age.

Chapter Fourteen

Teacher

Despite my promotion and regular servings of bread and jam, after more than a year in the Evans establishment, my heart was still in a sorry state of disrepair. At night my head was filled with dark matter, longings, the words of letters. They was prayers I wrote all day in my head. *Dear Dutch, Dear Joe. Hallowed be thy names. Do you still remember me your sister Axie who cared for you and raised you. She (our mother) is dead I tried to save her. Maybe she got some peace. I do not know what happened rather I do, but can't say not in a letter it is not right or decent. It was the stupidity of her assistant. We had a little sister God love her she is gone too so she is.*

One morning I pilfered some paper from Mrs. Evans's desk and wrote a selection of lines to Dutch before anyone in the household awoke. I put them folded in the crevices of my cot. At night I wrote more.

> *I work as a housemaid for a doctor and his wife they are very kind. Mrs Browder has got me new stockings and other things such as boots a cap and apron. The doctor has a wart on his eyelid his wife has a top not. I have been let to read some books in their library Dutch it has a ladder to the ceiling you would like Arabian nights so you would I read it every page.*

As I wrote I imagined my sister crying at the words of my letter, pulling a spring of her corkscrewed hair so it recoiled like her shock at my news,

that Mam was dead. Our Mother who named her Dutchess. As I wrote I
pictured how my sister would race with my letter through the cold marble
halls of the Illinois house to her false Ambrose family. She would stamp her
little foot wearing its kidskin boot and demand to go to New York, to find
me, and her true family. I wrote her pages of sentences and news.

> *I know how to cook a turtle soup and how to make biscuits rise.*
> *Also how to mix throat powder and the plaster for gowt. I can do*
> *remedies and medicines. Our mother axed would I find you and*
> *Joe. It was her dying wish dearest Dutch I do not know where*
> *they buried her or Kathleen but I promised a solemn oath to find*
> *you and Joe. She made me swear I would and I will.*

How I would get the letter to Dutch, I didn't know. It never occurred to
me to write to Mr. Brace or search out the Dix, so I wrote not expecting my
words to find their intended reader.

> *Dutchie where is Joe? I have not had no news of him nor you*
> *for these two years. Please tell me how you are and do you still*
> *remember me? I promised our Mother I would take care of you*
> *but that promise is broken. Before she died I promised again to*
> *find you. Far away there in Illinois do you think of me? I am*
> *called Annie now. Please write back to me please. I am sorry for*
> *the news of our Mother and having to tell it to you.*
> *Love your sister Axie Ann Muldoon.*

It was an ignorant attempt written by a low girl of the wretched class
but that was not my concern. What I cared about was my promise to Mam
and how would I get my letter to Dutch? I folded the pages and tucked
them beneath my pillow. The paper was crumpled and stained from days
of labor, and there it stayed for weeks as I sucked my tortured thumb and
gnawed my knuckles through all the nights, and every day worked upstairs
and downstairs and grew further into a small weedy girl with a head of
long black hair which I kept braided and under my cap like a secret tangled
fury to be unraveled. My own face surprised me when I caught a glimpse
of it in the mirror with its big red mouth and dark fringe of lashes and the

look of an angry wound about the blue eyes. Red spots erupted from my face like evidence of the terrible wrongs inflicted on me. My fingers was grimed with ash from the grates and blacking grease off the stove. Some days I sang Bantry Boy in the kitchen with Mrs. Browder and other times I banged the pots and cursed, so that she called me Axie the Dread. She watched me lately like she wished to catch me up to no good.

—What is this? Mrs. Browder demanded one morning when I came in from the clothesline. —What is the meaning of this?

I was frightened, for Mrs. Browder had a temper when she drank and had marrowed me good on occasion, once for eating all the grapes and another time for hoarding crackers in my apron. She had an apple in her hand and three walnuts, along with the pages of my letter, the paper gray with pencil and effort.

—I moved your cot to retrieve an onion that rolled underneath, and this dropped out from the folds of the bedding.

—It's only the one apple. I swear it.

She brandished my paper. —What is THIS?

—It's mine. Give it to me.

—You never said you had a sister. Or a brother.

I began to cry.

—There now love, there there, tell Mrs. B.

—I am not your love. I am no one's love.

—There now, sure you are, so you are. She coaxed me until I told her at last about Mr. Brace and the two Dix and the orphan train and the Reverend Temple and his wife. She listened with watery eyes and murmured Poor Lost Lamb, then took me by one hand with the letter in the other and pulled me up the stairs to Mrs. Evans, who was reclining on her sofa. She sat up and blinked at the light. —I'm just resting, she said. A dew of sweat was on her forehead.

Surely I would be put out now. For lying. For stealing Mrs. Evans' good paper. For saying in the letter that Dr. Evans had a wart on his eyelid.

—Read this, said Mrs. Browder.

Mrs. Evans read. Her face grew soft and she put her fluttery hand on the flat bone of her breast. —Why didn't you tell us you had a brother and sister?

—I'll never do it again, I told them.

They were not angry. Mrs. Evans gave me a lozenge, as well as an envelope and a stamp, and showed me how to address the letter so it would go to the General P.O., in Rockford, Illinois. Kindly Forward, she wrote on the outside in her witchety writing.

—You should have asked us to help you find them, Mrs. Evans said. —I'll write to the Children's Aid Society myself. Your Mr. Brace is very famous, did you know?

I did not know. I did not care. His nose was an eggplant.

Then she told me to run down the street and post the letter, which I did, fast as my boots would go.

That night in a corner of the kitchen ceiling the ghost face of my mother Mary Muldoon floated above my cot in a gauze, the fringe of her eyelashes dark against her pale cheek. *You must find them,* her spirit said again as it always did. I chewed my sheet and nursed my thumb till morning.

Weeks passed and then months, but I heard nothing. Not a letter or a word. Mrs. Evans got a communication from the Aid Society: We regret to say that we are unable to keep records of all the orphans who travel on our trains. They did not have any address for either Dutch or Joe Muldoon. It seemed my sister and brother was lost to me for good now, worse than that Clementine in the song Mrs. Browder sang sometimes while mixing tallow and lye for soap. *Dreadful sorry. Gone forever.* But Don't Despair, said Mrs. Evans, for the mail kept arriving regular, didn't it?—One day when you least expect it, you will get word, said she. —Someone will turn up.

It was true that strangers turned up on our doorstep daily, and while none of them was a Muldoon of my dreams, Frances Harkness arrived at 100 Chatham Street one May evening when I was fifteen years of age. It was Sunday, Browder's day off. Mrs. Evans and the doctor were gone to see a play on the Bowery. I was in the library reading by the last light of the window—The Principles of Midwifery, a chapter called Plurality of Children or Monsters about mongoloids and attached twins—when the front bell rang.

—Go away, said I under my breath.

My instructions was never accept a patient when nobody was home. I kept reading in my struggle with words such as parturition and ligament. I was eager to get to the chapter called Case Requiring the Crochet. The bell rang again with great urgency.

—D*** you, I cried and flang the book. Through the window I spied a bonneted woman leaning on the door and doubled over, her hand across her mouth. I went and opened the door.

—You must help me, she said, gasping. She was about twenty years of age, freckled, with ginger hair in ringlets.

—The midwife is not at home.

—Please, she said through her teeth. —Help.

—Mrs. Watkins of Lispenard Street will attend you.

—Please, let me in. Her face contorted, and she pushed past me into the house.

—Oh my, she gasped. She sank to her knees and reared her head back. And I am sorry to say she reminded me of a cur baying at the moon. Her breathing was rapid and keening. —I am going to have a baby, she said, like I hadn't guessed. —Please cover me.

I ran to the clinic and came back with a rubber sheet and a blanket, and as she tossed and turned, in a sweat of fear I placed the rubber sheet beneath her and the blanket over her knees. Though I now had traveled twice with Mrs. Evans to attend a laboring female and witnessed the PARTURITION of two more mothers lying-in upstairs here on Chatham Street, never had I acted the part of midwife at the blessed event itself and now I prayed mightily for Mrs. Evans to get here fast and spare me the spectacle. But the guest on the floor was wasting no time and with embarrassment she requested quite urgent that I help remove her undergarments, PLEASE NOW, so I did, but not willingly. The sheet made a tent over her knees. She moaned and carried on so I was afraid that because Mrs. Evans was not here, this girl would die like Mam. I did not know her name. I only held her hand for dear life and ran for water and a cloth to bathe her head, but she pushed me away viciously and labored on, until she was in one long spasm too far down in her own pain to shoo me off. The veins stood out in her neck till her face was the color of beetroots. *Press the right hand steadily against the fundament below the birthplace* was the lesson I remembered, and so while I was revolted to look, I done what I could by pressing firmly to prevent her rupture, so nervous and disturbed. Remembering a further lesson I felt gingerly around the little neck for the navel string and did not find it. As there seemed not more for me to do I held on to the stranger's hands till she gave a curdled cry and lay back.

We both was crying now for different causes and it took a moment before I mustered the courage to lift the blanket while she cried, —Don't see! Then I raised a corner of her damp skirt, and there in that mess of blue roping and red gore was a baby boy. I picked him up. He was slippery but I laid him on her stomach and folded a corner of the blanket around his naked form. —Do not move from there, I said, like she might escape.

In the clinic I found the catgut sutures and the bandage shears. My patient remained spent and breathless on the floor.

—What are you doing? she cried when she saw the shears.

—The cord. You have to cut it.

—Don't cut anything, she cried in fright. —You are only a child.

—I am the midwife assistant, I told her, promoting myself.

Helpless against me, she closed her eyes. For the second time in my young life then, and no less frightened, I tied a baby's umbilicus, cut between the ties. I brought the infant to the mother's shoulder and settled it there naked. At last we heard the Evans keys in the door.

—Mrs. Evans!

—What's all this? the doctor said.

—Annie, what's happened here? Mrs. Evans knelt down beside the patient, who looked up with fear.

—She nearly had it on the steps outside, I said. —I had to let her in.

Mrs. Evans gave me a peculiar look. —Run and get a basin, then. Go on, quick.

I ran and got the basin. Mrs. Evans was on her old sorry knees and had her hand on the patient's abdomen, but addressed me now, instructing, —See here, Annie, watch. You must never pull the cord to expel the mass, but only press on the stomach gently. Mrs. Evans pressed on the patient as she talked. —You'll wait till she delivers the afterbirth on her own, hear? It's only when some fool comes along and pulls that you get the flooding and fevers, because when it breaks and a portion remains behind it festers until it's deadly.

Which happened to my mother, I thought, and prepared to ask a question, but Mrs. Evans ordered, very brisk, —Now Annie you'll bring me gauze pads and bandages.

When I came back, she handed me the full basin, covered with a cloth.

The bowl was heavy as I brung it down the stairs and the mess in it sloshed about. In the kitchen, I lifted the cloth and there lay a reddish pudding in a translucent white sack, with veins like dark worms branching from a stalk. This was the mystery then, was it? Afterbirth. A dark mess of meat. Out back the pit was covered in black flies. They jumped up and swarmed when I dumped the bowl. I buried the whole works over with dirt and went back inside, up the stairs, where my employer handed the baby to me. —You'll clean him up with a damp sponge, she said.

In the clinic I laid him on the table. He was no bigger than a minute. His black eyes stared at the air like it was interesting. The branches of blue veins was a netting under his scalp, and his heart beat in the soft fontanel there. I stroked his wee cheek and his mouth turned toward the touch of my hand. I washed him and brought him back to his mother, whose face broke with helplessness and wonder.

—Mrs. Harkness will stay upstairs tonight, said Mrs. Evans.

With great effort we got Frances to her feet. She smiled very weak at me and said shyly, —I do not know your name.

—This is Annie, said Mrs. Evans. —She is my assistant.

Thus without ceremony nor a raise in my salary of ZERO dollars was I promoted official.

In the early morning two days later I went upstairs to lay the fires, and there Frances was, nursing her infant. —Good morning Mrs. Harkness, I said.

—Good morning, said she, very quiet, —but I am not Mrs. anyone.

—Why not? I said.

—His father died.

—I am sorry for your loss.

—I loved him, she said, and looked down at the child in her arms. —I still do.

These words startled me, as I had not heard this variation, about Love. Previous to now all I heard was about Liars and Sweet Talkers, and Good-for-Nothing Sots such as Mr. Duffy, and Scoundrels who Forced a girl alone in a room. I busied myself at the fireplace, adjusting the damper, and listened for more such information. I was not disappointed, for while Frances Harkness did not linger long at Chatham Street, she taught me a lesson I carry with me to this day.

—Could you help me to get out of bed please, Annie?

I took her hands and pulled her to her feet.

—Thank you. Slowly she went to her satchel and removed a packet of papers, which she put under the pillow of the bed.

—Those are his letters? I asked.

—You are very forward.

—I was raised wrong.

—Well. Since you asked. He wrote me every day. A poem or a letter.

—I am sorry for your loss.

—Thank you, she said, sadly. —Not everybody is.

—Who isn't?

—My mother and father. They did not like him. He was a schoolteacher.

—I never did like a schoolteacher myself.

—Ha, she laughed. —Then you don't like me.

—You're a schoolteacher?

—Not since I was found to be in disgrace.

I got up and took the coal scuttle with me toward the door.

—Can't you stay for a while? she asked. —I used to read poetry in the evening with my students. Would you read with me? A book was open on the bed beside her.

—I am not so good of a reader, I said, shy in front of a schoolmistress.

—I will teach you then, indebted as I am to you for your kindness in my hour of confinement. I do love Elizabeth Barrett Browning. Do you know her Sonnets from the Portuguese? Sit a moment longer. It's been so long since I had any company. Please stay.

She made me sit beside her on the bed and opened her book and had me read aloud very halting.

If thou must love me, let it be for naught except for love's sake only
Do not say, I love her for her smile—her look—her way of
*   speaking gently . . .*
Love me for love's sake, that evermore thou mayst love on,
through love's eternity.

—You see? said Frances, her eyes brimming. —It's *love* that matters, not what salary a man makes. Or his lineage. Or whether her parents might approve. Or whether . . . whether death may part them, such as Matthew and I were parted. But only love. Only love matters. Do you see, Annie? If I could teach you this at your young age, perhaps you will find the happiness that I had, and now have lost.

I stared at her like she had grown a beard. Her words was electric to me. Love! Love's eternity! It was a fine thing. Sure it was. And like all fine things it was far out of my reach, so I wanted it.

—You may borrow the book, if you like, Frances said. I thanked her and took it down to the kitchen, where Mrs. Browder screeched at me about why wasn't the wicks trimmed in the lamps? That night I read the Portuguese Sonnets over again by the embers of the fire and thought that if the poem was right, that Love was all, then what would become of me? What of love did I have? I did not have a father nor mother, a sister or brother, and certainly not a true love, neither, or a hope of one. And yet, all my life I remembered Love's Sake Only, and Mrs. Browning's poetical lines. One in particular tormented me, where she wrote, Behold and see What a great heap of grief lay hid in me, And how the red wild sparkles dimly burn Through the ashen grayness.

Chapter Fifteen

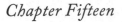

Sleight of Hand

On the morning of May 21, 1863, I dragged myself out of sleep into a stew of self pity. It was dark. It was my sixteenth birthday. Mam was gone three years already, her absence like an arm missing of my own. My brother and sister was a leg gone as well. I had no road, no ticket, no notion how to find them, and not a brown penny to my name. Happy birthday. There wasn't nothing to look forward to but fetching slop pots of blood. I laid the fires in a grump. I went to the market and returned with sacks of flour and rice. By nine I went to bring the linen off the line in the back and brooded over my future. It appeared all ashen grayness without no wild red sparkles.

—Annie! said a voice from one yard over. It came from behind a row of sheets hanging off a line. —Annie. It was the German saucepot Greta from next door. I could not see her till she emerged giggling with a bedsheet wrapped around her like a Roman. —Annie Muldoon. She threw a clothespin at me.

—Ya dirty cat. I threw it back at her, wary.

—Do you like the dried cherries? She had a cup of them in her apron and offered some to me.

—Thanks, I said, surprised.

She poured cherries onto my palm and stared at my red sore hands. —Tsk, she said, and showed me hers. The two of us compared the skin of our mitts, how cracked it was, from the ash and the lye and the scrubbing, and while she talked I tried not to laugh at her sauerkraut way of talking.

—Every day ze vashing, she said. —I hate it.

—It's s***.

—Every day to bring ze vater. She spit out a cherry pit.

I spit one, too. She laughed and gave me another handful.

—Before now, she said, —I hate you.

—I hate you more.

—You are chust der little scullery maid next door.

—I'm sixteen. I spit another pit.

—I am twenty. Much more old. Alzo, I heff a problem. You can help me? Sometimes I need a medicine for Ladies pains. For der *monatliche Schmerz*. You know. The troubles. Maybe you borrow for me from Herr Doctor one day?

I shrugged. —Sure. I ate more of her cherries, thinking her problems was less than mine, for at least she had a salary, money to spend.

Now she looked at me, curious. —Do you ever see ze little babies murdered in that Evans house?

—Excuse me?

—Everybody knows. Your missus does killing of ze little *Kinder*.

—She doesn't! I cried. —Who told you that? She never would. She's a midwife.

Now Greta raised her eyebrows suggesting something wicked. —Frau Pfeiffer says Evanses helps der hoors und Magdalenes and whatnot. You don't hear them cry out?

—It's only normal to cry out when a baby comes, I said, quite the expert.

Now Greta smiled at me and whispered, —She does der fixes, you know. If the girl is *schwanger*. She fixes a girl up.

—She'd never harm no babies never, I said with my chin forward. —I seen her nurse one with an eyedropper one time.

—She scrapes them out, all bloody, mit the Fräuleins screaming, Greta whispered, —und she kills them before they're alive.

—Stupid. How can you kill something before it's alive? She'd never. Greta was wrong. Was she?

—Think what you like, Greta said. —Anyway I heff to meet a fella on Broadway tonight and why don't you come out mit me?

She tossed her hair, dark and shiny as a lick of paint. Her eyes had a sleepy look and she held her mouth with the lips slightly apart, as if she was just about to sip a mug of sweet cider. Her appearance gave the impression she was not clever. Possibly wanton. Mrs. Browder said she was a Gypsy. When I saw her on the street, walking past the pawnbrokers and the trinket sellers and the used clothing merchants, she swayed her hips, and men looked at her and remarked, —Nice bit a bloss there.

Now in the yard she was acting the part of my friend. She raised her arms to the blue sky in a pose like she was on a poster for the opera, and sashayed around the clothesline in her bedsheet wrap. I had to laugh at her.

—Mein Gott, Annie, come out mit me up Broadway tonight.

—Why should I?

—Because you will love it.

You vill luff it.

—Come. She thracked me very playful with a wet pillowcase.

—If I went out at night alone, Browder'd sack me.

—*Gott im Himmel.* You von't be caught. Them old doctors won't never notice. Who cares what they think? They are murderers. Und Broadway is *verwunderlich.* Vonderful, so.

—Can't, I said, and stubbed at the dirt with my toe, angry.

—Are you on the tear, or something?

—It's only my birthday.

—Your birthday! she cried. —I'll drag you out by der laces then.

She did not have to drag me. All of a sudden I was hellbent. I would get out and do as I pleased.

That night, when the Evans was tucked in, with the doctor's teeth in the glass by the bed, I met Greta on the stoop. We neither of us had aprons on, or caps. Our naked hair unfurled in the night wind. I felt plain beside her. Greta was a beauty same as Dutch, with an imp in her eye. In the lamplight, I seen that she had rouged her lips. —Psst, Greta, I said, and passed her a bottle of Medicine for the Female Complaint which I had stirred together that afternoon in the clinic, laudanum diluted in spirits of wine.

—Thank you, Greta said. She wore a plum color jacket waist and a petticoat that stuck her skirts out.

—You're quite the article.

—Mrs. Pfeiffer's old petticoat. Greta curtsied. —A present she give to me.

—I never had one. Not a present nor a petticoat neither.

Greta frowned, perplexed, and ran back inside the Pfeiffer's shop. When she came out she carried a pile of ruffles. —Here. This one alzo is belonking to Mizzus Pfeiffer. Do not tear it.

She handed it to me, and in the shadows of the stoop with Greta standing guard, I pulled it up under my dress, so it stuck out now like the branches of a pine.

—Oh Du Tannenbaum, Greta said, laughing at me. —You're a Christmas tree.

—Get Away with you, I said, and pushed her, but she started singing a German song full of *Vögel singen* and *Sonnenschein* and *Blumen blühen* so it made me laugh. Without a clue to the words, I sang along and went out with my new friend. Oh Blumen bloomin', the night air was flavored with a smell of charred meat and spilled poteen from Crook's Restaurant down the block, an odor of wickedness and adventure. Oh yes, Blumen bloomin'. We sang it out whatever it meant, and strolled uptown.

—My fella will meet me by Haughwout's on Broadway, Greta said. —He is Mr. Schaeffer who come to the shop last Monday and asked me to come out mit him.

—Mrs. Browder says a lady don't go out alone.

—A lady don't. So lucky you're with me.

On Broadway, the lamps was golden all along the boulevard, little colored ones dangling off the carriages, amber and ruby and green. Each shop was lit outside with gaslight that pierced the dark above us, and the windows lit inside to display such things as you could only slaver over, silverware and ribbons, doodads and trinkets. We walked up and down from Leonard Street to Broome and listened to the minstrels, fiddle music spilling out of the shebeens, the cackles of drunks and strumpets. Greta spent a nickel on a paper of candied nuts that smelled of honey and vanilla, and we ate them, strolling just to gawk. The throng was packed so tight you was jostled and stepped on worse than cattle in a market. —Excuse us, please, we said. We was giddy with the street party and hampered by our petticoats, tripping on the curb. You could not cross to the other side of the

road without risking death under the wheels of a carriage. So many han-
soms, landaus and victorias was packed axle to axle, their horses whicker-
ing and restless. The sidewalks was jammed with walkers, gents and ladies
who slid their eyes at us, and we likewise did the once-over at everybody
we passed.

—I'd have that parasol, Greta said, nodding at a ruffled one.

—I'd have that cape, I said.

The two of us was pickled with envy. How plain we was compared to
society. How low. Even the men were tricked out. You never saw such a
variety of dandies, with their stovepipes and mustaches like the feelers on a
beetle, their broadcloth jackets called Swallowtail and Cutaway. Here and
there was an Officer in Union blue and bric-a-brac. We seen a lady in a
headdress of trembling ostrich feathers, we seen flounces looped up with
roses, silver tassels on a handbag, a cape of lace. We linked arms and pressed
against the windows of the stores and lingered outside the Marble House
off Canal Street. We seen carriages pull in front to disgorge females like
birds alighting from a gilt cage, their feet so tiny, their waists cinched above
enormous bustles like the rumps of cats in heat. Finally at Spring Street
there was Haughwout's famous dry goods store, where Greta was supposed
to meet Mr. Schaeffer. It was a building like a wedding cake, with fluted
columns and many stories of arched windows, each one blazing and sparkling. We went inside, our mouths agape, never so astonished. Silver, glass
and china glinted like sun off icicles spangling every surface. Fiery drops
lit by jets of gas sent shatters of brilliance around the room. I looked up to
see how it was done, and there was a fairyland article dangling from the
ceiling, all gobbets of ice. This was a crystal chandelier, high over our heads.
I gasped, staring above.

—Ooh Gott, said Greta. —It's brilliant. I want one all for myself.

Ooh Gott, I wanted one too. But I did not say this aloud. I only let the
craving eat down like a secret weevil tunneling in my foundations.

—Greta Weiss? said a gentleman coming upon us.

—Mr. Schaeffer, she said, smiling, so pretty, with her dimples and curls.
—This is my friend Miss Ann Muldoon.

I was not jealous to see Mr. Schaeffer. He was a porky nimenog in pin-
stripes, maybe thirty years of age, with a red face and dark yellow mustache
that drooped over a small mouth, small lips. Greta took his arm and winked

at me. —I'll meet you outside in half an hour. They strolled off to look at the millinery and soon was lost in the crowd.

The store smelled of lilacs and money. It struck me dumb. Reflected in the silver of a gilt-framed mirror I saw my watery face, so sharp-chinned, the black hair wild and loose, and the blue eyes dark with the hunger. I was no longer a pocky stripling but a young girl made sick by all the crystal and the dazzle of the merchandise. I walked the display of china like it was a foreign country, and lifted a dainty wee cup, painted with roses so delicate, the rim edged with gold. I placed it carefully down and picked up another, with forget-me-nots.

—Miss! cried a floorwalking porter, rushing at me. —DO NOT handle the goods. His small eyes was crazed with authority.

I reared back. —I'll handle 'em if I want, ya bungstarter, said I, wounded. —Ain't I a customer?

—That's it for you, then miss. He took my elbow and escorted me toward the door in a hustle.

—Lemme go, I said, fighting him. —Take your mitts offa me.

In the midst of this humiliation, I heard my name shouted in a man's voice.

—Axie! Axie Muldoon!

The fella calling me was about twenty years of age, trim and compact. His trousers were narrow in the leg as was the fashion, and he wore a flash jacket well fit over square shoulders, with white collar and cuffs. He had a luxury mustache and dark hair worn long over the ears. He held a cap in his hand, the color of rust. The cocksure way he carried himself was familiar and likewise familiar was the devil in his eye. I recognized the Dangerous Orphan, Charlie.

—Miss Muldoon, he said again loudly. Yes it was him. There was the slight underbite of his jaw, the darting minnows of his eyes.

—Charlie! I said. —It's you.

—It ain't Abe Lincoln.

—Come along now, miss, said the little rooster of a porter.

—Apologies, mister, Charlie said, and bowed very proper, even as he took my arm. —My sister here ain't quite right in the head. She suffers from fainting fits and dementia. Also she has a weakness in the blood which makes her simple. She has spells, you know.

I adopted a vague glassy look.

—She had a hold of the merchandise, the porter sniffed. —Without intention to buy.

—She doesn't mean any harm, Charlie said. —It's the shiny stuff she likes, the poor thing, you can't blame her. You know how the female is susceptible. They can't help it. I will take my sister off your hands and set her straight.

I smiled sweetly at the paltry little guard, and away he went to cavil and snitch. Charlie and me made our way through the throng till we stood outside in the night air where Charlie stared at me like I was something a cat had dropped at his feet.

—So, I said, —your sister, am I?

—There is a resemblance, he said, grinning. —You could be.

—In your dreams.

—You've not changed, I see, Axie Muldoon.

—I have. I'm a baroness.

He laughed. —Oh Your Highness, you should've seen your royal face when that cove grabbed you. Red as roses.

—You shoulda seen yours. You obviously was lying through your teeth.

—For a good cause I'd lie on Sundays. I'd lie on the Bible, but I don't have to since I have a crib now over at Sixth Avenue where Mrs. Sheehan keeps a boardinghouse. How's that for circumstances?

—Not bad for an orphan off the train. Where've you been all this time? I asked.

—I been down the Nile. I been to Staten Island. I seen Paris in the springtime. Yourself?

—Not on Cherry Street.

—I know that already. I came looking for you once. A year ago or more. So he had showed up, despite we had no cherry blossoms.

—That Duffy told me about your Mam, Charlie said, quiet. He leaned toward me and put his hand on my wrist then so my blood turned spiky at the touch of his fingers, which I seen were cracked and stained dark around the nails. —Sorry to hear it.

—Thank you, I said.

We stood awkward on the sidewalk like stones in a stream, with the crowd of walkers eddying past, the light of the bright windows in a pool around us.

—You've blossomed into a red, red rose, Miss Axie Muldoon. Haven't you? With those scarlet cheeks?

He stood with the left side of his mouth cocked up, squinting in appraisal, seeming to mock me and my furious blush.

—I'm called Ann now, I said, haughty as possible.

—Aha. Now he started to sing the Annie Laurie song, his cap over his heart and a look in his eye that was half a leer. —Her brow is like the snowdrift, Her neck is like the swan, Her face it is the fairest, That 'er the sun shone on . . .

I rolled my eyes at him uneasy and moved along the sidewalk.

—I must confess, Charlie said, —that just now I watched that mug grab you, and I didn't recognize it was you, and then on second glance, I seen you were none other than that chickenhearted orphan train rider who wouldn't stand up on the roof with me back in days of yore.

—Only an idiot such as yourself would stand on the roof of a train.

—Time has not made a lady outta you, I see.

—It hasn't made a lady outta you either.

—It's made me a gentleman.

—Has it then?

—I'm a typesetter at the *Herald*. He spread his inky hands for my inspection. —All the letters of the alphabet at my fingertips. All the stories of the world. I can set five lines in a minute, hundreds of lines an hour.

—Well ain't you grand?

—I ain't no shoeshine boy.

A wicked flash was in his eye when he said it, so that when he looked me over, I felt it like a hand on my skin.

—And yourself, Miss Muldoon of Gotham? Are you the queen?

—I am an assistant to a doctor in Chatham Square.

—You're a bonded girl then?

—I am not. I am an assistant.

—Assistant. What's that then? Do you hold a poor cove down on the floor while the sawbones cuts off his leg?

—Of course, I says, —I keep 'em quiet with a hot poker.

—Just as I suspected, you've no heart at all, Axie. Have you ever stitched a man shut? Ever seen a tooth pulled? Ever lanced an abscess?

—What I seen is what I seen, I said, not about to tell him the details.

—Assistant. He regarded me with frank respect. —Who'd have thought it? Such a long way from Illinois.

—Don't talk to me of Illinois.

—I'm talking about how you and me escaped.

—I wish everybody did.

He closed his mouth, and by his look of honest sorrow I knew he saw what was in my mind, my waxy heart. *Joe and Dutchie.* He smiled then and reached behind my ear to withdraw a penny. —For your thoughts, he said, and handed it to me.

—How'd you do that?

—Magic. Observe.

He showed me his palms, empty, yet he found a pencil between the strands of my hair with just the sleight of his hand, and balanced it on the end of his nose. I was nearly fallen out on the pavement with astonishment. The passersby turned their heads to stare. Among them was Greta, wearing a new hat but without Mr. Schaeffer.

—Annie, *mein Gott*! Greta said, noticing me there at last. —Where've you been? I've been up and down the place looking.

—What? Charlie said, looking back and forth between us. —Is this young lady that sister of yours then, all grown up?

—This is my friend Greta. She's a German, God forgive her, but don't you mind about that, I said, to razz on her, —she don't even like sauerkraut.

Greta gave me a pinch and sized him up with her saucepot eyes.

—Charles G. Jones, he said, bowing. —Pleased to meet you.

Jones, I thought when I heard it. So he wasn't plain Charlie anymore, he'd got a last name somewheres along the way.

Greta tugged my arm. —We have to go, Annie, *mein Gott*. It's late!

—I'll walk you, ladies, said Charlie, —so's you don't have to travel alone.

He took my arm on one side and Greta's on the other, and we jumped the streetcar. He rode with us in the back, squeezed up against the rail, and whispered in my ear so the hairs rose along the back of my neck and down along my arm. —Point me out which one's your doctor's place, he said.

—Number one hundred Chatham, there, I said, when it came into view.

—Ah, he said in my ear, —you've a nice pair.

I startled, for his meaning seemed wicked. —A nice pair of lanterns out front, he continued with a smolder in his eye. —I won't forget them.

—Won't you? I said, some upset taking root now in my system.

—I'll call on you then. He waved his hat as we hopped off and ran home, my borrowed birthday petticoat swishing around my legs.

—He's a dodgy fella, Greta said, running.

—No he ain't, I said, not sure.

—He's one of those danglers and he'll dangle you, miss.

—I known him from way back.

—Still, she said, —you gott to be careful.

—You're the one with the new hat, I says. —Where'd you get it?

—Nothing wrong mit a new hat. Be careful is all I'm saying.

—Right, I said. —Be careful yourself.

Chapter Sixteen

Student

*T*wo nights later came a knock on the back door. There was Charlie Jones, holding a penny paper of fried oysters.

—Hungry? he asked, chewing. He threw an oyster in the air and caught it in his mouth. —Come along out with me.

—Shhh, I says. —I can't.

—Why not? Chicken?

I looked behind me. Inside was the dark kitchen and the remnants of supper to clear. Mrs. Browder had gone home to Archie for the night. At present no ladies was in confinement upstairs in the spare rooms and the Evanses' lights was out. I had found no evidence of murdered infants on the premises and decided that Greta was full of b. and s. But I was on my guard and did not wish to invite trouble. —You can't come in.

—You're scared, he says.

—Hardly.

—Mind if I sit?

I shrugged.

He sat in the open doorway surveying the bare dirt yard and mentioned how oysters will make a man thirsty. —Have you got any cider? I went inside and brought out a jug of it with two cups. He patted the spot next to him and I sat there. He offered me an oyster and I bit down on it. It was chewy as rawhide but salty.

—Where's your employer the doctor, then?

—Asleep.

—Tired from bleeding the populace? Does old Sawbones lance boils all day and treat the piles and cauterize the suppurating wounds of accident victims?

—It's Mrs. Evans I assist, with her patients.

—Is she short-tempered then? he said, pleased at his joke. —PATIENCE, get it?

—Very funny, says I. And he was, though I barely gave him the satisfaction of a smile, only brushed at my hair with my fingers, nervous.

—So you're assistant to a midwife? You must've seen . . . things. And he wagged his eyebrows suggesting what I seen was dirty.

—It ain't a man's business.

—ISn't, not AIN'T. Listen to me, Student, speak like the upper crust.

—I'll speak how I want.

—Here, now, Student, eat this.

He held another oyster in front of my mouth. My jaws opened automatically and he fed me like I was a baby starling. I tried not to bust out laughing but was not successful. His boyish manner and his charm worked under my skin. The grease off the oysters made his lips shiny.

—Open. He fed me another bit, then another. He licked his fingers. He said, Oysters is an Aphrodisiac and I said, What's that? and he said it was a Liver Invigorator. He thrust another one in my mouth.

In this manner, Charlie wooed me on the back step. He fed me and trained me to talk proper. Isn't not ain't. Doesn't not don't. Saw not seen. Brought not brung. I done my best to learn, but it was DID my best, he reminded me, so that I was flustered and embarrassed and flattered, with his rewards of oysters, and how he called me Student. With his braces loose off the shoulder, he was a man, a stranger, though I had knew—had KNOWN—him, four years. While we sat there, the long train West and back again snaked under and around us carrying all our d***ed past with its sorrow and shame, my lost brother and sister left behind, the scars of a farmer's whip on his back. And flashing like a light on the last train car was Mrs. Dix's warning to me, how I must not succumb to the influence of wild unruly boys such as orphan Charlie, fathered in sin and mothered by the streets. No good will come of it, she had said. No good. And yet the night wore on in the dank yard with me and him laughing and the garbage pit still smoking and the laundry lines crossing to the trunk of a haggard half dead sycamore that grew there. The stars came out overhead, needle pricks stitching the dark. Charlie bragged of his job at the *Herald* where he started as a lowdown newsboy fresh back from the prairie. He told how he hawked papers in the wind and snow and worked his way up to the composing room, where he made a point to read everything he set in type and thus learned to speak like a schoolmaster.

—What do you mean, set in type?

—It's like this, Student. We use cast metal sorts, and compose them into formes until each page is set. You gotta be fast and precise and accurate and have your type and your leading all sorted in your tray. He folded his left hand palm up and stroked the thumb in quick movements, counting off. —Thumb thumb thumb, each one in order on the jobstick.

—Speak English, I said. —Not this jobstick and whatnot like a foreign language.

—Listen, Student, you gotta go top speed yet never bung it up, because the foreman'll come after you for every flip.

He stared at me, grinning.

—Flip?

—Flip, he said, very slow, and locked my eyes in the tongs of his gaze. —You have to think about the typeface, he said, quiet now, —and the shank, the point size, the shoulder, the nick and the groove.

—I don't have to think of that, not at all, so I don't.

—What do you think about, then, Miss Axie? he inquired with a crooked mouth.

What did I think about. The night around us was loud with peepers and soft wind, the scuttling of rats in the alley. A cat mewed and hissed. Charlie waited for me to speak and while he waited he leaned back on his hands, his face turned upward to the rooftops. He stretched his legs long in front of us, and his flank brushed against mine as he shifted so I shuddered at the touch. Behind my hunched shoulders his gaze burned me. When I turned to look at him his eyes was on my face, devoted and intent on listening for what pearl or ruby of secret thought I would confess.

—What worries trouble your little head, eh? he said.

I ran the hem of my apron back and forth, between my thumb and forefinger, until finally I brought the cloth to my face and pressed it against my eyes.

—What? Hello, now, Chickenheart, what's the matter?

—Nothing.

—Nothing, nothing, says the maiden, Charlie whispered, —but yet something makes her hide her face. What are you thinking?

—Shut it, please, I says, shy and miserable under my apron.

He was quiet. I heard him sigh and suck air in a chirp through the crack between his teeth, and he said so softly, —You think of your Mam and your pretty sister and your little red-hair brother. Don't you now?

I wept then, through the cramp in my throat. He had known me so long, since way back then, and knew Joe and Dutch and Mam. As for himself, he had no Mam or sister and brother of his own to think of, and it was all this that made me cry.

—Here, then. He put his arm around my shoulder. —Go on and sob away if you want to.

I shook my head and stayed stiff so you could not whittle the apron off my face with a pocketknife. He pulled at it careful as a surgeon, till it was peeled down to reveal my wretched expression. Charlie allowed me to cry into his neck. The collar of his shirt chafed against the socket of my left eye. The bone of his cheek rested against my hair.

—There now. That's a good girl.

He poured me a cup of cider and held it to my lips. I dried my tears on my sleeve.

—We'll find those two, your sister and brother, he said. —One of these days we will. Mark my words.

I marked them. I put them in my pocket and kept them there for years.

Now Charlie leaned in, toward my face, the kindness of his eyes so trustworthy or so dangerous, which? How could I know? His head tipped over my sorry mouth, looming near, so it seemed he would _____, and I was panicked so flustered as he reached his hand toward my hair, when just at that moment I heard the front bell ring, a fast knocking. I jumped away. A light came on inside, and I heard the feeble mew of Mrs. Evans calling. A patient was at the door, and I had to go.

—Well, Student, Charlie said, —I'll be off. He slipped his braces over his shoulders, put his arms through his jacket sleeves. He stood, looking down at the puddle of my sorry self, and striped my nose with the tip of his forefinger, the way you would do a puppy. —Too bad you wouldn't come out with me. Perhaps another time.

But for weeks there was no other time. He did not come again. He did not sit on the step nor bring me no more oysters or a lesson in proper English or let me cry again into his warm neck. What did he want with me anyway? He was a jagger and a dangler like Greta said. Was he? I did not know and had no way to know. Once before he said he would be back before the cherries bloomed and then looked for me too late. He had touched my hair, his eyes so soft, then had pat me on the nose like the stray mutt I was. The month of June wore away and there was no other occasion to borrow a petticoat or gaze at a chandelier. Greta met Mr. Schaeffer on the corner now and strolled out with him bold as brass. Several times I jealously saw them, arms linked, Greta laughing and saying, —*Oh mein Gott*, so loud that surely the populace would peer down from their windows and see her go off with him into the night. She had another new hat and a pretty necklace with a charm on it. The spring was hurtling on toward summer and it seemed Charlie was not my suitor, but only an empty pair of braces with tricks up his sleeve. He had showed up and then disappeared and while he was there I liked him but when he was gone I hated him. It would take me years to see it was a pattern.

But then one evening at last, Charlie arrived scuffing the dirt outside in the yard with the toe of his boot. —Axie Muldoon! he cried, rapping at the open door. Mrs. Browder got there before me, brandished her ladle at him.
—And who wants her?
—Charles G. Jones. He bowed like Lord Muck. —At your service.
—Does she know you?
—She does, I said. —I do.
Mrs. Browder turned to inspect me with suspicion. —How?
—I known him from my childhood, I said. —He met my Mam.
Mrs. Browder always liked when I talked about my Mam. —Is that so? Her face was softer now.

—It is, he said. —Her Mam fed me a lovely dinner one night when I was a youngster.

—Charlie is a printer at the *Herald,* I told her.

—Is he? Hmmp. I read the *Police Gazette,* myself. She dried her hands, pushed the door half-to, and pulled me into the kitchen. —And how did this man discover you here in Chatham Square?

—By coincidence at Hegemann's the chemist's, I lied.

She held my chin in her floury fingers and fixed me with a stern look. —You'll be back before the sun sets, is that clear?

—Yes ma'am.

—And keep your eyes forward and your hands folded in front of you or in back.

—Yes ma'am.

—And look out he doesn't finagle you.

—Finagle me?

—You know exactly what I'm talking about. And take your apron off. And brush your hair.

She watched me as I took out the pins and brushed my hair and twisted it up again. —It's about time you went out. She pinched my cheeks till they were pink. —Very pretty, she said, and shooed me toward the door.

It was my right to treat Charles Jones with frost and ginger after his neglect of me, and yet it was himself who stomped along in a dark mood. He did not wink. He did not whistle. He did not boast or correct my ain'ts, or find a penny behind my ear, or ask for my thoughts or feed me any kind of oyster. For several blocks he scowled and strode along so fast that my short legs could not keep up, and I felt small, like I was to blame, and did not muster the wherewithal to ask where had he been for the month of June?

—Student, he said at last, scowling, chewing his lip. —There's a war on.

—You don't say, Professor. Has been one on these past years.

—The point is this: them Republicans have a Conscription Act now and they're about to draft every cove with two legs to go fight, UNLESS we can pay THREE HUNDRED dollars for a substitute to take our place on the battle lines. It's a rich man's war and a poor man's fight and that's a SCANDAL.

—Three hundred dollars?

—Who can pay it? If you're a three hundred dollar man, you're a swell or a squire. Not a working cove like myself, right? And so I'm doomed to go to war against my will.

—Mrs. Browder's Archie had his arm cut off at Bull Run, I offered.

—There you have it. Poor Archie the slub. Meanwhile the rich boys buy their way out or pay a substitute. The blackies get a cakewalk. It's true! No Negro is required to fight and yet the Federals have gone and given ME a number in the draft lottery. It ain't fair and I won't go. The boys in the composing room won't neither, draft lottery or no draft lottery. Why should I lose one of my arms? One of my two legs? How would I tie my bootlaces? Tell me that. How would I dance?

—You can't dance now, Charles Jones, so what would be the difference?

With that he stopped short. —You think I can't dance? Is that what you think? It seemed he was furious till he grinned all of a sudden and grabbed me around the waist and whirled me once in a jig right at the corner of Duane Street, so I was confused whether he liked me or not at all and had to beat him with my little drawstring purse and push him away for decorum's sake, all the while laughing despite how the passersby stared and clucked. —Mr. Jones!

—At your service.

—Where'd you get that name, anyway?

—Off a street sign. Great Jones Street. There's a block with that name, near here, by Cooper Square. Great Jones! It's a name like P. T. Barnum would have up on a balloon. But I don't use the Great.

—Why not? Charles G. Jones. Sounds right.

—So you think I AM great then? I'll be greater still one of these days, you'll see.

—And not too proud of it, I said.

—Am I bigheaded?

—Like a watermelon's under your hat.

—I'll be writing for the paper soon. Starting with ads, and straight on to the articles with a headline here and a byline there. He flourished his hands like he was setting his name in type in the air. —By Charles G. Jones. You watch. Watch now.

He adjusted his cuffs, then reached slowly toward me like a mesmerist and pulled a handkerchief from behind my ear. —Behold, a Gentleman's pocket square. Chinese silk, spun personally by the Emperor's silkworms in the gardens of Shanghai, with a hand-rolled edge, and the bluest of indigo dye from the fabled lands of Araby. Available only from behind the delicate ear of Miss Chickenheart Muldoon.

He snapped it in the air, and I snatched it, tucked it in the bodice of my dress.

—It's mine.

—It's not yours. He eyed the nest where it was stowed.

—It is now.

—Well I won't argue with you.

—You better not, I said. —I'd win.

He was suddenly quiet. Not smiling. I was wary of him again. His beetled brow and his narrow eyes. —I would win, I repeated, shy.

—You won already, he said. —You won me.

—What? I did not hear him correctly.

We were stopped in the shadows of the St. Andrews Roman Catholic Church on the corner of Duane and Broadway. It was quiet, with just the clack of somebody's boot nails on the cobbles, and fiddle music drifting out of a saloon. On the sidewalk we stood rooted with the air thick and strange between us. I did not know where to look. The muscles of my arms and legs were shot through with dropsy.

—You won me, he said again. —Some poor prize, right? About to be packed off to the war to be fodder for the enemy. You'll pray for my mortal soul, won't you? Say you will, Axie.

—Everything I pray for the reverse happens. You'll wish you never've asked.

—Not true. He pulled me through a gate, into the dark recess of the empty churchyard, where the shadows were deep and holy. We were hidden by the hedge along the spiked iron fences but God watched through the windows as Charlie turned to me.

—You're my girl, he said softly. —Are ya?

All I gave him for an answer was just the lift of my chin, and he took it in his hand and pulled my mouth to him like my face was an apple he would eat. He kissed me then and my heart flew up into my throat so he took that too and swallowed it down.

—Axie you're a snap of a girl, he murmured. —You know it.

He held me in his arms and kissed me again, so my legs faltered and turned to aspic and his whiskers were a soft good burr against the skin of my face. I was water down a drain. We stayed still and pressed together. Far away I heard the sounds of wheels out on the pavement and men singing in the shebeen. Only the hush of our breath was loud and near, the thump of his blood wild as my own careening in the cages of our bones. —Sweet, he whispered. The heat off his neck smelled of tobacco and ink. His hand stalled on the curve of my back. We rested standing so quiet in the church-yard and my limbs trembled like it was cold out, when it wasn't. —You're my girl, he said, kissing me again, and he was smooth and professional in the way he went about it, so it was plain he knew his way around a kiss, and even as I was afraid of him and his dangerous knowledge, the flicker of his tongue started a jolt of molten liquid straight down my center so nothing was ever the same again. —Kiss me, he said, and I did, sick with kisses, and time went away till at last he took my arm and led me out of the shadows. We strolled, altered now and shy through the gaslit streets. The uproar in my very linings was surely visible.

At the back door of 100 Chatham Street Charlie took his hat in hand. —I'll be needing that handkerchief back.

—Then you should not have lost it behind my ear.

—I'll come fetch it soon. I'll go looking right where you stowed it.

—How will I know you are not a liar? The cockles of my heart already had begun to form their hard shell of suspicion. —Who's to say you won't disappear again, only to come and ... take a girl to the churchyard?

—Did I not say you were my girl? he asked.

—No, you ASKED was I yours?

—And you ARE, ya suspicious cat. Then he blew me a kiss off two fingers and went backwards away down the lane grinning. You'd think he won a raffle. When he was out of sight I closed the door behind him and leaned against it in a faint.

—Are you sick? Mrs. Browder asked the next morning.

—No, I said.

But I was. I spilled the tea. I stared at motes of dust.

—Are you in love? she asked.

—I'm not.

—I have only one thing to say to you. And I'll say it again.

—What's that?

—Don't go out nowheres with him after dark. If I catch you I'll welt you till you're sorry you ever heard the name Browder. You won't go out.

So I didn't. The next night when Charlie came late to the kitchen door and whispered my name, I heeded her advice and invited him to come in. We did not stroll outside but soon found ourselves sitting on the hard bench at the kitchen table with cups of cider and something else between us: last evening in the churchyard. While Charlie blathered on about the d***ed Conscription Act, it sat there like a red apple on a white plate.

—Two boys in the composing room got called up for the draft lottery next week, Charlie said. —I'll be next.

—I hope you're wrong.

—It's not that I'm afraid to die.

—Don't talk that way.

—If you're drafted in this war, it's as good as a ticket to the grave.

—You can't die, I told him, quiet so he looked hard at me. —You mustn't die. These three words caused just the smallest of reactions in him, a swallow.

—Do you mind, he asked, with his brown velvet gaze, —if I kiss you again?

My mind had nothing to do with it, I discovered, so it was not long before we found ourselves down entangled desperate on the floor where slips of onion skin were fallen in the cracks along with a dropped raisin from a pudding, a hairpin, the peel of a potato. It was hard wood planks beneath us and the rafters above. It was private. It was available. It was dark. It was somebody's arms around us. With our eyes closed we were carried away, away on top of a fast train. We were orphans murmuring and grappling and where we went was the only place that belonged to us. And then his fingers found the buttons at the neck of my dress.

—No, I said, and swatted him.

—Annie, Axie, oh Annie.

—No.

—Will you take your shirt off then?

—No!

—Just let me see them.

—No.

—Just a look. The rosy nibs.

—Stop. But he would not. My face was on fire by his questions, all my parts.

—Just a look, he said. —Lord have mercy just a wee look. I'm aching for it. How bothered and stirred was I by his wicked talk. *The rosy nibs.* And so passed that night till I shooed him away and another night, another assault on my buttons till at last one time shaking, I said, just a look and allowed him. How he gasped and trembled. Such Beauties he said in a holy voice while I cried, clutching the sides of the corset closed in the dim light. It was wrong I knew but it didn't feel wrong, it was _____. Please may I kiss them? he pleaded so charming and coaxed at me. I held him away. I was a girl of sixteen, torn every which way, by the warnings of Adelaide and Frances, and by the lurid texts and dangerous diseases of Dr. Gunning's book, and then tormented a different way altogether by the running of a printer's hands along the skin of my leg.

In the weeks after Greta started up her rumor of bloody murder at the Evanses, I observed my employers with suspicious eyes and listened outside doorways. I examined the waste bin and looked in corners for evidence or weapons. But while I found no sign that either of the Evans was a killer and argued against Greta, she would not leave off twitting me, saying, —You are Hausmaid to der Murderer. *Der verrückte Abtreiber.*

—Does Mrs. Evans murder babies? I asked Mrs. Browder one warm day, while she prepared a haunch of beef.

—Who told you that? She swung around to me with a cleaver in her hand, her eyes fierce.

—Next door Greta says it's all hoors here and Missus fixes them if they're you-know.

—Listen to me, young filly. Your Mrs. Evans has the kindest hand in the city and you will never brook a word against her, hear me? She'd no more murder a child than you or me. Tell your fine Greta to stop listening to Mrs. Pfeiffer who is nothing but a bitter old catamaran. People like her never stood in the shoes of a desperate girl or a mother facing her grave like your own Mam in childbed. I'll tell you, said Mrs. B., —men have war to bring them their sorrows and pain, and we have our own physiology, so we do.

—What physiology?

She sighed very heavy. —Mrs. Evans delivers the afflicted. And I myself wouldn't be standing here now today if it weren't for her favors.

Mrs. Browder stopped and looked off into the murk of the kitchen. By her silence and the way her face buckled and righted itself it was plain she knew something private about the shoes of a desperate girl.

—What she does is only scraping, Mrs. B. said. —Before it's quick. It's only to unblock the girl and return her courses to the natural rhythm.

—Scraping?

—You're the assistant. Ask her.

All through the hot early days of July Mrs. Evans did not teach me anything to do with scraping, but Mrs. Browder had, just by the force of her conviction, relieved me of the fear my teacher was a murderess, so I was free to brood on more important matters and moon about the premises preoccupied. For while Mr. Jones did not further breach my buttons, he did not cease his attempts, nor did I operate a moment of the day or night without an ache in all my parts, filled with unspeakable depraved craving and the taste of dread like metal in my teeth. One evening, when the night was thick with the smell of warmed garbage and the heat was trapped down amongst the buildings, my suitor came to the back door so handsome in his shirtsleeves, his jacket hooked over his shoulder and a grocer's bag in his hand.

—What do you have there?

—A picnic, he says, and opened the bag to reveal twists of salted bread and a bottle of apple wine.

We sat on the back step facing the coal alley and licked salt off our lips. The wine had a hard swooning taste new to my tongue, and I can't say I liked it but I matched him sip for sip. The moon shone in curdled light behind the clouds, and when Charlie the wanderer wandered his hand in my direction I was not sorry, I was eager, yes I was.

—What have we here? He pulled a penny from inside the warm neck of my blouse. —And what's this! he cried, and took a foil of hard candy from my sleeve. He put it in my mouth then retrieved it back from me with his own.

Thus our game was invented, Hiding and Seeking, tricks with sleeves and secret objects. Whether he had played it before with another I didn't know, nor would I ask, too proud even as I doubted him. Behind my ear he found another sweet, and fed me it.

—See what you can find, yourself, he whispered, and hid his tongue in my ear, his hand under my corset.

—No.

—Axie.

I stood up, mussed and bothered, and went inside the steaming kitchen, down the ladder to the cellar where bricks of ice chopped out of lakes months before were delivered by wagon. Frost rose up when I opened the top of the ice chest, and I stabbed with the pick to crack off a bowl of frozen chips, already melting as I brought them up the ladder to find Charlie standing by the cellar door. He reached for the bowl and with a swift movement put a chip of ice down the front of my dress. I shrieked. He clapped his hand over my mouth.

—Shush.

A snail track of cold traveled along my sternum southward. —Oh Lord.

—Shh. Be quiet.

Now I placed a sliver of ice on the back of Charlie's neck. —Ah, Mother of God, he said, his shoulders hunched up to his ears. He took another bit of ice and ran it up and down the skin of my arm till I shrieked but quietly so he stopped my mouth and sank me down to the floor where we traveled ice along the pathways and lanes of limbs and it melted in the steaming heat between us. All the while the awful force and the lure of what lay beneath our clothing had me in a panic. The words Danger and Downfall were plastered like signs on the inside of my eyelids when I closed them.

—Please Axie Jesus God. Please.

—No.

—Please God I am dying.

—No, I said.

—Have mercy I will die.

—Die then.

He held his heart like I stabbed him. He pulled away from me and his face in the dim light was the face of the orphan boy Charlie stumping down the road in bare feet, secret welts on his back.

—You wouldn't care if I did.

—I would.

—Nobody never loved me. Nobody.

—Not true, I said.

—Who loves me then?

—Who loves ME?

—I do, he cried. —Say yes.

— . . .

—Chickenheart. You're so beautiful.

It was finagling and flattery like I was warned against.

—Your wild black hair.

—Your wild sorry arse, Charlie Jones.

—I always loved you.

—You didn't.

—Since the day I saw you, he said. —You are the rose of Chatham Street.

—Pshht.

It was all talk. Honey and milk.

—Please Annie. I have set you as a seal upon my heart, and safe all the days of your life.

It was blarney and quotes off the Bible he was feeding me, fibs.

—If you loved me, he whispered, —you'd believe me.

—If you loved me, liar, you'd tell your fingers to stop with them buttons.

—See what they found, though? Now he pulled from his pocket with great solemnity a shiny chain, a necklace dangling a trinket shaped like a heart. —It's only tin. I wisht it was diamond such as you deserve.

—It's beautiful.

—Not as beautiful as you.

I held it glittering up to the candlelight and he took and fastened it around my neck. —Nobody never gave me a present.

—You deserve it, my own beauty.

Charlie laced the strands of my hair between his fingers, combed it out long so you would think it was silk, and whispered, —A rare girl like you should have whatever she wants forever. Sure you should. Pearls and white bread. Garnets and fur.

—Oh Charlie, d*** you.

—Trinkets, he said. —Spangles and honeycomb.

The words weakened me worse than the wine.

—If I should be drafted and die in the war, I'd die happy if you only loved me.

—Don't speak of it.

—You love me. He pulled the chain at my neck with the tip of his finger, roped me toward his mouth. —Do you? Say yes.

—Yes.

—C'mon then, he said, with just his breath. —Say it.

Yes would ruin me.

—Will you? His eyes so fevered were helpless against my answer, and sad as only an orphan's eyes are sad. —What if I should die? Say yes.

I never did say it. Still there was no doubt in that minute, then. I did not care about ruin or falling. I thought only how he might die or leave me, how it was that everyone left me. I thought of *love's sake only,* the wild red sparkles, the garnets and fur, that I was a rose of Chatham Street. The heat slicked our cheeks. The ice melted on the skin over my ribs. He spread his coat beneath me. The infernal clothes were in the way now. I did not care. I laughed. I helped him. It was a desperate hurry. He was everything I was warned against. Finagling. His hands clamped the sides of my face his knees clamped my knees. The laces of my corset snapped. His arm would not come free of the sleeve. And then it was free so fast I gasped. Son of God in heaven. The sparse pelt of his scrawny boy's chest pressed against my skin. He pulled away. He stared at me so naked in the pale circle of candlelight.

—No, I said and covered myself from his gaze.

—Yes, he said, his breath sharp and hoarse.

—No. But it was too late.

—Closer. Like that. He shifted my hips beneath him. He never took his eyes off mine or his trousers off. —Oh my angel. My sweet love.

We had no need for instructions or expensive lessons. It was free of charge. It was abandonment to the movement of the planets such that my limbs and hips and his were matched to the tides and I had no say at all anymore, opened as I was and carried away with him.

—My darling, he said, so tender, and closed his eyes. —My sweetheart.

His cheek was wet with my tears.

—Shh there my darling love now.

There on the floor of the kitchen we was transported to a private country where we were not orphans no more, not cast off nor lost. He took my chin with his fingertip, his eyes black pools of tar. He had me. Because he found a penny in my blouse. Because my resolve was melted with ice. Because he had got me on the floor. Because nobody loved me. Because nobody loved him. Because he gave me apple wine. Because he gave me a necklace. Because he was going to die in the war. Because I would lose him. Because he ordered me. Oh my angel he said. At last the secret of the ages was revealed and it was s***** congress. He had me. It was because he said Love and I thought I saw it like a mark on him. I did not know what it meant, only that if he forsook me now I would be an even worse kind of orphan, barefoot and shamed on the pavement with eyes flat and empty like the pelt of an animal long ago run over by the streetcar.

Chapter Seventeen

The Plethoric Habit of Body

*J*ust hours after he left in the dark of the morning, the city exploded. The buildings broiled on a hot spit of weather, and for a week that July of 1863, gangs of men took to the streets in a riot. I heard them at eight that morning as I fetched water from the square, a mob banging pots running toward Bowery. I hid in a doorway as they chased a Negro down the alley. They smashed windows and set buildings on fire. The next day the *Police Gazette* and the *Herald* said the rabble was enraged over the lottery for the Army draft, the same one that had Charlie ranting. Furious cowards strung up Negroes by the neck and hung them from lampposts on Clarkson Street. If it weren't for the Negroes there'd be no war, they said, and complained it was injustice that these same blacks didn't have to go fight like the rest of the miserable hordes without money to buy off the draft lords. The rabble sacked Park Avenue houses where the rich boys lived, the three hundred dollar men. They burned the Colored Orphan Asylum and the Brooks Brothers store at the corner of Catherine and Cherry not five blocks from where I first drew breath. All that week, Charlie stayed away from me while livid packs of brutes stormed his workplace and mobbed Crook's Restaurant on the corner of Chatham Street, shouting they would kill all the Negro cooks and waiters, who hid in the basement. At last on the third day, the army left the war to come and stop them, marching into town with cannons.

But I did not care one skerrick about the troubles of the world. I had my own troubles.

Four weeks passed, and my courses had not returned on time. Nor had Charles G. Jones. He was the worst form of b*****d. He'd left me so I was no better than stupid Adelaide or poor Frances, or any of the cow-eyed females who appeared on our doorstep. I was a Magdalene and fallen as Mrs. Dix had warned. Yes, these summer weeks was a time of war and riots, fire and purgatory, and not just in the streets but right there in the kitchen on my cot by the stove. Those days formed me for life as good as a blacksmith's forge. For I saw now what force had me hostage, and how strong is the hard fast chemical rule of s***** congress. If my own orphan resolve could be overcome only by a man saying LOVE, then no body was immune. If I was in trouble as a result it was no fault of my own but the fault of a demon pooka who was a Certain Man. I lay awake, bargaining with devils, Jesus God Mary, if only I was not.

Men have war to bring them their sorrows and pain, Mrs. Browder had said, and we females have our own physiology.

But I seen the females had war, too, oh yes we did. It was a hard lesson that came home to me every which way then, that it was us who was doubly grieved, by war and anatomy, both. Everywhere you turned in that year you saw the widowed wives in their weeds, and mothers following flag-wrapped caskets. At our door we got the mothers left alone with one too many fatherless runts who could not afford another. We got girls whose Johnny was gone for a soldier and now they were carrying his parting gift. Because of the war, Mrs. Browder whispered, there was many more such misfortunates. So now was I among them? Mrs. Evans relieved several of these afflicted but offered few lessons, saying I could not assist the premature deliveries, as she called them, till I had a child myself. Should I myself now go to Mrs. Evans and ask would she fix me up? Could I take a long spoon or a crochet hook or some such and fix myself? I could not face neither idea no ways, but I seen with new eyes then, for my OWN shoes was the shoes of a desperate girl, and I known I for sure was not a hoor and so what if I was? It was only half my fault yet I carried all the blame. If Mrs.

Evans did fix me it would be a mercy. Oh my teacher. She came to seem
an angel then in my eyes, saving girls from doom. All those weeks I turned
in my cot with thoughts of tragedy and shame. What would my sister and
brother think of the state I was in (if I was in it)? Surely the Evans would
not like me as an assistant in such a condition. Or afterwards. They'd throw
me out and I'd throw myself off the Battery rather than have a child in the
streets or die of having it like my poor Mam so it would be left an orphan.
There was too many orphans already and I did not wish to be an orphan's
dead mother. All night I gnawed my knuckles till they bled. If I ever saw
Charles G. Jones again, I would throttle him. I would claw his eyes. Where
was he, why had he left me? And why did my courses not return?

After another week of torment, I made my way out of the kitchen and up
the creaking stairs in the small hours of the night, across the hall to the
clinic. In the cabinet so orderly and alphabetized, behind the lobelia drops,
and between the pills for Lazy Liver and the Laudanum tincture, was a
small bottle marked Lunar Tablets, "for the relief of Female Obstruction."
In the prescription book, in Mrs. Evans shivered writing, I read how Lunar
Tablets was a remedy for all manner of womanly affliction, "esp. to loosen
the constriction or blockage of the womb and to restore the nervous system
to its lunar rhythms."

I pocketed the bottle and later in the kitchen I swallowed the tablets
down. In the morning I awaited the red flag of desired results, but none
was evident. Only a dizziness, a disturbance of the lower regions, cramps
and pain, headache and sweats. They was terrible symptoms and I would
be glad to endure them if only they included the one I longed for. But I
suffered with no relief. Next, in a secretive search of the library I turned to
Dr. Gunning's book, Diseases of Women, and there I found an article on
Suppression of the Menses.

> Cold, perhaps, is the most common of all the causes of
> suppression. Young girls subject themselves to serious illness,
> by placing their feet in cold water while their menses are upon
> them, and many a fair creature, whose morning of life was

serene and beautiful, has found an early grave through this rash and thoughtless act!

But it was not my feet nor where I had placed them that concerned me.

Prognosis: Serious, if not fatal consequences may result from continued suppression, especially in a plethoric habit of body.

Fatal, it said. I would die. Surely my habits was plethoric. I'd follow Mam to an early grave. But then as I read the words over, I saw that Dr. Gunning did not possess the sense of a codfish. If a woman's turns was suppressed each time she put her feet in cold water, there'd be an epidemic of fishwives complaint. Viz, I hadn't been near a cold foot bath in many weeks, yet my turns were suppressed worse than a sneeze in church. Still, in case Gunning was right, I noted his remedies with confusion:

For the Relief of Suppression: The diet should be strictly vegetable, and the patient should take a styptic footbath of warm water, cayenne pepper, and mustard. Failing relief, blood must be abstracted from the arm.

A footbath. Did the doctor not say that bathing the feet had CAUSED the suppression in the first place? It made as much sense as a herring. But such was my mission to restart the Catamenial Discharge that late that evening after a vegetable dinner of cabbage and roots, in secret I filled a tub with warm water, cayenne, and mustard, et cetera, and according to his prescription, bathed my feet in the mixture. This did nothing more than make me smell like a ham.

In an excess of panic, I downed another bottle of Lunar Tablets. For two mornings I had a loathing at my food, and a furred tongue, and felt twinges in the lower extremities and fits of languor, but no Restoration. Thus I had no choice but to follow the more drastic of Dr. Gunning's remedies. To take blood from the ARM seemed to me to be the height of ignorance, when the obstruction lay elsewheres. But it was the last hope, and I steeled myself.

When Mrs. Browder had gone to the fishmonger's, I took the paring knife and rolled up my sleeve. With the knife I struck and cut down a nick into the white underbelly of the wrist. I cursed Oh MotherF***, and blood welled up and dripped and I caught it in a teacup. I wished every trace of Charles G. Jones would drain out along with the blood from that soft place on my arm, which he had kissed so tenderly.

When only a meager teaspoon had seeped from me, there was commotion at the door. It was Mrs. Browder. —Annie Muldoon! she cried. I hid the bloody teacup under a mixing bowl and looked for a dishrag to clamp on the wound. But Mrs. B. came barreling into the kitchen with a basket of cabbages on her hip, and important news on the tip of her tongue. When she saw the gore on my arm she stopped cold, horror on her face.

—Annie! she shrieked and rushed to my side. —What have you done, love?

—I cut myself, peeling the potatoes.

—Don't lie, don't lie to Mrs. B., she says, and clamped her fist around my elbow. —It's a terrible sin what you've done! You mustn't never think of harming yourself.

—I wouldn't.

—You've been in a black mood of despair.

—I haven't.

She held my arm fiercely with her meaty hands, pressing a cloth to the cut, and stared me down with tender concern. My eyes welled over. —I'm perfectly well.

—You're not _____? Are you?

—No! Sure you don't think—

—I won't say what I think. But there's no reason to harm yourself.

—I haven't harmed myself.

—You wouldn't be the first. Don't deny you are pining after that printer.

—I'm pining after my sister and my brother who I've not seen in three years.

Strangely, Mrs. Browder smiled now so she broke out in wrinkles. —Is that all? She searched her pockets. —What do you think this is? You'll never guess.

—A crystal chandelier.

—No, you great lump.

With ceremony, she now handed me an envelope with AMBROSE printed on the return address, Rockford, Illinois. —Your sister at last, Mrs. B. said in triumph.

The letter rattled in my trembling hands as I lapped at the pious hooey my sister had wrote.

> *Dear Axie,*
>
>   *I was pleased to get your (very many!) letters. I am terribly sorry about your mother. Mother says that she is in heaven now and we must all try to be thankful she has found peace at last. I go to school in the sixth grade. We are learning psalms. I wrote one out for you. Number 105. They say Joe is well but I have not seen him in a long while. They say he has moved to Philadelphia. Thank you for writing to me,*
>   *Lillian Ambrose (Dutch)*

Mrs. Browder's face was greedy with expectation. —Well?

I stood reading the letter over, turning it by the kitchen stove as if the heat might reveal in lemon juice my sister's true nature and longing for me, which was nowhere evident in her script. She wrote *your mother* as if my Mother was not hers as well. She called herself Lillian Ambrose which bore no mention of Muldoon. She had not called me Sister, nor signed herself Sister or sent her affection. After three years, she had written one infernal psalm by hand but said not a word about whether she thought of me even once.

—Joe has gone to Philadelphia, I said to Mrs. B.

—The City of Brotherly Love, she said helpfully.

—My sister did not give me no address for him. In a stupor I handed Mrs. Browder the letter to read for herself.

—This is good news, she said, reading it, —don't you worry. She's alive and well and so's your brother. Write to her again.

So when I was somewhat recovered I took a pencil in my fierce grip and wrote:

Most beloved SISTER, Dutch MULDOON,

Why have you sent me no news but only a psalm? Please send another letter, expecially with word of our Joe. It was our mother's dying wish for me to get you and him and be all three of us together again as a family. Do not forget the songs our mother sang Whiskey in the Jar and Carrigfergus. Do not forget you are a Muldoon AND my sister. Do not forget to write back. Especially do not forget me.

LOVE from Your SISTER
Axie (Ann) Muldoon

—There now, Mrs. Browder said. —You'll post that in the morning. Don't you feel better?

But I did not feel better. I felt worse. My cut arm throbbed as if my heart beat there and might leap fishlike out of the wound and land on the table gasping. The letter and my Suppressed Catamenial state and my jilting by Charlie Jones that b*****d rankled me worse than devils. None of the remedies I had tried so far would fix what ailed me.

BOOK THREE

The Principles of
Midwifery

Chapter Eighteen

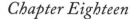

Reprieve

*C*ontrary to what the lying weevils and scandalmongers of the New York press might have written about me, my great good fortune in life has not been piles of money or property. It's not these pearls at my throat, this lace at my cuff, this china or silver plate here at the sideboard. My great fortune has been the second chance. The last minute rescue from disaster. And so it was in those days many years ago, on Chatham Street, when all signs and events of my young turbulent life seemed to point toward further misery and ruin, abandonment and destitution. But amnesty appeared in strange forms. First the letter arrived from my long lost sister Dutch. Second my FRIEND returned. And third, I received some news from the *Herald* but not off its pages.

I never will know for sure whether it was the mustard footbath or the Lunar Tablets, the scant spoon of blood that dripped from my arm, or the tears I cried in my cot at night, but by some intervention, divine or not, my courses was set to rights, as it sometimes happens with young girls in the throes of dramatic emotion. It seemed I was not p*******. I was not only saved but now newly resolved, as there is nothing like a near calamity to harden the will and shore up the walls of the fortress of so-called Feminine Virtue. Never again, I swore. Never again. From that day forth, no body would tempt me. Not pretty words or a chain of silver. Not Charles G. Jones or any man.

Except. Lust was a weed, a nightshade vine, a nettle, impossible to uproot as the mugwort I pulled in the fields of Illinois, so while in the daylight I was a flower of virtuous resolution, at night I was motherless in a cold kitchen, starved for the warm arms of a sweetheart and pretty words of approval. Worst, was the thought of (. . .), that grappling which had occurred between me and Charlie, so that in the dark carnal pictures swam behind my closed eyelids till I was swooned in longing. I took the silver chain off my neck in a fit of disgust but then put it back on. I hated Charlie with a concentrated fury, then craved in depraved longing to have him, such that my own physiology was a torment to me. I traced his initials in flour dust, then erased them. He did not knock. He did not send me a note. He disappeared in a mystery. Was he drafted? dead? I was abandoned again.

One late afternoon in September, on the excuse of running an errand to Hegemann's the chemist's, I walked toward Printing House Square, up Nassau Street, past Beekman. Outside the *Herald*, I stood at the revolving door to the building and watched men leaving in their workaday togs. The ones I picked out for the writers was rumpled and distracted, sallow, with pocky skin, patchy beards, and scrags of hair poking from under their hats. The typesetters and press operators had fewer teeth and more swagger, more plaid in their coats and more dust on their boots. I looked at their faces to see was any of them Charlie, and looked at their hands, next, to see if they was stained with ink, for these would be his colleagues.

The first inked hands I saw belonged to a ferret of a man with his features bunched in the center of his pointy rodent face, his eyes small and shifting. His hair was red.

—You, mister, I said, stepping in front of him. —Please do you know the whereabouts of a typesetter named Charlie Jones?

—I might just. He looked me up and down with his polecat eyes. —You're a pint of ale, ain't you? Tell me your name I'll tell you the game.

—Axie Muldoon.

—Bricky Gilpin at your humble service.

—Where is he? Charles Jones. Where could I find him?

—He's locked up, Bricky Gilpin said with a smirk. —In the Tombs.

At this news the fish of my heart flapped entirely off the dry dock where it had laid injured and gasping and now swam in cool water again, seeing as how I had been wrong about Charlie. He was not a renegade but a falsely accused prisoner of the law. Oh, happy day, it was all a misunderstanding, and I went from jilted to worried in a snap.

—Why did they take him? I asked Bricky Gilpin. —How could they?

—He was in the crowd that seven weeks ago attacked the Colored Orphan Asylum.

—You're a liar. Charlie would not attack nobody, least of all an orphan.

—It was a whole mob of us. Bricky shrugged. —We was all over the city banging pots and closing down the streets.

—I heard it. You was a bunch of mongrels.

—Why should the blackies get off the draft and not us? Why should we pay three hundred dollars to get outta the Army, and the darkies and Knickerbocker boys getting off? Found a whole mess of colored children in the asylum and burnt it to the ground.

—You didn't, I said.

—They excaped, them pickaninnies, said Bricky, and sucked his teeth. —But Jones didn't. The traps picked him out for the ringleader.

—He was never there.

—He was there and he'll admit it himself. Claims he was doing a report for Mr. Horace Greeley at the *Tribune*. Told the traps he was writing up the riots so the paper could print it. Which ain't a bad alibi, writing a report. Was he?

—If he says so, he was.

—He has only to prove it in a court, said the miserable messenger. —The *Herald* won't help him since he says he was writing for the *Trib*, and the *Trib* never heard of him. Meanwhile, Bricky Gilpin is here at your service. His leer was such that I could see the spaces for teeth he was missing. —If I was you, miss, said Bricky, —I'd just invite me for a cheese samwich and forget about Charlie Jones, because he's gonna be cooling his heels in the quod for a while unless they draft him outright.

I turned on my own heel and walked fast away from that Gilpin.

—Not even a samwich for my trouble? he called after me.

If I had a sandwich, I'd have given it to him, just for bringing me the message that I was not jilted. Only when I was safe away from Bricky with his leering, did the news settle on me like a layer of ash. Charlie was locked up or drafted into war.

* * *

Every day now I stared into the distance full of rage, at policemen, judges, warmongers, the rebs, God, and experts from Aid Societies who deprived me of every solitary soul who knew my real name. I posted letters to Charlie in the Tombs and for what? No reply. I smashed the pots in the kitchen and cursed with the mouth of a sailor, until Mrs. Browder said, —Watch your step young lady or we will be looking for your replacement.

I did not give two tacks what she threatened. Charlie was in jail and I did not hear a word from him. Greta the German was my companion now. The two of us was soaked in a lovelorn marinade of rage and longing. She pined for her own sweetheart, Mr. Schaeffer. She blushed when she described his attentions and flowery courtship. We hung the wash while Greta went on about him.

—I cannot even eat, she said. —I am sick with luff.

—Luff never killed no one, it's what comes with it that'll snuff you.

—Och, she said. —I told you your fella was a no good dangler, didn't I?

—He's not.

—You said yourself he is locked up, she smirked.

—*Pugga mahone.* Charlie will get away. He'll be back here to me fast as can be.

—Don't count the days. She reached in her bosom and withdrew a lace handkerchief. —From Mr. Schaeffer, she said, showing it off.

—Will he marry you?

—I expect yes, she said, with a smile like chocolate was melting in her mouth.

Perhaps it was. Her sweetheart gave her truffles and mint crèmes, until such time as he gave her a case of the nerves. By October, she sat and bit the inside of her lips, so that her red Kewpie mouth skewed sideways, little teeth gnawing on herself.

—Oh Annie, she said one day when the leaves were nearly gone. —I cannot see him. We cannot meet.

—Why?

—He is married already. Her eyes were feverish.

We two was hopeless. Through the cooling months toward winter, us young housemaids sneaked out after dark, into the razzle-dazzle of

Broadway. The windows of the hotels and shops were full of pretty things right at our fingertips. We were boiled in longing, and also contempt for ourselves, just two creatures of the wretched classes each with one dress to our name, and no money for a new one, let alone the Hindoo muslins or the French crepe maretz, the Llama jackets for sixty dollars and the princesse day robes for two hundred, the traveling skirts made of pongee or piqué for a hundred and sixty, or the evening robes in Swiss muslin and velour that would cost you three hundred. The stores had fashions for croquet-playing and for horse races and yachting. They sold Saratoga trunks the size of coffins. To Hold Sixty Dresses, said the ticket featured with the price tag.

Sixty dresses. Without no pay nor inheritance I did not know how I would ever get a new one let alone so many. When I was not dreaming of cream-colored satin I was filled with boiling resentment. I would never know the feel of these soft and shiny materials. I'd be apprenticed and sleeping alone by the stove for the rest of my days.

It was fall, now, and Mrs. Browder's legs was worse than before. She had an inflammation of the lymph, she said. The old badger would not go up the stairs for love or money which left Yours Truly toiling at the old up and down. Mrs. Evans was in her bed half the morning. Mostly it was the doctor's callers who rang the bell, no more than two most days. But one December afternoon the bell rang and there was a woman with a bruise on her face and paint on her lips. —I've a pain, she said.

—Whereabouts?

—In the cellar, she said, glancing downward. —Is Mrs. Evans at home? I shown her in. —Wait here.

Upstairs, Mrs. Evans lay in her daybed, a layer of sweat on her brow, and did not stir when I spoke. —Mrs. E., a lady's here to see you.

—Examine her yourself, please, she said, her voice languid.

—Myself? How would I, missus? I've not had that lesson.

My teacher sighed and rousted herself out of bed, her hands trembling. Her translucent red nose glistened with dew drops, and she wiped them away with her little pocket square, beckoning me to follow.

Down in the clinic Mrs. Evans appraised the patient, a peach-skinned woman named Beatrice Kinsley, with powerful limbs and a swelling midriff outlined under her skirts. She stared about the room like a spooked horse as Mrs. Evans questioned her about her monthly turns until at last my teacher instructed the patient to remove her underthings.

—It's just a small pain, Beatrice said, most reluctant.

—Small pains have a way of becoming bigger pains, said Mrs. E. quite firm.

After some persuasion, Beatrice did as she was told, first removing her scarf. We seen bruises on her neck with marks that resembled the print of fingers.

—Come here, Annie, Mrs. Evans says to me, —for your lesson. Explaining that I was the assistant, she secured me by the patient's knees. To my mortification, she took my hand and first placed it over the patient's abdomen and ran it up toward the wishbone of the chest, where she placed two fingers across. —Now, the fundus is here, you feel the rise, yes?

When I nodded, feeling the hard round under the ribs there, my instructress showed me how to measure. —Shush there Miss Kinsley, she said, —we'll only check your condition. Then despite my discomfort she took my other mitt and shaped the thumb and forefinger into an L, then guided this under the skirt toward the patient's monosyllable like it was only us out for a Sunday stroll. How studiously I looked away into the ether as the patient gasped at my touch. I likewise gasped, for how surprising was the warm animal feel of what lay under the petticoat, how familiar and yet unnatural.

As my teacher instructed me I waited, mortified, for the floor to crack open and suck me down to the root cellars of h***. My hand came away bloodied and when I blanched Mrs. Evans clucked, saying I was not the cause of it. To my teacher this lesson and her own cheerful intrusions on the poor lady seemed as ordinary as stuffing bread crumbs into a chicken. She cleaned her hands on a tea towel and I copied her, not knowing where to look.

—Sit up now, love, said Mrs. Evans to Miss Kinsley, who hid her scarlet face in her apron, weeping. Mrs. Evans put her arm around the patient and indicated I should do the same. We held her up like bookends.

—You are going to have a little baby in about three months, Mrs. E. told her, while poor Beatrice shook her head and said No no no, like Mrs. Evans could be talked out of the verdict. —I can't have a child, she whispered.

—Have you interfered with yourself? Mrs. Evans asked her.

—Ma'am?

—Some damage has been done to the internal apparatus, said Mrs. E., —which is the cause of your pains and of the bloody show.

—But you will fix me up? cried Beatrice.

Mrs. Evans' eyes was wet with either sympathy or the effects of her Sanative Serum, and as she stroked the bruised cheek of her patient, she shook her head sorrowfully. —I'm afraid I can't help you, love, until such time as you are to be delivered. Then as midwife I will ease your trials as best I know how.

—But Mrs. Watkins on Lispenard Street sent me to you, Beatrice pleaded. —She said you could CURE it. You could fix me up if it's not quick. It's not a crime.

—The law is written, said Mrs. Evans, —such that quick or no it IS a crime.

—But you've fixed everyone, she says. —If it's a crime, why aren't you arrested?

—The police don't bother with the law. Mrs. Evans shrugged. —They leave us alone. Nobody who comes to me complains. Would you? And second, who can prove anything? Women bleed and sometimes don't, and blood is blood, and no one is to say why she's bleeding or not, and nobody *would* say. It's her own business, isn't it?

—So you will help me.

—Not if it's quick, said my teacher.

—It is not, whispered Beatrice Kinsley.

—I'm afraid it is, said Mrs. Evans, very sad. —You can't deny you've felt a kick within and that's the sign you've quickened.

—I can pay you what you want, Beatrice cried.

Apologizing, Mrs. Evans left the room while her patient sobbed on the table.

I stayed quiet, and after a minute Beatrice asked, quite proud, —Do you know Peter VanKirk? He is first assistant to the governor, with a house on Fifth Avenue. He has kept me two years in a grand place off Washington Square. She fingered the bruise on her cheek. —But if I continue in this condition, he's through with me. He has a wife and two girls and I told him I'll spill everything to the wife if he won't help me.

—I could give you tablets for the Obstruction, I said.

—I have tried tablets already.

—I have tried them, too.

—Have you? Her face brightened. —And did they work?

—They must have done.

—I'll try them again then, she said. —Because if I don't, he'll be rid of me.

Her stockings sagged about her ankles. She pulled at them, reaching over the protrusion of her midriff. —If he does throw me away, where will I go? she wept. —I've no family at all. With a child nobody'll have me. Not even as a servant.

I sat alongside with nothing to offer. —Could you go to the poorhouse?

—Phh. She looked at me full of scorn. —The Womens House of Industry? Never. They chain you in pens. They farm you out as wet nurse for the rich mothers and your own child left to starve, stuck till you die on Blackwell's Island with the lunatics and the smallpox and murderers and thieves.

She cried and cried. —Why won't you help me? You're the assistant. You fix me up, then. Why not? Please, miss. I'll pay you anything.

The room was wet with her tears and I burned up with pity listening. —I don't know how to do a fix. If I did know I'd help you.

—Oh dear God, she wailed and pulled my clothing, fell to her knees on the floor so awkward and fat praying to me like I was powerful. —Please miss. Try. Do it please.

I couldn't stand it. I left her and ran after Mrs. Evans.

—Missus, please, the woman says her fella will kill her. She got nowheres to go. Help her, why not?

—But the child is quick, Mrs. Evans said, shaking her head. —I cannot.

I stared at her. —Did you never do a murder, then, missus?

—Murder? Mrs. Evans looked at me, her old eyes watery. —No! No, child, not exactly, no. But in her swallowing and perspiring and the break in her voice was a complication to her answer that she did not explain. —Listen, she said, —always help them with the premature delivery if they come to you early. Just to restore the natural functions. Otherwise, they'll do it on their own and—

—What?

—They bleed to death. You saw how Miss Kinsley interfered with herself. She is lucky she did not puncture her insides. You see them using anything. A corset stay. A turkey feather. A bit of bone.

—It's not a murder?

Now my teacher rose trembling from her couch. She took up both my poor paws again and turned them over in her own. —You have small hands. You have a soft heart and a curious turn of mind. But you don't know yet how it is with us. The female. You'll learn. You'll have your own trials. But if you are a midwife . . . and I think you will be, Annie . . . you won't be afraid.

—What trials?

My teacher sagged, but when she lifted her gaze to me she smiled very lovely, even with her eyes shot red, her gaze on me was soft, and I did not forget it.

—Remember Annie love, said my teacher, —that the soul of a midwife is a broad soul and a gentle soul, and she delivers the greatest blessing the Lord bestows on us poor creatures. But, a midwife must also keep comfortable with the complexities. What I call the lesser evil. You will learn not to judge too harsh on others. If you don't learn this, you're not suited to the work.

The intricacy of sorrow and mercy on her face made me wish to cry. I waited for her to speak more, but she was done with that lesson, about Good and Evil and Complexity, and while I mulled her words many times in years to come, it was a long while before I known enough to understand for myself what she meant by it.

—Then will you help Miss Kinsley? I said.

—Someone else might but I cannot, said my teacher. —The child is quick.

Some weeks later, the *Police Gazette* reported that Mr. VanKirk, first assistant to the governor, was arrested, accused of the murder of a Miss Beatrice Kinsley, age 25, of Washington Square, who was found floating in the East River, dead of stab wounds. At the time of her death, the newspaper said, she was seven months with child.

The item gave me a feeling like a stranger's hand was on my neck.

So far in my education I had learned that a baby will kill its own mother, that a father will turn out his daughter, that a schoolteacher is not a fit husband for a genteel lady, and that life is worth living for love's sake only. And now from Beatrice Kinsley I learned that to turn away a desperate woman was to imperil her life, because first, she might interfere with herself and die, and because, second, the father of an inconvenient infant might murder its mother and get away with it apparently. Mr. VanKirk was soon acquitted of charges and went on in later years to become Undersecretary of the Navy in Washington. The lesson of the murdered Beatrice floated through my nightmares forever after that, her yellow hair a seaweed.

Meanwhile, at Mrs. Evans' elbow, my practical lessons carried on through that year, so that in addition to pining for my lost family, and brooding over the fate of Charlie my lost suitor, and traipsing about Broadway with my friend Greta, I became expert in the subterranean sanguinary aspects of feminine existence, assisting at all hours of the day and night, for no pay.

This education wore on me, so that one day, when the front doorbell rang for my mistress, I was fed up to the gullet. I found Mrs. E. asleep again on her daybed, her face pale and sweated. —Missus, it's a lady caller again for you.

Mrs. Evans gave a wee hum and pulled at her blankets. Her vial of Serum was on the table. Just yesterday I'd mixed eight ounces of it (Thebane Opium extracted in wine, drops of nutmeg, saffron, ambergris). Now here it was, empty already.

—Missus?

—Go now and examine her, and then you'll come and tell me what's the matter. There's a good girl, now.

Perhaps it was the number of stairs I ran that day or maybe it was that I was on the tear, but when she said I was good something evil came over me and I snapped at her.

—I ain't a good girl. I'm a servant to you without no payment nor pocket money and I ain't got but two dresses and not ever allowed to go nowhere. Greta next door gets five dollars the month and I get f*** all and yet now plus the chores, you say I am the Assistant, Examine Her Yourself. Well I don't care if you send me back to Cherry Street for saying so but I am not your good girl nor no one's.

Mrs. Evans sat up alarmed, with grains of sleep in her eyes.

—You only want me to clean up the bloody linen, I said. —It's a CRIME is what it is.

I had meant the drudgery but she mistook my meaning. —Despite what the law says I don't believe it is a crime, said Mrs. Evans, raving a little. —Not till the child is quick. Anyway, if there's trouble, you just pay a bit here and there and they leave you alone.

Those words You Just Pay a Bit was another installment of my legal education. My financial education, however, was uppermost in my mind. —But sure it IS a crime that you don't give me a new dress or a nickel or a penny. It's slavery, sure it is.

She was silent, wiping the damp dew of her disease off her forehead. With some effort she got out of bed and traveled over to her dressing table. With a key she opened a small drawer there. I thought she might pull out a gun and shoot me. But instead she had a wad of money, which she flattened and fanned, then plucked out three bills, each worth ten dollars, and then handed them to me. —We intended to give you a settlement when you reached the age of twenty one, she said, pink with the strain of congratulating herself. —But if you would prefer to have part of it now, we don't object.

I had never held even five dollars of my own, let alone thirty, and now here was Money. —Thank you, I said, awkward.

—You're welcome. She made for her bed.

—Still there's the lady caller to see you.

—All right, she sighed. Fighting dropsy, yawning and fumbling, she got ready to provide me another lesson.

With my thirty dollars safe in a pouch under my cot, I went along now on Mrs. Evans' good days when she took me out to help her in the bedrooms of the city, where women labored and dropped their infants worse than rabbits, night and day. The Bible says in sorrow she shall bring forth children, but sorrow is a quiet humor and my apprenticeship was not quiet. I heard noises from girls like cats being killed. Worse. The battle of Gettysburg where boys was gored through by swords and felled by cannons was surely a match for the sounds of agony as came from these rooms of mothers laboring, and the slicks of blood was so equally sanguinary that you would expect Morrigan the fairy of war to land on dark crow's wings by the side of every female in confinement. Before I reached the age of seventeen, I knew the rudiments of my trade just by watching and listening and placing my hands where Mrs. Evans tutored me to place them. I reached in and helped along a breech boy to be born, his little red feet emerging and his chin stuck somewhere up the chimney so I worried would his head snap off. I seen mothers give birth drunk as sots and I seen them quaff the Sanative Serum like it was cider. I seen twins delivered, and an infant born with a caul, filmy as the skin off steamed milk, veiling the face. Its mother put that filament aside in a tobacco tin saying she would sell it to a sailor.

—A caul will save you from drowning, said Mrs. Evans.

She tutored me always. While I was helping out with the births I wasn't yet allowed to assist her in the premature deliveries for the Obstruction, but she had me observe and listen to her narration as she scraped a blocked woman called Mrs. Torrington who had eight children already. I observed again as she deobstructed another broken-down nag Mrs. Selby who had seven boys. Neither one could afford another squalling child, and both of these ladies no matter how much My Teacher hurt them only thanked her in the end. It was my sorry task to empty the bowl and on one of these occasions I seen amidst the gore a pale delicate outline of a form such as what you see in the smashed egg of a sparrow, not bigger than a thumbnail.

—What's wrong with you? cried Mrs. Evans when she seen my woeful face.

—It's been killed.

—It was never alive, said she quite firmly, and dragged me home to her Bible where she pointed me out a lesson from King Solomon and said, —Ponder it.

> If a man fathers a hundred children and lives many years, but his soul is not satisfied with good things, and he does not even have a proper burial, then I say, Better the miscarriage than he, for it comes in futility and goes into obscurity; and its name is covered in obscurity. It never sees the sun and it never knows anything; it is better off than he.

And she ordered me to go look in the street at the poor wee bundles of rags having their childhood in the alleyways of the Bend and ask myself what was meant by Charity and to read the verses of Ecclesiastes again, so I did:

Behold I saw the tears of the oppressed and that they had no one to comfort them; and on the side of their oppressors was power, but they had no one to comfort them. So I congratulated the dead who are already dead more than the living who are still living. But better off than both of them is the one who has never existed, who has never seen the evil that is done under the sun.

Under sun and moon both, Mrs. Evans schooled me about evil and good and the practicalities of administering them and all remedies in between. A few drops of opium will save the mother pain. Palpation of the belly will determine a breech presentation. A glassful of spirits will restart a stopped labor. If by feel you determine the head is rotated wrongly, coax the mother on her side and push with the hands to turn the child. If the face is presenting place one hand within and the other without, and push inside to tuck the chin, while outside pressing the head forward by a stroking motion across the belly. Small hands is a blessing. A steady hand is a blessing. A firm hand is a blessing. A warm heart is and so is a soft voice. Mrs. Evans had these all, whereas my heart was guarded and my voice was mostly silent. I watched and listened and did what I was told.

—You will see mothers die of prolapse where the u*****'s falls right out, Mrs. Evans said. —You will see them die when the child is stuck in the canal. Mothers will die of fever and they will die of hemorrhage. Their soft parts will rip and tear. They will die just of exhaustion. And remember, she said, —till you have a child of your own, no woman will accept you for a midwife alone.

I went along to thirty births. Sixteen boys and fourteen girls. The mothers moaned and carried on but when they were through most of them smiled and looked down at their raw new infants with wet eyes glinting. —It's a beautiful gift of God, Mrs. Evans said, her own eyes crinkled with wonder. —Such a wonder.

And it was. As disgusting as the Blessed Event seemed to me at first, I soon was dumbstruck at the power and workings of the female machine and never got tired of the drama and the miracle, even when I seen Mrs. Kissling die in her husband's arms, her newborn wailing, not even when I seen a mongoloid. I saw all manner of effluvia manufactured by the feminine anatomy, including blood, the Liquor amnii, p*** and s***, vernix and vomit. Plus all manner of womanly afflictions, swellings, growths, lacerations, fistula, bruises and the burns of a cigar. But the worst I ever seen was left on the doorstep.

I heard the bell and looked out, early on a Friday morning just as the sun rose. On the stoop was a plain woman in a dark bonnet carrying a cloth satchel. I went to answer the door. But when I opened it, I saw her hurrying away in the crowd. —Missus! I called out, but she did not turn. She had left her satchel behind.

As I began to chase her with it, I heard a sound, like a mew, and thought for a second she had dropped off her cat. But it was clear soon enough what had been left. Inside the bag was a runt no bigger than a teardrop on a rose petal. He lay wide-eyed, kicking his matchsticks under a blanket. I lifted him out and up to my shoulder.

—What the devil, mister? I said, soft, and carried him in. A note was pinned to his shirt. It said, Please take care of him for I cannot. His name is Johnny.

—Oh poor Johnny, I whispered in the oyster shell of his little ear. I brought him down to the kitchen to Mrs. Browder, all agitated. —Look what's left on our stoop.

—What next? she said, up to her elbows in suds. But when she seen Johnny, she cooed and let him suck on her finger, clucking her tongue. —What'll we do with him?

—We'll keep him, says I, and made a nest for him in a drawer. But he was hungry, the bugger, and we had no way to feed him. His shrieks was pitiful. I gave him a rag soaked in sugar water to suck but it angered him. I fed him cow's milk from a spoon, but it only choked him. He coughed and gagged on his own tongue and did not stop his cries.

Mrs. Evans heard the noise, and when she came down the stairs and seen the baby, she picked him up and tendered him on her shoulder, and I thought we'd keep him then. But, no, she said, since none of us was a wet nurse, the Sisters of Mercy on Twelfth Street was the only choice to save him, as they kept wet nurses at hand. —We're not an orphanage. You'll have to bring him, Annie.

—He'll only die there, I said, stubborn. —I won't turn him over.

—I'll bring him then, said Mrs. Browder, —if you won't. She picked him up and put him back in the satchel with his mother's note and his blanket. —Let's go Johnny, now, off with you to find some milk. She started out the door with him, waddling. On her weak legs, she would not even get to Bowery let alone Twelfth Street.

—All right then, I said. —I'll bring him.

Mrs. Browder handed off the satchel. —There's a basket in front of the hospital. You'll put him in, and ring the bell. They send the orphans out to nice families.

—They send them out on trains is what they do, I said. —If they live.

Their likely death was a fact known to me because news about orphans was my special interest. Everything to do with them I read with zeal. The *Police Gazette* that year wrote that ONE HUNDRED AND FORTY FIVE babies was left in six months with the Sisters of Mercy, and none but eight survived. It made no sense to have so many orphans and no one to feed them. Still, without a better plan and full of misgivings, I took Johnny and set out, straight up through Washington Square to Fifth Avenue and across a mile of blocks, hoping I would turn and find his mother chasing after me.

Holding him on my shoulder where he whimpered and squalled, I sang to that pitiful skippeen Whiskey in the Jar, and as I led him to his fate I told him, —Never you fear, Johnny, you will be playing soon in the green fields with your pony and eating your pie, climbing a tree in the country, yessirree, and folks'll give you a toy wagon and tin soldiers and you'll grow up to be a strong big lad of the prairie. I don't know why I fed him this pap. He was so raw and new, it seemed a shame to scare him with the truth.

At Twelfth Street at last I came to the Sisters of Mercy, and there in the vestibule I saw a wicker cradle with its plain white curtains and a little sign that said Please Ring the Bell. When nobody was around I put Johnny in the basket thus abandoning him for the second time already in his short life and rang the bell thinking surely Johnny would die like the rest of the babies who was laid there and what could I do about it, or anyone? I ran away from that place with my heart full of ugliness.

Chapter Nineteen

A Proposition

Baby boy Johnny rode on trains through my dreams. In his bunting he flew across the countryside heading West where nobody wanted him for he had no teeth in his gums and his baby arms was not meant for driving a plow. On the train he cried for his Mam, out of the hollow globe of his mouth. You'll never see me again, Baby Boy Johnny said to me, no more than you will see your own mother or your sister and brother, or find a replacement that could be called kin. In my dream I got on the train and climbed to the top with his little form in my arms and leaped off its speeding roof onto the white plains and woke when my feet startled out straight in the bed, the hard landing of a nightmare. In the cold of the morning I calculated how many years since I seen Joe or Dutch (four) and how many months (nine) since I sent a reply to my sister and had no answer. Seventeen years of age I was, without love nor money. I pictured Charlie's jail cell as an old potato hole. Was rats crawling on him in the night? Did he feel the hot breath of murderers on his cheek? After eight months in the Tombs, did he think of me?

It seems he did.

At the end of May, when I was settled on my cot for the night with my hair loose on the pillow and my nightdress on, a rap came on the kitchen door that made me startle up.

—Who's there?

I went to the door and the knock came again in a rhythm. Shave and a haircut.

Two bits, I tapped back.

—Axie? said a voice.

I swallowed. The knocking came fast now, the same as my heart when I flung open the door.

Charlie stood there on the step in the rain, silver grains of it shining on the dark mat of his hair. His suit hung off his bony skellington like it belonged to a fuller man. He was poorly shaved and the collar of his shirt was stained with a ring of grime. The fury of his expression struck me like a hard slap. It was not the reunion I pictured.

—Come in, I said.

He did. He fixed his angry eyes burning on my face so I had to look away. I went to the peg for my shawl and threw it around my bare shoulders to cover them.

—Don't. He came toward me and pulled the shawl so it fell away. He stared a long time. —Why'd you go with him? he said through his teeth, watching me.

—I didn't go with no one.

—You DID. You went with Gilpin. He said you did.

—He's a liar.

—I went to the *Herald*. And after I talked those b******s into taking me back to my job in the printing room, first thing I see is Gilpin, and he says, 'Jones, I met up with your doxie. A girl named Annie.'

—I went looking for you.

—Gilpin said 'I tasted her and she's a nice piece of cake,' is what he said.

—I asked him where you went to.

—He says you went with him.

—In his dreams.

Charlie's eyes were hard with suspicion and his fists flexed like they was warming up to strike me. Rain dripped off his coat and formed a puddle on the floor. A wet wool smell came off him, an odor of dungeon, like gruel and mildew. He was not a fella who liked to be cornered, he said once, and he'd been cornered now a while. —Why did he tell me then that you went with him? he hissed.

—I wouldn't look at that eel Gilpin. Not if I had ten eyes.

He stared me down so hard I needed ten eyes to hold steady against him. In the staring match I seen the wariness of a beat animal in his face, and he seen the set of my jaw softening down out of anger at him. We both of us blinked and looked off a ways.

—I didn't go with nobody, Charlie, I said again very gentle.

He sagged, and I seen he was still an orphan same as me. Neither one of us had a trusting fiber of muscle, only expectations of the next betrayal.

—Take off your wet coat, I says.

He flang his coat on the back of a kitchen chair. I plucked my shawl up from the floor and wrapped it around myself again. He paced and rested his palms against the sideboard, bent over, taking small fish gulps of air. A current of warning came off his hunched shoulders. At last he walked to the table where he sat pressing his thumbs against his eyes. I fetched Mrs. Browder's stashed bottle and poured a glass of whiskey and brought it to him. He quaffed it in one swig. I went to the cupboard and took out the plate of cold potatoes and lamb left over from supper. He did not speak even when I put it down in front of him.

—What happened to you? I asked.

His eyes were bright and skittish. He shoveled his food and drank so the apple of his throat rose and fell. He wiped his mouth with the back of his hand.

—What happened?

—The Tombs. The fumes off that word hung in the air.

I cleared his plate. —What else?

—They tried to recruit me for a Union soldier but I acted the cripple.

—What else?

—A pen and paper, and no more questions.

I confess to disappointment at his answer but was glad I'd made him jealous over Bricky Gilpin. It was good revenge for the suffering he put me through. I crept upstairs to the library and brought him down the articles he requested. He thanked me and began to write, scratching away so furiously that sometimes the nib pricked through the sheet, spreading blots like smashed huckleberries on the white page. In the oily lamplight I scoured his plate, took up a sock to mend and listened to the scratch of his writing and the wind outside the door, the slatting rain.

—There now, he said at last, —I'm done.

He extended the paper toward me. Life in the Tombs, an Exposé by Charles G. Jones, was written in a headline across the top.

> *Like a great cesspool of all that is worst about humanity, there*
> *sits downtown on Centre Street a terrible haunted building,*
> *which houses the most wretched and friendless souls on earth.*
> *This Hades is called The Tombs, and no more apt moniker could*
> *be found for the place. Inside its granite walls, human beings are*
> *interred without justice and left to rot and crawl with maggots*
> *as in a grave. It was there, in a damp cell the size of a pigeon*
> *rookery that I spent nine grim months without favor of a trial,*
> *and this is my story.*

My eyes grew big with horror as I read.

—Like it?

—It's terrible.

—So I am not a writer, then.

—No! The Tombs is terrible. Your account is not.

—That's just the first page.

—The first page of what?

—The report I'll publish in the *Herald*, or whatever paper will pay me the most for it. It's an exposé. Of corruption. The skulduggery of judges and policemen, the wickedness of prison guards and thieves. Right from inside the heart of the beast.

—An exposé?

—Of a scandal. They kept me without no trial, all this time.

But it was worth it, the jail time, if he could have a story out of it, Charlie said. It was his dream, to be a journalist. I saw it raw on him, the way he talked that night, telling me how the traps locked him up, how he was nearly drafted, how he got out of it because of he faked a bad leg, and how he talked himself back into his job at the *Herald* because they knew he was a first class printer. Soon he'd be a first class newsman, he said. —Will I? Do you believe it?

—I do. Sure I do, Charlie.

He stepped up close and put his hand on my hair. He ran his palm along the fall of it, down my arm, then without warning he clamped onto my wrist and held it so fiercely I cried out.

—You're still my girl? he said though his teeth. —Are you?

I nodded, frightened.

He held my jaw in his hard hand and kissed me without tenderness. I hit him and struggled and called him names and full of rage we were carried away to the floor as before where we rolled and pitched over the boards. We crashed into the milk pail, knocked over the broom. I was overcome with the weight of him, the smell that clung to his clothes, his rough beard chapping my cheek. He clawed my skirts.

—Don't, I said.

—Oh God. Jesus.

—Don't. I roared at him.

—All right then.

—So stop.

—You didn't miss me.

—I did. I did so.

—Axie.

—I said NO.

—I dreamed of you. All that time in that place.

—I won't.

—Jesus.

—I'm serious.

—I see that.

—You'd better see then, you b*****d, I said.

—Kiss me anyway. His old smile was back then, sudden, crooked as the finger he beckoned with. He took the blankets from my cot and spread them on the floor. —Axie Muldoon, he said, grinning, —you're a pistol, aren't you just?

He was changeable as hats. A shiny coating of charm now came over him, and he flirted with me and said I was so pretty till I kissed him when he asked me to and fed off the tender flesh of his earlobes and handled him according to his directions. I was happy and not ashamed, bold so it deranged him. —You are a wild woman of Madagascar, he said. —Sweet Jesus. Whatever he asked of me I obliged him. Except. Not that. I learnt my lesson. Please Jesus God Axie, he cried out. But he could not get the drawers off me. They were a poor defense, and it was my good luck that I did not succumb to the roar of (. . .) or the hot liquor in my veins, and also that he remained a gentleman.

—You win, he said at last.

We lay exhausted by the hearth amid the barrels of dried peas and barley and Indian meal, and when he smiled at me in the dim murk, a happiness took hold of me that was unfamiliar as a fine white Riesling is to the mouth that knows only pump water.

—Marry me, he said.

Chapter Twenty

Shield

*I*t was well knownt that one who has kissed a salamander will not be harmed by fire. So perhaps, since me and Charlie both was salamanders who had crawled out from the ooze and offal of Manhattan Island, it was some pull toward survival that threw us to each other. We knew the other's secrets. We had come through on the orphan train and seen ourselves in the other: me a stiff angry girl mirrored by Charlie who was a flash talker with tricks up his sleeve. His head was full of dreams and mine was full of schemes or vice versa. Anyways it seemed this was more than rhyme enough, and so we married.

The event took place the Sunday before my eighteenth birthday, in the year of 1865, and no matter to me that it was the year the President was shot dead and the year P. T. Barnum's museum burned and the year Joseph Lister performed the first surgery with antiseptic. What was more significant was that Miss Ann Axie Muldoon and Mr. Charles Great Jones was married before witnesses in the front parlor at 100 Chatham Street. It was not fancy nor splendid. There was no choir, harp, or even a monkey grinder with his accordion. There was no mother nor father to give me away, as they had gone and done that long ago. There was no sister Dutch nor brother Joe to hold my ring or my train, as I had neither ring nor train to hold, and Dutch and Joe and all other remnants of my Muldoon life was lost as ever. It was just me and my boy-o with the Evanses and Mrs. Browder and next-door Greta there as witnesses. A pocky minister named Robinson with a flask in his pocket and a dust of white dander on his dark jacket that Mrs. Browder had invited was the official. I wore my new dress, a gift from Mrs. Evans, made of cotton muslin with cap sleeves in a lovely shade of cornflower blue.

—Married in blue, she said, —you will always be true.

Always true, yes, but I'd always feel a disappointment over the dress, for yellow was the color I coveted. Me and Greta, perusing the pages of *Godey's Lady's Book,* had seen a wedding dress described so prettily that the words imprinted on my memory.

> . . . a rich yellow brocaded silk, trimmed with three flounces carried up to the waist, so as to appear like three overskirts. The body is trimmed with a double berthe of Vandyke lace. The gloves are long, the hair arranged in what the French call English ringlets.

I wished even then for English ringlets and Vandyke lace. Later, I would have both, not to mention brocade silks and velvet capes. But that Wedding Day, thoughts of Parisian flounces were canceled by the sight of Charlie by the parlor window, his hair slicked down and his dark eyes fixed on me. I found it a chore to be serious. Likewise my Intended. When I came to stand next to him, he ratted his teeth over his bottom lip like we used to do as children imitating the ridiculous Dix. I laughed and the dipsomaniac Robinson placed our hands on the Bible and said to Charlie, —Will you promise to love honor and worship?

—I'd be a fool not to worship at the feet of Annie Muldoon. I will.

—Will you promise to love honor and obey? Robinson asked me.

—I will, I said, ignoring the word OBEY which would give me trouble later on.

Robinson uttered away about the power of God and the holy sanctity of this and that, but we were not paying attention. It was all we could do not to laugh or cry. There was no ring of pearls nor no spray of orange blossom. There was a wedding cake Mrs. Browder made, dark and full of brandy and mace, with lumps of candied citron throughout. We ate it and were through by eleven o'clock that morning. The whole affair lasted a half hour. I was Mrs. Jones now, with all that entailed.

*   *   *

I would pull the curtain of modesty around the marriage bed but we didn't have no curtain. We didn't have a bed. What we had was a poor room at a William Street boardinghouse rented for five dollars the month. We possessed a shakedown pallet, a broken table, a couple plates. Nothing else but the same argument over again.

—Please, he said.

—No, I said.

—We are married.

—I don't care. I will not.

—Why?

I wept and carried on and turned my face to the wall. —I don't want to be a mother only to die. I don't want to bring an orphan into the world.

—What orphan? For Christ's sake. You're my wife.

—I don't deny it.

—What do you want then?

—Not to suffer! Like the whole groaning parade of girls bleeding at Chatham Street.

A red flush formed in two round patches on Charlie's white complexion. —Bleeding? It's only Nature is it not?

—It's only natural to wish to avoid it! I cried. —Just for example I don't want to have a FISTULA.

—Fistula?

I wouldn't never explain to him fistula is a tear in the soft parts of the female caused by childbirth so she leaks like a fishnet all the rest of her days. —It's not for a man to know, I says.

He sat up in the bed and lit his tobacco, naked and blowing smoke at the ceiling. —But we're married. A man has his desires. Don't you love me at all?

—Who else would I love?

—Well then if that's so, carry on in the manner of a WIFE.

He did not force me. God love him. He could have, but he didn't. The poor man had a point.

—Christ Jesus Axie.

—Not yet. Just a little time longer to stay alive. Just to spare my life.

—Oh for f***'s sake.

We were married three months, and I did not give in. One morning as we spooned and wrestled in a torture of longing I stopped him again and he roared. —Jesus! You're all peppery and ready the one minute and the next you're cold as a dead mackerel, he cried. —We're married, d*** you so OBEY like you vowed to do at the wedding.

—It will kill me like it killed my Mam.

—I'll kill you first. He got up red-faced, pulled on his trousers.

—Charlie!

In a fury he stormed out of the place. The ceiling swam overhead through a gauze of tears. He would kill me or leave me. It was unfair, this bargain. What he wanted. What I didn't. Before we had wanted the same thing, to not be orphans no more. To not be cast friendless upon the earth. And now we were not friendless or cast out. We were married. Charlie had his journeyman job at the *Herald* and I had only the one block to walk to the Evans where my cot was no longer by the stove but folded away upstairs. I had my jar of money and promise of more in three years when I turned twenty one. There wasn't nothing in our way but for this business of c**j*g*l relations and how they might put me in my grave. At last I dressed and went heavyhearted around the corner to Chatham Street.

Mrs. Browder was sweating in the kitchen over a joint of mutton. —You're late.

I hung my coat on the peg.

—What's the matter?

—Never mind, I said.

—Young lovers' troubles, is it?

—He's always after me.

—It's your duty as a wife, love.

—Then I won't be a wife.

—Good luck to you then, she said. —What else will you be?

What was there to be but a wife or a servant? It was all the same. And where was the wild red sparkles and love's sake only and the beauty of the wild ungoverned heart? Mrs. Browder gave me a little white pamphlet called Advice to a Wife and pointed out where the author Mr. Chevasse wrote his main counsel:

As soon as a lady marries, the romantic nonsense of school-girls will rapidly vanish, and the stern realities of life will take their place, and she will then know, and sometimes to her grievous cost, that a useful wife will be thought much more of than either an ornamental or a learned one.

Well no doubt I was useful but it was the part about the grievous cost that had me in a stew. I slammed the kettle and carried breakfast upstairs to Phoebe, a big lump of a patient who rested indisposed on the fourth floor. She was large and puffed, her child a week past due. It would kill me to be in her place. Her ankles was the size of birch stumps and I knew she had the milk leg for sure. I brooded the whole day. Toward evening, when I had taken the linen in off the line, and wrapped the scraps of dinner in a dishcloth for our supper, I headed with it home to our room to face my husband, if only he was there.

He was not. There was the brown watermark on the wall from a leak upstairs. There was the hole in the plaster in the shape of a bird head. In the dirty light our two plates sat on the table waiting, one of them chipped. In the air shaft pigeons rutted with guttural noises, half obscene. Overhead the ceiling creaked with the boots of the upstairs neighbors. The reek of cabbage leaked through the cracks. Charlie's extra shirt was hung on the knob, and I put it on, smelling his tobacco and ink. I waited there wearing it, but he did not come. I did not touch my supper. I crawled to the corner and lay down where we had slept these last married weeks wound around each other, coiled as springs, but now I was a straight line again alone.

For six days, there was no sign of him. No word. —He's a bounder, then, said Mrs. Browder. —Once a man of the streets, always a man of the streets.

And she was right. Was she? Charlie for years before we married had spent his time in saloons and bookstores, talking politics, singing McGinty, having his drop. This was a husband who loved to hear himself talk, jawing over a pint foaming with his opinions. It appeared I had no choice but to change my ways, if I wanted him to change his.

Toward morning of the seventh night, Charlie returned. His key rattled in the lock. He cursed and stumbled while he unlaced his boots. His breathing was loud, slow and heavy, through the mouth.

—Mrs. Jones? he cried. —Are you my WIFE?

—Yes.

—In name or in fact?

—In fact and name both, I said, so quiet.

—Well, then, said he, thickly breathing. —I have something for you. See what I have Mrs. Jones? He sat on the edge of our poor mattress and leaned over me. The smell off his clothes was pure whiskey. —A present. He reached down to his trousers.

Here it comes now. I quaked and steeled myself, but then with his other hand from behind my ear he withdrew a sealed wax paper packet the size of a silver dollar and pressed it to my palm.

—What is that?

—French letter, he said, weaving where he sat.

—We don't know nobody in France.

—It's not a letter at all. It's a shield.

The waxy paper crinkled and I was afraid to see the thing he unraveled. He did not explain its purpose. He didn't have to. It was plain right away. It was a comical sleeve made from sausage casing, with drawstrings.

I staunched the urge to laugh. —Where'd you get it?

—Off a hoor in the Bowery, he said, like it was funny.

I recoiled away from him. —Don't come near me, you scut. You're a cheater and a lout off the street and the nuns never taught you no morals and I should've listened to Mrs. Dix when she warned me against you. I faced the wall.

—Now, Mrs. Jones, I was joking with you. In truth I got it off a cove named Owens. He calls himself a freethinker. Belongs to a society over at T. W. Strong's bookshop on Nassau Street where I found him the other night with a bunch of abolitionists and Hungarian Laszlos and Tammany shoulder-hitters, and these past few days I cooped down with him hanging around the bookshop and listening to them Professors all wag their beards on an assortment of anarchical plots and radical notions. The Rights of Man. The stupidities of priestcraft. The beauty of Free Thought. The Beauty of Free Love! You'd have been happy to hear they was all for the latter.

—Free Love? I cried. —For sure it's not free at all.

I was not listening to his excuses. The lie that he slept at a bookstore? Not likely. And I did not like the sound of Free Love. I did not like the sound of Rights of Men.

—Since when does a person need a freethinkers society? I said. —Any fool can think for nothing.

—Not true, he said, up on his soapbox now. —How many fools line up to genuflect without question before the altar of church prattle, with no more proof of truth than a sorcerer?

—You'll go straight to hell if you talk like that.

—No more than you will, Mrs. Jones. Opinions ought to be based in scientific fact and logic, not just because some set of whiskers says it, or because it's tradition, or church order. You see? The freethinker's philosophy.

To me it sounded like a philosophy of carrying on with miscreants and cancan girls and hot corn sellers with a trade up Cupid's Alley on the side. I had married a faithless lout. Had I? At the moment it seemed yes. I did not trust him.

Seeing the woe and suspicion on my sorry phiz, Charlie began to swear to me his loyalty. —Quit your doubting, Mrs. Doubting Thomasina. Why would I go with the professional trapes off the street? They've got the Venus-curse all of them and there's not one that won't just as soon rob you as sit down with the queen for a cup of tea.

—How do you know that then, if not from experience? I cried.

—I never was a saint, he said, shrugging. —I lived off my wits and the kindness of strangers. Some of the strangers in the past were ladies, I won't deny it.

I glared at Charlie, but he did not apologize nor hang his head. He only stared at me straight on, his tongue working under his lip.

—Those days are long gone now I promise you. I'm a married man.

—Ha. You just was gone from home six days.

—You're my wife. You'll believe me or leave me, take your pick.

The fix in his eye was steady as a lantern on a windless night. I tried to look away but he took my chin in his hand and held it the way you hold the muzzle of a creature you would tame. We sat on the bed in the lamplight till all our turmoil was stilled down. Our breath was matched now and changed in its rhythms and our eyes dropped to the strange article still on the bed between us.

—You have to trust me, he said, and rested his hand so gentle on my cheek and worked his fingers up and through the thicket of my hair till I forgot my own motto was Never Trust a Man Who Says Trust Me, for I was weak as the thin pale ribbon of my nightdress as he unlaced it, and he kissed me while he unwrapped the French article like it was Christmas and he was offering me diamonds.

—Does it work? I said.

—It does.

—You swear?

—I swear.

We still did not have a curtain, but at least we had a shield, and we employed it then with all manner of language, none of it French.

Mrs. Browder smiled when she caught me whistling over the washtub.
—So you're a wife after all.

—What else could I be?

—A mother. It won't be long now.

I did not tell her about the letters from France.

Chapter Twenty-One

Lillian

*T*he letter from Illinois, however, was another matter. It arrived one afternoon like a late wedding present when I was sweeping the fireplace grates at the Doctor's house, my hands black with ash. The bell rang in front. —F. and S., I said, and answered the door to the postman, who handed over an envelope addressed to me.

> *Dear Axie,*
>
> *Mother and Father held a winter ball in Chicago! I know you would like to hear about it, for any girl, no matter her circumstance, loves to discuss fine things. My gown was a rose-colored glacé silk, with shoes to match. My cousins the VanDerWeils attended. The middle one, Clara, is a dear sister to me, so pretty and fashionable. Her older brother, Eliot, is going to Cambridge for university in the fall. He wears a gold pocket watch from the V&W Chicago Rail Co. (His grandfather is the founder.) I was allowed to stay for the dancing.*
>
> *For my birthday, Mother and Father gave me a silver locket, engraved with the name LILLIAN in the prettiest filigree. I do like to be called Lillian. Mother says it's a name of a woman of grace and beauty. I pray every day that the glory of the Lord is with you, and enclose for you His good Word. Blessed are the poor in spirit, for theirs is the kingdom of heaven.*
>
> *Sincerely, Lillian Ambrose*

Her words was light and frilly but they punctured me like hatpins. The Winter Ball and the silver locket. LIKE A SISTER TO ME. My craw was choked with insult and jealousy. *Blessed are the poor in spirit*. Ha. She thought I was only a guttersnipe. Her letter left me mad and smoking as lamp oil smuts.

—What is it now? said Mrs. Browder when she heard me cursing and slamming.

For an answer I emptied the coal scuttle in one toss. It raised an evil dust cloud near the clean white washing.

—You're a terror, she cried.

—I'm worse than that. I handed her the letter.

Mrs. Browder read it, her eyes drooling along the parts about the ball, the French silk, the silver locket. —Oh my drawers. Your sister lives in fancy circumstance.

—My sister lives in a fancy lie is what. And her name ain't Lillian.

—Well, love, I'm sure you're glad to have news of her at least.

I wrote my sister back in short order.

> *Dutchie: What do you mean you are called Lillian? What kind of a name is that DUTCH? And DUTCH do not even speak to me of somebody named CLARA who is not your sister. And here is a reminder who is: ME. Also don't send me no more high and mighty lines about how I am poor and blessed in spirit while YOU are blessed in lockets and balls. And if you are so fancy you should hire a detective to find our Joe, you should get BLOODHOUNDS.*
>
> *Your SISTER, Axie*

I tossed that letter in the fire. If I knew my sister and I did, she would pout. She'd say I was bossy. At last, with terrible effort, I wrote again, mealy mouthed and simpering.

> *Dearest Dutch, (Lillian)*
> *Thank you for your news. How marvelous that you all have so much fun in Chicago at the balls &c. As for me, I have married a dashing gentleman, Mr. Charles G. Jones, Esq. He*

has a pocket watch too! he is a writer for the Herald and his grandfather is a founder, also. Me and Charlie have a grand apartment in Gramercy. One of our favorite pastimes is strolling along the river on Sunday mornings and after church we take outings in the carriage to Connecticut in the heat of the summer, and just adore to see the opera in the fall. Oh dear Lillian if you might please devote some effort to finding our own Joseph Muldoon aged 8 years now. Like you said before, he is adopted by people called Trow who moved to Philadelphia surely you might find him so we might one day have a reunion, all three of us.

    Love,

       Your sister, Ann

If she would be Lillian to me I would be Ann to her. I mailed the packet of lies off to her in a blue mood, and not two weeks later, another letter arrived.

Dear Ann,

    Congratulations on the happy news of your marriage. I do wish you would write me everything about your wedding. I adore weddings! Did you have a honeymoon trip? You must write me all about it, and about Charles. However did you meet him? Mother says that the Herald is a respected newspaper in New York. She sends her good wishes and congratulations to the happy newlyweds.

    As for me, I have been busy with plans for our summer visit to the lake, where we have the most marvelous lawn parties, and go bathing and sailing in our little skimmer. Cousin Clara will be there, along with her brother Eliot. Clara has a darling new dress of white piqué. Mother says she will have several white dresses made for me, too, one of Swiss muslin, with a double skirt, a ribbon of pink satin through the hems, and Greek sleeves. Have you any dresses with Greek sleeves? I do adore them. I must go now to study être in the subjunctive tense. Quelle horreur. Que je déteste les verbes français!

    —Lillian

P.S. I am so sorry to report we have no idea of the whereabouts of Joseph Muldoon, but I will ask my Papa what he might discover.

My sister's words made green ribbons of jealousy run along the hems of my bad temper.

—Don't trouble yourself over it, Mrs. Jones, said my new husband.

—How would I stop troubling myself if I wanted to?

—We'll go to Chicago and find them.

—You said that before.

—One day we'll show up at the Ambrose lawn party in our yachting costumes.

—And our little French muslins.

—And our little French letters, he said, his lips on my neck.

I swatted him. —Stop now.

—Say stop in French and I will.

—F*****g stop.

—No, he said, and I was grateful for his persistence for he distracted me from the sorrows and preoccupations of the past. When I recovered from his ministrations, Charlie helped me write my sister back.

Dear Lily,
Last evening was unforgettably divine, for I danced the German at Mrs. Cropsey's party on Fifth Avenue. I can assure you darling Dutch, there is no more popular dance in all of New York. Oh how I wish you and Joe could visit us here! We would have a grand time.

Me and Charlie wrote to Dutch regularly now, long, lying accounts of our rich and opulent life. We matched her lawn parties line by line with charades and possessions.

. . . We have purchased a splendid pair of sorrels, such handsome horses, don't you agree? The carriage Charles selected has fine upholstered leather, and the curtains are made of damask. . . .

. . . Charles is just home from a reception at The Century
Club, where he dined with Mr. Astor and Mr. A. T. Stewart,
who inquired of an article Charles wrote on the Reconstruction
effort. Mr. Astor was of the mind it was as fine an editorial as
he'd ever seen. . . .

Charlie provided the details and the sentences. His handwriting was all flourishes and fancy legs on the downstrokes. He knew everything. Which clubs to mention. Which parties was the flash. He was a walking newspaper, with the ink on his hands to prove it. But he wasn't yet a writer at any journal, only a typesetter, and a journeyman at that, working when they called him, once or twice in a week, for a wage of twenty two cents an hour. His exposé of the Tombs had gone straight to nowhere. Some Editors, those pompous bloviators, had read it and said, Who cares about prisoners? It is not a story for our readers. Two weeks later, the *Herald* ran An Exposé of the Tombs under another writer's name, and more than half the words was stolen from the pen of Charles G. Jones.

So Charlie remained a printer. His earnings was never more than two dollars in a day. Still, he wrote away. He'd show them, he said. He'd make them sorry. He'd have his own name in type yet. He frequented bookstores and the inky haunts and drinking establishments of poets and rebels. He came home talking of Reason and Romance and Stoicism and Moral Physiology. The only comfort against my jealous suspicions was the idea that hoors did not talk such high talk, so perhaps he was truthful when he claimed he was up all the night arguing with Philosophers or flattering editors. For sure it seemed he was always writing. Our room was full of his papers, scrawls on scraps. He practiced on anything, on those letters to Dutch.

—Tell her we dined on squab and truffles, I told him, and gave him the menus of our banquets and all my dreams of dresses straight out of the Ladies' Book. —Say I worn a stole of marabou feathers and patent dancing slippers.

—Wore, Student, said my husband, —not worn. Speak like the gentry.

He was ever after trying to make me over into nobility and led me to believe he thought me Thick and caused me shame at my improper grammar, even as we enjoyed to write out together an uppercrust life for ourselves and send it off to Chicago.

Every three or four weeks Dutch wrote me back, pages of detail: about her governess, French lessons, wardrobe, social life, and them infernal cousins. Clara this. Clara that. Clara Clara Clara. The older one, Eliot, showed up, too. Oh, he was a dashing devil, that Eliot VanDerWeil, swashbuckling around with his mustache and his opinions, on the war, on railroad tariffs. *Eliot says young ladies ought to be in bed by nine p.m.!*

My sister in her writing seemed years older than thirteen. How I missed her.

The concoction of Big City stories that me and Charlie sent off to Dutch could not amend the worst fact: that Dutch's letters was pure truth and mine were lies. Envy grew soft and corrosive on my heart like mold on cheese. Now while I toiled away as a maid and midwife's apprentice, I coveted the life of a Chicago Belle. I longed for my sister Dutch and not this Lily. I hated Cousin Clara. I wanted Joe, to know where he was. He would be a wiry boy of eight years old in knee pants, hair the color of a brick New York building, like the one where he was born and belonged. He never had heard his name Muldoon or the word Carrickfergus nor the truth of how he was the descendant of the Kings of Lurg. I pined to see his dear face. Would I even recognize him? Joe and my sister was a preoccupation of mine such that my husband took to making wild promises to coax a smile out of me.

—We'll go and fetch them, Charlie whispered, and wound a curl of my hair around his fingers.—Dutch and Joe both.

—When will that be?

—Soon as we save up the train fare.

But it was all we could do to pay the rent. We scrimped along on Charlie's spotty journeyman wages, for two days one week, three the next, barely enough, and lived for the date two years hence when I finished out my service to the Evans at age twenty one, and would receive the rest of the money Mrs. E. had promised me. A thousand dollars we calculated. —*When you get your wages, darlin'*, Charlie sang, —*we'll have pie and pork, yes we will.* When you get your wages.

But I did not get wages. I did not get pie nor pork. Just a handful of tablets and a book of recipes. In the insult of it, what I failed to understand was, these items was as good an inheritance as a trunkful of Barbary Coast doubloons.

BOOK FOUR

A Useful Wife

Chapter Twenty-Two

Inheritance

*I*n the spring of 1866, when I was nineteen years of age, my teacher, Mrs. Evans, died in her sleep. God took her, said Mrs. B., but we both known it was more likely the vial of Sanative Serum on her nightstand that did it. Dr. Evans summoned me after the funeral to say that my services was no longer required. He sold the Chatham Street house to a carpet merchant and prepared to go lodge with his sister Mrs. Fenton in Yorkville, where I hoped a beer wagon from the Ruppert Breweries on Third Ave. would run him over for the manner in which he let me and Mrs. Browder go without so much as a paper of pins or a thank you. I stood before him in the library where he took off his spectacles to rub his eyes.

—Doctor, though, what about my wages? I demanded him.

—For these five years you have had room and board with us, the old unicorn told me. —You've learned housekeeping from Mrs. Browder.

—Skills such as every girl has, I said, —and none of them worth cash money.

—You are a married woman now. You live with your husband.

My husband was beside the point, as his wages was barely enough to cover the rent on a Vesey Street room the size of a tea towel. The roof leaked. There was rats in the walls. The privy was down the stairs out in the courtyard. A family of Gypsies was next door squabbling at all hours of the day and night. The smell of their dark spices drifted through the cracks and clung to the hair. I wanted to get out. I wanted another dress besides this one. I wanted to eat squab at Delmonico's and go to Niblo's theatre for shows and take the train at last to Philly and Chicago to fetch my lost Muldoons.

—A year ago Mrs. Evans promised me back wages to be paid when I left her service, I told the doctor. —She promised my mother as Mam lay dying.

—Wages? he said, very mild. —Mrs. Evans was not in her right mind.

—Her mind was right enough for her to deliver Mrs. Devine's baby not two weeks before, and it was right enough for her to play her Sunday game of whist just last week, and it was right enough for her to promise me wages when I left her service.

He blinked like a turtle. —I'm afraid there isn't any money. It's all taken in debt. He handed me twenty dollars and my notice.

The old gargoyle was a gambler, it turned out. His outings on so-called medical emergencies was in fact emergencies at the horse track at Jerome Park, where he dispensed bets instead of medicines. Mrs. Browder found out the facts after he shorted her pay, too, by four months.

—It's not right, she said. —We'll have ours yet, won't we Annie?

Packing up the trunks and crates of the household, we wasted no time helping ourselves. Into my gunnysacks went a bushel of apples and twelve jars of jam. A leg of mutton and half the potatoes from the potato hole. Also a frying pan, a sieve, and a good portion of Mrs. Evans' dresses, shawls and whatnot. The remainder of my inheritance came from upstairs: sixteen bedsheets with shadows of old blood faded in brown watermarks, four blankets, a sugar tin, and a slopper. From the library I took Arabian Nights and Dr. Gunning's Diseases of Women. From the clinic, I took Itch Powder, aloes to make a salve, and three bottles of Lunar Tablets for the Regulation of Female Physiology, as well as a bundle of medical tools, Mrs. Evans' syringe bulb and hot water bottle, all wrapped in a dishcloth. Out of spite, I pocketed the doctor's little book of medicinal formulas.

—What are these recipes? Charlie asked when he saw it later. —Are you going to poison me?

—Only rubbish, I told him, and soon had it hid in the cupboard.

                              *   *   *

Now I got up in the mornings and went out to find employment. I could sew a pleat and black a stove and rinse clothes with bluing. I could corn beef and make pudding from a piece of calf rennet soaked in a bottle of wine. I could say the psalm of David. And just by a hand on the abdomen, I could find the fundus of a woman three months gone or seven and could bind the chest of a nursing woman so her milk would dry. Armed thus only with knowledge, I knocked on doors. I went up and down Washington Square and all the way to Gramercy Park. For weeks, every door that opened had a maid or a shopgirl already behind it and none of them was eager for replacement.

At home in our bleak room I sulked over the scanty stew pot.

—We're doomed to live in the coal scuttle always, I said one night to Charlie, while he lay next to me, his hand on my right b*s*m, and his leg, so heavy-boned and furred, lay over my flanks. —We're poor now as we was the day we met.

—This right here is free, he said, and kissed me. —All you want, for no money. So saying, he helped himself. —If we could sell this, we'd be kings.

—Are you suggesting me, your own wife, to go out for work as a hoor for hire?

—Never. All's I'm saying, Mrs. Jones, is, I'd buy whatever you have to sell.

—If I had a scrap to sell I'd sell it.

—Sell them books that you filched from the doctor.

—After I sell them, and spend the dollar, I am poor all over again.

—Sell something else then, he said. —But not this.

And we carried on helping ourselves to free servings. There was red wild sparkles amid the gray garlicked murk of a windowless boardinghouse room. But also, there was bad nights when he didn't come home, and hot arguments over money, over the cost of his ale. Every day was a lesson in how love was a slippery fish between two anglers without no nets to catch it. Neither me nor Charles G. Jones ever had a working nuptial example to go by, so we proceeded by hook and by crook. Our money troubles was enough to turn us toward the second option, stealing apples off the cart, just to eat.

*   *   *

What could I sell? Matches? Muffins? I did not have the money for sulfur nor butter. I did not have tins or an oven. I had ten dollars left of the twenty that Dr. Evans had paid me squirreled secretly in the empty biscuit tin. One morning when my husband went off to his inky labors in Printing House Square, I went to the cupboard with the flicker of an Idea. Here was the notebook I lifted from Dr. Evans, stuffed with paper scraps in ink that had gone brown. Was there a recipe for me? The first page was a formula for Healing Remedy, Good for Man or Beast. The next page was the Spavin Cure for Human Flesh. There was Catarrhal Powder, followed by Lazy Liver Pills, Blood Cure, and there, just after that, was the one that had caught my imagination:

LUNAR PILLS (for Relief of Suppression of Catamenia): *Make a powder of ergot and Spanish fly. Make a milk of magnesia.*

With my secret stash of money I went through the hot streets to Hegemann's Pharmacy in Chatham Square. I bought beetle wings, magnesia powder, and the rusty fungused heads of rye stalks that was called ergot. In agony over the expense, I purchased three glass medicine bottles with cork stoppers. All this cost three dollars, a fortune I didn't have. All along Vesey Street I kicked myself over my spent money, gone on a gamble.

At home, I did the recipe. *Add a dram of ergot and a minim only of the Spanish Fly.* With the flat of a spoon, I crushed the emerald wings of dark beetles, loosened the ergot fungus off the stalks of rye and mashed it, wetted the white magnesia dust with water. My efforts left me a chalky paste on a plate. Without a pill tile I used a knife to shape my efforts into tablets, the way I done it so many times on Chatham Street. But there was no binding syrup such as we had at Evanses to use for the excipient so the mess only fell off the mixing fork. The whole effort was a mash of ruin, dried to a powder. A waste of money and now what? We was broke six ways till payday, and when was that?

In tears, I funneled my failed gamble into the bottles and stoppered up the necks. I stumped about the stove, chopping cabbage, boiling tea, flinging pots. I was Axie the Dread cursing and cooking. I burned the bread. It was our last bit till hell froze over.

When Charlie came in he was cocked off gin. He sniffed the burnt air and ranted away at the loss of his dinner. —What the devil? he cried. —Do we have bread to BURN? Are we MADE of bread?

—F. off. Are we made of HOOCH? What's the matter with you?

—Nothing you can't fix, he says, his rough beard at my cheek, his drag-on's breath of liquor.

I shrugged him off me, disgusted. —Get away. Leave me be.

—I WILL leave you, he snorted. —Then you could burn the toast whenever you please. You'll be well rid of me, eh? He stood holding the table's edge, swaying soused on his pins and staring at the mess I made, of powder and pill bottles, rye stalks and beetle wings. —And what's all this DUST? Is it dinner?

—It's meant to be sold as medicinal tablets, to relieve the female com-plaint, to loosen an obstruction of the female hmm-hmmm-hmmm.

—Whose obstruction? he said, his eyes narrow with suspicion.

—Not mine. And sure it's only a waste of three dollars now.

—You spent MONEY for this mess? he roared. —It's a fortune!

—It was YOU put the notion in my head, to sell it!

—Dust? You would sell DUST? Have you lost your mind?

—It was supposed to be TABLETS. What do you know about it?

—Where'd you get it, eh? Who gave you three dollars?

—I HAD it.

—Oh ho she says, she HAD it. And where would MRS. Jones get it? What did you sell, then, to get the money for your DUST?

He came and got me by the collar and wrenched me very vicious but I twisted away so he chased me. We circled with the table between us, yelp-ing. I made for the doorway.

—Mrs. Jones, he roared, and charged so I was maneuvered into a corner.

—Don't come near me, I said with my back against the wall. His arms was a fork to pin me there.

—Where did you get three dollars?

—From Dr. Evans. It was MINE.

—Oh ho. What else are you hiding then? Ya dirty shake.

—Don't come near me. Get away.

—Oh get away, he mimicked. —Oh keep away Charlie. His voice as he copied me was a high whine that slid fast down to menace. —You prefer a man who'll pay you. Is that it Mrs. Jones? You'd rather a paying customer than a poor wretched printer without a nickel, without a proper pair of boots, without a pot to p*** in.

—P*** out the window for all I care! I shouted. —P*** off.

And he stopped right there, breathing thick and reeling. —Oh is that what you want? Then have it.

In a swift jerk he lifted the table by the edge. Flipped it. —Goodbye then, Mrs. Jones, my husband said, and left our poor room.

—Good riddance, I cried. But just as I slammed the door behind him, he came bursting back only to fall out cold on the bed, his mouth slack and stains on his shirt. I looked at him snoring there and hated him too thoroughly even to cry over any of it.

That night in the dark while he snored I brooded with the thudding of the neighbors' boots above me mixed up with the mew of cats in heat and pigeons gargling on the sill. This racket was my only lullaby, for even married it appeared I was alone without no love or resources. Money was the one sure thing, wasn't it? Even if I'd prefer a warm nest of relatives, at least Money did not go off elsewheres in the night drinking hops and gin and coming home to fondle a woman and call her names only to pass out.

In the early morning while Charlie slept it off I examined my sorry bottles of dust. In my terrible hand I wrote MRS. JONES LUNAR POWDER on a label for each one, determined to sell the stuff no matter what. Ladies would not care if it was loose powder or tablets, as long as it did as promised. I trusted it did. The same ingredients had worked for me, or so I thought, and I wouldn't deceive a girl in trouble no more than I would rob an innocent child of milk.

Lower Broadway by City Hall Park was where vendors of every description went with their flotsam for sale, their bootlaces and buttons, their trays of meat patties, their whalebone needles and tortoise shell combs. There was nothing you couldn't buy: songbirds in a cage, clam liquor and beeswax, a nosegay of pinks sold by a dirtyface girl, such as I was not long ago and might be soon again.

That day the clouds ahead were dark as eggplant, but the sun lit them from beneath so they were tinged with gold, looming and purple. Such weather seemed a bad sign as I settled down on the sidewalk of Chambers Street and arranged my pathetic wares in the lid of a discarded pasteboard box plucked from the trash. On the front was propped an advertisement, hand-lettered by me.

Mrs. Jones' Female Lunar Powder, Cures What Ails a Lady.

*Not to be taken during p*******y, as M*sc****ge may result.

$3 $2 Only While Supplies Last

I began to call out in my timid cheep. —Mrs. Jones' Lunar Powder, I whispered. —Only three bottles left. Cures what ails you. This way, ladies.

In five short hours by a miracle I had sold my stock. One swank princess in a velvet cloak bought two bottles and the other was bought by a molting brood hen of a woman toting four grimy children. —If I have another it'll be the last of me, said she. And just like that I had six dollars for five hours' work. Six dollars. It was a fortune. Running home I spent it eighty ways a minute. And there in our room was hangdog Charlie, sitting up with his tail between his legs.

—Why do you look so pleased with yourself? said he.

—Ha! I told him why, full of triumph and spite. —FOUR dollars!

—Four dollars for a pile of dust, he said, wary. —Will wonders never cease?

—It was not DUST. It was medicine. It brings on the turns.

—And how would you know, Mrs. Jones?

—I tried it myself when you was locked in the Tombs. I'd have tried anything then and I did. Look here.

For the first time I told him the true reason for the pale scar on my wrist where the kitchen knife cut. —I stabbed myself to be rid of it, I cried, and my husband, pretty sober now, traced his inky fingernail along the line. He sat with his head hung, shamed, rubbing the cords of his neck.

—You should be SORRY for the torment of it, I said, —and SORRY for what you done to me yesterday night, and for what you called me, and how you ran off and left me here alone. And I don't never want to be alone. Not EVER.

He did not look at me, but picked very guilty at the threads of the coverlet. After a time sighing and rubbing at his eyes he got himself up heavily and put his arms through his braces, tucking in his shirt. He came over behind my back and leaned against me, pressing his forehead against the bone of my skull. I stood still. He turned me and nested me in his arms, and I allowed it. After a while like that the heat of him thawed my furious shoulders down. We stood holding on awhile, afraid to move, like we was made of wax and had melted that way.

—I am a sorry son of a knacker, says he.

With his chin resting on the top of my head, he confessed his trouble. —I've had no printer's work at the *Herald,* nor anywhere, not for three weeks. I spent the rent money.

Our poverty put him out of his mind with worry and trouble, he said. So yesterday he'd had a pint for the nerves. Then another pint for bravery. Then another several. —All to muster the wherewithal to come home and tell you the news. That we're broke as beggars.

—You called me a dirty shake.

—It was the whiskey called you that.

—It was your lips that drank it, and said it.

—A man will drink his lush, and a man will have his suspicions. Why did you hide three dollars from me?

—Have you never hid a thing from me?

He did not answer.

—I won't be without money, I said.

—Are you hiding more money then? he asked, very mild.

—I told you, I got four dollars. I stared defiant at him. I would have my secrets as a hedge against his, that he spent the rent or whatever else.

He looked at me, shook his head and whistled long like I was some fancy girl on the street. —My, my, my. Four dollars just like that. You're quite the gooseberry pudding, Mrs. Jones.

Well. Was this Charming Charlie, back again? —Gooseberry pudding?

—You're Christmas and payday all in one, says he, all smiles. —FOUR dollars?! It's brilliant, to sell these powders. Selling dust for four dollars in a day only?

—A desperate woman would pay anything to put herself to rights let me tell you.

—Exactly, he said, excited. —And let me tell you that with the proper salesmanship, you'll have yourself a little business. Mrs. Jones' Remedies for

Sale. And we'll have to work fast to sell more of this DUST, Mrs. Jones if we're going to make the rent this month.

—I don't have the ingredients.

—But you do have four dollars. Off we go to the chemists, how about it?

—What about the rent?

—Oh right, he says. —A pity. I guess you're not up for a gamble. You'd never take a risk. Not if there was a pot of gold sitting the other side of a deserted train track in the middle of the wild open prairie.

—Ha. A pot of coddle, more like.

—Chickenheart, he said, daring me on. —The rent is six.

That day I showed my husband how to mix the powders, and after that, when he wasn't trolling for journey work at the print shops and newspapers of the city, Charlie mashed beetle wings or wrote me out neat labels *Mrs. Jones' Lunar Remedy, $2.* He wrote instructions in flourishes of penmanship. *Mix with a half cup of water and swallow 1 scant teaspoon a day for six days.* He made a proper sign, telling me, —Yours looks like a child wrote it. He had to take over and boss me, saying, —See, Student here's what you do. Thus I seen—saw—his superior education, wrote out also in the little newsprint ledger he showed off, writing Expenses over one column of figures and Income over another column. After six weeks, in a miracle, he explained, —We grossed ninety dollars and netted seventy five dollars. This sum he wrote in a new column called PROFIT. —Gross is the total, Student, while Net is what we caught for our dinner, he said, like a Schoolmaster, so I never felt so ignorant. And wasn't the whole enterprise my idea in the first place? Still, we were in business. There was no more arguments now over money or dust, though I squirreled away a nest egg just for my own, rolled in a stocking. Things was patched up between us, just by the plaster of industry. Or was it the plaster of money?

On my worst nights, I suspected my husband stuck not to me, but to the profits of the enterprise we begun that day. What I didn't know then was that to have a common venture was a good cement for Marriage, an institution held together by financial operations same as it was by operations of the boudoir. It was a lesson it took me years to learn, believing as I did so fiercely in the wild red sparkles of Love's Sake Only.

* * *

Mrs. Jones' Remedy was good as fairy dust, molded into tablets. Within a few months the stuff transformed Mrs. Jones herself like a sprinkle from the pixies. One day I was a pitiful trape in the square, a shawl around my head, a wet cardboard box in front of me with a solitary bottle displayed, and so forlorn you would think by the holes in my stockings I was scranning a handout. Not five months later, I had new stockings and a wooden pushcart. Charlie had bought it off an onion monger and fixed it up for me with a proper sign: Mrs. Jones Lunar Powder, $3, painted in Chinese red over the old lettering that read, Onions, 5 Cents.

—WHILE SUPPLIES LAST, I called, in my new bold voice. —Halloo there madam! LOWEST PRICE ON THE MARKET. The customers circled, approached quite furtive with their baskets.

—You don't look old enough to be Mrs. Jones, they told me.

—She's my gran, so she is.

—Give me a bottle then, dearie, and tell your Gran it better do the trick.

The coins landed softly in my jam jar of profit, and the bills that stuffed it looked green and minty through the glass.

One year and one THOUSAND DOLLARS later, I wrote the latest installment of news to Dutch:

> *Dear Lillian,*
> *We have the most swell new apartments. Decorated throughout with draperies and such, in the fashionable Greenwich Street which is all the go. You should see the windows and especially the expensive harpsichord in our parlor it is lacquered black and painted with golden CHINOISERIE by which is meant Chinee painting.*

Chinoiserie was all the rage, Charlie informed me, for he knew everything about the money class.

> *I have wrote to the Children's Aid Society demanding to know the whereabouts of Joe. Won't you get your Ambrose family to help us find him? if you get his address we will stop in*

*Philadelphia to fetch him on the way to Chicago to see you quite
soon, dear little sister, and be reunited at last like Mam wished
for us all to be.*

The only lie was about the harpsichord. But the Greenwich Street apartment was true and so was our intention to look for Joseph in the City of Brotherly Love on the way to Chicago. The money jar was full and I was hellbent to round up the Muldoons at last. I mailed off the news to Dutch with our new address prominently featured. And this time, the reply was instant. Not at an interval of weeks, but by return mail.

Dear Ann,
*   It would not be an opportune time for a visit to Chicago, for
the winters are cold and the lake frozen. In addition, Mother is
in poor health and says we may not have visitors till the warm
weather arrives. It would be best to wait until summer. Oh, don't
you love the summer? It is ever so warm and sunny.*

Such tripe was never written by a girl before nor since. Ever so warm and sunny? Well of COURSE summer is sunny and warm. It is the SUMMER, you halfwit. After EIGHT years apart, why didn't she write how thrilled she'd be to see me? Instead she wrote of Cousin Eliot. His mustache and his riding breeches.

*   He has a velvet waistcoat and patent leather dancing slippers.
He is going to study business. He is very jolly, but such a terrible
tease! He calls me Miss Lillian, and all manner of other names:
Lilliputian, Silly Lily, and Mistress Sillypants.*

Mistress Sillypants indeed. It was enough to make me lose my toast in a teacup.

Charlie said,—What do you expect? Sixteen years of age and corrupted by the Decadent Society. No wonder she writes nothing but c***!

I comforted myself by writing regular to Dear Mr. Brace at the Aid Society, asking did they know of Joseph Muldoon, taken to Philadelphia, etc. A Mr. P. Claridge wrote back promising to communicate directly should he hear any news. So we had no choice but to wait for summer to rescue Dutch. As it turned out, we were to wait longer than that, through many events, small and large. The first of them was very large indeed, although it weighed just under six pounds, about the heft of a good joint of mutton.

Chapter Twenty-Three

Derangement of the Uterus

*A*t first it was only a cinder of fear. But then came the clues like steps leading down to a cellar. The taste of chalk at the back of my tongue. A sudden odor off things with no odor: stone, water, wood. One morning I woke queasy. In a panic over it. I knew the symptoms and remembered a night when our shield fell to pieces for we had wore it out and now I feared the consequence. What if I was _____ ? Please not. I was twenty one years of age and too young to die. I selected a bottle of my own Lunar Tablets and swallowed them down, waiting for my turns to arrive. I wished on the evening star. I soaked a rag in burberry oil and placed it on my forehead. I left a saucer of milk on the windowsill, as Mam advised to do, so the *sheehogues* would keep trouble off. But no god nor fairy heard my pleas this time. The medicine did not take. There was no change in my state. I was still sore in the chest, still sick in the a.m., grim in the evenings.

—I am on the nest, I blurted to Charlie one night in our bed.

He was reading a newspaper. He did not hear me or pretended he didn't.
—Hmm?

—Because of you, I am _____.

Now I had his full attention. —You're not joking.

—Do I look like a clown to you?

—Sweet Jesus, no, you look like the mother of my son. It's true then?

—It's YOUR fault, I cried.

—I hope it's not nobody else's.

He was grinning. He could not stop himself. He took me in his arms proud like he won a game of skill, strutted with his feathers cocked up, a rook inflated with the news. I stayed stiff and turned away and picked at a piece of loose skin by my fingernail, pulled it off so the blood was bright in the lamplight.

—Aw Missus Jones.

—I'll only die, is all. My mother did.

—Not of having you, she didn't. He fitted me under his wing. —Chickenheart.

—It's not you that has to have it, I cried.

—It'll be fine, he said, for he was lately optimistical and full of plans. —Little Joneses all over the place. It'll be swell.

—For YOU it will, I said, miserable. It made no difference knowing that all the time I'd assisted Mrs. Evans I'd only seen one woman die, and of eclampsia, which was not common. What was a baby but a ship built in a bottle? You couldn't get it out without breaking the glass. I was narrow-hipped and small-boned and my mother's daughter. I would die.

—One out of a hundred mothers died in childbed just in the last year of 1868, I told him. —I read it in the *Police Gazette*. It's carnage, so it is.

—Well the *Gazette* never met Axie Jones, did it now? He tucked me down tenderly as a nestling.

In the morning, Charlie hummed and patted me on the rump, a new kind of smile on his lips. I went around pinched and gray, full of doom. —You look like yesterday's fish, Charlie said.

—In seven months I'll be dead as haddock on Friday.

—You're not going nowheres, Mrs. Jones. That wee Master Jones in the oven there is just the first of the rest of the Great Joneses of Greenwich Street. Of FIFTH AVENUE. We'll have a house on Washington Square with a room for each little Jonesie. Money in the bank and horses in the stables.

—Ha! I brushed him off. But from under my pillow, I listened.

—You WON'T die. These ladies with nursemaids and carriages, such as you, Mrs. Jones, they don't die.

—I seen Mrs. Kissling die right in her husband's arms. And he was a banker.

Charlie sobered a little so I thought he might miss me if I departed this life, but then he gathered steam, talking himself into his own argument like he could issue a decree. —You can't die, Mrs. Jones. It's the lower orders that go to the grave, whereas the better classes with the three rooms, such as YOU, the ones with the plumbing and gaslight right in the hallway, such as you: they don't die. They've got doctors. Medicines. Elixirs. Doodads. All the finest remedies and SCIENCE. Likewise, so do you. You're not living in Cherry Street now, do you hear me? Or ever again.

It would be nice to believe the picture, what he said. The family with stables and bank accounts. The elixirs and the pomades and the doodads. It was all I wanted but I didn't trust it was real. None of it. —Not possible, I said.

—You wouldn't trust the sun to shine or the moon to rise, said my husband.

But why should I? Just because we had some coins in the jar to call our own? To me trouble was regular. Everything else was only temporary.

Strangely, as my form grew misshapen and enormous, my dread and fear shrunk down. Maybe it was Charlie's persuasion, his confident talk of science. More likely it was something else: the child was quick. Lying down, dozing, I felt the hard thump like a heart, low in the abdomen. I lay in the darkness of the early morning, five months gone, with Charlie asleep beside me, and put my hand to the spot low down by the hip where I felt it. There. And there again. A flutter. Not bigger than a hiccup. I smiled in the darkness. So this is what is meant by quick, I thought. Alive. It's come alive. My own heart beating somewheres else in my body.

Hello, I said in the dark, but not out loud, and began to allow myself a dream of a girl with eyes dark as huckleberries looking up. I would be a mother. Would I? Already wee Jones had a sense of humor. I pushed my belly, then came a push back. We made a game of it. Push. Thump. —Feel here, I said, smiling, and took my husband's hand. He circled the round hard lump through the wall of my middle.

—What the hell is that?

—Kicks.

—Mother of God. It's a boy no question.

*   *   *

My stomach was so large now it could have its own moon. Sitting at my cart with my bottles displayed alongside the big round of it was not a good advertisement for the regulation of anything, esp. the female physiology. Nobody bought my wares. On a Friday in July I lumbered home and sat on the bed with my feet straight out in front of me. They was swollen sore and cracking, ruts in the heels like dried mud. Mr. Jones came home and found his wife was a beetle pinned under the weight of her own Self.

—How many sold today? he asked.

—Not one. At this rate we'll be on Cherry Street again in a wink.

—Quit that talk.

—What use is it hauling the cart all the way to City Hall, I cried, —just to sit there broiling for not one green dollar? I'm fat as a tick and all the housemaids turn up their noses like they've no use for tablets. Not a penny in the jar all week. It's hello Cherry Street for us again. The Childrens Aid will send Mr. Brace after us and that pooka will put the child on the train to Illinois.

Charlie did not like when I talked about our poverty nor Cherry Street or to be reminded of that train. He paced the room, stroked his whiskers. He was having a Great Thought, you could see it come over him. He took a pen from his vest and began writing in the small notebook he carried with him in case he might stumble upon the story that would get him printed in the pages of a newspaper. The man was possessed, I thought. As he worked, the pink tip of his tongue protruded between his lips, which reminded me, always, of something about to be born.

Something was, of course. His grand idea.

—Look at this, then, he said after five minutes. —An advertisement.

I took it and read what he wrote.

FEMALE PILLS. Mrs. Jones, renowned Female Physician, informs the ladies that her pills are an infallible regulator of m****s. They must not be used when p*******, as M*sc*****ge may result. Prepared and sold only by herself. $4 a bottle, including instructions. Inquiries and orders to 148 Greenwich Street, NY.

—Am I supposed to wear this on a sandwich board then? I asked, disgusted.

—There's not no board that would fit a sandwich the likes of you.

At this I threw my shoe at him.

His brown eyes flashed with the love of his own joke, and some new feverish intent. He retrieved the *Herald* from the chair and turned to the end page. —We'll put a notice here, he said, and pointed to the ads selling all kinds of remedies: HUNTER'S RED DROP for the effectual cure of v*****l diseases. SAND'S REMEDY for Salt Rheum. JAYNE'S VERMIFUGE for Worms, Worms, Worms.

There were advertisements for every reason under heaven.

> THE ORIGINAL MADAME R— tells everything, traces absent friends, causes speedy marriages, gives lucky numbers. Ladies, 50 cents; gentlemen, one dollar.

> A RETIRED SWEDISH PHYSICIAN, OF FORTY YEARS' practice, discovered, while in India, a sure remedy for consumption, bronchitis, colds, etc.

—Every one of them advertisements is by a European fancy type, I said. —A Swede and a German and also a Vandenburgh and a Portuguese. Who am I to advertise in that company? Nobody. I'm Mrs. Jones, just.

—Well so you will be MADAME Jones then, Charlie suggested. —The famous French female physician Madame Jones.

—Jones is about as French as a piece of laced mutton.

—Not many laces big enough to go around this mutton.

I flung my other shoe at his head.

—Madame Broussard? he tried. —Madame LeClerc? Madame DuBois? Madame DeBeausacq? He dreamed up Madames and wrote them on a list.

I pictured myself as a Paris lady. —What's that one there? I pointed.

—DeBeausacq? You will be glad to know that Beau means beautiful.

—I'll take that one then.

—Beautiful sack, he translated.

—Ha. Sack of misery, more like.

—Won't be long now, he soothed me with tender ministrations and sips from his bottle of ale. He was altogether now a more attentive class of husband as my confinement grew closer. —It will all be fine, he said, which aggravated me, and I prickled at him and did not trust him and suspected he was only nice to me because I was going to die. He would miss my earnings, that was it.

—I am ready to burst, I whispered. —I'm a kernel of corn in a fire.

However, I was not corn but more like biscuit dough, rising in the oven of our sweltering August rooms. Climbing stairs required me to haul myself up by the banister. Pain stabbed at the small of my back while I walked or moved about our kitchen making bread. Sitting, lying, the child shifted in my belly. You could see it. A knee or foot or elbow protruded in a knob of flesh. It was a cat in a sack. It kept me up nights with dyspepsia and fear and the sensation of bubbles rising through my middle, fillips of air like the wee somebody was laughing, the sound turning to fizz within. Perhaps I would like the little squibben after all, its fingernails like tiny slivers of moon. But it was an outrage, the whole condition. The bloating and the thrombosis. The vomiting and swelling. The red chap of the cheeks and the ominous dark line that appeared on the belly like a carving mark.

We were cows. I was.

The summer slid into autumn, and as it did, envelopes slid into our mailbox common as leaves off trees, thanks to the many new advertisements Charlie placed in all the papers. While the mail did not bring the letter I craved from my sister, or any communication from Mr. Brace with news of Joe Muldoon, it did bring countless orders for Madame DeBeausacq's Female Remedy, and inside the envelopes were folded bills, cheques and pieces of silver like miracles every day, along with letters to freeze the blood of any woman expecting a child, as they froze mine. For example.

Dear Mrs. Debosack, I have ben Married 7 yrs. and have All redy had 4 live children with 2 in the Grave. My last child is 9 mos. I had no doctor for 2 hours after she was born and I layed

on the floor and nearly got Blood poison and am still suffering
from Milk Leg ever sinse. I am All most Broken down Aged 25.
Please have you a Prevention? —Mrs. Sophie Peck, Erie, Penn.

Dear Madame, While I love my six children there is no joy
in living. I am only twenty-eight and am penned up till I can't
have half an hour to myself. I am almost a prisoner. Please,
please help poor people like us. It is so hard in the winter time
with so much coal to buy and winter clothing. If we have any
more I don't know what we will do. —Mrs. Arlen Livermore,
Flemington, N.J.

Dear Mme. DeB., I have the fear of pregnancy on my mind
all the time. If I try to stay away from my husband, he is terrible
mean to me and says awful things. He doesn't think what I have
suffered having my babies and what a terrible worry it is when
they are sick and how hard it is to make over old clothing and I
don't know what else. I could go on with my troubles and fill a
book, but here is three dollars for your tablets it is my last money.
For God's sake please help me, so I need not have any more as I
have heart trouble and I would rather to be here and raise these
four, than to have more and probably die. —Mrs. A. P. Kelly,
Troy, NY

I sent out orders of tablets, and out of charity returned to the poorest
ones, such as Mrs. Kelly, their three dollars along with their medicine, for
who could take a mother's last money? But even with such small acts of philanthropy, our income grew daily. Thanks to the advertisements, I no longer
went to the street with my cart but instead stayed inside our rooms working
away. I was a factory, not just of wee Jones' bones and sinews, but of powders and pills. Charlie lettered the labels and brought them to his printer
friend Harold at the *Herald* to set in type. Herald Harold as we called him
did not charge for the printing but asked instead for a bottle of Mrs. Jones
powders for his wife (he said). With spruce gum I stuck the labels on the
brown glass, my hands and hair sticky. For hours, with a folded paper as a
funnel, I counted out thirty tablets per bottle and stoppered them down. I

waddled off to the post office to mail out parcels wrapped in string to my poor ladies, the most of which seemed to be married, mothers already, anxious to prevent another confinement. They was all of them desperate. Our profit now was steady and immediate.

—Pinch me, I'm dreaming, I says to Charlie. He pinched me and we laughed, running our hands through coins like they was common dry peas. Our fortunes were shifted overnight, such that some two hundred dollars a day poured into our pockets. We was getting along now like the best of friends. With money in the bank, Charlie was jovial, his temper gone away same as the old mattress we burnt to replace with a feather one. How bittersweet, I thought, that I might die in my own soft bed, with a husband at my side and cash in my pocket, and not like I had long expected, on the pavement alone with a gnawed bone between my teeth. My time would be soon upon me.

Chapter Twenty-Four

Vessel

*I*t was like a belt or a clench tightening from the back around to the front. I was dreaming. The covers of my bed were twisted in the dark. Was this it, then? No, it was nothing. False pains. I slept and woke again. The belt tightened and cinched. I stirred and sat up and still the muscles across my midsection were rigid then flexing.

Charlie woke. —What is it?

I did not need to tell him. He knew. He got his pants on. His shoes. —I'll fetch Dr. Vachon, he said, and that started up our running argument.

—No! Get Mrs. O'Shaughnessy. Vachon's a peacock, I won't have him.

—He's a man of science.

—He's a man of snails and garlic. I won't have any man. Not of science or anywhere, not even France.

Dr. Vachon was an old beast with hairs grown out of the sockets of his ears. I didn't want him near me with his notions about *accouchement*, and his foreign savage practice of using a forceps tool to pull a child out by the head. He had the nerve to lord it over ME who had previous assisted a midwife at thirty births. But Charlie was all for anything mechanical or scientific and did not care that these metal contraptions was a terrible invention that ripped the ears off infants and left their heads in the shape of strange fruits, according to my teacher, Mrs. Evans. Worse, she said, they tore the parts of a woman and left her in such a condition as to prevent any future living with the husband, since her injuries were a bar to marital relations. Charlie was half-persuaded by this last threat, but told me to stop my silly Irish balderdash.

—You'd believe anything, he said. —That a caul will save a drowning man, or that the touch of a seventh son will cure the bite of a mad dog.

—It's true, says I. —Mam always said.

But his French Vachon had scientific theories. Delivery and parturition, as he called it, was a disease, he said, a *maladie* to be relieved by doctors.

—Hooey, I told him. —A delivery is a function of nature. Mrs. Evans says what's best is to find a female midwife who's schooled about it.

But Mrs. Evans had died. Mrs. Watkins of Lispenard Street was known as a charlatan and Mrs. Costello was worse. That left Dr. Vachon or Mrs. O'Shaughnessy, and between them, I'd rather have an Irish washerwoman such as she was with her nine children than an entire hospital of Vachons, but that didn't matter to Charlie. We argued over it even as I clutched my middle and he spouted his theories.

—It's the French and the scientists who's the experts. I'll get Vachon.

—I do not want that poodle here, and if you bring him I'll pelt him good with fish heads. But Charlie went off clattering down the stairs, leaving me to stew, hoping he would not come back with some Monsieur of a medical man and afraid he would not come back at all, leaving me to die alone. In the dark I went to my dressing table and put a drop of lavender water on the hard bone behind my ear to ease pains. I dipped a napkin in warm milk and applied it to myself down below for it was said milk would ward off scrofulous diseases. I made a tea of raspberry leaves and drank it to hurry labor. And last, I went to the window and put a saucer of cream on the sill there, to keep the *sheehogues* out of mischief.

Pain came, then left, but it was not the worst pain. Not yet. I lit the lamp. I hummed a tuneless hum of nerves. I spread a rubber sheet on the bed. I placed a pillow down. I arranged the string and the knife nearby. For distraction, I made pills, mashing the ingredients together with the water, molding tablets, seized regularly with constriction. I stopped till it passed. Grit my teeth. I brushed my hair. I boiled water and made a pennyroyal tea. I drank it. I took a dosage of castor oil, as Mrs. Evans instructed, to clear the b*w*ls. My palms was clammy with dread. Charlie did not come.

I opened all the windows to let in the dawn smell of the river. Outside now was the sound of crows, of pigeons hooting, the rattle of bottles off the milk wagon. A drover lifted paving blocks off a flat cart. —Motherf***, he said, and heaved. These are the sounds that will greet new baby Jones and accompany my death, I thought, the grunts of ratty birds and clanking jugs, the curses of laborers lifting heavy loads.

Where was Charlie? Sure he had gone all the way to Twenty Third Street to fetch the poodle. But even walking there and back didn't take one hour. Likely Vachon was lost and Charlie set out after him. Ridiculous. To go off searching for quackery. Why did he not come?

A boulder was at my center. The weight of it pressed through me and broke the sac of waters in a flood as I stood at the window. I remembered how the steam rose around my mother's legs years ago in the cold of Cherry Street, her life leaking out. The floor below me was drenched that way, my skirts were. I got on my knees with a dishcloth and blotted the floor, while the belly hung under me heavy and solid, a hive dangling from a thin branch, filled with stings and danger. *Oh honey,* I thought to my child in there. The pains came in steady turns. The belt tightened and stopped my breath down where I was on my knees and hands. The pain was liquid, the sick deep pulling of a terrible undertow.

Charlie. Where was he? How much time passed I couldn't track. Five hours. Six. I swallowed ergot. It will bring on the hard labor, Mrs. Evans said, her voice in my ear like she was there in the room. Just swallow this down dear. Needles stitched me a lining, a sick fur of pain sewed right to the canvas of me, so I was seeping, torn at the seams. Then it came hard and regular, crashed in waves now that lasted, crested, lasted, peaked, crashed. I was swept under. Crawled to the bed. Got in it. Climbed out. I clawed the mattress. Bit the sheet. Where was Charlie? Whether he came or not I was alone. Just a vessel like Mrs. Evans said. This pain. Oh honey. It hurt. I chewed the flesh of my own arm, while something within turned and ground twisting like a fist pulping an orange. I drank a glass of whiskey. Vomited. I drank another to blunt the edge. Where was Charlie? I hated him, terrified.

Light smudged the edges of the city outside the window. The outline of rooftops was lit behind by sunrise, so that in the pinkest part of the morning, I lay myself down. The waves came now with no break between them, and the fist, that fist, twisted, pushed out through a great burn opening the bones.

Charlie crashed into the room. He was winded. Dark smudges of sweat stained his shirt. He got down on the floor where I labored.

—Axie! I can't find anyone.

—Get away from me.

—Don't die. Don't leave me.

—Get AWAY.

He went across the room reeling, saying some mess about how he went all the way uptown and he couldn't find Vachon for hours and then he went over to Canal for Mrs. O'Shaughnessy but she was gone with another laboring mother. —So sorry, he said, fretting at me, he was exhausted, he was so worried for me, he was beside himself, begging, —Please don't die, my darling wife, and—SHUT UP, I says to him—SHUT YOUR GOB, and then paid him no more attention as I was sunk down so far inside my own linings bearing down in the waves. Mrs. Evans voice played in my head:

Don't push.

YES.

Not yet.

YES.

Not yet you'll tear.

The pains were waves of whitecaps on the top of whitecaps. Still my child was not fished out from the terrible sea of me.

Push NOW.

I did. I bore down. It was for nothing. If this was torture to make it stop I would give in, reveal any secret, betray the names of all my loved ones, where they were hiding. —It hurts, I cried like we all cry all us cursed mothers giving birth to the human race.

Axie now PUSH.

I pushed another last time. And another. Each time was the last. Every fiber pushed. In my neck I pushed and my eyelids and my teeth, down through the marrow of my bones. I shrieked. Death would kill me this way, exposed. Used up. Freezing with sweat.

Push. There love. There. There's the wee head born.

Mother of God I was convulsed. Legs in tremors, so cold my arms qua-
vered. Shaking like a ribbon in wind.

When you feel it again bear down one last time.

There. That's it.

And all in a great slithering slip of mess I delivered my daughter alive. It
was the first of October 1869. I was twenty-two years of age.

Charlie stayed over on the wall, a skittish dog. It was the quiet that brought
him over and the whimpering of the warm girl on my chest. He crept up
to where we lay.

—Oh sweet Jesus, he said, looking down at us. He was shaky. His eyes
were eggs of fear.

—Use these scissors, now, I said.

—I can't do it.

—You could if you had the baubles you was born with, I said, faint, and
cursed him.

He followed my instructions, sick with the task of tying the cord. Cutting it, he nearly fainted. When he was done he sat back on his heels, his
head down, swaying so it seemed he might keel over.

—I thought I'd lose you. I never seen such blood all over. Like a murder.
He swallowed. Nerves blotched the flushed skin of his cheeks with white
patches. I seen how he was out of his wits with fear and was that love? He
thought I might die, that the child might, too. It was there like terror on
him, same as it was on me. He pulled the flesh around his lips and huffed
air out of his mouth in big sighs.

—Stop, I said. —Look at her.

Our girl gazed up like she already knew the secrets buried in the salt
mines of our heart. Charlie looked down at her and looked at me so tender
and his eyes were bright with words he could not say, his tongue tied for
once in his life. He put out one finger only and touched her cheek like it
might burn him, and then he cupped his palm around the perfect orb of
her head.

—Well hello little itty bitty bean, he said at last.

*   *   *

On her birth certificate proudly filed at City Hall our daughter was named
Annabelle Gwendolyn Felicity Jones. —Belle is French for beautiful, her
father said, and we chose it so our daughter would have a bell and not an
ax in her name.

We inspected the kernels of her toes and admired the serene waters of
her gaze. She weighed not more than a sack of dry peas and her head was
a round peach under the palm of her father's hand. We gazed at her by the
dark of the fire and the light of the window, and despite evidence that she
was wrinkled and slit-eyed with the rumpled phiz of an old man, we pronounced her the Baby of the World. By the time she was six weeks of age
she was round and pink, but bad with the colic. She carried on crying with
a sound like the screech of train wheels on a steel rail. I picked her up and
put her over the hard bone of my shoulder, patted her back.

—Hush hush now, I said.

While I had seen babies born, I did not have an inkling of what to do
with one after it arrived, and I wished for my Mam so that she might tell
me. The poor infant screeched, I suckled her. She screeched, I burped the
wind out of her. She screeched, Toura loura, I sang. Daddy will buy you a
mockingbird. But no portion of singing or cooing would shut her tiny yap.
I nursed her. She sucked the life out of me, down to the roots. Taking her
own life right out from me even as I loved her. She was a leech. A barnacle.
I made her of my bones and my blood and my milk. I would die for her. I
would drink boiling whale oil straight from the lamp if necessary to save
her. Standing in the kitchen I suckled. Sitting exhausted I suckled. Lying
asleep I suckled. For months she hiccuped and shuddered, fretted her face
into folds like a crumbled ball of paper.

—Shush sweet baby, I said, so tired, and mixed her gripe water with
whiskey and dill weed, but it did no good, so I seen now why lullabies was
all about cradles falling from trees, oh dear, when the wind blows, down
will come baby, whoops too bad, but at least it's quiet. I seen why the ladies
wrote me letters of their despair and said Please Help I Have Enough
Babies, and also why some mothers threw their infants out the window, or
left them for the nuns. But luckily I did neither of these, and after some
months found I was born to be a mother, tacked down by a warm lump of
girl so peaceful across my chest, her breath sweet with milk, even as I was
her prisoner. In this time, I learned for myself as my teacher predicted, how

it is these two extremes—that we are transported by love and jailed by it—
that are ever impossible for mothers to reconcile.

Even while I toiled nursing and tending my sweet infant, Madame
DeBeausacq did not rest. Every day now on the back pages of the *Herald* and the *Times,* Madame's advertisement appeared, a small gray box of
type in the corner. While it was officially a misdemeanor under the statutes
of New York since 1846 to administer a substance designed to produce a
miscarriage, so what? This was not a law the authorities of 1869 bothered
to enforce, for how would they prove anything? Certainly it was legal to
advertise a Lunar Remedy for Relief of Obstruction, for not all obstructions was due to the Delicate Condition. It was a thrill to see our notice
among the many hundred others in the paper.

Madame DeBeausacq, it said, Renowned Female Physician.

She was me. She was Axie Muldoon Jones and she was famous just by
Charlie printing the word RENOWNED. Envelopes arrived through the
mail slot full of money. Just on medicines alone we sometimes had fifty
orders a week, at an average three dollars each which was six hundred a
MONTH. At that rate we might some day be making more than seven
thousand a year, Charlie said, and while I couldn't hardly believe him, the
numbers were the carrot that kept the stick of hard work at our backs, filling the orders for Lunar Remedy till all hours of the night. *Please Madame
advise if your remedy is a good preventative?*

There was no law against Prevention at all and we began to sell preventatives, too, female syringes, newfangled rubber pessaries, and French
letters. We did not hear complaints, not one, despite the nauseating effects
of the cantharides and the tansy oil in our medicines. Everybody knew the
tablets we sold was not fail-safe. But, they offered the best chance of success
short of an Interference. Especially now with my wee daughter gurgling on
my shoulder, Interference was nothing I wished to be part of.

Our money jar filled up and overflowed. On a Friday evening, Charlie
came home from delivering a lot of orders to the post office and asked for
it off the shelf, the glass green with cash. We two poured it out between us
on the table and counted. Little Belle laughed at the sparkle and clink and
reached her tiny hands out, grabbing.

—She likes it, Charlie said, and propped her up next to the pile of money.

The baby hummed, sucking something like it was a peppermint. I fished my finger between her four milk teeth and retrieved a silver dollar.

—Give me that, ya wee thief, I said. She howled in rage.

—She likes the taste of silver, Charlie said.

—So do I. And that made three of us.

Late into the night we stacked the change, flattened the bills into piles, entered numbers into a ledger. Our dreams was dressed in silk and velvet now, not shoddy nor mungo no more. We had money to travel to Chicago in style, and I felt sure that when my sister got a look at the French lace at my sleeves, she would sit me up beside her on the leather of her carriage perch, and we'd ride out with harness bells ringing, and velvet around our shoulders to find our Joe. It was bound to happen now.

But on a September morning in 1871, the postman brought me a letter that squelched that plan. It was a packet of news from Dutch, and it was not her usual list of parties and fashions, but tiny pages torn from a pocket diary, written over the years in miniature handwriting, in the haste and despair of a kidnapped prisoner, pressed into an envelope.

Chapter Twenty-Five

A Fraud

February the twelfth, 1868

My Darling sister Axie,

*I have just made the most terrible—wonderful discovery.
While sitting at Mother's dressing table, I saw some torn bits of a
letter in the wastebasket, and peering at it I noticed a scrap with
what appeared to be your name. Mother was not around, so with
a pounding heart I gathered up the bits of paper and put them in
my pocket.*

*Imagine my shock to find when I assembled the pieces that they
constituted a letter from you.*

*Oh Axie! I am sorry I have not written to you in all this time
but you must understand my terrible reasons: I was told you were
dead. I know no other way to say it.*

*From just after we parted until now I have gone about my
life believing that you were in heaven with our Mam, and the
discovery of such deception confounds me no end. Still (if only for
myself) I will try to explain Mother's conduct and tell you as much
as I can of what has happened to me since last we saw each other.*

*You see, I have no address for you. There was no envelope
to be found, and I have searched in vain for it. I am beyond
distress, for even as I write I see no way to get word to you. I
scarcely believe you are real. It's as if I have been touched by a
ghost. As if I write to a ghost.*

March, 1868

*I resume, again in haste. It is only safe to write in this diary
when there is no one about. It would be terrible if anyone found
it, or discovered that I know the wonderful secret, that my sister
is alive! but I cannot stop thinking of you, and am determined to
write this chronicle in hopes you will one day read it.*

*It pains me to think how Mother has deceived you, writing you
news of me and pretending that I was the author of the letters
you apparently received. Since my discovery of your letter I have
tried to understand why she might do this. From listening to the
servants talk, I know that many years ago, in Rockford, Mother
lost a child, a girl who would be around the same age and
appearance as myself. I believe that as far as she is concerned, I
am that child.*

*Please do not get the wrong idea about Mother. She is a lovely
lady, but very delicate in health. I have seen her faint dead away
at the slightest suggestion of pain, or the least idea of strife.
Everybody knows not to upset her, for she turns terribly pale, and
has miserable headaches and tempestuous outbursts. Oh nobody
loves me! she cries until we calm her.*

*So, on strict orders, I have never been allowed to talk about
you, or Joe, or Mam, or New York, not to anybody. Father says
do not make Mother upset, so all these years I have tried to heed
their wishes. Mother says she cannot be happy unless I am her
own daughter, Lily Ambrose, and so I have been, dutifully. I
must say that it was easier to do this before, when I believed you
to be in Heaven. But now, I am overcome so profoundly by this
evidence of you I hardly know where to turn except to this little
diary.*

*That first summer—eight years ago! every day I asked when I
could see you and our brother. Whenever I asked Mother became
very sad and had to lie down on her couch.*

*Let's not talk about that, she said. One day, in town, she told
me to wave goodbye to the train pulling out. Then, as it left,
Mother said, Do you know that your sister, Annie, was on the*

train? She said you were going back to New York, to take care of our mother.

And I cried and was sad that you would leave me and Joe. But Mother said, Oh, now, Lily, let the past be the past. She did not wish to discuss these matters any more and said we should think about nice things like Christmas. She said she had prayed for a good little daughter, and here I was. She asked over and over did I love her? and if I said yes she would smile, and her eyes filled with kindness the way warm water fills with the color of tea, when it steeps. You'd do anything to make her smile on you. I tried to be good, Axie, I learned all my psalms as Mother wished. I did my lessons, and kept my stockings neat. But it was hard to please Mother as she liked me to.

One afternoon, she led me to a seat next to her on the sofa. She said she was afraid she had some sad tidings from New York. And she said—I will never forget it—Your sister Ann Muldoon has passed away. I'm very sorry.

Mother explained that you had found our mother, but a few weeks ago you and Mam were stricken with fever, and died. She said you two were angels in heaven now. I did not cry then. All I remember is that I pressed the end of my pencil hard into the velvet upholstery so it pierced the fabric. Horsehair poked through and Mother heard the sound of fabric ripping. I was only a girl of seven.

What have you done? she scolded me, and because I was still unschooled, I said, I ain't done nothing. It always made Mother so unhappy when I spoke that way. She told me again quite heatedly that I must not say "I ain't" or "I haven't done nothing." It's a double negative, she said, for if you have not done nothing, why, then you have done something, isn't that right? Yet all the time it was Mother who had done something wrong, and lied to us both.

Only when she heard me crying for you my dead sister and my dead mother and my lost brother did she take me in her arms and soothe me down, and so I loved her then, what other choice did I have?

I must end this entry fast—my mother's carriage is in front, earlier than expected, and I must hide this journal where she will not find it and pick up again when I get a chance. Please forgive this scribble.

September

Mother always hated the town of Rockford. There was nothing to do, she said. What life required was chamber music in a beautifully appointed room. A person had to talk about literature and fashion! But where would she do that on the terrible prairie? When she talked that way I would comfort her and say Poor Mother, but she was not easily consoled and suffered hysteria and took to her bed.

The year when I turned eight, Father put Mother and me on a train to Chicago. We were moving there, he said, and he would join us in a month.

On that journey, Mother told me that I spoke so properly now, and was so refined, that no one in Chicago need ever know that I was an adopted child. It would be so much easier for me if I never mentioned it. People could be unkind, she said. There was no reason for them to suspect my origins. She said I was their own little daughter Lillian Ambrose, and any talk of anything else was forbidden. She asked me to remember please not to kiss my thumb or cross myself or any of that Papist nonsense.

And so I never did mention any of my past to a soul, and, I am sorry to say, for years I lost sight of where I had come from and thought only of the present. There was so much to see and do, and I hope I do not sound ungrateful for my good fortune. We moved to a new home on Lake Shore Drive, with a carriage house and a garden. You can imagine the whirl of parties. When I was not in school, I was at a dress fitting, or going with Mother to buy dancing slippers. There is not much to report on those years.

Axie, I do not know how I'll ever see you or Joseph again, or even be able to mail these pages. Why should I bother to write

*more? Mother watches over me so carefully. If I asked any of
the staff to research your whereabouts, surely she would hear of
it. They are like spies against me, Axie. I cannot go to my room
without a maid following to ask after my welfare. (At the moment
I write this in the lavatory, where I am supposed to be taking
a bath. I splash the water to deceive the housemaid.) I am not
allowed to visit the other girls from school unless my governess
is by my side. It is too awkward an arrangement, and so I have
few companions but my cousin Clara, whom I seldom see. I
don't know what to do. It seems no use to continue writing this
account.*

March 1870

    *I scarcely believe it but after two years I have found another
letter from you in Mother's reticule, and by some miracle this
time it is in an envelope with the address clearly marked. I am
trembling with excitement. My sister! I admit I had begun to
believe you were dead after all, that the scraps I found was only
a dream. But today I know you are real. You live on Greenwich
Street. You are Mrs. Charles G. Jones and you have a little girl.
Your letter was in Mother's handbag, so full of news about your
daughter and your wish to see me. I am overcome reading it. I
should not have been searching her possessions, but in truth
I was only hunting for a hair comb and there it was. And now I
know why all my previous efforts to discover another letter from
you have failed—it seems you've been writing to the address
downtown at my father's office—which means that he has gone
along with this deception. I would like to condemn him and my
mother but I cannot—for they are kind people and have been
good to me. You must please promise never to reveal me. I know
I can trust you. I will attempt to mail these pages as soon as I
can devise a way. Oh Axie, I feel that something will happen
now, at last.*

October 1870

*Dear Axie, forgive the long time since I have added to this
account but something HAS happened, and I must report on the
most exciting news of my life. I am engaged! Perhaps Mother has
written you all about the reasons for my distraction. My fiancé
is Eliot VanDerWeil, Jr. He is my cousin—my father's cousin's
son, really my second cousin. Oh, I can scarcely believe it. Just
now he took me for a drive along the lakeshore. As we sat there
on a bench, he proposed to me so gallantly, down on his knees. I
thought at first he was joking, and I said as much. But he had a
ring in his pocket—a gold band with pearl and diamonds—and
he put it on my finger even before I said yes. Oh if you could see
him. His green eyes do sparkle! Mother says he is quite the catch
for any young lady, and I must say—*

May 1871

*Please forgive the abrupt end to my words above—now almost
a year old. I was too distracted and unable to write again till
now. I can only assume that Mother has told you all the details of
my wedding to Eliot. Just now I came across my diary hidden in
a trunk, and at last have found a moment when it is safe to take
it up again.*

*My plan was to tell my dear husband the truth, once we were
married. But if anything, I fear discovery even more, for as
Mother explained, Eliot is a wealthy man, and quite active in the
Methodist Church. If the family should discover my origins, he
could disown me on the grounds that he had been deceived. He
might disinherit any children we will have, knowing that I was
born a ~~XXXXXX~~ She has convinced me that she is right, and
there are any number of reasons for me to keep our secret. Really,
it is not difficult. We have kept it now already for ten years. I
will attempt very soon to mail these pages to you with an address
where you might write back.*

*You must understand that Mother is only trying to protect my
future and to maintain good relations within the family, and she
has succeeded admirably. Eliot and I have a lovely home. We are*

*always at parties and concerts. (Did I mention to you that I enjoy
singing lieder music?) We have traveled to Paris and London.
We are sure to stop one day in New York—and even now I
scheme about how we might meet. It is still nearly impossible to
find time alone, for Mother often travels with us, and Eliot is as
jealous of my independence as she ever was, but I am determined.*

September 16th 1871

Axie!

*God forgive me I am here now, TODAY, in New York, and
will try to pass this account to the Hotel clerk to deliver to you
before we sail for Calais the morning of the 18th. I pray that
you still reside at your address in Greenwich Street. Please meet
me tomorrow evening (the 17th), in the lobby of the Hotel Astor,
at eight o'clock in the evening, as my husband will be at his
gentlemen's club. If anyone should ask, please say you are Mrs.
Ann Jones, an acquaintance from my school days at Crawford
School for Young Ladies. If I am with a gentleman or anyone
else please do not speak to me, I beg you. If you ever should
identify me as your sister I feel certain I would be in danger of
losing everything. —Lillian*

Chapter Twenty-Six

A Chance Encounter

*S*he was here. My sister.

I read her packet of pages with a sick loose feeling like I'd swallowed bitter aloes and would now come apart at the joints. The delicate small pieces of paper trembled in my hands. A whiff of rosewater came off them, and one of the pages was stained, with tears I figured, spilled by Dutch for the ten years gone past, while she believed I was dead and I thought she had forgotten me. Now she was a married lady of nineteen, here in New York. I might meet her in a hotel as easy as walking out the door. I sat down in my chair and held my head in my hands. She was here.

—What is it? Charlie asked, when he came in and saw my face.

I handed him the packet and while he read it he whistled through his teeth.

—Charlie, I said, trembling, —my sister is only down the street.

—Let's go find her right now, then, he said, and went for his hat.

For a shiny minute, I had a picture in mind of us two sisters flying across a hotel lobby, past the potted palms and the bellhops, catapulting into each other's arms. But no, fate's cruel fingernails had come to rake me across the face.

—The date, I cried. —What is today's date?

—The eighteenth of September, my husband told me. But it was the SEVENTEENTH she'd wanted to meet me. I had missed her. The letter arrived too late. She had sailed for Calais already this morning, off and gone to the backside of the moon. I set her pages down, and covered my mouth with the flat of my hand. —I've missed her.

Charlie put his hand on my shoulder. —At least the dirty deeds of that lying excuse of a so-called mother of hers have been exposed.

—All this time she thought I was dead.

I went in a rush off to the Hotel Astor to find her in case of a mistake, but the clerk informed me the VanDerWeils had departed. I could not be consoled. That night the ghost of my Mam visited me keening, full of reproach while my sister floated in my dreams, wearing pearls. Despite my husband's leg draped over mine under the covers, and the round bundle of the sleeping Belle warm in the bed between us, a dark bile of longing covered me along with the blankets. I loomed around the house lost in blue thoughts and when I worked filling orders for Lunar Remedy often my attention was drawn to the far distance, gazing off like relief was there if only I knew how to look.

—Sweeten up, said my husband when he tired of my black mood.

—Easy for you to say, says I, snappish.

—He who dwells in the past robs the present, he quoted, Mr. Philosopher. He would not coddle me or humor me, he was too busy yes he was, for Madame DeBeausacq's remedy required special ingredients in large quantities, and Charlie had found a farmer up the river whose rye field was corrupted with ergot and he'd contracted to buy the lot at a discount. Off he hurried in great excitement to Poughkeepsie to fetch it, while I toiled lonesome over the stove, the pill press and the washboard, a toddler at my skirts. He talked of ergot and advertisements and profit whilst I mourned my sister and worried that when he was out of my sight somebody would steal him like all my loved ones was stolen, some Poughkeepsie Polly in pantaloons. He only laughed and promised he would bring Annabelle a present. And what would he bring me? I wondered. While at Mrs. Evans' I had seen ladies whose husbands brought them a case of the Venus Curse, a ghastly pox that made the hair bald in patches, the skin all over pustules, and worst was they gave it to the babies. Some present. That Curse was the reason so many children were born dead. And now Charlie was in Poughkeepsie, and while wondering what he'd bring me, I took the train of mistrust all the way from a present to a pox, suspecting my husband even without no evidence, expecting betrayal at every depot.

What he did bring me was the news he'd met a Private Detective, Mr. Renaldo Snope, a swashbuckling fellow, Charlie said, who claimed for a hundred dollars he would find Joe Muldoon Trow and bring him to us in a matter of months.

—Did you pay him? says I very eager.

—Half, says Charlie, appeasing me. —And the rest on delivery of information.

So I pinned my hopes on Snope, till it became a little rhyme with us. Heard from Snope? Nope. While the joke was funny the reason was not, and in time the joke was not either, for it seemed Snope had absconded with our deposit.

In those bewildered days, it was my little Annabelle who brought me the most of comfort and peace, and the business of Madame DeBeausacq which brought me distraction. One fine morning when Charlie was off and away somewheres, I put my two year old daughter on my hip and carried her out to the street. She babbled and razzed as we went along, her nose wrinkled in mischief.

—To Market, to market, to buy a fat hen, I sang to her.

—Hen! she cried.

At the butcher's I ordered for the week just like snapping my fingers. —A rump of beef, a pound of neat's tongue, and six blutwurst. No more scrag of mutton or neck bones, for me. I was a lady.

—Will that be all, Mrs. Jones? Oppenheimer the counterman asked from beneath the ledges of his mustache.

—Yes, thank you, I said, and paid him.

At the bakery I bought Annabelle a cinnamon bun. The brown sugar smudged on her lips and she hummed at the taste. The shop assistant laughed. —That's a lovely girl you have there, Mrs. Jones.

We went out of the shop quite proud, past the fond envious glances of the women filling their market bags. They cooed at my daughter admiring how the April sun shone off her black curls. Though her blue eyes were bright with mischief, she had a fairy beauty like my Dutch so that sometimes when I looked at her I was struck mute by memory and cramped with despair over where was my sister?

At the grocery I bought a pound of sugar and some coffee. Mr. Pingree chucked the baby under the chin and asked, —Should I put it on your account, Mrs. Jones?

I had an account. I was Mrs. Jones. I paid our bills in full. My calfskin boots laced prettily up the ankle and carried me past the misfortunate and the wretched of the street. I did not look at them. They would grab me by the throat. They would drag me and my Annabelle back to the gutter where they grumbled and stank and begged. The weight of her on my hip was the same as our Joe's when I lost him. As we came from the grocery with our packages, we passed a heap of urchins in a corner, shoeless and crusted with disease, the poor orphan castaways of a bad world. An old soldier crutched along with his leg cut off and his eyes dead. We passed a man spatchcocked in the alley, his beard crusted with dark matter. Ahead was a woman limping with her one hand out, the other clutching a boy not bigger than my daughter. You could hear his crying from a ways off.

—Baby cryin', announced my daughter. —Baby's sad.

The limping woman turned and came back in our direction, and as she approached I saw with a lurch how well I knew her. She was Greta, near unrecognizable. I turned on my heel fast and walked the other way. My stomach was sick with blame. Her eyes bored holes in my back. I turned again. —Greta, I cried.

She saw it was me. I saw she had a scab on her chin. After three years we was face to face again, our fortunes told, children hanging off our hips. The crowd teemed around, dogs at our ankles, carts rattling, peddlers crying out.

—Greta. I threw my reluctant arms around her. The smell of rank circumstances, grease and suet rose off her clothes, out from her skin. Her hair that was once so glossy was dull now and straggled. When she pulled back I seen dark rinds around the nails of her fingers, the collar of her neck.

—What is your boy's name? I said.

—Willi.

I gave him the half a cinnamon bun out of Belle's hand. He reached for it like a little organ grinder monkey and ate it steadily still hiccuping in tears. When she saw him with it, my daughter let out a screech. —No, now you've had enough, greedycat, so you have, I scolded her, dug in my pocket and thrust a fistful of money at Greta.

—I won't take it, she said.

—I have a business, I said. —Selling medicines.

—Good for you, then. She bit her lips and her chin dimpled with ingrown tears.

—What happened? I whispered. —What happened to you?

—When they saw I vass . . . *schwanger* . . . they threw me out the door to the street, in the night time, mit nothing, only the boots on my feet.

She stood with the light slanting through the buildings behind her, holding her filthy boy.

—Where did you go?

She shrugged. It was a long story painted in the gray color of her face.

—Where do you stay now?

—In the Bend. At the basement of Ratzinger's.

Ratzinger's was a cesspit, famous as a fortress of thieves and diseased hoors and murderers and hopeless hopheads, disciples of the pipe. Nobody who landed there lived many birthdays. I searched her for signs of pox and though no scabs nor ulcers was apparent yet I figured she was good as doomed.

—You'll need this. I pushed a handful of money at her. —Take it.

She did not meet my eyes as she took the coins and started away, her gait slow.

—Come with me, I called after her, regretting it even as the words left my mouth.

She didn't protest, only followed me home. I didn't ask her more questions because I known the answers. Where she lived? In a hole. How? By such means as necessary. The father of her boy? A scut.

What would she say when she saw my five nice rooms, lace curtains in the parlor, the beef barrel full in the corner of the kitchen? She said nothing, only slumped in a chair with her son, eyes dull. I made them tea and boiled eggs. She and Willi ate quietly, his small teeth tearing at bread. Then, while Willi slept, she told me her sorry details, so ashamed.

—Now again, such *Kümmerniss,* she said, —I'm in trouble.

—Trouble.

—Two months.

I received this news flinching, very quiet, and put my hand out to cover hers. She took it away. I went to the crate where tablets were labeled, packaged for mailing. Without her asking me I gave Greta two bottles of Lunar medicine, as it was a fact that her delicate condition was a grim sentence for her and Willi and whatever child was mustering in her to be born. They would not last long in Ratzinger's hole. —Take these five times a day for three days.

—I heff tried them, she said, her voice dull. —They don't work.

—They sometimes don't. I'm not going to lie to you. But they sometimes do, too.

—And if they don't?

I hesitated. —They could scrape you.

—Who?

—There was a woman on Lispenard. Named Costello.

—I can't pay. Now she thrust her chin forward, pointing at me. —You, she said, very fierce.

—Me?

—Do it, she said, her eyes burning. —You sell the medicine but what about when it doesn't do what you say? What do you do then? Greta stared me down across the table. Her son had fallen asleep on her lap, his fingers in his mouth. Clear strings of drool fell from his lips. My own child was asleep in her crib.

You said once before it was a murder, I said, faltering. —You said Mrs. Evans does murders.

—Pphh, she snorted. —So I was wrong.

Were you?

—You're the one Axie. You said you can't kill a thing before it's alive. So. Do it then.

I looked away from her. Swallowed.

—Do it right now, said Greta. —Right now.

—I never have. But it's true I felt a type of thrill. Like a power, because I could help her. *Always help the poor things if nobody else will,* my teacher said.

—Everybody knows you vass the assistant, Greta hissed.

—I only watched. I don't have the practice.

—You'll practice right here then. You know you can. You know.

I began to shake. —You could die of it. Just of the scraping.

—I'll die anyway. And after that so will my son.

—Greta don't ask me.

—I'm asking.

—It hurts, I said. —It'll hurt you. Terrible.

—Pain now or pain later. No difference.

Pain later was pain I knew and it was worse and lasted longer and there was more that could go wrong. It was well known Mrs. Evans said that *more ladies die struggling their babies to be born than ever die from premature delivery* but that fact did not make such premature delivery procedures safe nor tidy nor something I'd like to try now.

—No, I said.

—Already I can't feed Willi or myself. We're good as dead now. Look at us. And you say to me NO?

The boy stirred in her arms, so thin, a crust of dry blood at his nose, a red rash on the exposed shank of his leg. His eyelashes made dark half circles on his cheek, and his lips were slightly parted as he breathed. He was a pure beauty even filthy as he was, so dirty that flies might rest on his eyelids as on a carcass, and his mother no better, just a husk left of her. Still when she looked at her son a softness came to my friend's face so I known she was not depraved nor fallen to a state of infamy such as the Dix claimed was the condition of all hoors.

—This new one, she said, —it will be born in winter. Outside how do we live? We will die, and for why? For nothing. Because you say no.

—Don't ask me.

—They're asleep. The *Kinder*. Do it now.

—I don't know how.

—You can't deny me.

—Greta.

—If you don't, she said, —I'll do it myself.

It was the look in her eye. Raw. Clear and burning like spirits of turpentine that could flame up and consume her.

—What if I do it wrong?

—This is what I want, for my son and for me. I'm asking. How can you deny me?

It was Mrs. Evans' voice in my head that afternoon. I heard her at my shoulder, the cold sun streaming down on Greta Weiss through the window of our humble parlor. *You do not need light, only feel your way, and give the girl a glass of spirits as stiff as she can stand.* I poured Greta a glass of Barbados rum that Charlie kept, and poured her another. I kissed her. I took the kit of tools from the cupboard and unwrapped them from the chamois cloth. We placed Willi asleep next to Annabelle napping. My patient slipped off her rancid underthings with a grim face not at all resembling Greta the bright servant girl who gave me a petticoat and went gaily with me into the night of my sixteenth birthday.

—I don't want to hurt you, I told my friend.

—I don't care! Even if I say stop, do not stop.

—All right.

—Hurry, she said. —Hurry.

The girl is placed across the bed, with her feet resting on two chairs.

—Feet up, I said, tense.

Greta was obedient, but in the eyes she was fierce and determined. I sat on a low stool between the chairs, below her skirts. I got a curette from Mrs. Evans' kit and wrapped it at the end with gauze. I had a basin ready.

Pass the two fingers of the left hand within.

Greta's eyes were shut. She bit her lips.

You will maneuver the left hand fingers, and using them to enlarge the portal, with the right hand you will pass along the instrument using your left hand fingers as the guide, and finding the resistance there at the neck you will come to a second resistance, but through the opening you will push but not forcefully, and maneuver the instrument upward around a bend. This is the tricky part which is why the curette is a crooked tool. Whatever you do don't go back straight or use a sharp probe. If you do you will perforate the woman and she will die. You are only to perforate the sack. When you sense you're past the obstruction you will discover what matter is there. It will be soft as the liver of a chicken is soft but moreso even than that. The walls are firm but delicate. You will scrape gently two or three times.

I done all this, listening for the faint gritted sound.

Like cleaning the guts of a pumpkin.

Greta cried out. She thrashed her head. The neighbors would hear, I thought.

Withdraw as much of the obstruction as will come away.

Greta pulled her hair and suffered, but what she said when she cried I

didn't know as it was in her hard language and I made my ears slam shut
against the sounds even as my nerves was peeled raw by her sharp breath
and her high whimper and her scream.

—I can't do this, I said, and stopped.

—Don't stop, Greta said, so wild. —I told you.

I began again.

*Do not listen to her cries. Focus down hard on the innards, the twists and
turns you must follow to relieve her. Just say, You're doing fine, missus. Say,
It won't be long. It will only be a longer torture Axie if you stop each time she
winces. You don't stop until you've got it. If you leave any behind it will fester
and she will die.*

—Stop, Greta shrieked.

*When she cries out remember all the ladies who have stood worse and longer,
and remember that it is a woman's lot to suffer, and she will not die if you do as I
say. Only say to her, Shush, there, there, love, soon it will be all over.*

—Shh, there, there, I said, shaky. —Soon it will be all over, love.

I was nauseous. The smell of fear was on us both. Greta cursed me in
German like a witch. I grit my teeth and felt the sap drain out of my muscles so I was weak.

*If she loses her mind or will not cooperate you will tell her BE STILL, for if
she thrashes too much she will only endanger herself.*

—Axie, she said, and vomited.

—Don't move do you hear me? I said, harsh. —You'll make me puncture
you.

I feared her little son and my Belle would awake at the noise and come
and see her lying there like I seen my mother, with Bernie and the bloody
bowl alongside. I wanted to hurry *but you cannot hurry,* Mrs. Evans said. *You
must take the time it needs.*

*Withdraw the instrument, and discard any contents in the bowl and rinse the
interior with a solution of ergot in vinegar.*

Now I mixed the solution and took the female syringe from among
Mrs. Evans' tools and filled it. I brought it to Greta by the window. Little
stutters of breath came out of her.

—I will have to bathe you now, I said.

Greta did not speak, only looked at me with eyes white and bulging like
a horse gone down in the street. —Do it. Hurry, Gott d*** you.

I administered the solution directly into the narrow neck of the organ within, pressing the bulb and as I worked she moaned and vomited again and I was sick myself. I went across the room and was sick where she did not see me and then went back to her. Her skin was pale as eggshell and clammy. Shaky I fed her sips of water while she whimpered and was so dizzy, she said. I gave her the last dose of laudanum I had left over from Mrs. Evans. —Keep that down now it's all I have. It will dull you down.

After you have cleansed her you must grip a roll of gauze which again with the long instrument you will guide into the opening, but only so far as where you can pack it, leaving just a tail of material about an inch or two protruding down into the cavity for it will open the portal and nature will ease the rest of the way. I done this with trepidation and difficulty over fifteen minutes as my patient thrashed and tossed her head wild on the pillow, the sheet clamped between her teeth.

—There, there, shh. Done, I said at last.

My friend wept. I climbed next to her in the bed. —I am sorry, I am so sorry. I stroked her poor infested hoory head and cried along with her. It would be a choir when the babies awoke, I told her, the four of us crying for a bottle. —If only you and me had ourselves some gin, I said, and she laughed at that but not for real.

—In thirty minutes, I said, —maybe longer, the bleeding will start up strongly, and you'll have cramps so terrible you will feel you are dying but you won't die, and after some hours you'll remove the gauze plug and be relieved of the rest of the obstruction once and for all.

—If I die, she said quietly, —you will take Willi.

—Yes.

—Promise.

—Yes.

—Thank you, she whispered.

Many hours later while she slept at last, I took the basin. Inside was no more than small clots of viscera, soft like giblets. I tried not to see it but failed, and whether it was from accident or some terrible fascination I could not avoid confronting the fruits of my mercy. It was a red clump not bigger than a walnut. There in its midst was a pale tracing outlined in the shape of a hand, like the stump-fingered hand of a wee monster or a fish if fish had hands, the bones translucent. It was the tiny mitt of a salamander which is a fairy spirit who lives in fire. To the fire is where this sprout was given, for it was not alive yet, no more than a seed is alive, never quick at all, at all. What came to mind then was that Bible Mrs. Evans read, the words something like *better the miscarriage, for it never sees the sun, nor knows anything, and better is the one who has never existed for it knows not the evil that is.* And I reasoned that to deliver it now was only to prevent a death or a doomed orphan, to save my friend, and my friend's son. Still I shuddered, for a spirit had passed its touch along my spine. Did I feel I had done a murder? No. I felt I had done a mercy. And yet I was altered ever since, for the tracing of bone I seen was the outline of what might have been and now wasn't, because of me, and I knew myself after that to have the soul of a midwife, who could live with the complexities.

Chapter Twenty-Seven

Assistant

*S*ome hours later Charlie's boots thundered on the stairs, and then he was at the door hungry for his dinner. I went with our daughter in my arms and stopped him.

—Don't go in.

—How can you keep me from my own house? For what reason? His temper was up, fast. —Out of the way.

—Greta's here. In our bed.

—With a customer? What? Have we started a cat house?

My nerves was unraveled enough already and so when he called my friend a flagabout I flown straight off the handle and shot him across the face with the flat of my hand. —What do you know about anything? I cried, shocked at myself.

And he slapped me back, right across the cheek.

Annabelle started up crying and he'd have struck me again, if she hadn't. —Da, she sobbed, with her two year old tears, —Da! as he reeled away, into the hall.

—I'll be leaving now then Mrs. Jones before I wale on you again, he said, flexing his knuckles.

—Charlie.

—I'm gone. He started down the stairs.

—Da, Annabelle cried, her voice echoing in the stairwell. —Wheresa mousie, Da?

Charlie stopped. He clutched at his heart for she had got him right in it.

—Mousie? she said. It was a game Belle had with him, for he'd convinced her he had a creature named Whiskers in his pocket. —Da?

Unable to resist her Charlie returned, smoldering at me and winking at his daughter, the whole family in a welter of confusion. He reached in his pocket where he pretended to find the mouse. —Here he is! he cried. —Whiskers! Acting like he was not furious he placed the pretend creature on Annabelle's head, and ran his fingers down her back and pointed toward the floorboards. —Look! he cried, as if it had run off. —Gone.

And our little girl laughed and laughed. It never failed. —Again!

I quieted her and sent her toddling back inside where I could hear her call for us through the door I shut, so she would not see her father leaving her mother once and for all because of what I done. —Mam!

—There's no call to use your FISTS, Charlie said, his voice scary.

—There's no call to say Greta's a HOOR.

—She is, though, ain't she? I saw her myself in the streets flagging about in her petticoat.

—And you never mentioned nothing of it?

—It's well known in the taverns your Greta's a dirty shake, Charlie said. —AND she has a child.

—That same child is here too. Her boy.

My husband cursed. The print of my hand was red on his cheek, his eyes dark. —The devil is going on, he said, helplesslike and confused.

—Charlie, I cried now very quiet so the neighbors would not open their doors for a free drama. And I told him. What I done. Scrape, I said. Blood. I said it was in the bin.

—H***, he said, and worse. —You want to tempt the devil on us, is that right? And the traps?

—Greta ASKED me.

—If she asked you to light yourself on FIRE, would you do it?

—It's what she WANTED. To save her own life. And the boy's too.

—But it's not right.

—It's not wrong neither, is it? If I didn't, she'd've done it herself, with a piece of whalebone from a corset.

—Then LET her do it herself. Do you want to bring the traps on us and lose everything? All our earnings?

—She would die, don't you know? What's more the traps don't care and never bothered Evans and they won't bother us over this neither. It was the one time.

—Is that what you were doing there, then, on Chatham Street?

—None of your business, I said. —It's women's private matters.

He stared at me like I was a stranger. Like he imagined in grim pictures what I done with Mrs. Evans. What I done for my friend. I feared what he thought of me, and how I would disgust him, and that he would leave me. —What else would you have me do? I cried. —Leave Greta on the road? With her boy no bigger than a minute? Weren't me and you orphans once? And don't we know their chances? And don't we see them on every corner? The little ones with no mothers?

With each of my questions he flinched. —Well, he said, and steadied himself against the banister. —I've seen her boy—

He stopped then. In all the words he didn't say it was plain he was brooding about when the traps found him years ago, starved on the docks, singing McGinty, three years old, same size as Willi and dirty as a pigeon nest. He never did know why his own mother lost him.

—I'll be off then, he said, very gruff. —It's not a man's place.

He didn't say where he was going or if he'd be back. He only took off clattering down the stairs, despite my calling after him and our wee girl crying inside for her Da and that Mouse.

I made supper. Greta half slept on the bed with her boy quiet beside her. Annabelle played on the floorboards with her bucket of corks, the stoppers of malt bottles and mustard jars, all of them made into cork dolls by her Dad. He'd carved heads in the corks and drew faces on. No matter that she had a real china doll now like I never had, buttercup hair and rosebud mouth. She liked these poor corks better, giving them nonsense names: Gagala and Glowpin. Watching her play so sweet I cursed my own hot temper, sorry I hit Charlie and argued. For sure he'd never come back this time because of what I done for my friend.

And my friend was in a bad way. She stirred in the bed and then stood up gingerly. She glanced at us where we ate our salt pork and apples and walked over to the chamber pot. Vomited right in it.

Her son sat on the bed and whimpered. —Ma.

—Axie, said Greta. She held her belly doubled forward, and I went to the bed where I gave her whiskey and took her boy up in my arms.

—C'mon son, I said, and brung him over to Annabelle playing on the floor. The two *Kinder* as Greta called them watched each other very solemn. Annabelle then presented the boy a cork. He took it in his grimy fingers. Tasted it. She smiled and tasted one, too, copying him. They had a laugh over it, the monkeys.

Greta was back on the bed now. —Pull your knees to the chest, I said. And she folded herself into an egg, her eyes shut. All night the poor woman bled and moaned and cursed. I lay alongside her and crooned soft words. I helped her to sit and walk and helped her back to the bed. I emptied the basin. She would die, I thought. What had I done? There was nothing left of her. Her face was the boiled color of suet.

Charlie did not come home. Not by supper the next day. Not by midnight. He was dead drunk in a cat house. Was he?

Annabelle asked, —Where's my Da?

I snapped at her, —He's back when he's back.

—He'll have some trinket on the side somewhere, Greta said, with a smirk, feeling better, evidently. —*Ein kleines Schmuckstück.*

—Don't say that. Don't say *Schmuckstück* to me.

—They all do.

—They don't, I said. —Not all.

—I would know.

—So you would, wouldn't you? I said, very nasty, but she gave me a look so hurt I took it back. —Sorry. Still, was she right? The idea had its rat teeth in me again. That Charlie had a piece of trade somewheres. *Schmuckstück.* He was with her at this minute. While I emptied the bin in the gutter and bottled tablets in the kitchen, he whispered in her baubled ear. He loomed over her painted lips in pictures formed by my jealous demons. I was half mad with imagining it.

*   *   *

Days passed. My friend and patient Greta was not dead. She was well, brushing her hair, minding Willi and Annabelle. There they were on the floor, banging spoons on pots. Willi was cleaned up nice, too. His hair was the pale color of wax beans, not dark like his mother's. She said his father was a big Swede in military boots. She sang the children beer hall songs and called them *Liebchen* and made them little rolls sprinkled with sugar called kugel and irritated me with her habit of eating sunflower nuts and dropping the cracked shells like black scabs all over the floor. I was more than irritable, I was beside myself.

At dinner on the fourth day Charlie walked in.

—Halloo, he said, wary like he might sail off again if the wind was wrong. —How's the women?

Belle charged him and he swung her up and kissed her. Greta left us alone, taking the children to the back room.

—Did you miss me? Charlie said.

I kept up chopping the cabbage, shredding it to white ribbons.

—Mrs. Jones, I asked a question. Did you miss me?

—Where've YOU been? My knife whacked the wood block with angry chops.

—In Trenton, New Jersey, where I contracted with an agent to sell your Remedy. Thus earning us fifty percent of what business she does, so don't cast your disbelieving eyes on me, Mrs. Jones.

—Four DAYS you were gone.

—Four days is a blink. A swallow of spit. Four days. Pfft.

—Where were you in FACT?

—Like I said. Contracting an agent in Trenton.

—What more was you contracting?

—You're a jealous f***ing cat, aren't you? Where ELSE was I supposed to go, then, with you running a hoors' hospital here in my own home and saying it's a woman's place not fit for a man?

—YOU said that, not me.

—Who would blame me if I sought comfort elsewheres? he cried —Which I did NOT. Instead yours truly was sleeping on a hard bench of a traveling coach in my working boots and laid up in a terrible inn and here I am back now. And yet when I ask, did you miss me? you chop the cabbage like it was my own head! A fine fiddler's welcome. He stormed about the room, swallowing whiskey, flinging his shirt off, collar and cuffs, so I seen the old pale scars on his back again and was reminded anew I wasn't the only one with no mother. The two of us never would trust no one, I thought. I nursed my suspicions over him and prepared for further argument.

—I won't put Greta out, I told him, —if that's what you're thinking.

—Why'd I be thinking that?

—You said we wasn't running a hospital.

—Is that what this is now?

—Maybe. She and Willi got nowhere to go.

—So let them stay, he said, with a shrug. —We'll employ Greta to make tablets, so's she won't have to flag about, then.

And thus he undid me, for instead of a fight, Charlie employed my friend, and retrieved the children from her watch. He went down on the floor to play with them, saying he was a lion, and was hungry. —Some nice tasty children for my dinner! he roared, so they laughed. Charlie never mentioned nothing else about What Happened, and all was well again on Greenwich Street.

Now Greta had a bed in the nursery with Willi and Annabelle. Charlie didn't appear to mind her there. The babies trundled around the premises like whelps vying for scraps and took naps side by side, their fat wee fingers laced. While Greta fussed at her boy and coddled him, Charlie roughed him about boxing and riding him horsie on his knee. Willi called him Uncle and called me his Auntie. Our place was jolly for a time, till Charlie was off again on another mission, he said, to deliver a batch of Madame DeBeausacq's Elixir to Newark.

—It seems Madame is your excuse to wander, I accused him when he returned a week afterwards.

—You could say Madame is my mistress, he said, all smilinglike.

—You say such things deliberate to hurt me.

—But she is you and you are she. You're my wife and my mistress both, Mrs. Jones.

I did not like his reply for it was too clever. Soon, off he went once more, this time to Brooklyn, claiming to conduct the business of Madame far afield, while I conducted it right in the kitchen, toiling as usual. He was a man out in the wide world and I was tied by my apron strings to the laundry boil and the soup pot, simmering, me and the soup, both. But at least now I had an assistant.

—I'm glad for helping you, Greta said, while we went about making our tablets. I showed her how to pick the black grains of ergot off the heads of rye, and how to mill them to powder. I showed her how to measure the chalk of magnesia and roll the mixture into a round long pipe, and how to use the press to cut the pipe to pill size. She was a good worker. She filled the bottles with such German speed that within two months we doubled our sales, and she was glad for the small wage we paid her, and glad later on for the room we rented her on the floor below.

One morning as we worked she stopped, very sudden, the pill press in her hand. —Mit out you, I'd be eight months, she said. —Eight months and on der street. In winter.

—Eight months gone, you mean?

—Gone and dead. I was that close. She rested her hand on my arm. —Thank you, that's all.

But it was not all. One day she came back from the market and with her she had a broken down nag of a diseased hoor called Cecile. Cecile's nose was red as a bunion from the cold and her eyes had blood cracks in the white. One look I knew what she wanted. —No, I said to Greta.

—Axie, listen—

—No, I says.

Now my friend pulled me off a ways from her hapless companion who stood by the stove warming her hands. Small Annabelle studied the visitor boldly. —Hallo, hallo, Lady, hallo, my girl said to the hoor, and in turn the hoor patted her with a tear rolling down her cheek. —Lady cryin', said Annabelle, and she was right. Lady was cryin'.

—She has nowhere, Greta said.

—I said no.

From over by the stove, the hoor Cecile watched me and Greta arguing about her fate. A hank of greasy hair hung down from under her bonnet. —Axie, Greta said, fierce.

—I'm not in the business! I brung you in and Willi. But not so the whole city could traipse through my door.

—She'll die if you don't, in winter, in the street. Greta spit the word, pronounced it *vinter*.

Cecile was shaky under her paint, her eyes skittish. —Madame, she said, —See Voo Play.

It was please in her language. See Voo Play. Greta put her arms around French Cecile and Cecile cried on Greta and at last the hoor looked me in the eye and again it was that look. A glaze of misery and helplessness. If you seen it you would help. Jesus himself had pity on the hoors, they was not called Magdalenes for no reason, and while I did not want to be anybody's savior, here she was asking me. Please. It was what she wanted. *If they ask you you must help them.*

—You'll pay me then, I said in my last effort to discourage her. —Three dollars.

But the fee did not deter her. She paid me. I fixed her up. I said it was the last, but it wasn't.

My husband said only one thing about it. —Perhaps you should have charged her five dollars? And not long after, there was Mrs. Tarkanian from downstairs knocking at the door at suppertime to borrow a saucepan, quite evidently in the family way. And Charlie says to her, —My wife here can help you, when your time comes. She's a fine little midwife.

Mrs. T. glanced at the two children under my feet and smiled through the gaps in her teeth. I was accepted as her accoucheur then and there as Mrs. Evans said I would be, for I was a mother myself.

A month later, Mrs. Tarkanian had a breech presentation, and a terrible time of it, and yet I remembered to stand the mother upside down, and also how to move the infant with my hands to turn it, so my patient delivered a seven-pound boy headfirst and happy. After that his proud mother went around the neighborhood trumpeting about how I saved her, and thus I got up a little reputation as a midwife and soon it went around, too, that Mrs. Jones of Greenwich Street could help a girl in trouble.

BOOK FIVE

Liberty Street

Chapter Twenty-Eight

My Enemy

*W*hile women knocked at my door, while I did what I could for them and toiled at pulverizing the wings of Spanish flies for their medicine, while I attended their deliveries and changed the diapers of my little daughter, while I washed the linen and went to the market and fetched the coal and water, while I scrubbed the floors and sold bottles of Remedy and sang Who Put the Overalls in Mrs. Murphy's Chowder— my Enemy was busy too, as a carpenter ant chewing passageways into the very walls of the house.

As I labored all these years, oblivious, the pious young bachelor Tony Comstock was selling textiles not even twenty blocks away at the dry goods emporium Cochran & McLean, 464 Broadway, off Grand. One certainly hopes Crusader Comstock did not sin in his thoughts as he fondled the merchandise of ladies' delicates, or observed the merry housewives handling the stockings made ready-to-wear. It seems that all his life, well before he persecuted me, Sin was on his mind like a hat. He was so distressed by his fellow clerks' interest in girly pictures that he eventually founded himself a club called the Society for the Suppression of Vice. But even by 1868 he was already responsible for the destruction of his first bookseller: a fellow named Jakes. Poor Jakes was a good Christian man, a churchgoing taxpayer. Jakes' error? He sold a picture postcard. What was the picture of? A statue, just. A famous naked statue from Rome. For that, Comstock had the poor cove arrested and hauled off to jail. My enemy ruined Jakes and began his rampage, to stamp out the smutty book business wherever he found it.

In those early days of my practice, the LAW pertaining to midwifery sat gathering cobwebs in a corner, a relic of the Forties. It said that anybody who would ADMINISTER a woman any drug or medicine, or EMPLOY an instrument with INTENT to produce a miscarriage of a quick child— unless it was necessary to save her life—would go to jail for a year or pay a fine. No right-minded trap or smirker of the courts could be bothered with it, as it could not be effectively enforced. Without a witness, Intent could not be proved, let alone a fact like Employ or Administer.

In the 70's, My Enemy took matters into his own paws. He dreamed up new laws that later would catch me, but in them days, I and other female practitioners who assisted our afflicted sisters was still left alone by the brothers of the Judiciary.

Sitting here now in my elegant parlor amongst the potted lilies I have enjoyed reading a published history about what a righteous bunger My Enemy was. Were it not for his undoing me so long ago, I might extend a word of charity to him, knowing he was once a little tyke grieving for his mother, dead of childbirth, a grief we have in common. But thanks to the recent publication of his diaries we can confirm that Anthony Comstock, by his own admission, was not the paragon of virtue he pretended to be, just only an unctuous hypocrite and weevil. At age 19 he wrote:

Again tempted and found wanting. Sin, sin. Oh, how much peace and happiness is sacrificed on thy altar. I am the chief of sinners.

And on another day:

This morning was severely tempted by Satan and after some time in my own weakness I failed.

What sin he refers to we can only guess but the easy money would be on the sin of self-abuse. He was only a man wasn't he? And yet, despite being the confessed Chief of Sinners, the whiskery Crusader was marching around telling others what to do, disgusted at ordinary habits. While serving the Union Army, young Tony spent his energy organizing church services. *Have been twitted several times today about being a Christian,* he wrote. *Heard some persons speaking against me. Will not join with them in sin and wickedness; though loose all of their friendship.*

In his righteousness, he refused to drink his Army ration of whiskey and delighted in pouring it on the ground in front of his comrades in arms. He scolded them for cursing. And no, he would never smoke, he wrote in his journal, not even to keep the mosquitoes off him in the swamps of the Confederacy.

The poor slub. For all his moralizing and sermonizing, he was teased and tormented. He was a lonely killjoy and wrote how everybody loathed him even then.

Seems to be a hatred by some of the boys, constantly falsifying, persecuting and trying to do me harm. Can I sacrifice Principle and conscience for Praise of Man? Never.

Still, he found a woman to love him, his little Maggie, a full ten years older than he was. Reports of tiny Mrs. Comstock said she was an eighty-two pound invalid, dressed always in black. And it must be said to his credit that for his own beloved, Tony had an uncommon tenderness. In his diary she was his Little Wifey, his Dear M., his Precious Little Wife. And as much as I may loathe the hideous man and blame him outsize for all my grief, I can say sincerely that the cove has my admiration for his devotion as a husband. He also has my sympathies for the loss of his baby girl Lillie, who died when she was not more than six months of age. His pain was not less just because he was a first class bunger. While I suspect he then adopted a child rather than risk carnality, the b*****d gets some respect for one reason: he rescued an orphan from a tenement in Brooklyn and named her Adele. While I do pity poor Adele for having to spend her life with a moralizing liar of an Inquisition for a father, what he done to save one child is more than I did for the thousands of misfortunates living on the corner. In my defense it must be pointed out that me and Charlie was at one time intending to adopt our own stray larrikin, but was rudely deterred by the hounding and endangerment of Mr. Comstock and his ILK. Such are the complexities of Good and Evil. My Enemy cared for this daughter Adele, who was feebleminded, with tender understanding, as he did NOT care for me or his other victims, for example the smalltown Brooklyn saloon keeper Chapman who he ruined in 1870. Why? for the simple reason he did not like that Chapman's Saloon served a drop on Sunday. For this he tormented the barkeep in the courts and had him jailed till the poor man dropped dead in his cell of a heart attack. It was the first death Comstock would take credit for. I wish I could say mine was the last. It wasn't.

We two, me and Comstock, was barreling toward each other, each one on a mission. It would be years before we would meet, and despite the fact My Enemy relocated for a while, far off to Summit, New Jersey, the infernal man got closer to me every day, his hot breath a prickle at the back of my neck.

Chapter Twenty-Nine

Offices & Boudoirs,
Saloons & Salons

ANNOUNCED. MADAME DEBEAUSACQ, the French physician, has removed her offices from her residence at 160 Greenwich Street around the corner to 148 Liberty Street, where Ladies can purchase FEMALE PILLS. They are an infallible regulator of m****s, and combat violent and convulsive headaches, derangement of the stomach, gnawing in the side, burning in the chest, disturbed and feverish sleep, frightful dreams, languor, debility, deathly, sallow and inanimate complexion, want of appetite, in short, the utter prostration of the enjoyment or even endurance of life, engendering that depression of spirit that makes existence itself but a prolongation of suffering, and which, alas! not infrequently dooms the unhappy victim to the perpetration of suicide. Not to be used when p******* for the ingredients may act upon particular functions. Compounded and sold only by herself for the price of $4. To the poor, half price. To the very poor, nothing. Advice, gratis.

—Ad in the *Sun*, the *Herald*, and the *NY Times*

As our fortunes increased, Greta took on the duties of receptionist and nurse at the new offices at Liberty Street, around the corner from our Greenwich Street home. Liberty Street had rooms for lying-in, a proper Female Hospital. The outer waiting room where Greta sat we had appointed with a sofa and armchairs for the comfort of the patients, a carpet, a canary in a cage, and two framed prints, of a pair of swans. It was not a SUMPTUOUS PARLOR as the *Times* later described it, nor was it a GATEWAY TO THE CHARNEL HOUSE as the *Polyanthos* wrote. It was just an office such as you might see in any reputable enterprise, for I was now established as female physician to the finest ladies of Manhattan.

—Would you prefer the blue room, Greta asked when a lumbering mother came to spend her confinement, —or the yellow? It was Greta's task to explain the blue room cost more, for it was larger, and had a window overlooking the street. When ladies called, Greta now kept track of the appointments and took payments by bank cheque or in cash. She sat at a French oak writing desk with fluted legs, where in her childish writing, like the scrawl of a halfwit, it must be said, she took down patients' names if they would dare to divulge them. They arrived dressed anonymous in their veils, sometimes double veils, while some came with their aprons still on under their coats. Some were parlor maids and some was out-and-out lulus with the paint still on their faces. More and more they were elegant wives with jet buttons on their jackets and a barouche outside waiting. I was a midwife same as Mrs. Evans, though I sought a finer class of patient, the carriage trade now. They came with all manner of complaint from every ward between the Battery and Bleecker and beyond. From New Jersey. From up the Hudson in Dobbs Ferry or up the Sound in Norwalk. Some of these ladies were round and pink with the new life stirring in them, knitting cradle bonnets as they waited for my instructions about their forthcoming labor. They wished to inspect the new rooms upstairs, to interview Madame about her skills. But then there was others. These ones came early in the morning or after dark. They were tightlipped and nervous and glanced sidelong at each other, cats guarding a secret.

Though my husband said she was None Too Bright, Greta compared favorably with the best of these customers, as she was again a good-looking lady, known as the Widow Weiss, with the story that Willi's father was a sea captain lost in a storm at Cape Fear. She was usually outfitted in the latest fashion, her hair glossy in dark finger waves or side curls such that I was jealous of her stylish appearance and copied her. Many patients confused her at first for Madame DeBeausacq when she greeted them in the office. But Greta dismissed this idea with a German snort.

—I heffn't the skills of der female physiologist. Madame is the midwife, und I am her assistant.

She was loyal to me as a cocker spaniel now for saving her off the corner and paying her a decent wage, always complimenting my skills to the women who came through the doors, telling them, —Ya, ya, you're in good hands with Frau DeBeausacq, ya, she's very knowledgeable, she'll put you right in no time, missus, she can fix you up.

Despite what had happened to her in wretched alleys and the back rooms of saloons, Greta most of the time was cheerful, singing beer hall songs picked up at Scheutzen Park or Luchow's or the *Lagerbier* palaces where she went with her suitors. But she was also prone to dark moods and fits of crying. One morning, her boy Willi had to trot around the corner from their apartment on Cortlandt Street, saying, —Auntic, please come for my *Mutter*, please come, and we two found poor Greta curled in her bed and had to pull her upright and splash her face in the bowl.

—I am zo ashamed, she wept to me later. —No man ever will marry me. My son is a b*****d. Promise please never to tell no one.

—I promise not to tell that you was once a hoor if you promise not to tell I was a ragpicker daughter of a one-armed washerwoman grown up to be an adviser on such things as can't be discussed in polite company, such as ____. I whispered in her ear though what I said remains unmentionable in polite writing, yet me and Greta fell over laughing just to speak of it.

Wisecracks usually worked to make my friend revive, so she laughed like the same saucepot girl hanging the wash next door and was cheered enough to go off to our day's work with the ladies of Gotham. With her German efficiency she kept the appointment times on a schedule, and the stack of gauze bandages cut neat, into squares of just the right size. She knew me, knew my ways, and I knew hers. As a nurse she was never subject to fits of emotion, always calm, good with swaddling up the newborns quick and snug. But despite her small hands she never could stand to get near the ____ ("monosyllable," as we say) of a patient, not even to tell me how many fingers open was the laboring mother. You'd think, Once a hoor, never shy. But *Nein nein, nein,* she'd say, with a shudder, if ever I asked. And so I stopped asking. We stationed her up at the north end of the patient, me at the south. We was partners. An old married couple. For their part, Annabelle and little Willi was good as brother and sister. Many an afternoon the two young rabbits took their naps and their tea together in the nursery of the new house we purchased in 1872, at 129 Liberty Street just down the block from the new office. All four floors of it we got for a sum I could have never dreamed only two years before, when we was all lodged together, we three Jones and Greta and Willi jumbled as odd socks in a basket.

Now on Liberty Street it was plain we was arrived. Nobody common could live in such a building. Built in the Federal style with protuberant dormer windows up on the gabled roof and black painted shutters, our home had a respectable appearance. You might say if the house was human, it would be a burgher from the Metropolitan Club, an upright pocketwatch gentleman type with a generous stomach under his cummerbund. Up the stoop you went to the front door, which featured a big American eagle knocker of brass kept polished by Margaret McGrath the parlormaid called Maggie, who I had helped some years before when her dear mother brought her to me: the girl had got in the family way with a longshoreman she said, and would I help her please? Since the longshoreman was long offshore, and Maggie could not return to her father's house without the risk of his murdering her, she had never left my establishment from the day I met her, and now each time I smelled lemon polish on the gas lamps and linseed oil on the moldings I rejoiced it was not me who done the polishing.

The swish of my skirts was a whisper of refinement over the parquet in the vestibule, where I removed my bonnet and glanced to the front parlor, so distinguished with brocade upholstered sofas and lace antimacassars on the backs of tufted armchairs in crimson Genoa velvet. No street rat or kitchen drab like I once was could ever hope to be crossing the wide mirrored landing where I saw myself framed in gilt, twenty six years of age, and mistress of the house. It startled me every time, to confront Mrs. Ann M. Jones reflected like a member of the gentility. Whenever I found myself alone on the landing I had to admire the figure cut there. *Hello, and how do you do, Mrs. Jones?* I said to myself. *Fine thank you, yes indeed, a pleasant good day to you too, you codfish Axie, don't get too fond of it.*

In truth I didn't trust the mirror at Liberty Street to hold this swell picture of me very long. Ever suspicious of good fortune, I was always after thinking some fever of consumption would come in the night to steal my breath. Despite that certain procedures was going on against the law, behind closed doors, all over town, and nobody was ever arrested for it, it was sure as sin if Somebody was caught, it would be myself. But meanwhile fortune had smiled on me, so why shouldn't I smile back at my gilt mirror and my French doors? Through them was the library. The backstairs led down to the kitchen. Upstairs were rooms for Maggie and the cook Rebecca—another of my former patients—who shared quarters on the fourth floor. On the third level was the nursery with a doll's house and a chalkboard, where my daughter Miss Belle Jones played her spinet and did her letters with the nursemaid, Sallie, likewise once a patient of mine. Down the gaslit passage was the bedroom for me and Charlie with damask at the windows, a carved oak mantel over the fireplace, and the bed that featured a rosewood headboard so royal with crests and crockets, cornices and cusps and finials.

Queen Jones, Charlie called me, when I sat there on the pillows regal in my nightdress, and he came burrowing under the feathered counterpane where we played at Your Majesty and Your Highness and enacted the Royal Protocols of Jones (a sleeve is removed first to reveal the white shoulder of Mrs. Jones, and another sleeve to reveal the hard egg of muscle at the biceps of Mr. Jones, whereupon custom, not to mention the chemicals of passion, demands the rest be removed in haste). On these nights Charlie was to me a flame inside the glass globe of a streetlamp, burning all doubts of him in a puff of smoke, so sometimes in the daylight going about my routine in the clinic or offices I would double over practically in a cramp of soreness and memory, recalling how he had feathered me and tarred me with his kisses and sweet words. I was in a swoon till he went off overnight somewheres and my jealousies took over again.

We did not have more children. We had abandoned any methods, French or otherwise, of prevention, yet every month the red banner of our disappointment appeared and despite the quantities of black cohosh root and teas of raspberry leaf I swallowed, despite a sticky remedy performed regularly with egg white, and charms uttered for the *sheehogues* and prayers to God on my knees, salt thrown over my shoulder against bad luck, I remained barren as the sea stretching out from the Battery on a frosty morning.

Each time I suffered the turns I was doubled up with pain and could find no remedy for it. My condition was called unpronounceable in the medical book of Dr. Gunning and when I read about it I was disgusted at the cause and dismayed by the treatment:

> Dysmenorrhoea consists in the exudation of coagulable lymph coating the cavity of the u****s and thrown from the cavity in fragments, hence the extreme pain so characteristic of the malady. The treatment consists of the local abstraction of blood from over the sacrum every two weeks, together with free purgation and vegetable diet.

The esteemed author Dr. Gunning was down in the papers as the most famous medical man of the century so I did what he said and Greta, bless her, bled me from over the lower backbone as recommended though she complained more than I did, the cat. I followed the grim vegetable diet as recommended and purged myself, &c. yet still my turns invariably sent me to bed sick with headache, cramps, nausea. I had no more children. My child Belle had no sister nor brother as I had none now either. I was in despair over finding Joe or seeing Dutch, who had sailed away and never wrote more. Not even her false mother Mrs. A. bothered to correspond. Why? No doubt she had discovered that Dutchie knew about her lies. My sister's origins as a Papist Orphan Guttersnipe was exposed, and she was thus disowned by her husband. I worried Dutch was angry with me for somehow I had exposed her. As for Joe, No Other Information Is Available, said a Mr. J. Morrow of the Childrens Aid Society who wrote to me, *Dear Mrs. Jones, more than two thousand children emigrated west from New York in that year of 1860 alone. We do not have the field agents to keep track of them all.* He and the Aid Society then stopped answering my letters hectoring them about my siblings.

The size of my longing for a safe big family with our youngsters playing by the hearth and the cousins and the uncles and aunts all around was measured by the holes in the circle around me and Charlie, with our Belle in the middle. She entertained us with her chatter and her stories. At four years of age, she had a dear lisping way of speaking, and an imaginary brother named Cocoa.

—Cocoa is nearing his confinement, she announced one day. —He is going to have a baby girl.

—But, I said, —he is your brother.

—Yes. With RED hair.

—But it is only ladies who have a confinement, says I, very patient, and thinking of my own carrot-head brother. —A little boy cannot have a baby.

—When he grows up, he can.

—When Cocoa grows up he might become a father, true. But he will not have a confinement.

—Cocoa does. He is laboring all the night long.

Charlie laughed at this and we decided Belle was too skilled an eavesdropper to come along any more with me to the offices. —We should try to get her a brother, said my husband, a gleam in his eye. But still none was forthcoming, despite the steam of our attempts over the months.

—Perhaps we should adopt a child, I says one night to Charlie as we lay in the dark. —Aren't there occasional candidates born right here in this house? Or sleeping on the corner in the Bend?

—Give it time, Annie, he says. —A man might prefer to carry on trying in the natural manner, if you take my meaning. There's plenty of time.

But he agreed, sure, if some lady was lying-in and couldn't keep her baby for the usual reasons of shame or poverty, he'd consider adopting. H*** why not?

—Well, they die, don't they, the infants, without a wet nurse, I said, thinking of Baby Boy Johnny then. —So might be we should find an older orphan.

—Depends on the circumstances, right? Charlie said. —Keep our eyes peeled.

The both of us had our eyes peeled, indeed, wide open to the possibilities and the pitfalls too. On my bad jealous days I suspected my barren state was the reason for Charlie's wanderings. Maybe he was a fox who would find a new mother for his kits, out so many nights, his half the bed cold and flat, a hollow there where the husband was supposed to lie. —A man needs his freedom, he explained. —I'm no different than any other husband.

To me that was no recommendation.

No different except for how he capitalized on his wife. Years ago he gave up his wish to be a newspaperman and now was devoted entirely to the business of Madame DeBeausacq, keeping the books and managing the mail orders, writing the ads. He went to Philadelphia and Boston. He went to New Haven and Newark, Providence and Baltimore, drumming up business, gone for nights at a time. —It is only to *support* Madame, he said, —that I must regretfully leave Madame.

He was raised to roam the streets, he said, and liked them the way he liked his egg in the morning and his newspapers lined up perfect on the table and the anarchist pamphlets he read with a pair of spectacles perched on the end of his nose. He liked to pass Saturday afternoons in Matsell's bookshop or The Freeman's Club, and evenings at The Billy Goat or the Harp House. He was frequently at Chickering Hall or the Ethical Culture Society where he listened to the preaching of radicals and Jews and Fanny Wrightists and spiritualists, and went out afterwards with his friends to argue about such topics as the morality of war, the population question, and the rights of workers. Meanwhile, I festered over his absences and pestered him. He didn't smell of perfume nor bring a strand of another's hair home on his jacket. There was not a crumb of evidence against him. Yet my jealousy would not quiet.

One morning eight years into our matrimony he arrived under the covers just as the sun was leaking through the window curtains. The smell of tobacco and gin came off him. —Where have you been? I cried. —Where do you go?

As he lay his head upon my pillow I gave him a sharp elbow in the ribs and a piece of my tongue, which was a buggy whip of hurt feelings and fury.

—For the love of God why don't you never trust anyone? he cried, holding his injured spleen. —Once an orphan always an orphan, is that your song Mrs. Jones? Well get over it. You're a married lady in a brick house, aren't you?

—I'm tired of you coming in smelling like a growler.

The salt of my tears changed his tune. —Axie my Annie, he crooned, —you know I'd never deceive you, pretty doxie. My silky sparrow. Earth's own angel.

—Don't give me that velvet no more.

—Christ woman. Here I am traveled this week all the way to Pittsburgh and back just to sell a wagon of medicines to a doctor there and advertise

the good name of Madame across the countryside, and you can't even warm
the cockles of my poor and lonely heart after a long tedious journey.

—It's not those cockles you want warmed, sure it isn't.

—D*** you! You'll have to trust me, won't you?

Never trust a man who says trust me. It was hard advice to overcome, and
I was hard-pressed to try.

—Come now, I'm freezing, Charlie whispered, thawing me out with his
cold bony feet. —That's my Annie. That's my girl.

Such was his arts of persuasion and since I had no other choice, we was
friends again by breakfast. But it was the same argument all over again six
months later, to trust him or not. With Charlie I was always a woman on
edge. It was as if, when he led me up on the roof of that train so long ago,
we never got off it.

—Who are these friends of yours? I asked him one evening as he straightened his collar on his way out the door.

—Yes who are YOUR friends, Papa? cried Belle.

Instead of answering he repeated the question as a song for our princess
who was four years of age and bouncing on the bed. —Oh who are these
friends? he sang, —these fine friends of yours?

—Willi is my friend! Belle cried, —and Liebchen and Schnitzel and
Cocoa.

Liebchen was her dolly and Schnitzel was the wooden horse in her nursery. She had German names for everything, thanks to Greta. My daughter
knew more about *spätzle* than she did about the proud Muldoons of Carrickfergus or a good pot of coddle. And it was just as well, for a working
knowledge of Irish would not be the key to any doors in society that I
wished for her to open.

—I do not have a friend named Schnitzel, said Charlie, —but I do have
a friend named Will who is not the same young larrikin Willi who is your
playmate.

—And who might he be, this friend Will? I asked. —Why have I never
had the pleasure of his acquaintance?

—Because he is Will Sacks who frequents The Mighty Unicorn saloon
where a woman's not welcome.

—Then bring him here, I said, —and the rest of your unicorns. Have your saloon where I can see it.

—A saloon! Why not? It's all the rage with the upper crust, only they call it a salon. Or a soiree. Whatever French they can muster.

Well Charlie liked anything French, and so did I, such that the next Saturday night, I put on my burgundy-colored crepe de chine and a pearl necklace and entertained a salon of men in our parlor. PHILOSOPHERS, Charlie called them, including Will Sacks, and David Arguimbeau. Also Andrew Morrill, a lawyer, and Bill Owens, a tall gasp of a man, asthmatic and stooped.

—You will like these gentlemen, Mrs. Jones, Charlie told me. —They've an academic interest in female physiology.

At first I kept my mouth shut, pouring their claret, for I wasn't yet accustomed to the niceties of salon society. But the one called Owens motioned me to sit beside him, so I made my way over through their pipe smoke. He stood and kissed my hand.

—*Enchanté*, madame, he said, like I was a genuine French lady. —Your husband says you're in the business of selling female remedies, is that right? I applaud you for it.

—If only all men had as much sense to applaud as you.

Owens laughed. He was an old cod, with his bulging eyes and fins for ears, but he talked with an eloquence that made him half goodlooking.

—This population question is exceedingly pressing, he said. —Don't you agree?

—All I know about the population question, I replied, —is there wouldn't be one if certain matters was left in female hands.

—Exactly! A full half of all the world's problems is directly caused by our animal desires, am I right? He leaned toward me whispering. —I have long been fascinated to interview you, Mrs. Jones, about your medicines. What can you say about them? We are at pains to discover the proper methods of . . . *prevention*. Control by masculine restraint alone is flawed, don't you agree? simply by the fact that the practitioner suffers no consequence if he fails at it.

—Only the female suffers the consequence.

—Sadly, yes. But the *baudruche* is in every way unreliable, and inconvenient.

—YOU may find it inconvenient, sir, I said, blushing, in a huff, —but your lady friend finds it a shield against her downfall.

—And what do you prescribe for your own patients?

—To become nuns.

He laughed and stared at me with admiring eyes. —You may be frank with me, Mrs. Jones.

—Well then, I said, very frank indeed, —what is required would be more common use of a pessary, like the sea sponge I sell for a dollar, or the rinse by syringe, or some other practice controlled by a lady. Then she does not have to trust a man. For how many men is trustworthy?

Owens seemed affronted. —The great majority of us are gentlemen! he said, as if I was asking him a question of a personal nature. —For example, your husband Mr. Jones. I've never known him to be profligate in his habits. On the contrary. He has often bragged to us of his wife and her successful midwifery practice. He appears devoted to you to the point of uxoriousness.

Whatever it was, uxorious, it appeared I should be glad to hear it. Indeed, Owens' notion of a devoted husband was entirely foreign. Had Charlie truly bragged of me? With new eyes now, I noticed him watching from across the room, while his friend and I talked and sipped our wine all smiles and rosy laughter. Soon he came over to where we sat.

—Mr. Jones, your wife here is enlightening me about certain questions of feminine physiology, said Owens.

—Didn't I tell you she would be knowledgeable? my husband said.

Well this was new, too, that he thought me knowledgeable, for he was always the know-it-all, calling me Student. And now here he was sitting down quite close beside me with a possessive hand on my chair while Owens interrogated me on the fine points of preventative powders. Charlie watched me as I spoke boldly of the benefits of tansy oil and Spanish fly, and the syringe, —Which can also serve to baste a roast, I said, quite tipsy now, as Owens roared.

—Like the missus says, it's good to water the plants, Charlie told him, and the two of them had a laugh over the idea of a female syringe giving the ivy a good spritz.

That night was the first time me and Charlie had opened our parlor for a party, but very quick we developed a taste for the company and the talk. We woke the neighbors with our laughing, the chatter spilling out to the street after, the guests reluctant to leave.

—Owens is taken with you, said Charlie, as we blew out the lamp later.

—He's taken with the sound of his own voice, I said. But a secret triumph bloomed in my heart for not only was my husband proud I was knowledgeable, I saw also that he was jealous, even of a fellow so old he resembled cheese left over from biblical times.

After that first soiree, I found myself often holding forth to a roomful of men and soon discovered that these acquaintances of my husband were famous in the bookshops and at The Mighty Unicorn for philosophizing on the Population Question and the like. The group consisted of Owens and his wife Ida. Mr. Sacks and his lady friend Millicent, Dr. Arguimbeau, Mr. DeLand, Judge Baker and his daughter Roberta, along with Andrew Morrill, the lawyer who would later come in useful to my cause.

These were our friends now. We frequented their parlors and they frequented ours. Charlie liked the talk and the argument, whereas I liked especially to dress up in finery, to see the insides of drawing rooms decorated with flocked wallpapers, lit by colored lampglass, rooms where I was not a servant nor a midwife but a guest drinking sherry. When they came to Liberty Street, I liked to parade our Anna-bee in her sausage curls and pantaloons. She would sing McGinty and the ladies would feed her sugar lumps like she was a trained pony, until the day came when Mrs. Owens suggested, —Perhaps McGinty is not a proper song for a young lady four years of age to be singing.

—Why not? I cried. —Her father taught it to her. It's all he has of his ancestors.

And it was then she took me aside with the idea that I might wish to hire a governess, as it was all the rage in polite society to have one. And so it was that Ellen Nickerson the governess came to our household and the next time we had guests, our Annabelle came in to greet them with a pretty curtsy only.

—Say your good nights, Anna-bee, I says to her, and she kisses me so lavish, saying, —Oh You are My Pretty Mamma, till Ellen admonished her.

—Only a peck is proper, the Governess pronounced.

—Nonsense, says I. —Our girl will have her good night kiss. And I wrapped her in my lap and whispered in her ear that she was my own Anna-bee, the baby of the world.

Ellen extracted her off to the nursery, with a huff of disapproval, and just in time, too, for here came Owens approaching with the philosophers' favorite subject in mind. —Mrs. Jones, tell us please which of your remedies serves best as emmenagogue?

—I can't answer for any sort of gogs, I told him, which caused him to roar laughing so his whiskers trembled, —but I can say that tansy's the best elixir I know for obstruction. The problem is it does harm the system worse than any rotgut if the dose is wrong. Some of these ladies drink it like lemonade.

—Tsk, said Owens.

—I've seen a few who bleed from the perforations and some have seizures.

—Why then do you sell such medicines?

—No one knows a better one. Besides, if the dose is proper it serves the purpose only, far as we can tell. But no lie, sir, we are in need of a better class of medicine.

Owens agreed while I wondered, What was his motive? Surely with such probing questions about de-obstruction these fellas was interested only in how they might have a rogue life with all the burden on the LADIES and none for themselves. Why else would they question me so closely about purgatives and procedures? So I was surprised that they soon showed a true concern for female virtue and welfare. Mrs. Owens herself had suffered greatly in four incidents of childbirth, and her husband divulged to me he feared another confinement would surely kill her. Mrs. Arguimbeau had had six children, only three living, and she likewise wished to limit her family size, if not just her waistline. It was from the talk among these friends that over time I learnt how they saw me: not just as a midwife, but a soldier in a BATTLE.

—I tell you, Mrs. Jones, said Owens one evening, —when it comes to human reproduction, you midwives are warriors on the front lines. We must fight to take society from a night of blind prejudice and brutal force into an age of rational liberty and cultivated refinement.

—I am in favor of any kind of refinement, I said, —but against all forms of battle.

I did not like the picture of myself as warrior. I was a small woman, no more than ninety pounds, with small hands, which were not weapons, only instruments of relief.

Then one night, over a game of whist, the philosophers made a proposition offhand that was to have a great impact on our fortunes, and drafted me unwitting into the very battle I declined. It happened as a result of my entertaining the assembled men with a tale from my workaday practice.

—Today I saw the new young bride Mrs. M., I says, while they listened. —The poor chicken came to me with a pain and swelling. From eating oysters, she thought. All's she knew of where babies came from was about the cabbage patch. Till her wedding night she thought it was the fairies who brought a baby. Imagine her horror when her husband showed her the truth? And so, when I told Mrs. M. what she was expecting, and how the package would be delivered? she had never heard it. Imagine.

—Such ignorance! these fellows laughed and muttered under their mustaches, and in the corner Charlie whispered something into the ear of that horsefly Millicent, who came with Arguimbeau but buzzed about all the men till you wanted to swat her. —Haaa ha, they snickered, —oysters and fairies, indeed.

—It's not funny, I says. —The point is Mrs. M. was a girl in the dark. It was my task to tell her it was not OYSTERS. She was going to have a little dumpling quite soon, and she had no idea about it. I've even seen fine newlywed ladies off Fifth Avenue just as ignorant, crying in my office over certain shocking events in their boudoir, when all they are referring to is You Know What. Don't their mothers warn them?

—Exactly the problem, said Mr. Arguimbeau, wagging his head.

—If only all prospective brides could hear you, said Sacks.

—Send them over, I said, as if it was a tea party I had in mind.

—Mrs. Jones should run a little school, said Owens, —to educate the ladies.

A school! the philosophers cried. I should run a classroom, they said.

I should instruct the ignorant female populace on the functions of their own physiology. I should discuss hygiene and demonstrate the workings of certain apparatuses, the cunicle and the thingum, ho ho, the baubles and the undercarriage. They laughed with wicked chuckles as they said the words and left our parlor that night congratulating themselves on their enlightened attitudes. I admit I enjoyed their jokes and attention but it was Charlie who took what they said and wrung money from it, for that was a talent he had.

When they were gone he lay back on the sofa. —Madame DeBeausacq's School of Wifely Arts, he said, running his fingers in the air like it was printed there in type. —Twenty ladies at five dollars per class, each.

—Ladies will not like to discuss such things.

—You'll educate them on matters of physiology. A classroom.

—Never. They will not like to be seen attending such a place. Maybe it would be better if I told you what they need to know and you just wrote it all down in lessons.

In the mists of tobacco that hung over the room I saw my husband smile as a Grand Idea stole over his phiz. —Woman, he said, coming near to nuzzle my neck, —you're a clever bit of business. I will write little pamphlets and sell them for a dollar! Enlightenment and profit all in one go.

So now Charlie launched himself on his career as a pamphleteer. Practical Advice for a Wife and Mother by Madame DeBeausacq, priced at $2 a copy, was soon in the hands of every female who walked through my doors. Charlie wrote:

> It is but too well known that the families of the married often increase beyond what the happiness of those who give them birth would dictate. Is it desirable, then, is it moral? for parents to increase their families, when a simple, healthy, and certain remedy—well known to all citizens of France—is within our control? Estimating the vast benefit resulting to thousands, the celebrated female physician from France, Mme. DeBeausacq, has opened an office where married females can obtain the

desired information. Hours of attendance from Ten o'clock in
the morning till Nine in the evening.

By advertising we sold ten thousand copies of Practical Advice in six
months, mostly through the mail. In new quarters that we added to the
rear of our office on Liberty Street we now had a small factory and dispensary for medicines and built yet another room above for mothers spending their confinement. Our business on all fronts was brisk, such that we
employed a nurse, and a pharmacy aide. I held little classes in the waiting
room now and then. I talked to the ladies about nipple inversions and false
labor, about belly braces and the importance to new mothers of opening
the bowels. Charlie wrote a guide for newlyweds, and another with instructions on the use of the items sold in our advertisements. Money had long
since overflowed our glass jar and into several accounts. —One with my
name on it, I insisted to Charlie. And he did not object, for it seemed now,
where money was concerned at least, we did not quarrel but only agreed:
that we liked it.

Our address was now popular as a tree of nesting birds, its branches full
of peahens and parrots. But it must be said that while these ladies' plumage
ran from plain to fancy, their distress and ignorance, their fear and their
questions, were all the same no matter their station in society. How could
they start a baby? or prevent one? or stop one growing before it was quick?
or birth one into the world without danger? They came to me in a variety of
states, uninformed and afraid, weeping and bleeding. Their shapes was distorted, feet swollen, the face bloated, waist gone. A black line divided them
down the middle of their bellies. They walked lumbering, hands pressed to
the smalls of their backs. This one had short breath and that one had red
hands. This one's heels was cracked and raw. Another one had piles.

Can you help me? they asked when they walked in, and Thank you,
they said, when they walked out, lighter. Tell no one, the half of them said.
Never tell. And I never did. Never said a word or listed their names in
public or held them up for shame. That was not ME who did that. While
I had them I held their hands. I fed their infants rosewater in a dropper. I
was merciful and fast. They would tell you I was quick about it. *There love
it's almost over, there you go, you're a brave girl.* They all was brave. Every one.
Patient as beasts. They cried and groaned and sweated and bled. There was

a great lot of blood. Still, I say without no false modesty that to my knowledge, not one woman ever yet died at these hands, for they had got very
skilled, sorry to say.

The law didn't come up, not at all. Was it a crime to talk to my ladies? Was it
a crime to give them information and medicines? Was it a crime to protect
them from the dangers of childbirth? Was it a crime to unblock their sup-
pressions, to restore their catamenial rhythms, to protect them from ruin
and the false promises and lusts of men?

Not in my book.

But the leathery books of the judicial whiskers who made the rules told
a different story. In their pages it was a crime to interfere at all with the
machinery of a female *enceinte,* and the law said anyone who did so was
subject to a fine of one hundred dollars and a year in jail. If the child was
quick, well—that was not my line of work to fix a quickened lady. And, also,
it was Manslaughter, and four years in jail.

In those days, I did not worry. Them officials lived in a world of smoke
and pronouncements, rooms full of throat clearings and whiskey breath,
whereas we, my customers and me, lived just in our own flesh, the blood
and bones. We were factories of blood and bones, in fact. These authorities knew nothing of us and what went on in our private country. They
could not be bothered. How were they to guess which woman was interfered with by me and who wasn't or why? Blood was blood and women
was bleeding regular all the time. Who was to know the difference? Who
would come forward? Who would tell? No one. There was no need. There
was nothing but shame in telling. It was for ourselves, in danger, that we
decided. And for our children. It was not the business of men, despite the
kindly philosophers' parlor pontifications on the subject. These matters was
now, and always was, for a female to determine. We knew how to keep our
secrets. Our lives and honor depended on it.

Still, evil would find me. It came in through the door like mud on shoes.
You'd never have suspected who brought it. A girl called Susan Applegate,
her name a springtime orchard, her face a blossom. There wasn't no way to
see what worms were lurking in the fruits of my helping her.

Chapter Thirty

Trouble Named Susan

For someone who would ensure my notoriety and drag me to the clutches of My Enemy, she was unremarkable, just a bland girl with cornsilk hair and eyebrows that made hardly a shadow above her watery blue eyes. Her lashes was near to colorless.

—Your name? Greta asked her.

—Susan Applegate, she replied, and Greta later said it should be Apple-blossom, so pink and white was her appearance.

While the young lady waited, Greta gave her to read several of our new circulars including one called Practical Advice for Newlyweds, by Monsieur Docteur Gerard Desomieux, also known as Charles G. Jones, my husband. He was especially proud of the philosophy he put forward—French Common Sense, he called it, and he used this philosophy—and this pamphlet—to sell his wares for gentlemen.

It is well known that the French always have intervals of three, four, or more years between the birth of children, and this is because no Frenchman would abstain from the use of Desomieux's Preventive to Conception. The same result is attained by a complete withdrawal on the part of the male previous to emission. But this mode is attended with insurmountable difficulties. In the first place, few men can control themselves in this respect. Thus, Desomieux's Preventatives are the best relief. Complete instructions as to their use included in every box. $1 a dozen, by mail, Dr. Gerard Desomieux, 148 Liberty St., New York. Boston Office, 7 Charles Street.

Susan Applegate read these words with what Greta later told me was a great fretting of the hands, and she flung the paper away from her in such disgust that Greta feared we had lost a patient. (And I wish we had.) But at last the young Miss Applegate came in the office, and by the high swell of her stomach I judged her to be eight months along and carrying a boy. She'd've been pretty above the neck if not for the way she shifted her cheeks left and right the better to gnaw at them. Poor young Susan was eaten away by trouble.

Her trouble's name was Adolphus Edwards, she said, a man she'd known since her girlhood, the son of neighbors. Her father was the personal physician to his family, whereas she, Susan, had lately become the personal plaything of young Adolphus. He had promised to marry her, but now his promises lay ruptured as poor Susan's virtue, not to mention her heart, for Adolphus was indeed engaged, only not to her, and he was on his way to the Antilles where he meant to make a fortune in sugar. Susan was left behind, her problem growing more evident by the day.

—Can't I have an . . . operation? she asked. Spots of embarrassment stood out on her fair skin like stains. —A renovation such as you advertise?

—Your child is quick, I said, softly. —You yourself know that.

—But I've only now had the chance to find you and—

—Miss Applegate, said I, sorry as could be, —you are quite evidently about eight months gone. You've no choice now but to see it through.

—I cannot! she cried, collapsed at the news. —Please, won't you help me?

—Had you come earlier, I might have been better able.

—I meant to come right away—but my father confronted me and kept me in. He said he knew what was wrong with me because I was sick in the mornings and complained of dizziness.

—Is he a doctor?

—My father is Dr. Samuel Applegate, president of the Columbia University School of Medicine.

—Is he now? I said, only curious, and failed to see a WARNING right there.

—I asked him to help me, said fair Susan, —but he said that I was ruined, and beat me, while my mother begged him for mercy. Still he locked me away and said my only choice is to marry his revolting old friend Doc Benjamin, who will say the child is his. Oh horrible Doc Benjamin!

Poor Susan. She recounted how Doc Benjamin was an ancient geezer with great gravy eyes who lived in a house that smelled of cats. He bored her. His hands had brown spots. He talked of nothing but his remedies and theories. She would rather marry a goat.

—I told Mother if she would not help me then I'd do the fix myself, Susan said. —So I beat myself with a dustpan. I drank vinegar! I threw myself down the stairs.

—Poor lamb, I said, wincing, and did not tell her I heard of a woman once with a broken neck from that same trick and seen another who put lye in herself and one who drank peroxide with horrible results.

—I have five hundred dollars from my mother to pay you if you'll only help me.

—At this late time, I can only help you deliver your child.

—I cannot have a child! I cannot marry that Doctor but if I have this . . . this . . . who else will have me? Nobody. I would soon as kill myself, along with the—

She couldn't utter the word (baby) but left it hanging.

—There is one other possibility, I said, reluctant to offer it.

The pale Susan leaned forward with desperate eagerness.

—I could help you find a placement for it. I might know a wet nurse who would raise your child up, and be a mother to it, and you won't never see it afterwards.

Even as I said these words I felt their terrible weight and saw how they hurt her. I had never yet gone so far as to find a placement for a baby. The thought of taking a child from a mother wracked me to the core and brought to mind Mr. Brace. How he sorted us out and gave us up. But now? Now I seen what he was after. The lesser evil and the greater good, &c. How he lived with the complexities, same as me.

To confess, it must be said that in my secret heart I considered a question: Would I take in her child? I admit I thought how I might claim it, raise it up, while Susan looked away from me, gnawing her cheeks.

—I would rather have no child at all than give away mine to a stranger, she wept so bitter. —But there's no other recourse.

So at last, in great torment, she decided she would surrender her infant. I led her upstairs to a sunny room and told her my terms, the costs for room and board, for midwife service, for a wet nurse. I did not tell her of the quickening of my heartbeat, how already I dreamed it was me and Charlie who took her child in. Not even Charlie heard that idea. I kept it for myself for now, eyes peeled. Was this our chance?

Upstairs, Susan spent many days sobbing. At meals she kept apart from the other ladies—there were two or three other patients during that time—and declined to read the novels or newspapers around the place or even the Bible. I sat with her when I had a free minute and showed her the poems of Elizabeth Browning, but she was indifferent and alone. Though she was raised rich and had the coddled look of a china doll, her troubles was as heavy upon her as the troubles of any barmaid.

While Susan awaited her time, I contracted a wet nurse named Catharine Rider, a fleshly young costermonger's wife I assisted one recent day at the market when she had gone into labor behind her vegetable stall and delivered a little girl who she named Annie, after Myself. I returned to the market now and found Mrs. Rider and her new Annie sitting amongst the cabbages. She greeted me groveling with gratitude and pressing parsnips into my arms.

—How's your milk, then, Missus Rider? I asked her. —Are you nursing all right?

—Yes, Madame, she said, and showed off her girl, cooing at it.

I explained my proposition then, that she adopt new Baby Applegate and feed both the infants, for the price of four hundred dollars.

—Four hundred? she cried, in excitement. —Four hundred dollars?

Such a lump was, for her, a half year's earnings, at the least.

—And Mrs. Rider, I said, —might be we could take the child off your hands when you wean him. If you was agreeable.

She said she was agreeable, for sure, yes, whatever I asked. I did not give her further explanation, but seeing how willing she was, I determined to speak to Charlie after a time, if circumstances proved right, for now here was a chance for a child.

Catharine Rider thanked me, kissed my hand. —A boy would be nice.

Well, it was a boy. —I don't want to see him, poor Susan wept so terrible, when he was delivered. —Don't let me see him.

I hardly dared look at him myself for the guilty thought he could be mine one day. Then an hour later Susan changed her mind. She wanted to hold him. —Now, please, bring my son, oh please, Madame.

I brought him to her, and she nestled him down and gazed at him with the look of the Madonna, all wonder and moist eyes and trembling. It broke your heart to know she'd give him up. Despite my earlier fantasy, I myself now wished she would keep him, rather than watch her grief. —You still want to place him out then?

—Give me just two days with him, she said. —Oh please. Two days only.

I looked at the fusty little man there in her arms, and with a sinking heart I said, —All right, keep him a while, and sent the kitchen girl to tell Catharine Rider not to come till Thursday. It would be the worse for everybody, the longer Susan held on.

For a week, Susan Applegate refused to part with her infant, called Davey. She nursed her son and cooed over him. She slept with him swaddled in the bed next to her and sang him a song about bluebirds. She held him up to the window and watched him blink in the sunlight.

Did I shoo her away? Did I insist she surrender the boy? Did I charge extra? No.

Did I RIP THE BABY FROM ITS MOTHER'S ARMS like the *Herald* accused me? No. I stroked her hair and comforted her and we cried over him, the both of us. Our Annabelle came in to visit, for she liked to see the newborns and thought Davey was a big live dolly. She counted his wee toes in her singsong voice. —One, two, four, two, FIVE! Can we keep him for my brother?

Conflicted with sadness and selfish reasons, I didn't reply. I wavered very guilty. Every day I asked Susan, —Are you sure? and every day she

replied yes, she would give him up at the end of the week. I didn't sleep.
Baby Boy Johnny returned to haunt my nights. Charlie took my hand and
shushed me.

—You're grinding your teeth, he said.

The soul of the midwife must live with the lesser evil.

When the day came, Susan Applegate handed me one thousand dollars,
four hundred for Mrs. Rider and the rest to me for room and board and
services rendered. She thrust the money at me with a degree of rage I did
not think she possessed.

—Take this from my dear mother and the rest of it is blood money from
that wretch Adolphus! You know I hate him! she cried. —I hate him! To
him it's only money. He pays only in money, whereas I pay with—

She stopped, choked on her own dark thoughts, of a woman's currency.

—Poor young Susan, I said, and pulled her to me. —Mrs. Rider will be
here tomorrow after supper, if your mind is made up. And after that we'll
stop your milk.

I did not sleep. Catharine Rider came at six. She was bursting her dress
buttons. It was a comfort to think little Davey would have plenty of nour-
ishment. We went up the stairs where Susan clung to her little boy. —My
son, she whispered and wept so tears fell on his face. She took a silver chain
off her neck and put it over his head. —Remember me your mother who
loved you.

—Are you certain? I asked.

—Take him, she said. —Take him now. Fast. Before I lose heart. Take
him now I'm begging you.

She thrust the child in my direction and turned her face away, so I
did it. I took him from his own mother and trembled as much as she
did, sick in the gut with this project. It was what she wanted. I did not
SNATCH the child. I did not *wrest* him. She gave him over to me. I
gave him to Catharine who took him as natural as if he was hers, and she
fussed over him and called him a big handsome fella, wasn't he? yes he
was, yessirree, sir. —Don't you worry, ma'am, she told Susan. —I'll love
Davey good as my own. She bundled him into the night, and after she
left I went up to wind a sheet across Susan's chest to stop her milk, if not
her bitter weeping.

In the morning, young Miss Applegate kissed me, sober but no longer tearful. —Thank you Madame. For everything. For your kindness.

—Where will you go, child?

She would go home. Her father and mother would take her back. Nobody would know, except the family, and the beast Doc Benjamin. She was so glad she would not have to marry him. I embraced her and wished her well. Then Susan Applegate was gone, and as I watched her depart again the question came over me, would I speak to Charlie about Mrs. Rider, and little Davey, and whether, when he was weaned, we might take him? In truth, I had lost the stomach for it, as all I could picture was a child torn from a mother's breast once more, and this picture did not rest easy on my spirit.

Because of Susan now I seen in a raw new light the sorrows of my Mam, and the fingers of Mr. C. L. Brace brushed the back of my neck. I had brokered the surrender of a child to another mother, and I could feel the part not just of the child, and of the poor mother who lost him, but now also the part of Mr. Brace who had said all's he wanted was to do good. Such thoughts put me in mind to write to him again:

> *Dear Mr. Brace, have you any new information about my brother Joseph Muldoon? He is a lad 17 years of age and despite your good intentions he has been deprived of his sisters and his birthright. As I am now a wealthy woman you can be sure I will pay any sum at all for some news of his whereabouts.*

I mailed off my note, but, with little faith it would make a difference, the next day I proposed to Charlie to try hiring another detective. —Not a Snope, I said. And so Charlie agreed he would inquire at the police department for a reputable man, and this time we'd offer a reward. That night I dreamt that Mr. Brace himself came to the door. —*Here he is, your little wayfarer,* said he, holding the hand of my small brother, as if all these years, Joe had remained a child.

*   *   *

Four months later, at my door instead was Susan Applegate again. Two gentlemen waited in her carriage as she knocked. —I've come to get my boy, she said.

I invited her in, noticing an altogether new kind of pink in Susan's cheeks that day. She was an Apple Blossom for sure, and sporting a diamond on her finger, so excited to tell me that her father had coerced the bounder Adolphus Edwards home from the Antilles, and he had done the honorable thing by her. She was Mrs. Edwards now.

—We will raise our son, she told me, tearful, —little Adolphus Edwards.

—Well that's a fine thing, I said, smiling bravely at her Happy Ending.

So I would not have the boy I plotted for. It was a disappointment, sure, but just as fast, it was a relief, for I was not the one who now would have to surrender him. Catharine Rider was. And I knew that would've proved too grim for me, to hand him over once I'd claimed him. I was spared that grief, at least.

Susan went off smiling to Mrs. Rider's address to fetch her baby and I watched at the window as she drove away. I imagined a Sweet Reunion. You can imagine my dismay not an hour later to find Susan, along with the two gentlemen now, returned to the office in a lather.

—The thief Catharine Rider is not to be found, announced the older man, —and neither is the infant.

The speaker was Susan's father, Dr. Samuel Applegate, a florid old fruit who brandished his finger at me while Susan wept. The other cove, who I correctly guessed to be the redeemed scoundrel Adolphus Edwards, picked at a piece of lint on his cuff.

—You, Madame, Dr. Applegate said, —produce the child.

—It was not I who produced the child, but these two, I reminded him.

—I want my son back, squawked Adolphus, a young genteel. —If you don't return him at once I shall haul you down to the precinct and have you thrown in prison.

It was the first time I was threatened with prison but it was not the last.

—I don't have the child, but I'll find him, I said, and went to comfort poor Susan.

—Don't come near her, you monster, said her father, and snatched the girl away from my arms. —I know all about you. Your terrible Satanic practices. Your life of crime. It is well known you sell the corpses to resurrectionists! You are the horror of all of us in the medical establishment.

—Oh ho, I said. —Do you think so, Mister? I run a respectable clinic.

—You are not qualified to run a chicken coop, madam, Mr. Applegate said. —If you do not find my grandson, you will rue the day you first drew breath.

It must be said that my desperation to get the boy back was nearly the equal of Susan's, as I had suffered spasms and nightmares and guilt, separating mother and child, questioning, was my own motives selfish? And while I did not take the Doctor's threats lightly, it was Susan's tears that motivated me. I did not yet know she was in the claws of gargoyles, ready to fly down off their cornices and pounce. We set out to find the boy. The Riders' neighbors on Delancey Street told me that Catharine and her family had moved to a place called Sleepy Hollow, on the Hudson, but left no address. Charlie set out up the river to find them. He was gone for weeks.

—Where's Papa? Annabelle asked. —Has he found a baby for us?

I had to explain it was not for us he was looking and felt more sharply the loss of the children we did not have. But it was on this very mission to find the Edwards baby that Charlie took a fancy to the village of Sleepy Hollow, where the finer classes had their castles. Knocking on doors, Charlie happened upon the riverfront mansions of robber barons such as Jay Gould, and the playhouse of Washington Irving, called Sunnyside. He did not find Davey or Mrs. Rider. Was it because he spent more time ogling real estate than searching?

—Why did you take two weeks away?

—Annie, I tell you we'll build ourselves a castle above the Hudson that's the equal of Lyndhurst, he said. —Turrets. Arches. The long carriage drive. We'll retire there at Sleepy Hollow in country splendor one day. You should see the gardens at Sunnyside.

—What of Mrs. Rider?

—I tramped the whole area, and nobody knew a Rider. Nobody'd heard of this wet nurse. She isn't to be found.

*   *   *

—The trail is cold, I told Susan Applegate very sad.

The poor girl lost her senses then. I don't blame her for that. What I do blame her for is how she returned in short order and sat there with her father, telling him lies. —Madame DeBeausacq stole my baby! She took him against my will! She locked me in a room. Oh Papa I heard him crying for me! It was terrible. Ladies were bleeding and begging for mercy all night, and that woman, Madame, told them to go to the Devil.

—Susan, I reproached her, pained. —You know that is not true.

—She wrapped a plaster over my bosom, she sobbed, —and stood hardhearted while my baby cried to be fed. She's sold him to a Satanist, Papa, just as you feared.

Dr. Applegate quivered and clenched his hands so ferociously it seemed he was practicing to strangle me.

—Susan, I said, —my own heart breaks to see your distress, but please look to your conscience before you tell such tales.

Tragically, them two Applegates preferred lies to the truth, and while I refunded them all the fees I had charged, and forked them over a nice BONUS sum of a thousand dollars, they would not keep quiet. They marched out and took their fabrications to the newspapers, and thus began my dangerous days.

Chapter Thirty-One

Slander

Infant Abduction

Madame DeB_____, a Notorious she-devil, the keeper of a stylish house for the slaughter of "petit innocence" has stolen a young boy from his mother's bosom, presumably with plans to sell the infant, or fling it off the docks into a watery grave in the Hudson. Susan Applegate, still weak in the aftermath of childbirth, clung to her baby as it was wrested from her arms, and despite her cries of "My child! My child!" the well known Madame persisted in removing it, and will not reveal its whereabouts. The public will now make Liberty Street too hot to hold this wretch, unless the child is forthcoming.

—Susan! I cried aloud when I read this vilification in the *New York Herald.* —How could you?

She cut me. I helped that girl. I did what she asked, wept with her and coddled her, and now she repaid me with libel and publicity. What I'd reply to her if I could give her a piece of my mind would not be printable. Charlie tutored me what to say instead, how to address her falsehoods with reason and science. But he did not warn me how the roaches of Printing House Square would write a slanderous headline for the letter I wrote, and label me a monster:

From the Pen of Madame DeBeausacq, the Wickedest Woman in New York

To the editor:

The truth is that Miss Applegate applied to me for help during her difficulties, and being a midwife of longstanding practice, I gave her room and board until she delivered a healthy child. The mother then asked me to find a placement for her infant, as she could not raise it herself. I found a wet nurse, and Miss Applegate surrendered her child willingly. The arrangements were made between the mother and the nurse, and it seems preposterous, does it not? to hold anyone else responsible for what may have ensued after the child's birth.

Sincerely, Madame J. A. DeBeausacq, midwife

The newspapers ignored the truth. They said I ripped the Applegate child from its mother's arms. They wrote how I threw it off the docks at South Street. They wrote how I had killed another, different mother and deposited the remains in a secret sewer that flowed underground from my home to the Hudson, so that I might dispose of bodies without detection. They wrote how I sold infants to witches for their Satanic sacrifices. It was exactly what Susan's Papa had tutored her to claim. A resurrectionist, the *Gazette* wrote, had been seen leaving my premises, with grisly packages! They had me trafficking with grave robbers. It was a steaming horse pile supplied to the papers by Applegate.

—It's only hacks, said Charlie. —They can't hurt you. What power do they have?

I took what he said for an article of faith. The press was toothless. Charlie knew the papers, right? Still I did not like that it was MY name dragged through the gutter. Maybe I was Mrs. Ann Muldoon Jones but also I was

Madame J. A. DeBeausacq, and proud of my success. And so it was with dismay that one day I opened the *Sunday Morning News* to see that a certain Doctor, a man called Dr. B. S. Gunning was gunning for me, now, too.

On the Ignorance of Midwives
by Dr. Benjamin S. Gunning

In light of recent lurid information pertaining to the tragic disappearance of an infant at the hands of one Madame J. A. DeBeausacq, a self-proclaimed midwife, it behooves the medical establishment to speak out against such nefarious practices as are all too common in our grand metropolis. It is precisely the quackery and ignorance of those old women who imperil the wives and daughters of the better classes, at the most delicate period of their existence, the time of parturition.

Gunning went on to write that only a doctor with a diploma was qualified to attend a birth. Meaning only a man.

It is for us, gentlemen of the educated medical establishment, to prove that human life is too sacred to be entrusted to the uneducated midwife, whose ideas are scarcely adequate to the management of a poultry yard! Meanwhile, we shudder at reports of a resurrectionist seen leaving the premises of that most notorious demon of Liberty Street, and we can only surmise she sells the corpses of her poor victims to this wretch.

A poultry yard. A resurrectionist. Where had I heard this before? From a certain Dr. Applegate. Didn't he say to my face I was not suited to run a chicken coop? Didn't he accuse me of consorting with undertakers?

—Gunning, I muttered the name. —Gunning. Gunning.

—Are you all right, my dear? Charlie inquired, over his egg.

—Listen, Susan Applegate was to wed a Dr. Benjamin and raise her child with him against her will. Could she have referred to Dr. Benjamin Gunning? Is he one and the same?

He was. I inquired about it. Gunning was a friend of Applegate and member of Columbia College Medical Hospital. He was the SAME Dr. Gunning whose book I studied at the Evans, and who advised the mustard bath and the letting of blood to restore the Catamenial Discharge, and the vegetable diet to relieve the cramps, and while it seemed this bad advice was alone enough to brand him a first class nimenog who would not know the difference between a bustle and a barnacle, still he was a very learned man. Very important. He delivered lectures at the University of New York. He was the president of the American Medical College. He wrote books. Now he wrote against me. Who was I, an orphan girl from Cherry Street, to go against him?

—Perhaps Gunning is right, I said. —Perhaps a medical doctor is best.

—Hooey, said Charlie. —Is he a woman? Does he know the cunicle from the crinkum-crankum? Can he divine a breech child with the pass of the hands like yourself? What does he know that you don't?

—Charlie, Gunning is an expert author. You yourself have read his book.

—So? He should read mine. Charlie shrugged. —You're not to worry about Dr. B. S. Gunning. Nothing will come of his b.s. or his blather. You know he is angry because he didn't win the beautiful Susan for himself. He and his cronies only want to take your business and cut the midwives out of it.

—Pfft, they won't get our business. Ladies always prefer to see a female.

Dr. Gunning was no threat to my livelihood, we decided. But what we did not bargain on was the power of his personal grudge. Dr. Gunning was angry at losing his Apple Blossom, and Dr. Applegate was angry at how I lost his grandson the wee Adolphus, and the two of them old b******s mustered all their friends, the white beard whifflers in their white coats, and then enlisted the inky bungers of Printing House Square to their cause. I know now they were in cahoots, just a bunch of knackered old animals fit only to be RENDERED, the drippings poured boiling hot down their own throats. They was all of them in high dudgeon. They set about to bring me down.

*   *   *

Now in the papers it was war against me. Madame was written up by the *Police Gazette*. I was called "A wholesale female strangler, a modern THUG of civilized society." My medicines, the paper claimed, was at best sugar water, and worst, probably poisons. They wrote that my interventions was worse than dangerous, they was immoral.

Their insults made me angry as a cut snake. I could not stop arguing with newsprint. —First, I said to Charlie, —Mrs. DeBeausacq's powders are made of the BEST ergot and tansy oil available which are known to relieve a woman of most obstructions if taken in a proper dosage. Second, the ingredients are the SAME as what anybody can buy at Hegemann's or any chemist.

—You will write them back a challenge, Charlie said, —argued in law and science.

He wrote it for me as I talked, as was our practice since our long ago letters to Dutch, which we did not write now anymore since I had lost track of her and all hope of a track. His eyes shone with his love of argument and I seen that for him this excitement was as good as the life of a hack he used to covet. Though I still had the grammar of the old neighborhood, Charlie made me sound first class. Then I read what he wrote in the fine print:

Editors:

What criminal evidence have you against me? What gives you the right to slander my good name in public? None. I hold myself amenable to the law. My medicines are known purgatives that are sold in reputable pharmacies. Therefore, let any of my lady patients for whom I have cared these past years come forward and say that my medicines or practices have been harmful, or that any of the good care that I have extended to them in my practice of midwifery be dangerous to their health, and I will pay you and them each one hundred dollars.

Sincerely,

Madame J. A. DeBeausacq

—We will PAY them? I cried. —You went and invited them all to sue me.

—Nobody will come forward, Charlie said, pleased with himself. —Even if a lady didn't like your medicines, who would admit she received your services? Or bought a remedy from you?

—Susan Applegate did.

—The only one ever, in years, and it was her father forced her. What can she prove? If you don't like the letter, don't sign it or send it. Let the papers say what they want. You can be a chickenhearted lily-livered quail or you can tell 'em what's what.

As usual when Charlie accused me of being a coward I had to rush right out to prove him wrong. I would not roll over, not for those Maggots. No, I wouldn't, so I sent that letter he wrote, offering MONEY to anyone with a complaint. Maybe I should've kept my trap shut as Mam used to advise me. —You're asking for it, she always said and it's what the papers said of me too. Ha! Well why is it every time a girl finds trouble it's her OWN fault? I seen enough trouble myself already. Why would I ask for more? I had my own child to worry over, an angelic picture in ribbons, only five years old and sewing her little sampler with hearts and flowers, or going along with me to try on a new bonnet at A. T. Stewart's.

—Oh Mamma you are a beautiful Mamma, said she, resting her warm head against me in the carriage.

Would I risk such happiness? Not likely. It was only letters. Only self defense.

The several letters I wrote to them editors did nothing to stop their fiery campaign against me and only seemed to rile them more. All that summer, the lies piled up in the papers, festering in the boiling sun same as manure in the gutter, where flies settled like the ignorant population on the dunghill of rumor. That winter, the *Police Gazette* wrote that I had killed a girl.

Has it ever occurred to law enforcement in this city that poor Mary Rogers, murdered last year, was the victim of that hag of misery, Madame DeBeausacq? The case remains unsolved, and yet it is well known that Miss Rogers worked as a cigar girl at

Anderson's Tobacco store on Liberty Street, not three blocks from Madame's house of death. It is entirely likely that she died at the hands of this notorious wretch, who then disposed of her corpse in the Hudson.

Mary Rogers! I had never laid eyes on the creature. She was the most famous murder victim in the history books of New York. The beautiful cigar girl. When they found her she was floating in the river off Hoboken, with her face smashed and her throat bruised, strangled. The *Gazette* claimed that it was ME, Madame DeBeausacq, who had killed the poor child in my EVIL DEN on Liberty Street. They claimed poor dead Mary's body floated across the river to New Jersey and that I planted her clothes in a Hoboken sassafras grove where they found them, or hired somebody to do so.

Yes, sure. Also I could fly and shoot a moose off horseback. I never BEEN to F***ing Hoboken. The slander of it. These papers turned me into a wasp of rage. Why ever would I strangle a woman when every day I ministered to the gentle sex with all the tenderness I possessed. Plumped the pillows. Mopped tears. Sopped blood. I was the SAINT of Liberty Street. Of all New York. And what did they say of me? The *Police Gazette* called me Evil Doctress and suggested that a cordon of officers be drawn around my house, to prevent the entrance of unfortunate and misguided females, who, they said, "so desperately seek to hide their shame."

Well, the newspaper boys underestimated female desperation. Nothing seemed to prevent my ladies coming to me. Not a cordon of police. Not firehouse dogs. In time, we had both out front. For now, thanks to Chief Matsell and his *Police Gazette*, with the helpful counsel of Doctors Applegate and Gunning, I was under threat, watched and hounded, the papers picking on me daily, a policeman walking a regular beat out front of the clinic, and still my ladies came to me for help.

—What if I am arrested? I says to Charlie.

—We'll bail you out and get the charges dropped, Mr. Optimist Charlie replied.

—And how will you do that? A magician trick?

—Friends in high places. Judges. Police lieutenants. A payment. That's how it's done, right? That's what your Mrs. Evans claimed.

—And if that fails?

—We hire a lawyer. But I STILL don't think any woman would testify. Why would she?

—But if you're wrong then it's a year in jail for me and do you think your daughter will like to have a mother in the Tombs?

—My darling, they are all talk and no action. What can they prove?

The answer was, nothing. Charlie was a salesman. He sold his argument to me, and really, what he said made sense. I trusted my ladies above all. They had good reason to be quiet, and that was my best insurance.

It was a chicken-neck cop, so young you seen where the pinfeathers was plucked above the neck of his uniform, who walked Liberty Street daily between my office and my house, swinging his shillelagh and whistling Toura Loo. One morning I went out with a market basket, to welcome him.

—Good morning, Officer, I said, very smiley.

He gave me a cold stare.

—Lovely weather, I said. Which it wasn't. The poor trap was blowing on his hands and stamping, his nose red, so when I returned from my errand I sent our Maggie McGrath out to him with a cup of hot cider, fluttering her considerable eyelashes.

—Madame DeBeausacq sent this, in thanks to you for protecting our establishment, Maggie said with no apparent sarcasm.

When the temperature dropped into the cellar so did Officer Corrigan's resolve, which finally was melted altogether by the heat of the soups we sent him from Rebecca's kitchen, and the warm lights of Maggie's smile. In no time, he was stepping in the back door to thaw his mitts at our fire, and we women was giving him pints of ale and remedies for his Mam who had the consumption, and contributions to the charity of his choice, namely his own pocket, and generally taming him down from Foe to Friend.

But Police was like roaches and when you saw one it was well knownt here was a nest of them under every crack of the floor. We advised ladies to lower their veils upon leaving, and not to speak to anyone, and to walk some distance the wrong way, to see if they were followed. Afraid as we was of the hairy hand of the law, we placed our trust in our own mutual interests: not to be exposed. None of them would tell. And so still the women came, or sent their husbands, or their sweethearts, or sometimes even a brother. These men scuttled in with their paws in their pockets, stammering, did I have a remedy for their sweet Martha? their Jenny? their Missus? Could I pay a house call on Margaret? Come quick please for Mrs. Roper? It touched the heart to see these fellas' concern and their relief as they paid me, pocketing the pill bottles and the pamphlets of advice, or hurrying me through the dark streets toward their ladies' trouble. I remember especially Mr. Bivens, a kindly fellow, hostage as any to his own masculine urges. He came fresh from praying on his knees in church.

—I told God my Ruby is in the family way again, said Mr. Bivens, —and if she has one more it'll surely kill her. Well don't you know He answered my prayer to say it was no sin to come and ask for your help as well as His, if it would spare poor Ruby.

Well his Ruby came to my door, too, some time after I sold her husband some medicines and preventatives, expressly to thank me for the improvements in her health (and, she said shyly, OTHER improvements). Her husband had read all of Charlie's pamphlets. —We're following the ways of them French, she said, —and have stayed with just our four children very happily since, and don't expect to have more.

If only such a happy ending was the result for every woman who crossed my threshold, but too bad, there was one or two of them ended up like poor Cordelia Purdy, which is one or two more than I care to remember.

Chapter Thirty-Two

Guardian

ordelia was just a small bony girl with a tumble of black hair like
scribbles under her hat. I put her age at the time to be sixteen years,
not more. When I brought her into the office she would not look at me.
She was nervous and sidelong as a bird.

—Is everything I say here private? she whispered.

—My dear Mrs. Purdy, you bury your secrets when you tell them to me.

She sighed and fidgeted very childish with the strap of her handbag.
—My husband has sent me here from New Haven . . . to procure an . . .
abortion.

She said the word so quiet I cocked my ear to her. —You have other little
ones at home then?

—We have no children. She squirmed and gnawed at a fingernail, twisting it between her teeth till it came away in a spot of blood. —You're sure
it's secret?

I nodded.

—Oh Madame, she cried, —I am not his wife, though I am called Mrs.
Purdy.

—I see.

—No I'm afraid you don't. He is . . . my uncle. I am his ward and niece.

—His ward?

—Yes, but he presents me as his wife. My name is Cordelia Shackford
but he calls me Mrs. Purdy.

{ 278 }

—He's your guardian, you say?

—He'll marry me soon. He promised. He treats me all right.

—Right as ruin, I said under my breath. —How many months are you, my dear?

—No more than three.

—Have you tried any tablets?

—They made me sick. He says it's the operation now or else.

—Are you committed to this course? It's not just your so-called guardian, trying to bury his shame?

—It's MY shame, she cried. —I don't have a choice about it. He's made it plain. If I don't do as he says he'll let it be known I have gone off with soldiers which I haven't. Uncle George loves me he says but he can't have a scandal, so the operation it is, again.

—Again?

She looked away. —I've been to Mrs. Costello before. Twice. If I refuse he'll throw me out and never marry me as he promised. We saw your notice in the New Haven paper and came since a girl at Costello's told me you was gentle.

—Three times! Your guardian belongs in jail.

—And what would happen to me if he was? Where would I go then?

I sat beside the girl on the sofa and put my arm around her narrow shoulders. She smelled of lilac water. She had tiny feet in tiny boots that buttoned up the sides. There was a plain ring on her wedding finger. He gave it to her, she said, so she could tell me and anyone who wondered that she was Mrs. Purdy and there wouldn't be gossip.

—Where's your mother, sweetheart? I said, soft.

—She died when I was fourteen. Two years ago.

I told her mine died too. For a while we sat very quiet, the two of us, thinking of our mothers, and how, had they not left us, neither of us would be having this talk.

—In her will, Cordelia said, —she trusted me to Mr. Purdy. To provide my education.

—And so he has provided one, the old ferret, though not the kind your mother hoped for.

—He has promised to marry me in two years, I told you, when I turn eighteen.

—Is that your choice then?

—It's no choice at all. I've to do as he says.

—All right then, I sighed very heavy. —Return tomorrow after dinner with the money, my dear, and I will relieve you of your trouble.

—Thank you Madame. She put on her blue shawl, the color of a hyacinth, and went out to the street chewing her finger, wary and hunted.

The next afternoon Cordelia and I sat together on the bed upstairs. —All right, sweetheart? I asked her. —Are you sure, then?

She nodded and rummaged in her bag, handed me the price, then smiled weakly.

—Ah there now, love, don't be too sad. You're a pretty girl and will have pretty children. You'll keep your kids one day.

—Oh, Madame, I pray it's true.

—You'll have a better class of man then, let's hope. I pushed the silk of her hair off her face. —Now Cordelia, sweetheart. I'm afraid I have to probe you.

—I know.

—And you'll be a brave girl.

—I will.

It was a difficult one. The probe could not find the channel. There was scarring thanks to the work of Mrs. Costello. My poor girl bit down on a piece of rawhide I gave her. Halfway through she fainted. Throughout, my throat was half-closed with panic and a chemical pulse of fear went through me as I worked, my heart pounding so fast, my hands damp. It never was easy for me, not once or ever, though I known my way around as expert as possible. Each time was different and each time could be the time of a terrible mistake and each time I cursed and wished for some magical elixir to send these poor ladies to oblivion whilst the task was under way. But there was nothing for it except for them to suffer. Thus I had learnt to make my heart a hard nut, like the Brazils or the filberts you could only crack with bricks, and though Cordelia cried, I did not crack. I said, —Be still. Hush. I was sharp with her, as I was sharp when I had to be, for while I was not even ninety pounds, they knew it was me in charge of them at that minute. What they did not know, my ladies, was that if they flinched wrong a nick could kill them.

—Stop that now, I said, when she set up a piercing cry, and after that she only whimpered. When I was done at last I spoiled her. I spoiled them all, but her, more. She was a lost wild girl of sixteen and her guardian would not guard her. I tucked Cordelia in. —Just rest now, *macushla*. I called her in my mother's Irish word for darling and kissed her clammy head and smoothed the black hair off her face. I brought her mint tea and fresh sheets. She drank the tea and vomited. I put her on the groaning chair with the basin below and she sat doubled over. She cried and I held her in my arms and called her wee babby, girleen, and sweet Cordelia, *aroun machree*. I called her child although she was just ten years younger than myself. She could have been Dutch, I thought, what if she was my sister? Something frightened about her made me feel she was mine to keep care of. All night she went back and forth from the chair to the bed. —Terrible blood comes from me, she said. I slept on the floor of her room. By morning, her head was hot. Her lips was dry and shiny with fever.

I thought she would die.

For two days, the fever in our little Cordelia Purdy had us running. I didn't go home to my Belle all the night long and sent word to Sallie the nurse to spoil her with a sugar lump after dinner to make up for missing me. How that child still at five years of age did fret when I was not there to sing her *shoul aroun*. Instead, I sang to Cordelia very soft. Me and Greta was up and down with compresses. Buckets. Water. Sheets. We fanned her. Her brow was hot and the pillow soaked. —Mama, she called out, and cried in my arms. We would lose her, I thought. The bones of her frame were so light when I held her, willow bones. The skin of her face was tight across her cheeks. On the second day I sent Greta for leeches from the apothecary. They were dark and meaty, thick as thumbs along her white skin. The poor patient did not notice. They lay on her skin drawing the fever out of her. She was listless. Her limbs were limp and her breathing shallow. On the morning of the third day when I pressed her abdomen it was tight across the bowl of her hips. There was a smell of old blood, musk.

—I'll have to probe her again, I told Greta, and so spent another night away from my little one.

*   *   *

In the morning afterwards Cordelia was better. After another day the fever cleared. We helped her sit up in the bed, and she was so damp and gray colored.

—If he doesn't marry me now, she whispered, —I'll kill myself.

—Aw sweet, I said. —Don't trouble your head about it.

—I will do it.

—No, now shhh, you won't. You'll come back here, lamb. You come here if ever you need a hand. For anything. You can always come to Madame's.

I don't know why I said it. Sure I wouldn't have, had I known how it would play out later. But I said it. You can always come to Madame's. There was plenty of girls desperate as Cordelia Purdy, as young and troubled. I didn't say it to them. But there was something about this one. Her motherlessness. And that black hair of hers in a tangle. It put me in mind of Dutchie. Of my younger self. And I thought of my sister across the sea with her fancy husband, probably dancing the valse in Vienna with the Kaiser, or back in Chicago with the Ambroses and their high society.

Three years had passed since our tragic missed connection. I did not write Dutch now for I had no safe address. I could not write Chicago no more because I feared exposing her secret, that she was not a natural-born Ambrose but A KIDNAPPED PAPIST CHILD, a New York Irish, apparently a fact so shameful it would be her undoing. Did my sister have her own babies to run after? Likely yes, and my brother Joe would be a man in long pants by this time. Was his hair thick as our Da's? Could he carry a tune like our Mam? Charlie had not contracted another detective for we wished to avoid police at all costs now, along with private dicks like Snope who'd only swindle. I cursed myself anew for my broken promise to her, yet still this longing for my old family was a cool moon, sometimes sharp like a scythe blade, other times round as a coin, a wealth I couldn't have, lurking far away behind clouds. I turned my nervous protections as best as possible toward my own daughter and all the troubled ladies who came to my door. Instead of a big pile of relatives, I had one little girl, and desperate females like Cordelia under my roof to watch over.

In the afternoon I fetched Annabelle from her school, and we brought poor Cordelia strawberries and a chocolate wrapped in colored paper. I plumped her pillows while Belle warbled in the corner, playing with the ribbons on her hat. —There now, Cordelia, love, I said. —You're all right now.

—Do you know how to make a man marry you? she asked.

—If you have to make him, then you don't want him.

—Mr. Purdy's all I have. There's no one else.

—You could work here for me. We are in need of a kitchen maid.

—Oh yes please, miss, said Belle, who was ever after listening in. —You are much more nicer than our Maggie who licks the frosting spoon ahead of me.

—A kitchen maid? Cordelia considered it. I watched her. You could see her dress herself in a uniform, the apron, wondering where does a kitchen maid sleep? *I could teach her,* I thought. Her hands were small. She would learn like me.

—I was a maid once myself, I told her, —in a doctor's house. Not near as nice as this.

—Oh, she said, —were you? Her smile was watery and distracted.

When she declined and said she was going back to her so-called guardian, I gave her an envelope of French letters. —He won't, says she. —He doesn't care for them.

—The b*****d, I says. —So here's another remedy to try then when he's after you: coat a piece of sponge with honey and put that where the sun don't shine. If you're lucky he'll never know the difference and it'll act as a pessary against a repeat visit, and if you're not lucky—well I'm hopeful, sweetheart, I'm hopeful for you.

Later, she came downstairs with her satchel packed and her hair swept into a knot. She embraced me tearfully. —Oh Madame. Thank you.

—Never mind, I said, fondly. —You're all right now.

—You're good as a mother to me. She kissed me. —I'll never forget you. Cordelia then squared her shoulders and departed my doorstep, checking left and right to see if she was watched. No one was about, or so it appeared.

Chapter Thirty-Three

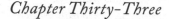

Warning

*A*t half past nine one morning not long after Cordelia left, I was returning home from a lady in labor on Duane Street, a heroine's effort all night, with a boy just delivered. When I turned the corner home to Liberty Street, there was my girl Belle, a wee trundle of black curls and motion. She was playing with a hoop, and as it rolled along, she chased after it. —Smelly Nelly! she sang, full of spunk and vinegar.

The white of her knee shone in a knob through the hole in her stockings and her ribbon was untied. —Smelly Nelly, she cried loudly.

Ellen, the governess who she called Nelly, sat on the steps of our house, watching with a well-paid eye. Annabelle did not like her.

—Smelly, smelly, smelly Nelly, my girl sang out.

Having now studied the Mother's Book by Mrs. Lydia Child, I known it was not proper for a young lady to shriek like a savage so I stopped her by surprise.

—Oh Mam! she cried when she saw me, and leaped into my arms. She clamped her legs around my waist, kissed my face and petted my hair. —I have a new hoop!

—Do you now, ya bad girl?

—I am not bad.

—Calling Ellen names! Shrieking like a banshee. Look at your stockings!

—I don't care. The cook's man gave me this hoop off a tar barrel.

She struggled out of my arms and rolled it away fast with her mighty five-year-old legs chugging. I watched her with a strange heart, afraid. Terrified always. A horse would shy and run her over. A buggy would. Fever would come in the night. Strangers would take her from me.

Instead, danger announced itself in the cry of a newsboy.

—The Charnel House of Liberty Street! he cried, just when my daughter passed him with her barrel hoop. —Get your paper here! The Charnel House of Liberty Street!

—My Mam has offices on Liberty Street, says Belle, and stopped next to him.

—Why then, ask her to buy you a copy of the *Polyanthos,* said the runt of a newsboy, pimples on his face like smashed raspberries. —Get your *Polyanthos* here! A nickel is all! The Charnel House of Shame. Liberty Street Scandal!

Full of foreboding I paid him a nickel and took Belle by the hand.

—We live on Liberty Street, isn't that so, Mam? she said, trotting along beside me, looking up, ready for a talk. How we loved to talk, us two. That child was an Axie like her mam. Nothing was ever so much fun for me as to tell her things and see what question she'd manufacture next. Now, though, I did not answer her chatter, when she asked What is a Charnel House? but stopped still at the headlines.

In the newspaper I held open there above my daughter's head, was half a page printed with a lithograph in a scowling likeness of ME, dark hair in ringlets. "Madame DeBeausacq, The Female Abortionist," it said below the portrait, with a skull below and bones crossed beneath my shawl. Right alongside this slander was printed a scurrilous pile of dung written by one George W. Dixon, editor.

> In our fair city lurks a Demon woman called Madame
> DeBeausacq who has been responsible for hundreds of wicked
> crimes! It is too well known just what her evil practices entail.
> This Bat, this bloodsucker, is a blot stain on humanity, her
> crimes are crimes against morality!

More c**p. The Applegate affair had faded away and there was nothing new for the jackals to feed on, so they was conjuring B. and S. against ME, while nobody, not ONE of those gargoyles, wrote how George Washington Dixon, the editor of the *Polyanthos*, was a man known to manufacture spectacle in order to sell his rag. He was known for dressing in blackface to sing the darkie song Zip Coon. Known for circus tricks and hypnotism, known to love a scandal, as tawdry as possible. If an actual scandal was not available, he drummed one up. Charlie had explained it all to me. How the papers worked. How the editor of the *Police Gazette* was none other than George Matsell, the Police Chief himself. The newspapers was good for nothing but fishwrap. They were not satisfied planting rumors and false-hoods about me. They wanted a riot. They wanted my head on a plate.

—What does it say, Mam? asked Belle, tugging my hand. —What does it say?

—Nothing true.

What it said was manure off the street. The cove Dixon was lucky, because if I was a bat or a demon I'd come for him in the night and carry him off to fester in a pig wallow where he'd be right at home, obsessed as he was with so-called female VIRTUE. As I read along, fury replaced fear, as I saw what this Dixon was up to. He'd have you believe it was WOMEN who corrupted themselves, all alone, and the MEN—so-called GUARD-IANS like George Purdy—had nothing to do with it. In Dixon's excuse for intelligent argument, he wrote that if it wasn't for ME, Madame DeB., the Ladies of Gotham would all be Virgins. But, because I sold certain medi-cines and services, they was hoors and I had made them hoors.

Men! You took to your bosom a wife, the image of purity, a thing upon which you think the stamp of God has been printed. Not so! Madame DeB*******'s so-called Preventative Powders have counterfeited the handwriting of Nature. You have not a medal, fresh from the mint, but a base, lacquered counter that has undergone the sweaty contamination of a hundred palms. Madame DeB******* will tell you how to swindle your husband or deceive your lover.

If you asked me, I and my Remedy saved more females from becoming red light sisters than any preacher on Sunday, and these b*****ds should get down on their knobby knees and thank me. Instead they blanked out my name like it was a curse and drew pictures of me as a hellkite witch. Then this POODLE Dixon of the *Polyanthos*, again called out the law on me.

Where is the grand jury? Where the police? We, the *Polyanthos*, will keep this woman's flag, with the death's head and marrow bones, at her mast head, until she is legally dealt with!

—Mother! said Belle. She tugged at my elbow. —What does it say?

—Lies and c**p my darling, I said, but with a new cold paw of fear on my neck. —It's all c**p.

—C**p, she said so prettily, and I had to kneel and explain to her ladies did not say such words, and that Mrs. Priscilla Lyle the headmistress of Lyle School for Girls would not like her to say them in her schoolyard. My angel nodded very solemn. —Why then do you say them, Mam?

—Do not ask so many questions.

—Yes Mother, says she, and we skipped up the front steps where I left her to Smelly Nelly the governess and went to the library to find my husband to show him these new words: Grand Jury.

—Death's Head and Marrow Bones my a**, Charlie said, reading Dixon's screed.

—But Charlie, more and more they talk of POLICE! I cried. —Mrs. Evans never once was exposed to the law, but now thanks to that Applegate, the papers'll have the traps on me.

—Not on you, Mrs. Jones. On Madame DeBeausacq. The point is YOU are not Madame. Madame is an old woman, an aged French lady who visits from time to time, when she's here from Paris. Sometimes she's in town, and sometimes she's not. They can't hang you for the acts of another.

—They have a picture!

—A drawing that looks nothing like you. Who's to say you are Madame?

—The police. They have their manacles and what have I got? Twaddle.

—You've got secrets. You know the name of every Society Gentleman whose mistakes you fixed. You know their doxies. You have a list. You have names. You have dates. They have no proof. They can't touch you. If they do, you'll reveal them.

—Oh, I said, slumping. I took a breath and remembered. He was right. Wasn't he? They couldn't touch me. I had a list. I wasn't Madame, I was Mrs. Jones. Again his confidence lowered my guard and draped a blanket of safety around my shoulders.

—Have you ever heard of a midwife getting arrested? he asked. —Have you? No. Morrill hasn't either, and he's a lawyer. You are safe.

Charlie's arguments renewed my resolve and worse, gave me contempt for my Enemies. The stupid b******s. I read Dixon's words, scoffing along with Charlie.

—How can Dixon say it is ME who corrupts? I said, in full cry, —when it's men, these wolves who do the sweet-talking and the strong-arming and can't control their urges. The only one looking out for the ladies is ME.

Charlie grinned. —Well argued, Mrs. Jones. It's almost like you'd been hanging around with a rabble of dangerous freethinkers or some such. He again bore down on his pen, and soon handed me a page. —Here's your letter to the editor, Madame.

> To: George W. Dixon, Editor, The Polyanthos
> From: Madame J. A. DeBeausacq
>
> Sirs,
>   I cannot conceive how men who are husbands, brothers, or fathers can give utterance to an idea so base and infamous— that their wives, their sisters, or their daughters want but the "facilities" to be scandalous. What! is female virtue then a mere thing of circumstance and occasion? Is there but a difference of opportunity between it and pr*st*t*tion? Would your wives and your sisters, and your daughters, if once absolved from fear, all become pr*st*t**es? I assure you, not, and I have their names and their letters as proof! In fact, the Preventative Powders sold by Madame DeBeausacq are well known to PROTECT the lives of mothers and women, and save them from VICE. Gentlemen! I urge you to eschew your OWN immoral conduct, lest you bring

shame upon that state of virtue which you value and prize beyond
any other feminine attribute.
    Signed, Madame J. A. DeBeausacq, 129 Liberty Street.

—You do have a talent for how to write me down, Charles Jones, I said,
and saw again by his pleased expression how he liked to hear sweet words
from me.

Included with the letter to the editors, Charlie had wrote out a list, simply called "patients," which consisted of names, disguised, as follows: Mrs.
John A., magistrate's wife; John P., financier; John L., banker; Miss Jane
W., Daughter of the American Revolution; Mrs. John N. T., wife of the
distinguished professor, and so on.

—The list, he said, —is the secret weapon. If they arrest you, you'll
threaten to release the names. Plenty of coves in this city—bigwigs and
fat cats—want that list to remain secret. They'll make sure any charges are
dropped.

The *Polyanthos* printed the letter the next day, but neither the letter nor
the threat of the LIST did any good, for published alongside my note was
MORE of Dixon's lies. That weevil was too cowardly even to print my
name. Instead the next day, it was Dixon who branded on me the rude
moniker MADAME X.

The Female Abortionist, by George Washington Dixon

No doubt, that with our efforts redoubled, this atrocious
foreign woman, notorious throughout this city, will soon be
brought to justice. Her nefarious practices will cease, so that
the ladies of New York will guard their virtue with more care.
But beware! When Madame X (whose francophone name is
too well known in our city to need reprinting, its very sound
a curse) is in the dock, awful disclosures will pour forth: the
names of the prominent and the wellborn, and the true nature
of the Gomorrah where we live will be revealed. Sinners should
tremble in their boots.

I was not the sinner but I trembled. —In the DOCK?

—It's . . . yes . . . a small risk, Charlie said. —Prison. A small risk. Right?

He caught my eyes with his. It was the first time he admitted it. That I could go to jail. The frank intensity of his gaze, as he said Risk and Prison, and the cut of his jaw beneath the short boxed beard he wore, and how he whispered to me now still had a danger in it that nevertheless confounded me with a thrill in the blood. He liked a risk. He always had, and it seemed now, thanks to his daring me, I liked a risk too. I would ride on the roof of the train. Would I?

—You know that, Annie, right? It's a slim danger. But it's real.

We two pulled away to look at that danger like it was a zoo beast, mulling around it to see if it might attack us, and as we done this Charlie began to talk again, like he could cage the menace with his words. —Trust me. The list will keep them off. Dixon appears to think so, or why else would he mention the prominent and the wellborn?

Hmm. A list would save me? How? Why would the fact I'd assisted Mrs. Phillip Pennybacker, wife of the head of the NY Stock Exchange, to remove an obstruction in her passages after the birth of her fifth child, or that I had relieved Lily DeLisle, the mistress of Mr. Randolph A. Havemeyer, cousin to the Mayor, when she found herself in need of renovation, save me? Why would ANY of the intimate services I had provided to the ladies of Fifth Avenue ever save me? But Charlie said they would. He said my ladies would defend me. And also lawyers would. —Morrill says the statute is a puny featherweight that never will trap you. And if it did, he says the charges are easy to beat. Your fears are piffle, Charlie said.

—Piffle? Not hardly.

—Listen: Susan Applegate's charges did not even come before a judge. And despite we offered MONEY to anyone with a complaint, not one woman has come forward. Not for a year.

—Charlie. Our child motherless. I can't. It's a year in jail.

—A year you won't ever serve. He was confident as a peacock.

—For sure YOU won't serve it. It's not YOU they're after.

He chewed that idea in his mind, nodding. —Right. But if you aren't willing to entertain the slim chance of prison, then quit. It's what they WANT you to do. Retire. They are after you to stop. Quit the practice.

—Quit? Now I was a bull and the newspaper slander was a red cape waved in my face. —It's our livelihood! And what about the ladies? Who would mind their troubles if I quit? Mrs. Costello? She's a butcher, I see when they come to me after she's mauled them.

—Then you are the one for the job, Mrs. Jones. Charlie lifted my doubting phiz between his palms. —Only you can say when you've had enough.

—Right. Because it's not you they'll hang.

—Stop the dramatics. It's not a hanging offense.

—Why's it an offense at all? Maybe the law don't like it, but it's only a lesser evil.

—Exactly. And you ought to know this: Sacks and Arguimbeau and Owens, especially, believe you must stand firm. They are your steadfast admirers and agree you're a great fighter.

—I do not want to be a fighter.

—But you're in it anyway. Aren't you?

I did not reply, but I seen he was right. I was in it. And he was in it with me. Thus the two of us after that chose to live alongside risk like frontiersmen do, with wolves roaming wild in the forest, keeping the children close and trusting providence.

—You're safe, Charlie said, with more hope than evidence. —Mark my words.

I marked them, but I was not safe. Cordelia Purdy wrote me a letter:

> *Madame,*
>
> *I must hasten to inform you that after leaving your premises a policeman followed me all the way home, and asked my purpose in visiting you. I told him it was a private matter. Still, he insisted on taking down my name and noting my address. I thought it best to warn you.*

Chapter Thirty-Four

Riot

*T*he day after the newspaper published Dixon's call to put me in the Dock, I was walking my daughter home from school, the two of us holding hands. Little Annabelle skipped and practiced her letters on the street signs. "Barber Shop," she recited proudly, "Hair tonic for gentlemen," "Shoe shine five cents." Only six years old and reading like a professional. Already she had the makings of the fine cosmopolitan woman she would surely become, delicate-boned and charming. We had already taken her to hear the Magic Flute opera at the Philharmonic Society and she declared she would sing like Ida Rosburgh. We took her to see Roman statues at the new Metropolitan Museum and she declared she would like to go to Rome. We dined with her at Delmonico's and she announced she would eat Charlotte Russe every day. My own dreams saw her whirling in cotillions and famed for her charm and beauty. She would have entry into the finest parlors, draw suitors from the upper ranks, live in a grand house on the avenue.

Now as she skipped along we seen a man tacking a notice to a Cortlandt Street storefront and mistook him for a common advertiser. He was clean-shaven and tall with a great black head of hair swept into a pompadour, pointy in the nose and chin. Annabelle brought me over to see what his notice said, and he scuttled away to tack another to a lamppost. I hoisted my girl up to practice her reading on his sign but I hadn't got three lines in before I put her down again in alarm:

Citizens! A Public Protest!

For the Enforcement of Law

Against Madame DeBeausacq of Liberty Street

A committee in formation to force her removal!

Assemble at Cortlandt Street

Tuesday, February 8, 1876

At 10 o'clock in the morning

—What is it Mam? my daughter asked as I tore the sign down from its post.

—Nothing, child, I said, and took her hand. —A committee.

—Committee, C.O.M.I.—

—Two ems, I said, cold and wooden. —Two ems, two tees, and two e's.

Annabelle skipped along singing and spelling. Several of the neighbors saw us and could not help but smile at the picture we made, swinging our hands. Did they recognize the picture of the wickedest woman in the city skipping past? Did they know a committee was forming to force my removal? Maybe they did know. Sure they did. Maybe these neighbors was the ones who later assembled, as the sign directed, and joined the mob that assailed me.

The next morning I delivered Annabelle to school. Mrs. Lyle praised my daughter for her posture and deportment, unawares that Mrs. Ann Jones sitting across from her was a Bat and Demon. —Although she should learn better not to fidget, Annabelle Gwendolyn is a refined child, said Mrs. Lyle, —and pure of heart.

I wore this praise of REFINED and PURE like a red feather in my hat and started home full of pride, humming that old song I learnt on the orphan train, *O children, dear children, happy, young, and pure* . . . as I often did. But still the winter sky seemed weighted, with snow, or something worse. At home I found Maggie McGrath filling the lamps with oil and Rebecca the cook making bread. Nelly the governess had gone off to a milliner's, and Charlie was already gone to Yorkville, to see to Madame DeBeausacq's agent Mrs. Prem, who owed us a sum of money. I was just preparing to meet Greta at the office down the street for the morning's appointments when I heard a noise outside, growing louder. Shouts and the beating of pots. The clang of a cowbell and the hum of rabid voices. I ran outside, but when I seen what was brewing I ran in again.

It was not a committee. It was a mob, raging down Liberty from the direction of Cortlandt, a swarm of roaches pouring from the cracks between paving stones.

—Maggie! I cried. —Rebecca!

Slam the door. Slide the bolt. Close the shades. Maggie and Rebecca hid in the pantry. Upstairs, through a crack in the shutters, I looked down at the street. A furious rabble seethed below, a crowd in front of my house. Women with bonnets and market baskets. Vagrant children with sticks, their tongues out, fingers in their ears, jeering. Men brandishing fists and brooms.

—A hag lives among us!

—Throw her to the dogs.

—Where's Susan Applegate's child?

—Revenge for Mary Rogers!

—Haul her out! Drag her out!

They seethed below me, their faces lifted like pale pocked moons to the windows looking for a glimpse of scandal, until they turned in a mass toward the sound of boots marching. It was a cohort of policemen coming up Liberty Street. Their leader was a large beast of a man, some three hundred pounds. I recognized the Chief of Police himself, George Matsell. Apparently it was not enough for him to crucify me in the pages of his *Gazette,* now he was here to crucify me in person, an editor in a cop's uniform, wielding his stick. Sure, he'd have his story tomorrow, for hadn't he stirred it up himself?

Matsell lumbered through the crowd to my door. His troops followed by the dozens. In the drab light their brass buttons had the glint of menace. Their boots was hard and loud as the rattle of swords on the pavement, and danger fogged the air along with their white breath in the cold. Matsell blew a whistle and twenty traps in dark blue lined up across the front of my house while the rabble screamed.

—Murderess! Deathmonger!

Somebody tossed something hard, a clod of mud or a bottle. It cracked against the window. They hurled whatever came to hand. Pebbles, chestnuts, oyster shells, apple cores, chunks of horse dung frozen to ice.

—This house is built on babies' skulls.

—A thousand children murdered in this house!

These people to me was ignorant lumps of coal. If all the tears shed on my shoulder would rain down on their cretinous heads they still wouldn't know a skerrick of what I knew, not the truth nor the doubts or the gore or the mercy or the thanks I got every livelong day. They craned their necks up at the house to see me. Neighbors who on other days whistled and swept the sidewalk, waved hello and tipped their hats, now threw open their windows, shouted, shook their fists, and cursed me for the devil.

—Murderess! Sinner!

—Haul her out and hang the hag.

The police formed a hedge of blue coats around my house as the rabble began a chant, their voices hard as bricks.

—Haul her out, haul her out. String her up, string her up.

Their white eyes was cracked red with rage. Their open gobs slobbered and foamed at the lips. The world's people was against me until they wasn't. Till they needed me. Then it was Oh Help Me, Madame. They was my neighbors and good citizens. Why did they hate me so?

Now somebody rolled a hogshead barrel in front of my parlor window. A hairy pompadour with a pointy chin climbed up top of it. Oh look! it was the very same COCKROACH who had posted the notices in Cortlandt Street the day before.

—Dixon! cried the rabble. —Dixon, Dixon.

Dixon? So. The whole thing was a staged play. I seen it with my own eyes. It was Dixon who posted the notices, who gathered the crowd, stirred them to a foaming frenzy. He was selling papers. He was a showman. He was not there to sing Zip Coon, nossirree, he was there to make speeches.

—Ladies and Gentlemen, Dixon says, holding his finger aloft, —I beseech you to remove this Blight from our midst! I refer to Madame DeBeausacq, the murderer and female fraud whose gold and riches are made off the bones of the innocent!

—Hang the woman!

—If Madame won't remove herself from the neighborhood, Dixon continued, —why, let the people take the matter in hand, let them storm the door, and haul her out!

At this a roar came from the maw of the crowd, and it rushed forward toward the line of police. This incitement to lynch me was too much for Matsell, for although I'm sure he in fact wished to see me strung from the locust tree out front, he was after all charged with keeping the peace.

—Disperse, now disperse, cried the Editor in his Police uniform. —Break it up, now. He was a haunch of meat on my stoop, smacking a billy club onto the flat of his palm. The mob heckled and cackled but they did not attack. They milled about threatening, so I was more than frantic over how would I escape? How would I fetch my daughter from school? How would I get a message to Charlie or Greta or Morrill the lawyer? Later I was relieved to learn that down the block at the office Greta had heard the rioters at the other end of Liberty Street and had shuttered the place, then gone to fetch Annabelle. My daughter stayed that night with Greta, playing with Willi, ignorant of the crisis at home.

—Murderess! Foul Murderess! the hecklers shouted, till at last, as the afternoon darkened, most of them scuttled away, back to the cracks and crevices where they would feed off garbage and gossip. By evening it was only a few of them about, muttering, sorry to miss the hanging. And then it was only the men in uniform outside.

—It's just the police anymore, said Maggie, still scared.

Hang me for a fool. The moment she said that—it was just the police— was the moment I recognized the red face of real danger. The traps were not there to protect me. Danger was the dumb hand of the dumb law and now here it was rapping at my door.

—Go and answer it, I said to Maggie. —You know what to say.

Maggie opened it.

—Madame DeBeausacq? said a voice larded with authority.

—Madame does not live here, said clever Maggie. —And my mistress is not at home. Who may I tell her has called?

—Chief Matsell, said my visitor. —Please tell Madame that we know she is at odds with regulations and is under advisement to cease her practices, or face the consequences.

—Consequences? said Maggie, and I could almost hear the flapping of her lashes as she coquetted and tipped her head. —Consequences?

—We're not above hanging her, he said.

Chapter Thirty-Five

Notorious

*T*he next day, the *Polyanthos,* the *Herald,* and the *Police Gazette* sold papers off the account of the so-called riot, not bothering to mention they started it themselves as fodder for their pages. The *Herald* reported in smug tones that I cowered inside my LAIR trembling lest the mob haul me out of my CHARNEL HOUSE and rip me limb from limb. The *Gazette* said, the SHE-DEVIL was not at home, but off selling a baby into white SLAVERY. The *Polyanthos* wrote how the mob had a noose made, ready to swing me from a lamppost.

That riot sold papers like hot corn on the corner. They wrote their lies and I read them at the breakfast table of the Astor House Hotel where Charlie had insisted, after hearing the events of the day, that we remove ourselves for safety. There we were joined by our friends the Owens, and the lawyer Morrill. Ida Owens patted my hand while the men harrumphed and bristled their whiskers with righteousness at the trumped up poppy-cock of fabrication printed about me. The cream curdled in my coffee as I read the *Gazette*'s account.

> Great excitement existed yesterday on Liberty Street in the
> vicinity of the house occupied by a certain Madame X, and
> was ominous of a deep feeling of abhorrence among the better
> classes, for the practices of this miserable female wretch, who
> hid trembling behind the shutters while a crowd called for her

removal. We trust from the expression of yesterday, Madame is now convinced of the necessity of closing her business; otherwise there seems to be a most fearful certainty that the end of outrage toward her is not yet.

—"Madame is convinced," Charlie read. —Is that so?

—ARE you convinced of the necessity of closing your doors? Ida Owens asked. —Pray not.

—Don't tell me you're done with it, said her husband.

—I'm done with it, I said.

—We're not going to let a bunch of costermongers rattling pots send you packing, said Charlie.

—We? You wasn't there, I said.

I known my husband was mortally sorry he was not at home during the Disturbance. He had only arrived well after dinner from his errand uptown and was so shocked at the news, so tender of me. —Poor Annie, never again, never again, he whispered, and wrapped me in cloaks and handed me up to the seat of our carriage, whisking me off to the Astor House Hotel. But now this morning while Annabelle rested oblivious at Greta's, Charlie was all brave talk again in front of his idols, the Owens. —It was only Dixon up to his tricks, he said. —It was only a staged spectacle for the press.

—Only!? You didn't see the blood in their eye, I said.

—I've seen blood, Charlie says. —I know what it looks like.

—It was MINE they were after, not yours. They have a likeness of me in the paper.

—Not even close, he says, all flattery. —You are a beauty yet they drew a hag.

—Are you giving up on them, then, Mrs. Jones? Owens asked. —Your ladies?

—Would you abandon us, your sisters, to ignorance? cried his wife. —Would you consign us to our fate at the hands of men?

—Mrs. Jones, so many depend on you, Owens said. —You know you have our profound respect and admiration for your bravery.

Owens, that wily cove, had found my weak spot. I was a sucker for praise. They was all goading me, the crew of them. And now Morrill joined in, bragging, —Madame, they have no evidence against you, but even if there WERE charges, I could beat them with one hand behind my back.

I played with a spoon, seesawed it on the white starched linen. Little oblongs of light reflected off the glass and the silver of the swank dining room. The clink of cutlery and the laughter of other people talking was a tinkle of piano music in the air. These other diners spoke of their ordinary days, their shopping expeditions, politics, opinions, pets and children. They were not talking about blood. Not about sad shamed women facing life and death. Not mobs. Not jail or hanging nooses. They ate their fruit compote off their spoons. They wiped their lips with their napkins. Ha ha ha they laughed.

—Eat something, my darling, said Charlie softly, touching my hand over the sugar bowl. —The papers would not like it if you starved, for what would they talk about? You'd no longer be in the headlines if you give it up. No knocking would wake you in the middle of the night. You'd have peace and quiet.

He waited while I thought about it and he was a clever b*****d for he knew I was not one for peace and quiet.

—These are the monkish days of mental darkness, Owens muttered, into his cup. —Imagine what they'll write when you retire and close your doors!

—Won't they preen and boast? said his wife, clucking. —Gloating and claiming they have shut you down.

I considered it, Dixon crowing. Matsell wheezing so SMUG. I didn't wish to give them one smidge of satisfaction. —F. them, I said at last, reckless. —The b*****ds can't drive me out.

Back home, sitting by the fire with Anna-bee on his lap, Charlie's idea was that we Joneses would show them one better. —All the really fine families are moving along Fifth Avenue, says he. —So we'll move right next door to the fancy folk to spit in their eye. They got empty lots uptown for sale, the size of a city block. We'll buy one. We'll buy four or five. We'll build a castle.

—A castle? cried our Annabelle. —Will we live in a castle?

—Yes, wee princess, said her indulgent father. —Château Jones. A castle with turrets, and a pony with silver bells, and a garden with fountains of chocolate.

—And a soda fountain! his daughter demanded, stamping her slippered foot.

—Shut your gob now, says I in the voice of my own Mam, who never did tolerate a whinging child. Charlie was ever after spoiling her and giving her sweets.

—Never mind pet, he said, —I'll call on a land-agent in the morning and arrange it. We'll have a deed in minutes.

—A deed, a deed, a deed, sang Annabelle, to the tune of Farmer in the Dell. She was learning to play the piano and kept up humming that tune till it grated the nerves. A castle in the dell, it soon became.

I on the other hand had no time to sing, nor dream of castles, for Liberty Street was busier than ever, thanks to all the free advertising we got from the riot and the press afterwards. The cries of the mob still rang in my ears, and we went about our business full of foreboding.

Still, when the bell rang at the office later in March of that year of 1876, I was expecting a lady in labor as usual, not a pickle-nose policeman in a uniform.

—Madame DeBeausacq? he says. —Madame Jacqueline Ann DeBeau-sacq?

—You have the wrong address. There's no Madame anyone here. I'm Mrs. Jones.

—Wo ho ho, he blustered, —that's not the story I heard. It's common knowledge you are one and the same.

To my alarm I saw he had a friend with him, another trap standing at the foot of the front steps.

—It's not a story, it's the facts, I says. —I am Mrs. Jones, and here is Mr. Jones, my husband, to prove it.

—What's all this? Charlie had come out of the dispensary at the sound of men's voices. Now he took my elbow and put himself between me and the police.

—I am Officer Hays, said the trap, —I have a warrant for the arrest of your wife.

—On what grounds? Charlie said.

—For providing a*******.

Charlie demanded to see the paper. —I'm terribly sorry, he said, reading it. —It says right here this is for a Madame DeBeausacq.

—Madame DeBeausacq is an elderly woman, I told the policemen. —Very rarely here, and currently in Paris. We don't know when she is next expected.

—Mrs. Jones is only an alias, said the trap. —And the papers have a likeness of Madame who is the very image of yourself.

So much for that defense, it was a wash, but Charlie stuck with it.

—Mrs. Jones is my wife, and this is a ridiculous charge.

—She'll come with me to Centre Street, said Officer Hays.

—The Tombs? I cried.

—I won't allow it, Charlie said.

—Come along, said the law, and we saw it was useless to argue.

—I'll fetch Morrill, said Charlie.

—Pray give me a moment, I said, in a panic, —so that I may change my dress.

The papers later noted the velvet and fringe of the Scotch catlin silk I selected, and the quality of my outer garments. "Elegantly attired," said the *Herald*. "Finely-dressed in cashmere and fur," said the *Polyanthos*.

At Centre Street after several hours, Charlie arrived without Morrill who was delayed in the grand jury. Without a lawyer I was brought up before Police Magistrate Henry Merritt, though what he merited besides a thumb off the nose I did not see, as he was just a mug in black robes. But when he spoke the name of my accuser, the blister of fear in my chest ruptured.

It was Cordelia. My little Cordelia.

—We have a sworn affidavit from one Cordelia Shackford Purdy, said Merritt. —She has sworn that you did procure an a******* upon her.

That cat had gone and reported me, after I saved her life, and how had that happened? They must have forced her. I was sure of it.

—It's a lie, I said, very fierce.

—Miss Shackford—Mrs. Purdy—has testified in a separate suit against Mr. George Purdy for desertion, that he did force her to undergo a******* at your hands, of a quick child.

—Not true! I cried.

—You are charged with Manslaughter in the Second Degree under the New York State Statute of 1846. The crime shall be punished by imprisonment no less than four years and not more than seven.

FOUR to SEVEN YEARS. Manslaughter. Why? If they arrested me for anything it would be a misdemeanor operation which carried a one year sentence, not FOUR to SEVEN. Manslaughter? Never. It was known I'd not go near a quick child except to deliver it. The blood drained from my face. I seen how now I was set up.

Charlie steadied me with a sweaty hand. —It's your word against hers. They can prove nothing.

—First of all, I told the judge, —this Cordelia Purdy, whoever she might be, has lied to you. I never set eyes on her in my life.

—The court will now set bail.

—I am the mother of a young daughter, Your Honor, I said, the terror in me rupturing like bullets in a fire. —Please release me. I have done nothing against ANY law let alone done manslaughter.

The judge rapped his gavel and set bail in the amount of ten thousand dollars.

—Ten thousand!? cried Charlie. —But it's a lie!

—Manslaughter, said the judge. —Ten thousand. With two sureties.

He rapped again and said I would be kept at the Tombs.

—My wife Mrs. Jones is wrongfully charged, Charlie said. —Bail in that amount is a mockery of justice is what it is. But I'll pay it now Your Honor.

—Two sureties, said the judge, and rapped once more.

Immediately, several matrons came at me like a swoop of bats.

—Axie, said Charlie, stricken, and watched as they clamped shackles around me, hurting the skin of my wrists.

—Get Morrill you b*****d, I said, as they pulled me away in a panic.

"Madame DeBeausacq did not flinch as she was taken away to the Tombs," wrote the *Herald* the next day. But I was all flinch, hard-pressed even to stand upright, as my limbs was boneless, filled with aspic. They took me to a paddy wagon so named for all the unlucky Irish before me, the fathers and the brothers named Paddy and their mothers, and even the children carted off to rot and suffer the outrages of apple pie American justice in the Tombs. That name was a grave for a reason. The matron, Mrs. Maltby, dragged me up to the second tier and unlocked a black iron door like the grate to a furnace and pushed me into a cubicle without light. I sat on the bed and leaned against the hard wall, so damp with the tears of all the many ladies who had languished here in indignity and squalor. And when the door was slammed and locked behind me, even then I did not cry, only cursed the names of my enemies, Matsell and Dixon, Applegate and Gunning, Hays and Merritt, each one a different uniform of the medical and legal and printing establishments arrayed against me. They was a pack of Aces against just a two of clubs. I prayed to Charlie to have me out of that place by morning.

At daylight, with a rattle of keys a jailer brought me a tray. The tea was dishwater and the taste of the biscuit was of weevil. I wouldn't eat it. I pressed my face to the orifice in the door and looked across an open gallery where meager light came down through a glass roof grimed with pigeon dung. The smell was close and savage. A terrible din echoed up through the center of the place, of women calling and weeping in their cages. Opposite was another row of cells where a guard walked. He had a pistol on his hip. I watched him strut and stroll.

It was all a mistake. Manslaughter. Four to seven years. Charlie and his friends had misled me. Egged me on. Belittled the dangers. Mocked my enemies as fools. My worries was piffle, he said, as he dared me, and I hated him now for it even as I longed for his face at the bars of my coop.

Instead of Charlie arriving it was a matron with a plate of potatoes the color of cement. I did not eat. She came back and took away the plate.

—Is my lawyer here? Morrill? My husband? Will you let him up to see me?

—Hah, she said. The dishes rattled on her cart as she wheeled it off.

Later through the bars she handed in a garment of coarse hideous fabric. —You'll wear this.

—I won't, I says.

—You will. Or we'll cuff you.

She went away and left the wretched article. I would not wear such a dress of c**p. I was a lady, Mrs. Charles G. Jones, not some dirty pigeon off a corner.

Time passed. It was a roar around me in the murk. Was it four o'clock yet? I wound my watch. Wound it again. When would they come? They didn't. Only the matron, her eyes appearing suddenly like blackeye peas in the window slot. —Prisoner out of uniform! she cried, and in an instant she was in my cell with her keys brandished.

—You'll put that on now, missus, or we'll put it on for you. She was at my buttons. She had her hands on me.

—Get off, I says. —I'm a lady.

—Not in here you ain't.

At night Mam's ghost spoke to me.

Axie are my children safe?

No children are safe. No mothers are safe. No one is safe nowhere.

Did you find our Joe? Where is Dutchie?

Lost, same as you, Mam. Same as my Belle now. Who'll sing her *shoul aroun*?

In my cell I nursed my knuckles, fiercely brooding. Annabelle slept without me in an apartment with the governess and I was full of fear and an ache like stopped air in the lungs. Home. It was all I wanted and here I was facing not just one year away, but Four to Seven. It was a betrayal of the worst order.

—Don't cry now Mrs. Jones, said the rosy young prison guard Elsie Reilly when she brought my tray in the morning. —Don't cry.

—I'm a mother, I says to her, so angry. —Ain't you a mother yourself?

—God did not bless me and Mr. Reilly with a child, says she, sorrowful.

—I'll tell you how to get one, I said, and beckoned her. She approached like I would cook her and eat her. But she put her ear at my cell door, and I whispered her the same lessons we had wrote down in the pamphlets, to count the days of her courses and three days after she finished to be with her husband for five nights lying for one hour afterwards with her hips braced up on a pillow. In addition she should take a raw egg white and place it directly in the cunicle while her husband had his way, and tell him it was very important he should have no spirits at all for the best result.

—For good measure you'll go over to 148 Liberty Street, I said, —to get a bottle of medicine from Dr. Desomieux. Take this note to him and there won't be no charge.

Dear Charlie, I wrote in it, *Give Mrs. Reilly some Elixir, and GET me OUT.*

—But why should I listen to you? said the little guard. —You're the devil's wife, ain't you?

—What have you got to lose? I told her, grinning, and she went off to deliver the message.

When I had been three whole days in the Tombs, I looked out the hole of my cell one morning and saw the Head Matron Mrs. Maltby coming with two men carrying a trunk. One of them was Charlie at last. The spectacled fellow with him wearing his beard in the chin curtain fashion was Morrill. Hallelujah.

—Ten minutes, gentlemen, said the Matron, opening the door to my cage.

—Thirty, said Morrill, and he took out his wallet.

Maltby simpered as my lawyer counted the bills into her claw. —Thirty minutes then, she said, and instead of releasing me she departed with a clang of metal.

Charlie wiped his forehead and looked around him with a rabbity eye.

—Why aren't we leaving? I cried.

—Mrs. Jones. Morrill cleared his throat. —Despite many rounds of entreaties, we have not been able to secure anyone to offer surety for your bail money.

—We have the cash to pay bail! And the property to guarantee it.

—This particular judge, Merritt, won't allow you to use your own property, Morrill said.

—We found Mr. Stratton and Mr. Polhemus, said Charlie, —but the judge rejected both on the grounds their land was not sufficient for so serious a case.

—So serious a case that I am charged with MANSLAUGHTER and face seven years. Not one, but SEVEN.

—My darling—

—You was WRONG. You said they would never charge me. You said if they did it would be only a Misdemeanor—

—Mrs. Jones, said Morrill, —we will have the charges reduced if not dismissed outright. For now we must get you bailed out.

—Have we no friends? I cried. Apparently, my husband and my patients and all of them parlor talkers had set me up for a battlefield hero, then left me like they was the cavalry in retreat.

—Our friends don't have that caliber of money, Charlie said. —People who do have it, they don't want the notoriety.

—God forbid their good name should be linked to mine, I roared. —God forbid that they should remember how Madame helped them in a desperate hour and God forbid they should help me in mine.

—Now, calmly, calmly, Mrs. Jones, said Morrill. —We'll find a surety.

—Calmly, calmly, yourself! Cool your own heels in this boghole, see how YOU like it.

—Judge Merritt rejected six bondsmen so far, Morrill said. —He has it in for you.

—At least the warden's friendly, said Charlie. —We brought you some comforts of home. Now he opened the trunk and removed a blanket. It was made of Kashmir wool, the color of a mourning dove and as soft. He placed it around my shoulders and kissed my cheek. Mr. Morrill turned away out of decorum. —Hush, wife. Hush, my love.

—I do not effing wish to hush. I wish to go home.

My husband did not reply, but took from the trunk silk sheets and a feather pillow, dresses and stockings, a robe and slippers, a bottle of claret and a selection of novels, tins of biscuits and dried fruit. Licorice. A lap desk and writing materials. Stores for a voyage. A rap came on the cell door and there stood a burly cove wearing overalls, carrying a crate. After Charlie paid him he broke apart the slats and revealed: a mattress.

—Stuffed with goose feathers, Charlie said, —from Gramercy Farm geese.

—Will I be here a month then? I cried.

—Best be prepared, said Morrill, blustering through the obstacles in his throat. —Judge Merritt is pigheaded in his resolve. The trial date is, ehm, set for, ehm, July.

—July? It is March!

Morrill now fixed me with a steady look and spoke in noble tones. —I will defend you, lady, with all of my energies, as an advocate and friend in the hour of your misfortune. We'll find a surety within the week. Trust me.

I did not bother to reply with my motto.

In the end, it was not our noble Morrill who betrayed my trust but Mighty Judge Merritt, who soon made it plain he would hold me in the Tombs until the date of my trial.

—Her crime, he told Morrill, —is one of deep moral turpitude. She poses such a danger to humanity and such a flight risk, with her ill-gotten gains, that you are hard-pressed to find a guarantor acceptable to this court.

And for five long months no guarantor was found good enough to please The Grand High Lord Merritt of the New York Criminal Court, and while he preened his side-whiskers, I festered innocent in my cubicle, pondering what turpitude could I be guilty of worse than keeping a mother locked away from her child for no good reason.

Chapter Thirty-Six

A Gilded Playground

A Scandal

Mme. DeBeausacq continues to live the high life in the Halls of Justice. Her cell is a gilded playground, with a feather bed and silk sheets. She dines on capon and squab, playing at whist with visitors. It is said by reputable witnesses that she never goes to church and takes her meals with the Keeper of the Women's Prison. Moreover, it is well known that when her husband visits her, she adjourns to the Keeper's quarters, where they remain for three to four hours at a stretch. What travesty of justice is this! to see this vilest of criminals spending her imprisonment rather like a lady in peaceful retirement than a convict. Is the Prison merely a means of emboldening a criminal in the pollution of her own sex? Thus the murderer of innocents will be sent forth into society with a charter from the officers of justice!

I read this B. and S. from the *Police Gazette* with my teeth grit, for the silk of my prison sheets was no defense from the tang of mold nor the teeth of vermin. The roasted capon Charlie had delivered to me weekly from the Beverly Inn on a tray covered with a white cloth could not hide the twin odors of dung and despair in that dark place or patch the holes of anger in my system. No feather pillow held in my arms was a substitute for my daughter who belonged there. No words in a letter would stand in for her voice. *Mama,* she wrote to me in a child's print, *Father says you are away helping poor misfortunate ladies but I wish you were NOT and would get home now we could sew our little samplers and make toffee apples I know how Rebecca showed me.* I wept when I read it, adding more misery to the din around me. It was a relentless symphony of wailing and catcalls. Mother of God, what did the Powers want of me? An apology?

—Stop them advertisements at the least, I said to Charlie. —They only bring more attention. Let them pick on Mrs. Costello or Mrs. Bird and not me.

He had come that morning to deliver me the newspapers, letters from my lawyer, from our friends, the Owens, and another from Belle, with a crayon drawing. That it featured a bird in a cage pierced me like a butcher's hook. Her father said she cried for me at night. —But I soon have her singing McGinty, he said, —so she's cheerful as a bluebird in the daylight.

—Aren't you clever? I said, very acid. —Apparently she don't need a mother.

—I didn't say that. I'm doing my d***dest to keep her happy, and the rest of them. The whole household's in a shambles.

—Oh the tragedy of Mr. Jones. The hardship and the sacrifice.

It was rough days for me and Charlie. My real enemies was not at hand, so the choice was to blame my own stupidity for trusting Charlie, or to blame Himself. I chose him. —You said they'd NEVER arrest me.

—Christ! my husband said. —Why don't you blame Morrill for a change? It was him who advised us on the law.

Now when Charlie visited and sat on my prison bed eating bread and cheese, crumbs in his mustache, I seethed in jealousy of his freedoms and imagined him up to all manner of tricks, sure he was motivated by finance and selfish designs. We bickered and sniped as we had not since the days when we had no money nor French letters nor funny little daughter to calm the matrimonial tempests. —Pull the ads, I said.

—For what reason? No law against ads. We'll lose half the business.

—It's all just business with you then, is it?

—You know it isn't. It's well more than that. He rummaged very weary in his pockets and came up with a page he had scribbled. —Look here. He showed me the letter of response he had written, to the *Gazette*'s outrage. He meant me to publish it in self-defense, under my name:

> *Gentlemen of the press:*
> *Ladies die every day in ordinary childbirth and are cast out on the streets destitute, and in shame, when they are the forced VICTIMS of men's debauchery, depravity, and rape. Moreover, while the MEN are not prosecuted for their part, it is the LADIES who suffer in jail WITHOUT FAMILY, merely on suspicion (trumped up!) of trying to come to the aid of the desperate.*
> *Sincerely,*
> *Madame J. A. DeBeausacq*

—I don't wish to sign this. Or publish it.

—Defend yourself, Mrs. Jones. These are your own words.

—YOU wrote them, Charlie. It's YOU who cares for politics. You enjoy to use me for twitting your old enemies at the *Herald* and showing off to your philosopher friends.

He rolled his eyes. —The letter's only what you told me many times yourself, Madame DeBeausacq.

—So? I don't want to be Madame DeBeausacq no more, I said, and felt the truth of it, the burden she was to me, with her French ways, her bloody trade, the laundry pile of terrible linens and the sodden handkerchiefs of weeping women. —I'm retired.

—Really? Are you serious?

—Yes. And I was. Or thought I was. —I'm done.

—I never thought you'd say that. Charlie slumped, seeming quite stunned, and for a moment in the midst of my self-pity I seen the rumple of his suit. The black of his hair was salted with gray. Scallops of darkness hung under his eyes. —Perhaps you're right. At least retire a certain aspect of the business.

—And which aspect would that be?

—The unsavory one. The one in question.

—F*** you. Unsavory? Is that what you call it?

—I don't call it that, no, he said, weary of me. —But the law does.

—The law is a steaming HORSE pile, and you know it.

—Wouldn't it be easier to have a simple midwifery practice? Charlie now grew animated, his eyes lit. The more he warmed to this new idea, of my partial retirement, the more suspicious I turned. —Listen to me, Mrs. Jones. When you are released, you'll practice as a happy midwife who only delivers healthy bouncing babies and dispenses only certain medicines and procedures but not others related in any way at all to the premature—

—Don't YOU say what I will do! Only I can say when to close my doors.

—Confound you! You said just now you would retire! You claim you don't want the LAW on you. Make up your mind! Retire or don't retire. I throw up my hands. I can't live like this.

—YOU can't? Live like what?

—Like a man whose wife is in the quod, whose daughter cries for her mother, whose house is run to ground by lazy servants in mutiny.

—My heart bleeds for you, said my hotheaded self.

—Our daughter cries for her Mam. She crawls into her bed at night and holds your pillow and says it smells of lilac scent like her Mamma, and—

—Stop it! I roared. —You only rub hot salt in the cut. You think I forget her? Not one minute passes I don't think of her.

—So you will retire. If you don't—

We stood staring livid at the shambles around us.

—So help me Axie, when you get out of here, if you return to practice as you did before, and you are trapped again, and sent away—

—What?

—I won't forgive you. You think I enjoy to have my wife in jail?

—Yes! I think you enjoy to do as you please and frolic with Millicents and—

He went to slap me. He raised his hand and it hung in the air, our dark chandelier of mistrust. We two was beat down and snarling thanks to the laws of Merritt and Matsell and Hays, the cunning of Applegates, the lies of Dixon. We was supposed to be warriors in a battle but no, it was a battle between US. Not a Grand Cause, but only mistrust and jealousy, the dirty currency of the sexes always.

Slowly his hand sank down. —Every night, Axie, I curse the forces that took you from my side.

—You only curse those forces because the business suffers without me.

He winced. —The business does not suffer. Even while you've been in here, Madame DeBeausacq has sold more than six thousand dollars' worth of medicines. Just in the mail. Just in a month's time.

—How about that? Six thousand for sitting in a cell.

—So the business is fine, he said, —while the rest of us—the rest of us are not.

—Then get me out. Get me out why don't you? I turned my back to him, my blood in an uproar. —It seems I'd have done better to jump off the roof of the train onto that prairie long ago when I had a chance, I said, and wept bitter into my bare hands.

This torrent was enough, it seemed, to extinguish what fire remained of my husband's anger. —Aw now, hush, he said at last. —We'll get you out.

And he came up behind me, clasped my rigid waist with the tines of his fingers meshed in front. His face rested by my unyielding neck, his lips at my ear. His breath made the hackles rise along my spine. —It's your birthday soon, my sweet, he said, —and I have a present in mind for you.

—In your mind? A lot of good it will do me there.

—It's a surprise. He said this with honey, so I known what he was after.

—Is it a key to this door?

—I promise. You will be vindicated at court. Don't worry. Shh, now.

His hands traveled along the rungs of my ribs, over the terrible drab mungo of my prison dress. And then he began.

To kiss my neck. To whisper, Ann. Annie. Axie sweet.

—Don't.

—Why not? His voice was a burr against my skin, the hard bone of his jaw clamped along my clavicle. He nuzzled in hard against my cheek and took the lobe of my ear in his mouth.

Delicate readers will turn aside now to avoid an indelicate scene. But to tell it is to save it for my private self, for proof of how it was with us. How fast he turned me. Confused me. Handled me and pulled me by the waist, by the lips. —Get off, I says. —Get away. He pressed on, the fabric of my wretched dress tenting back with the force of his knee between my knees, and I fought him off.

—Why not? he whispered. —Why?

—You b*****d. Get me out of here, I said, and pushed him.

He grabbed the shanks of my arms and pulled me against him so greedy and sank me down upon the feathers and there I was turned again. He kissed me and his breath was caught in my mouth, combustible.

—No, I said, my tongue lost and tangled. No. The guard would come. The door would open. We'd be discovered. The shame of it. The risk. —The matron, I says.

—Afraid, are you? he whispered. —Afraid, right? You won't, right? Why not? Come on. Come on Annie. He was baiting me. Circling. Stroking. Baiting me. —That's it. Thatta girl now. His caress. His whisper. His taunts. Soundless we was wild things, and even despite the danger, the cringe of depravity, my fingernails raked the bare skin of his back beneath his shirt, stuttered over the knobs of spine. His fingers was laced through the long hair at the back of my head, and then in a maneuver of his knee, the wrestle of his arms, he lifted me over him. Mother of God. How he loved this, the unholy surroundings. A drip of ooze down the wall. The words Lord Help Me scratched by a wretch on the stone. Color swirled darkly on the inside of my lids.

My husband pulled at my jailhouse garments and pushed them aside. —Afraid? he whispered. —Chickenheart, are you? He flipped me flat to the bed with no noise except for the rough breath of his craving. He'd show me. Sure he would drive his point home so he would, so I'd know the force of his needful passion and power and how these twin engines of his manhood couldn't be stopped and to be perfectly honest I had no intention or wish to contain him but lay angry plus ecstatic, afraid of the matron, the clang of metal on stone. It was panic now and a thrill of desperate craving. Dear God the key would turn in the lock. I helped with the buttons of his trousers. —Hurry, I said. How slow he was. How clumsy. I hated him. —Love, he said. The guards would be at us. It was dirty, it was delirium, the danger and the smell of him, shaving lotion and tobacco, a taste of sour apple, salt of blood where his lip bled, or mine.

Like hot bitters in a whiskey burn. Was that keys rattling in the hall? The boots of the guard. —Ssht, I said. We stayed still. My heart careened in my chest.

Charlie put his mouth to my ear. —I've paid, he whispered. —Fifty dollars so they'll not disturb us, I paid her off. Like I was a piece of trade off the street, how it excited him.

—You paid? I cried. —You paid you c***s**ker.

—I did. He drove at me and lifted me to him. —Love, he said, and I believed him, the b*****d was right it could not be helped, that force you could not arrest it or hold it for bail or contain it, not in prison or nowhere. He paid for it, a quick fifty. My own money. He bribed the guard. With a feel and a kiss he had turned me and yes I was right there with him. —Charlie, I said, with a gasp. My throat was thick with hatred of him and love. We were married. How needy he was the way he clung to me, like he could transport us far off from this terrible oubliette, till with a great shudder he rested so I was safe in his arms for the barest of moments, and then he stood to rearrange himself, to go and present himself again to the clear unfettered air outside my brutal cage.

A week passed, and he did not visit again. I had no word of him. All those days was another typhoid of jealous memory. I paced my cell and bit my lips so they turned raw. Half the time I thought Madame DeBeausacq could fry in jail for all I cared but I, Axie M. Jones would go home to my darling little one and never hear that name DeBeausacq again. Mostly though, I wanted to boil my enemies in a vat of lye to bleach their bones then run them through the mangle and hang them flapping from the line. I was punished for no reason.

And sitting there reproachful was the letter to the *Herald* Charlie had left for me to sign. *Defend yourself.* For days I ignored it. Then at last in a fit of fury I picked it up.

"While the MEN are not prosecuted, the LADIES suffer in jail . . ." Charlie wrote that. Ha. Defend yourself, he had said. It seemed, on that bleak day, that nobody else would. So I picked up my own pen and wrote more on the page.

Given the true facts of Miss Shackford's case, don't I owe it
to myself and my family, and to some very dear and true friends,
and to the ladies of New York City who adhere to me amidst
all the clouds of malignity, and also to that public who scorn
persecution and injustice, to point out the lies of your newspaper?
The charges against me have no merit, and I will be vindicated
at trial.
          Sincerely, Madame J. A. DeBeausacq

With no help at all I wrote out the whole thing, including Charlie's part about how *Ladies die in ordinary childbirth every day,* and signed it, and got the little guard Elsie Reilly to mail it to the *Herald* for me. Thanks to my advice and medicines, she had swole up in the family way and went about advertising me amongst the inmates and the wardens as an expert on female physiology, so that even in that wretched boghole I could not give up ministering to females on the topic of carnality, and all its attendant woes. Meanwhile, the *Herald* would have my letter, and them bungers could put their own b***s*** in their pipes and smoke it.

On a May day, Charlie arrived again in my cell, pleased like he hung the moon, waving the newspaper with my letter published in it, bringing me correspondence from Owens and Morrill and blue flowers from a hydrangea bush.

—Where were you? I cried.

—What else do you think I have for you?

—A writ of release, I growled at him, —or else get out.

His face fell. —If only it was such news. But instead it's your birthday present.

—My birthday? Was it?

He reached behind my ear and withdrew a chocolate, and then again under my shawl and withdrew a roll of paper tied with pink satin lace and handed it to me with a flourish. —Many Happy Returns of the day, Mrs. Jones.

—Twenty nine years old, I said, —and buried alive.

—Just look.

I took the ribbon off the paper and it unfurled before us. It was a draw-ing. Blue ink on blue-stained paper. It showed a house like a palace. Four stories tall with walled gardens and a carriage barn. Archways and columns at the entrances. Finials on the grand posts of the staircase, on the rooftops. Curlicues and flourishes around the windows.

—What is this? The picture startled me, the way the house sat there like a queen in all its beauty, so fancy and expensive. I wanted it.

—Behold the House of Jones, Charlie said. —The land is bought and paid for.

I beheld as instructed, disbelieving. All orphans dream of home and for Charlie and me this was the drawing of a dream. The house in the picture had three chimneys. Three doors. Forty windows. The rooms were named, each one for a separate purpose. Salon. Library. Conservatory. Ballroom. Boudoir. Office. My finger traced the blue lines of ink on the paper, like veins under my skin already. How I wanted to live there.

—Say something, said Charlie, smiling away. —It's your house.

—You have always been a wild-a** cove with no more sense than a bar-nacle.

—We'll live there in peace and luxury. We'll have a grand ball to wel-come you home where you belong, Mrs. Jones.

—If them baboons ever let me out of here.

He took out his handkerchief and pressed it tenderly to my eyes while I wept. It smelled of the sweet wide world outside.

—The land's at Fifty Second Street and Fifth Avenue.

—It's a cowpath, I said, afraid it wouldn't come true. —The middle of nowhere.

—Not for long. Archbishop Hughes is raising Saint Patrick's Cathedral two blocks away. He wanted the land for his own residence but I outbid him. Won't he love to have Madame DeBeausacq for his neighbor? He has denounced her already, from the pulpit. She's more notorious than ever.

Small comfort, to be denounced by an Archbishop, because at that moment I was not on Fifth Avenue riding in my carriage, but spending my birthday in a festering boghole. Our household was falling apart without me there to manage it. The appointments kept knocking with nobody to help them. And what of Annabelle? Charlie reported the child had taken to sucking her thumb and refused to go to school because she was teased there, for her mother's infamy. The governess had quit because of her tantrums. The piano teacher wanted a raise. Charlie said Greta had suddenly married a man named Alfonse Sprunt, a brewer from Yorkville, and it seemed she was as fond of his pilsners as she was of his kisses, for she had been at her desk drunk on several occasions and often came to work late or not at all, suffering her dark moods without a joke and a laugh from me to cheer her up. When Charlie scolded her she had told him she expected a bonus wage for running the office single-handed.

—Greta only cries and carries on complaining, said Charlie. —I'm apt to fire her if she keeps at it.

—Don't you dare.

—And what should I do about it, then?

—Get me out you b*ll*cks.

—I am doing my best, you pure devilment of a harpy, you know I am.

These were our dire days of feuding and grudges fueled by terrible circumstance and the bad faith of Judges. I waited for relief, through the spring and the turn of the weather, when the temperature in the Tombs reached a hundred degrees, and we females slowly cooked in the stewpot of the law that some called justice but I called s***.

Chapter Thirty-Seven

In the Dock

*A*t last in July came the Monkey Show of my trial. In the court of general sessions, I appeared before Government lawyer Frederick Tallmadge, Associate Justice Merritt, and two aldermen.

RESPLENDENT, the *Times* said I was, dressed in black satin with a white bonnet and white mantilla of Spanish lace. "Madame DeBeausacq," they wrote, "swept into the courtroom fashionably attired as if she were a gentlewoman."

Not so fashionable was my reluctant young accuser Cordelia Purdy, who did not sweep but slank through a door behind the judge's chair and took her place at a table to my left, where she shrunk down childish with her head hung and her tiny hands folded in her lap like it was not me accused, but herself. She was no longer the fairy sprite I seen when she came to my door, but a drab moth in a plain gray dress and a veil, which despite the hideous heat was heavy and black.

The front of the court was crowded with lawmen cloaked in dark robes. They stroked their beardy chins and cleared their throats so their Adam's apples dunked and rose. They rattled their papers and stuck their important hairy hands in their important pockets. Their eyes fell on me hard as pebbles off a windowpane, glancing. One or two lingered long enough on my face to cause the corner of their lips to curl. They was dogs who knew their prey was weak so I smiled at them, and in the skittishness of their gaze, the nerves of their tapping hands, the way they toyed with their mustaches, I saw they were scared of me.

As far as ladies went, it was only me and Cordelia there. Just by the space we took up, with our skirts wide around us, we was set off from the rest of the room, set up for judgment like turkeys for sale, surrounded by dark coats and the men's hard smells of Macassar oil and walnut military shaving soap and Blackwell's Bull Durham tobacco.

—Oye Oye, said the recorder.

—May it Please the Court, said prosecutor Tallmadge. A flap of his gray hair hung over his brow. Oh, he was a mighty unicorn, Tallmadge. A State Senator, so they said. A soldier in the war. Well I was a soldier too, in my own war, only I didn't have no muskets or gavel, only my wits.

—Miss Cordelia Shackford, Tallmadge called her before the judge.

Cordelia now was made to swear an oath, so reluctant you would think the Bible was a hot stove the way the recorder had to hold her hand down upon it.

—Your Honor, Tallmadge said, —I must inform you that the witness is hostile and unwilling. And then he began his terrible work on her.

—State the number of times you have been pregnant.

—Five times, she said, in a whisper of shame.

—Five! And by whom?

—By . . . Mr. George Purdy.

—At the time were you married?

—He promised he would marry me, sir, but the reason I am here is because the police said if I did not speak up I would be thrown in jail and I—

—Answer the question only! By what manner and means were you delivered of your children?

Cordelia did not answer.

—By what means? By what means were you delivered?

—I was not delivered of any children.

—You stated you were pregnant. By what means, then, were you delivered?

—By . . . abortion, said the moth, her voice a filament of wind through the dark lace.

—We request that the witness remove her veil, said Mr. Tallmadge.

—I prefer not to, whispered Cordelia.

—You will remove your veil, the judge ordered her.

—Please no.

—You must do as asked, said Judge Merritt.

Slowly, with her two hands grasping the edge, Cordelia lifted her veil and even from a distance you could see it tremble. The gallery sat forward. There she was, pale as milk, her eyes dark bruises in their sockets. A cry escaped her as she uncovered her face, and she hid herself with her hands.

—Explain please.

She swayed and appeared delirious and when she spoke it was in the thin high register of keening. —George told me I must have the operation, because he didn't want a scandal. And he promised he'd marry me. So I did it. Each time I did it. Now, just because you all FORCED me here, instead he's gone and married someone else, and I went to sue him for desertion in the court—

—Only answer the question, please, Tallmadge said. —And where did you go to procure such an operation?

—First Mrs. Costello. And then . . . I don't wish to say.

She looked at me fast and guilty like the sight of me stung her.

—You must tell the court, Miss Shackford, where you did procure this operation.

She fidgeted and quaked till at last she whispered my name. —Madame DeBeausacq. She looked right at me with eyes full of remorse. —But I'm so sorry, Madame, I'm not complaining of YOU. It's just they said they'd jail me if I didn't come today and I didn't mean t—

—Miss Shackford! The judge rapped. —Answer the question only. Had you been there previous?

—No. Previous times I went to Mrs. Costello.

—And why did you choose Madame DeBeausacq in this instance?

—Because it was said she was a professional who treated ladies with kindness.

—Describe the events of that day.

Cordelia shook her head, and her hands remained pressed to her eyes as she swayed in her seat. —No no, I can't.

—You must describe the events of January the twenty second, said Tallmadge again.

Cordelia whispered, swaying in the box. —Madame brought me to a room.

—And then?

—She told me to get upon a bed. She gave me a pillow and a tumbler of wine. When I had drunk it, she told me to lie with my feet upon two chairs.

The child spoke with long tracts of tearful silence between words.

—How did she effect it? Tallmadge pressed her. —Describe what she did.

—I prefer not to, sir.

—You must tell the court.

—I cannot. I would rather not. Please. No.

—Miss Shackford, Tallmadge said, — you are under oath.

My accuser sank further in her misery. —Madame said . . . she would have to probe me. She said I was a good brave girl and that for a moment I would feel . . . pain.

The newspapers next day wrote that "with much hesitation the witness proceeded to recount the treatment she received from Madame DeBeausacq, the details of which are so extremely disgusting and filthy we forbear to give publicity to them."

Let me say right now the papers was wrong on them details. The details are of Human Kindness. These judges, these police, these reporters, are squeamish low bloodworms, half of them, consorting with cancan girls. How I know this is because them girls come to me. So do their society mistresses. Also, their wives. I know them, daughters of Judges, sisters of Prosecutors. But these robes of the law did not wish to hear the filthy details of their own sex's duplicity, or dwell on the disgusting filthy things they did THEMSELVES, nor see the fair face of the ones they punish for their own masculine debauchery.

The court was breathless and still. No matter how they claimed otherwise, the neckties in that room was no better than the rabble that chased the fire brigades of the Seventh Ward to see buildings burn for sport. They leaned forward with the thrill of it, panting practically, to listen to Cordelia's torment.

—What did Madame do? said Tallmadge again.

—She put her hand.

—Where?

—In my . . . privates. And hurt me very much. I cried and she said it was nearly over. But it wasn't. She turned her hand or some instrument round in my body like she was breaking at something. Scraping. And it hurt me so I cried out.

—After it was over and you had got up, what occurred?

—She said for me to go to bed and rest, as she would feel anxious until I was relieved of my obstruction.

—And that evening?

—I was in great agony all the night. Madame slept with me, right in the room. She gave me compresses. In the morning, about daylight, I took a great flooding. I had been very sick also and vomited. She bade me get up and sit on a stool, with a chamber below. Whilst seated there I suffered violent pain, and Madame—

—Carry on, Miss Shackford.

—Madame inserted her hand again and said it would make it easier for me, though it gave me more pain. Every pain I had, I heard something fall from my body into the chamber. Madame said be patient. One more pain and I would be through. I then got on the bed as she bid me. She again examined me with her hand. She hurt me so. I hallooed out and gripped hold of her. She called me love and said I would thank her and call her Mother, and later I did thank her. She stroked my head and brought me a tray of tea and toast.

It was as she said. I stayed with her. But these were not the details that interested the whiskery officials. They did not care about my small hands, my swift skills, how I was expert at my profession.

—And when I left the premises, Cordelia continued, hysterical, —Officer Hays followed after me. He arrested me and brought me to the precinct where they had a doctor named Gunning.

Gunning? Gunning?

—And at the station the police and Dr. Gunning forced me to submit to an inspection without my permission, said Cordelia. —And they hurt me worse even than Madame and said the inspection proved what I did. But it did not prove a thing! And they said if I didn't confess it, it would be the worse for me—

So, I had been hunted and framed up by Dr. Gunning and his friend Applegate.

—It is Dr. Gunning also George Purdy they should arrest! Cordelia said.

By now the brave child was crying so fitfully, you could not understand her. Her words were mumbled. She was close to fainting. Exasperated, the judge rapped, and adjourned till the next day.

Outside afterwards, the crowd and the press by the courthouse was a pack of wolves, pointing.

—There she is, the ghoul of Liberty Street, they cried.

I was a ghoul to them but to my ladies I was an Angel of Mercy. If I'd have had those white wings I'd have flapped them in the face of all the ignorant coves arrayed against me that day and flown away to my daughter.

Instead Charlie came to my prison that evening, with a steak and kidney pie made by our own Rebecca, a bottle of sherry, and a lame condolence. —Perhaps they will only convict you of a misdemeanor. A year only.

—I served half that already, I said, and drained my glass trembling.

—Hush now. My husband put his hand on my arm. —Hush.

—YOU hush. It was you who advertised Madame DeBeausacq in New Haven. If it wasn't for those ads, that Cordelia woman would've never walked through our doors.

—Tomorrow Morrill will have no choice but to destroy her character. He'll say she was a prostitute.

—She was not. Jesus, she's a child. Tell Morrill don't put her through that.

—It's the only way to turn the jury's sympathy toward you. She's ruined.

—And so am I ruined. Unless you get me out.

—How would I do that, Mrs. Jones?

—You're the magician. Pull something out of your hat.

Charlie stroked his mustache. Then abruptly he swigged the last dreg of sherry, kissed me, and rapped on the door of the cell so the matron would come and release him.

—Where are you going?

—I'll tell you if it works, he said, and deserted me again.

"Madame arrived in dark blue silk," wrote the *Herald* about my arrival to court the next morning, "trimmed, apron-shape, with Brussels lace, gold and bugle, with one flounce, going all around the skirt; body and sleeves to match; sleeves looped up with blue satin ribbon." Justice Merritt was in a fine pickle when I made my entrance.

—You are late, Mrs. Jones.

—Apologies. The lock on my cell door was a bit rusty.

He scowled and harrumphed but did not become truly livid until my dear lawyer Morrill called the accuser Cordelia to the witness box for cross-examination. But, where was she? She was nowheres to be seen. The Government decided to call their star witness instead.

—Dr. Benjamin Gunning, to the stand, Tallmadge said.

Dr. Gunning! Imagine. Here he came trundling down to the front, a soft white man with a fizz of white hair receding on either side of his forehead, pale and blinking as a grub in the sunlight.

—State your position and expertise, please Doctor, said Mr. Tallmadge.

—Distinguished professor of Medicine at Philadelphia Medical School, said the Grub.—Founder of the New York Medical College, board member of the American Medical College, and author of books including Principles and Practices of Obstetrics.

—And a good friend of Archbishop Hughes, too, as I recall, laughed Tallmadge very chummy.

So our Dr. Grub was a friend not just of Susan Applegate's Papa but a friend of police and Archbishops. And now prosecutors, too, it appeared, from the simper around Tallmadge's mouth.

—Please tell the court your experience on January twenty fifth, Tallmadge said.

—I was called to the police precinct, where I found young Miss Cordelia Shackford under arrest in a delicate state. I was asked to examine her.

I stared at Dr. G. wishing I might roll him down a hill in a spiked barrel which Mam said the English enjoyed to do to the Irish.

—I found that Miss Shackford had been recently pregnant, Gunning continued. —When I asked where was her child? she lied and said she had not been pregnant. When pressed she said that she had had a miscarriage. Officer Hays confronted her then and she at last confessed—that Madame DeBeausacq had caused her to miscarry five times! She stated that these miscarriages had been brought about either with drugs administered by this fiendish trafficker in human life—he pointed at me—or, as in this most recent occasion, by one of her surgical interventions.

—Did Cordelia Shackford exhibit any signs of remorse at all? asked Tallmadge.

—On the contrary, said Dr. Grub. —She asked only if I might help her to sue her guardian, Purdy, for desertion, and while there's no doubt that Mr. Purdy is a scoundrel, my duty as a medical man is to stop such abominations from recurring, as indeed they would if such monsters as THAT woman did not ply her trade in our very midst.

The doctor stood and pointed his white finger at me again. My lawyer Morrill leaped to his feet shouting his objection. The judge rapped and barked. I was in an apoplexy. All the indignities and squalor of the last months in the Tombs was because of this man Dr. Gunning. He started it. It was not enough he had sicked the press on me and began a riot at my home. No, he must now put me in the pen on Blackwell's Island where I would pick oakum till my fingers bled to stumps. Without confessing his own miserable motives of revenge, Dr. Gunning blathered on and the judge allowed him to go on till adjournment.

The next day, the courthouse was packed more than ever with black-coated men.

—The defense calls Miss Cordelia Shackford, please, Morrill said.

There was a craning of necks, a holding of breath. But again Cordelia did not stand. She did not walk forward. Again she was missing. A police detail was sent to find her. —A hoor likes to sleep in, said one of the hacks under his breath, and the gallery cackled.

Four o'clock arrived but Cordelia did not. Morrill and Tallmadge conferred at the bench.

At last, at five p.m., very frustrated, Justice Merritt gave his gavel a rap.

—Counsel for the accused has applied for dismissal, on the grounds he is not able to cross-examine the principal witness. While I maintain that said witness Miss Shackford has come under the influence of the accused and has in fact been PAID a goodly sum by her to DISAPPEAR, there is not sufficient evidence to PROVE it. Unless it can be ascertained that Miss Shackford has left New York by the persuasion of Mrs. Ann Jones, alias Madame DeBeausacq, and unless Miss Shackford can be produced for the purposes of cross-examination by the defense, at this time I must declare the charges dismissed and the prisoner . . . released.

With no Cordelia in sight, Judge Merritt's gavel rapped the bench again with special fury. Thus was I freed.

Twenty minutes later Charlie and me was sweeping home in the phaeton to Liberty Street. He had a fat grin on his face.

—What's your secret? I asked him.

—Which one of my secrets are you talking about?

—The one you're so pleased with yourself over.

—I paid her, he said, whispering behind his cupped hand. —Gave her four thousand dollars to move to Philadelphia. I had tried to pay her off earlier but I couldn't find her anywhere till yesterday when I had the bright idea of appealing to your friend Officer Corrigan who's so sweet on our Maggie. For a fee he discovered where they had Cordelia hiding, and *voilà*!

—Four thousand? Four THOUSAND?

—Would you rather I had not spent it? Should I fetch her now from Pennsylvania so you can head back to the quod?

—I'm never going back. Not as long as I live.

Perhaps I shouldn't have tempted fate so boldly with those words, but I meant it and was happy in that moment, with the yellow sun on my face, the wind off the Hudson blowing through the window of the carriage, and my husband whispering in my ear how glad he was to see me, and just how he planned to welcome me home.

My daughter greeted me laughing and jumping, with a bouquet of dahlias.

—Mam! she cried, and rushed to clap her arms around my knees.

—*Macushla machree,* I said, as I lifted her.

She opened her mouth to show me the pale shoots of new teeth growing through her gums. —Look.

—Is it those fangs you're showing your Mam, young Miss Jones? said Charlie to our daughter.

—Father! Stop! She shook her finger at him.

—It's fearsome, Mrs. Jones, Charlie said, winking. —How a girl six years of age has grown fangs like a mountain lion. Look there, see the sharp points in her mouth? Maybe they're fox teeth!

—Stop, Father! It's not true! My daughter jumped down to scold him, then ran back to me. I held the good sweet weight of her while she kissed my face and patted my cheeks. —Mama, Father is all the time pretending I have fangs to tease me when I do NOT have fangs.

—He's an old wicked livermush, I said, —and what will we do with him?

—String him up! my daughter cried. —Away with him to jail!

Annabelle marched her father off to the prison, which was behind the balusters of the staircase. Charlie clung to the spindles like iron bars and peered between them scowling and rattling. How she laughed and clapped her hands and mocked him. —Father's in jail! He's a jailbird!

I laughed but the sound was hollow. Your Mother's a Jailbird was the words the other children used to tease my daughter. Them little hair ribbon girls was SNAKES and I wished St. Patrick would come and drive them off the face of the earth the way he done in Ireland. No one would hurt my daughter again if I was alive to shield her.

That night against all Mrs. Child's Advice to Mothers we two, Father and Mother, slept with our daughter in the bed between us, where the soft sound of my own small family breathing was medicine to me, a draught so strong I did not wake till noontime the next day, when the sun rose up over Liberty Street, and I was Home at last.

BOOK SIX

Luxury

Chapter Thirty-Eight

A Midge on a Summer Night

*T*he papers ranted how I was a Murderess who had Got Off Scot Free, but soon they lost interest. The rabid Dr. Gunning published one small letter saying it was Just a Matter of Time before my practice was closed, giving forth about dangerous female physiologists and how the medical profession would soon replace me and my ilk. "Modern Woman," he wrote, "will no longer seek out the ignorant midwife, and turn to men of science instead."

—Ha. No matter, I said. —I am not a midwife anymore.

With Charlie's evident relief and approval, I stayed home and enjoyed riding out in the landau with him and with Annabelle, buying her trinkets and licorice and ribbons. —You're my own sweet Mamma back home, said she. —You'll never go away again, right?

—Never, I swore to her. —You have my word. And as she nestled under my wing, her warm head smelling of tea roses and her little paws playing with my bracelets, I asked, —What would you most like to have in the world?

—A baby brother. Or, no, wait, a grand piano.

Well, despite our recent vigorous efforts, the baby brother was still not on the horizon, and how would we adopt one if mothers like Susan would only come to accuse us of cradle-robbing and put me in jail? So off me and Belle went to Steinway & Sons on Park Ave. and purchased a baby grand instead. How marvelous it was to hear such flights of music coming off the fingers of a child. —Mother and Father, said our girl, only six years old, —I now will play you Mr. Johann Sebastian Bach's Musette Number Fifteen.

Tears gathered on my lashes. It seemed she had become as fine a young lady as anyone could wish. I was content to hear her play all day and night and remained content as long as I was with her, learning the featherstitch as we sewed side by side, trading riddles, such as What walks all day on its head? A nail in a horseshoe. What is it that you can keep after giving it to someone else? Your word. I had given her mine and would keep it.

—When WILL you return to the office? asked Greta, visiting with Willi one day.

—Never, says I. —Haven't you heard me say that Madame is RETIRED?

She looked at me in a fine German Humph. —You are not retire, Axie. I heff told Charlie you are chust resting. I know you Axie. You soon are growink bored.

—You're wrong, I said, but Greta would not stop asking every day for my return, no matter how I ignored her.

Charlie was pleased to hear my refusals though he himself continued to go to the offices and sell medicines and other preventatives under the name of Dr. Desomieux. Madame DeBeausacq's advertisements had stopped as per my request. I was done with her. Amen.

But the ladies of Gotham was not done with me. After the publicity of my trial, there was more patients knocking on the door of the Liberty Street clinic than ever, of the most exclusive sort. Mrs. Landon Comfort and Miss Hope Hathaway &c. Were these ladies disgusted by the notoriety of Madame or put off by her time in the quod? No they was not. They besieged Greta with calling cards and requests for appointments.

For weeks I passed happy hours basking in freedom to do what I pleased, playing cribbage with the Wickendens, and attending the Academy of Music, where we saw a performance of Marcella Sembrich singing *Lucia di Lammermoor* which (except for the excitement of the Lunatic Scene) was three hours of horrible screeching and I did not need to pay money for that. Afterwards we dined at Delmonico's. Charlie and me had managed to plaster over our bickery days by talking of our new house, now breaking ground on Fifth Ave.

—The stables will hold four horses, he said one morning at breakfast.

—Why not six?

—Six, then. And stone pillars either side of a carriage drive.

—And a garden with a pony! cried Annabelle. —And a little puppy dog for me.

—Yes, my love, said her father.

—Do not spoil her, I says.

—Why not let's spoil ourselves, he said. —And have statuary indoors and out.

—And those French tapestries in all the bedrooms.

—Like at Versailles.

—And the physician's offices, I said, —on the basement level.

—I thought you retired, he said, wary.

—What if I should change my mind?

—I thought you were happy to be home again, in the bosom of your family.

—BOSOM, said Annabelle, who fell over laughing.

—Belle! I said. —Don't be naughty.

—Axie, my husband said warning me like I was the other child. —No offices.

I bit my tongue for a change. I took his heavy paw in mine and kissed it very sweet and dutiful. And thus with my own tricks I distracted him, and learnt to starve an argument rather than feeding it. Instead I fed Charlie a breakfast chocolate spiked with brandy. —Have another bite of truffle, dear, I says.

Well, it was truffles and honey, caviar and wine for us in those early days of my freedom. It was my genuine intention to carry on carefree, for now at last, Mrs. Charles G. Jones, shed of her connection to the Notorious Madame X, seemed poised for her entry into the finer drawing rooms of Manhattan.

Viz., very exciting, one morning at home the bell rang, and Maggie brought me the card of Mrs. James Albert Parkhurst, who was known to me as a prominent biddy of the Women's Municipal League. She was wife to the Very Rev. Parkhurst and mother of three little girls at Mrs. Lyle's school. I received her in the parlor. She was decked in such velvet I assumed she was arrived to invite me to luncheon with her refined friends. My future from now on appeared as an uppercrust one indeed.

—Mrs. Jones! said she, brightly, when we were alone.

—Yes, my dear Mrs. Parkhurst? I says, expectant to be anointed.

But the cheer on her face crumbled immediately. —Oh oh oh, she sobbed.

—What is it? I cried. But already with a sinking heart I knew.

—I never thought . . . she stammered. —Me of all people . . . would . . . I am a member of the Female Moral Reform Society. Never did I think to find myself . . . at your mercy.

—It's all right, dear, I says, sighing. —It happens to the finest.

—I have had seven children, but with only three girls born live. And now, I am with child again. Already I am deathly sick. I nearly died last year when our poor infant boy did not survive. Yet Reverend Parkhurst wants a son so terribly and insists for me to carry on trying, despite I have lost four of them and will likely fail altogether in my own health if I do. And it is a sin and I know it is a sin! But oh, Mrs. Jones, can you help me?

—I cannot. I am retired.

At this she sobbed so bitter she was a picture of despair.

—It is a danger to me to practice as a female physician any longer.

—I will not breathe a word. I can pay anything. Whatever your price. I have my own little inheritance. Please, Madame. I love my girls and only ask to live long enough in health to see them grown.

—Poor Mrs. Parkhurst, dear. There, there now.

Hers was not the worst story I had heard. It was only the most ordinary. Looking at her yellow pallor, her thin wrists, her anguished phiz, I considered the threat of Mrs. Hideous Maltby at the Tombs and Judge B*ll*cks Merritt and the Dungbeetle Tallmadge and those other oranga-tangs of the law. I considered my family. My girl. Then I said what came natural to me when I met a woman in Tabitha Parkhurst's shoes.

—All right, I told her, very heavy. —Come round to 148 Liberty Street tomorrow.

—Oh thank you, Madame, said she, but burst out in a fresh spasm of wailing. —It is a terrible thing I choose. Wicked. And yet I am resolved on it Madame.

—Perhaps not wicked. But terrible? Yes. Yes. Though maybe less so than other roads you could travel. I don't know. It's not for me to say.

We two sat reflecting miserably on wickedness and travel and the road we had agreed upon. Thoughts of Risk and Danger began to prick at me again so fast. Worry over what Charlie would say. Guilt over my daughter.

—Strange, said Mrs. Parkhurst, —I am sad and frightened, yet resolved and grateful, to know that you might relieve me. It is a contradiction I cannot reconcile.

—I know such contradiction as you describe and feel it even now.

She thought on this for a moment and wept afresh. —Bless you, Madame, for your bravery.

She paid me one thousand dollars in cash.

I was not brave. No. I was a sucker for a crying woman. Also the money did not hurt. I was still an urchin who once scranned for orts and rags. A thousand dollars was always a fortune to me. Who knows but I might need it? For their part, the ladies needed a midwife. And that was me. My services was mine to offer or not and I offered them. Yes I was asking for trouble. Yes I was afraid the law would snatch and swallow me away from my child, my house, my husband. He said if I was caught he would not forgive me. But now I seen with alarm that I could not forgive myself, not if I slammed a door in the face of a lady who needed my skills. It was a complexity, and I did not know how to live with it exactly.

—Madame has not retired, I hear, said Charlie, with a cold face, when I returned from the office next day after relieving Mrs. Parkhurst.

—No. I have not.

—What if I forbid you? A wife obeys her husband. I could stop you.

—You won't stop me. I know you, Charlie, and you won't.

—So you take the risk? Because if you do, you force us to take it with you, don't you?

* * *

I would take the risk, I told the fine ladies of Gotham, but they would pay me for doing so. More than ever I did not apologize for the money I earned. The rich patients I charged a steep price. The poor ones I treated for nothing. Advice I doled out to everybody *gratis*. Money, it seemed, had proved an indemnity against the forces of Gunning and Tallmadge and that barnacle Merritt. More of it, I reasoned, might offer me the protection I required and might provide a cushion of comfort to my daughter if she was forced to cope without me. I was cautious. The practice was conducted by word of mouth. Consultation was the only service I advertised anymore, so even though ladies still came to me for every necessity, I avoided attention. The fat envelopes of cash, and the occasional fruitcake slipped to our local Officers of the Law did not hurt our cause. For one reason or another, it seemed the press boys had moved on. The traps had gave up.

Within a year of my release, we again had an income of ten thousand a week, from our various efforts. There was medicines sold in eight cities from Boston to Baltimore, Portland to Pittsburgh. (And these we did advertise again after a time, but only as "Female Medicine.") Charlie's pamphlets of medical advice was so popular, he hired a new assistant, to print and mail them. This aspect of our enterprise made a sweet profit with little more effort than it took to glue a stamp. My husband, it seemed, liked the profits more than he disliked the risk. He had proved himself a moneyman, and his return on investments piled up in the bank, alongside all the earnings from Madame DeBeausacq's Female Hospital and midwifery practice. And just as the Newspapers had dropped the subject of her practices, so we had dropped the subject of her retirement.

Now on Fifth Avenue at the corner of Fifty Second Street, the Jones' new palace rose at a good clip. We drove uptown on the weekends to see the land cleared and the foundation set, a skeleton of beams rising. Charlie liked to discuss the particulars of the architecture, especially the stables, but I preferred to occupy myself with the decoration of the interior, all fancy curtains and mosaics and upholstery.

By way of assistance, I engaged the services of Mrs. Candace Wheeler, who had founded the Decorative Arts Society with Mr. Louis Tiffany. She advised the owners of the finest palaces in the city on all aspects of domestic decoration.

—Anyone can arrange her home in a tasteful, elegant manner, given the right materials, said she.

The right materials indeed. On a Thursday we went to Duveen's Imports and spent $11,000 on European *objets* and furnishing: tables and chairs, also vases, statuary, paintings, candelabra and assorted curios such as a fire screen of Berlin work done in beads, a bust of our nation's first President, George Washington, and one of Benjamin Franklin, a favorite of Charlie's for his writings on The Way to Wealth, and his invention of the lightning rod.

—I hope you will not be a lightning rod anymore yourself, my dear, said Charlie to me, as we surveyed our new decorations. —For the sake of us all.

—I hope so, too, I says, and he smiled and winked at me. He was Fair Weather Charlie again, flush with profits and safe with wife and child under the roof. The Tombs was an old bad dream. The newspapers had turned their attention to other scandals: the murder of Sarah Crane, a hoor of Prince Street, the scandal of Joseph Potts, a bookseller whose shop offered such smutty titles as *The Lustful Turk.*

I paid little attention to the headlines but went instead with the whole family to A. T. Stewart's on a Saturday, to purchase my heart's desire. There, in the lighting department, Annabelle twirled beneath crystal and colored glass. Before we walked out we had ordered the largest custom-designed light fixture ever sold in New York City: the Swarovski King chandelier, all the way from Austria, made with arm-to-arm crystal festoons and crosscut bobeches with almond accents dangling. If I could, I'd've run the glassy drops through my fingers like water. My chandelier.

—I wish I could eat it, said Belle, —it's rock sugar candy.

Belle and me went to buy fabric and trim for dresses, India and Swiss Muslin, cambric and batiste, pique and Irish silk poplin and all different laces, bullion and sarcenet ribbon, llama fringe and steel fringe, cords and tassels. We ordered fancy combs, and stockings, an ermine fur muff for Annabelle, and a stole of marabout feathers.

—Oh, Mother, said Annabelle, —I would like to wear the feathers to my school.

—And how, mistress, would Mrs. Priscilla Lyle react to such a costume?

—I don't mind what she says. It's the girls who will wish they had one, too.

—But they don't! We was both gleeful over it.

The fact is, we Joneses was good or better than any of them swells now and had the trappings to prove it. Half the pupils of the Lyle School for Young Ladies was jealous of my daughter, a child of orphan train riders. Mrs. Lyle herself had brought me aside upon my reappearance and whispered, —You must know our hearts were with you during your travails.

Still, at her school, there were certain Silks and Velvets who would not stoop to speak to me. Despite fancy Mrs. Parkhurst's recent bloody adventures in my clinic, she was frosty to me in public, a hypocrite LAPDOG. Others slighted me same as if I was a common bogtrotter. Mrs. Caroline Van Zandt and Mrs. Eleanor Gibson seen me in the morning, escorting Annabelle to the door, and when I smiled at them and said Good Day, the pair of them only grimaced and smirked. They were a couple of vain old ewes. You could see the coal tar at the roots of their hair where they blacked the gray.

Despite these snubs I befriended other ladies of the best class, such as Mrs. Sybil Gaskins and Mrs. Dorothea Becker, who secured me invitations to the grand balls of uptown and down. We three enjoyed a companionable stroll along the fashionable avenues and traded invitations to luncheon or to dinner with our husbands in the evening. Mr. Becker liked to play whist. Although Charlie said he was a snooze, Mr. Wickenden was knowledgeable about gardens (his father was gardener to the Vanderbilts). It was Matthew Wickenden who advised me on the plantings for our new Fifth Avenue house, and his wife Serena was my favorite, for she had been known to smoke cigars with the men. She taught me to suck the smoke just into the mouth without inhaling very deep, and I ENJOYED to do it—not the taste or the smell like poison but only the shocked expression on the faces of the men when they saw me puffing. It was a barnyard collection of New Yorkers we had in our parlor, theosophicals and Liberal Leaguers, phrenologists and psychics, and our old friends the Owens and the rest of that philosopher group from our Liberty Street parlor.

*　*　*

At last in April of 1878, came moving day. We drove up Fifth Avenue in our new barouche. The top was open to the sky, the better to display us as we arrived at One East Fifty Second Street, grand entrance on Fifth. This was the Palace of Jones, where the wide front steps rose up off the Avenue to full double doors under an entryway that was vaulted and arched like the gates of a kingdom. We got down from the carriage with the help of Devlin our new footman in full livery, who held his gloved hand to me. I picked up my skirts, to show Annabelle, eight years of age now, how a lady dismounted. She followed me, and her father came round to give us each an arm.

—Queen Ann, your majesty, he said, quite formal. —Princess Annabelle.

He escorted us up the grand stairway while passersby gawped. Inside I was gawping myself. Here was our home, a palace. Who cared that the *Times* called it the domicile of a "rough woman" who "mangles her speech with ain'ts"? Who cared they called it "monstrous, in an extravagantly rich and vulgar style"? No more did they like my choice of window shades which they called "tasteless floral monstrosities."—When they write that, Charlie said, you know it's only jealousy oozing out their pens. Truth, what they didn't like was the office down the basement entrance, its discreet plaque advertising only Female Physician.

The great front hall inside was done up with floors of marble in a mosaic pattern called tessellated. The main staircase ascended up a curve, with the polished mahogany banister gleaming dark as a ribbon of chocolate. In the entryway Charlie puffed his chest and his cigar.

Annabelle clapped and twirled so her skirts flared out. —I LIKE this home, said our girl, and went sliding on the polished marble in her stockings.

Home. It was true and not a delusion. There was my lifesize reflection in the walls of gilt-edge mirrors: Mrs. Charles Jones, a woman thirty one years of age, plain featured but fine figured, in a dress of a cobalt blue stripe alternating with a deep blue floral. The Ladies Book pronounced this style among the richest materials for street dress, and there it was on me, a LADY if ever one lived and breathed. In a trick to the eye, my image reflected in the mirror behind it, and thus it repeated in both directions, back and front, coming and going, in ever smaller reproductions, so there were thousands of me, into the distant past and on to eternity.

I ascended the stairs, where in addition to the family quarters, there was two apartments which served as places for quality ladies to rest during their confinements, but which belonged in my mind as a place where my sister and brother might still come to roost. Maybe the Police detective or the Psychic Investigator we had hired might find Joe. Maybe Dutchie would write me again. The Post Office had strict instructions to forward mail to our new place. The Childrens Aid Society was on notice that any word from Lillian Ambrose VanDerWeil, or Joseph Muldoon or Trow should be sent to me right off. *Joe,* I wrote, in care of the Society, *You might like to watch the carriages race in Central Park I know you would.* I was sure I knew this about him even though he was no longer the baby boy I remembered. *Dutch,* I wrote, in a letter I did not send, *You and your Eliot would be welcome to stay here on Fifth Avenue with us in your own private apartments.*

Every weekend now, we Joneses traveled out, trotting up and down the Avenue in the landau or the barouche with two or four of the most brilliant horses in our stable, two bays, a gray, and a chestnut, their harnesses of German silver. The whole of Society was out riding the boulevards, wearing carriage cloaks in magenta and gold, fuchsia and chartreuse. We paraded in the sunlight through the drives of the new Central Park and nodded at the gentry along the boulevards. Neither Charlie nor Annabelle cared as much as I did for this pastime. At every chance, I went out bareheaded under the blue sky with teardrop diamonds on my earlobes, the better to catch the light. The ladies looked at me so envious, and the gentlemen tipped their hats.

Except when they didn't.

Sometimes they stared quite baldly at me with hostile eyes, and regularly some female would lower her veil at the sight of me like I was a species of maggot. For a week that year, the outraged pages of the newspapers scraped together a picayune new scandal to pin on my name. Wrote the *Tribune*:

The shock of seeing such a dangerous individual as Madame X (whose name we cannot utter) out riding in our midst, bedecked and flaunting expensive millinery, is apparently not enough to bring the law upon her. She has the audacity to drive her flashing carriage down the boulevards, and we cannot help but think that we, as a society, are making a retrograde movement in morality.

This editorial appeared in Mr. Greeley's paper in August of 1878. Was I sorry? No. For what? riding out in public? F. them all. Reckless, I wrote back with a piece of my mind.

> *It is, really, too monstrous that such silly epistles should have found room in your paper. Can we not drive in public with two or four horses without spiteful comments published in respectable papers? I would leave it to every impartial, liberal, high-minded person, to decide whether these uncalled-for attacks partake not of the full spirit of persecution, if not of even worse motives?*
> *Yours, &tc. —Madame DeBeausacq.*

Charlie helped me only with the last bit, about persecution, and also suggested the word epistle, which was of a higher class than article, but otherwise the sentiments and locutions was mine alone, especially about their worse motives. What might those motives be? Greed and Jealousy. Dr. Gunning and his medical friends envied the money a midwife such as myself brought in and wanted it for their own. When they themselves was guilty of such subterfuge, wasn't it preposterous that they should protest my right to only ride in a buggy?

—If they do not like my driving in the park, I said to Charlie, —imagine what they will write when we hold our Grand Housewarming.

—Invite them, he said. —They'll come if only to get a peek inside Jones' Palace.

Mr. and Mrs. Charles G. Jones request the honor of your presence said the invitation. Within ten days, three hundred of New York's social order replied they would Accept With Pleasure, including every mother from Mrs. Lyle's school—even those old legs of mutton Mrs. Gibson and Mrs. Van Zandt who snubbed me. Priscilla Lyle herself sent her acceptance on rose-colored stationery. *An honor,* she wrote.

My gown was ordered from Paris, midnight blue with silver brocade; flounces trimmed with silver cord and tassel; lined throughout with silver silk to match. In such a dress I was royalty. On Saturday, I delivered Mrs. Constable's baby girl at five o'clock a.m., and at five o'clock p.m., I slipped my ballgown over my head, and Maggie pulled the laces tight. I took my jewels from the safe. Charlie watched as I selected a crown of diadems. Three diamond rings and jeweled bracelets for each wrist. Around my neck was a pendant, the big stone set with small sparklers, the whole works flashing and winkling like the secrets I carried and never would tell. At my earlobes were clusters of blue white drops, shaped like tears.

It was these same earrings she wore, the morning they found her in the tub. I took them off my own ears and placed them on hers. They were buried with her.

From behind the curtains on the second floor me and Charlie watched the carriages arrive in the dusk of the evening. The gold of their lanterns was a parade of fireflies to our door. The ladies dismounted and gentlemen in white ties and top hats extended their gloved hands as they climbed the stairs to the Grand Ball of the Joneses. The guests was all the swells, lawyers and physicians, brokers and financiers, aldermen and members of the political class. Too bad Mayor Havemeyer and his wife disdained the invitation. So did Mrs. Hottentot Astor and Mrs. Snoot Vanderbilt, and all the other old pedigrees: the Rhinelanders and the Stuyvesants, the Peter Coopers and the George Templeton Strongs. In the entrance hall we had a string quartet. Waiters in black coats circulated with flutes of champagne and caviar on crackers that was the style in Prussia. For the gentlemen, rosewood humidors full of cigars stood ready, and for the ladies there were finger sandwiches and cakes the size and delicacy of a daisy. In the great parlor on the fourth floor were banquet tables groaning under the weight of roasts and wheels of cheese, and étagères of small sweets, tarts and fruits spilling over.

At last we made our entrance. At the head of the stairs Charlie held his hand aloft and I placed mine upon it. The hem of my blue gown trailed behind so elegant, as me and my husband proceeded down the grand staircase. The strings played a tune suitable for royals.

—There she is, somebody said. —Mrs. Jones.

The sea of faces was lifted. Eyes on me. There was many I recognized. Dorothea and Serena with their husbands. Dear Candace Wheeler my décor adviser, and my lawyer Morrill and his entire law firm with their wives. Mrs. Priscilla Lyle and Judge Crittenden came and Fanny Rheingold and our disreputable philosopher friends the Owens and the Arguimbeaus and Will Sacks. We made our way through the throng, and the guests all came to thank us. Oh our lovely home. Oh our charming hospitality. Oh the tasteful music. At the peel of a little bell rung by Thomas the butler, the guests made their way upwards to the feast and entertainments. And oh, yes, you can bet they did enjoy themselves, the gentlemen in the billiards room and the ladies in the parlors. On the first landing everybody admired the giant frescoes, a scene of cherubs frolicking by a pool, darling wee babies, so rosy-cheeked. Mrs. Webb and Mrs. Frelinghuysen discussed its finer points.

—Two Italian artists took a year to paint this, can you imagine?

—Ten thousand dollars for one fresco alone.

—And this carpet is lovely, said Mrs. Webb, as we proceeded into the parlor.

—An Aubusson, I said, with proper pronunciation. —Three thousand dollars it cost. I had the satisfying impression that they'd never heard of such a price for a carpet. Mrs. Candace Wheeler had once suggested to me that it was not refined to discuss the cost of things in public, but I said to her that was c**p, for what was the point then of having money?

There in the throng now greeting us was Greta and her husband Mr. Alfonse Sprunt. He was a man who looked like his name, a sprout of a runt, in need of a barber, with tufts of hair like cattails in his ears and his thumbs hooked on his waistcoat pockets. They greeted me and Charlie with twin crooked smiles, so it was plain they both were cupshot already. Greta laughed and embraced me, calling me Axie.

—Remember when ve vass hauzmaids? she said, mashing the words with drink.

—Greta, dear, you're tipsy!

—*Sturzbesoffen*, MADAME. She laughed and stumbled off dancing, so I rolled my eyes and worried over her. Greta had taken a chance marrying her Mr. Sprunt, who was sour and mean now to little Willi, though while he was courting her he'd brought the boy presents, tops and tin whistles. From the corner of my eye I watched the merry Sprunts empty a pair of champagne flutes.

In the ballroom, Mr. Morrill approached us and exchanged pleasantries.

—And what do you think of this terrible new law? he said.

—What now? said Charlie. —No cigars after dinner?

—Worse. It is now a crime to send or receive certain materials through the mails. So called obscene matter.

—My thoughts may be obscene, sir, said Charlie, —but my mail is always clean.

—Charlie's pamphlets are educational, I said, —as you well know, Morrill.

—This law is sure to impact you unfavorably, Morrill warned. —It aims to punish the possession or sale of any articles to prevent . . . ahem. Conception.

—Says who, pray tell? I said.

—Mr. Comstock, he replied. —It's called the Comstock Law.

—Who is Comstock?

—A species of Postal Inspector, by special appointment, replied Morrill. —Mr. Anthony Comstock.

Thus it was in the swirl of the party that I first heard the name of My Arch Enemy. And do you know, reader, I yawned at it? It was a midge on a summer night. For the moment I would pay no more mind to Morrill's warning. I swatted it away and placed my gloved hand across my mouth. A postal inspector. Who cared? Music like a waterfall spilled down the stairs. Alcohol bubbles caused a fizzgig in my veins. I drank champagne like sipping stars and whirled around the dance floor under the woozy sparkles of my chandelier, in the arms of all the many gentlemen who requested a turn. It was a night of nights and it did not end till the small hours of the morning.

The papers were full of the spectacle, especially the *Polyanthos*:

> A certain Madame X, who needs no naming in these pages, infamous as she is for her nefarious practices, held a Ball last evening for the cream of the New Money Classes. Not an Astor or a Vanderbilt could she lure to her door, but members of the shoddy aristocracy were there in abundance. Mrs. Candace Wheeler the society decorator was one who did attend, no doubt proud to defend the occupants' choice of such tasteless floral window shades as adorn the mansion on Fifth Avenue. The interior of the house is a marvel of sumptuousness and unexceptional taste, full of curios, bronzes, statues, clocks, and two life-sized white marble busts of Washington and Franklin, surmounted by American flags.

—They noticed George and Ben, I cried to Charlie. —They noticed the flags!

—What so proudly we hail, he said.

Proudly, yes. For now it was published in writing for the world to see: the Jones family was righteous wavers of the flag and lovers of the liberties and justice for which it stands. It was not for nothing we had those flags and our busts of Washington and Franklin. We were patriots, and proud of it.

But no flag could serve as a defense against a steamroller like what was barreling towards us then. Mr. Comstock was over two hundred fifty pounds, while I was only two more than ninety. It was not a fair fight from the word go.

—You're in the news again, Mrs. Jones, said my husband very ominous at breakfast not long after our Grand Ball. He handed me the paper. —The *Herald* has dared Mr. Comstock to come after you. They call him the Roundsman of the Lord, while he calls himself the Chairman of the Society for the Suppression of Vice.

The expression on my husband's face was wary. I read the article with a knob of fear in my chest.

> Public decency demands that the state protect citizens from so-called "medical practitioners" who are no better than quacks. Thanks to the efforts of the crusading Mr. Anthony Comstock, the current pages of the Herald no longer contain advertising from such vile sorts, but these medical imposters continue to operate unhindered. The most notorious, Madame DeBeausacq alias Mrs. Ann Jones, of Fifth Avenue, is a case in point. She was locked up some years ago in the Tombs but escaped Justice, and who, if Justice were done, would now be in State Prison, instead of the owner and occupant of one of the finest dwellings on Fifth Avenue. Let Mr. Comstock bring his crusade not only to silence the smut peddlers of our city, but to go after such Hags of Misery, and shut down her evil den.

—They mean to come after us again, I said, a weakness in my legs.

—Tell Maggie and Greta to be careful who they let in the office, Charlie said. —Life could change again with just a knock on the door.

And it did, it did. But not as Charlie thought it would.

Chapter Thirty-Nine

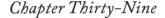

It's You

—Madame, there is a lady at the front, who refuses to go down around to the office, said Maggie.

—If she won't come in the business end of the place then send her away, said I.

—I tried, Madame. She insists I let her in.

—Likely she's one of those Females from the Moral Reform Society. —Tell her to find herself a real sinner.

—But she claims she knows you as a friend. Maggie dug in her apron pocket and brought out a calling card. When I saw the name engraved there, it floored me like a steam train.

Mrs. Eliot VanDerWeil, the card said.

—She's very grand, said Maggie. —She insists and insists.

The room fell away, and Maggie's voice was a garble beneath the roar in my ears.

Mrs. Eliot VanDerWeil.

—Are you all right, Madame? You are quite pale.

—Send her in, I said, so weak.

—Yes ma'am.

My heart was clutched by a fist in my chest. My hands were lost things patting the air, smoothing the sides of my skirt, touching at my face to see was it real? The air was sharp and clear as ice water. I waited, freezing, till after a minute, the click of boot heels echoed off the marble in the hall.

—Mrs. VanDerWeil, Madame, said Maggie.

And there she stood. I was drained of blood.

It was her and not her. She had a bosom. Her face was sculpted now, with cheekbones like you find on a statue. Lord she was a creature. Black lashes like a scallop of feathers against her flushed white cheeks. She took off her hat, blinking slowly, and fixed the blue lanterns of her eyes on me.

—Oh Dutch, I whispered.

—Axie?

We were in each other's arms. The smell of Lily of the Valley clung to her hair. Twenty years gone in a spray of perfume. I felt her stiff and formal, ladylike. When I reared back to look at her, her eyes were chips of the summer sky that had fallen into her face to rest there.

—Is it really you? my sister said. —Is it?

—I don't know. Let me pinch myself and see.

She laughed and I remembered her laugh. She bit one of her fingernails.

—You still bite your nails, you dirty cat, I said, to tease her.

—Oh. She removed her hand from her small white teeth like it was burnt. —Mother has always hounded me about that wicked habit. Not our mother, I meant—

—Shh. Never mind, Dutchie. Oh look at you. You're a fine Chicago lady.

—If so, then I don't know why your maid would not admit me!

—Maggie's a sly little cooze, so she is.

—I beg your pardon?

—Excuse my Portuguese. I explained it was Maggie's job to send anonymous callers round to the office door. —And to her you seemed to be anonymous.

—I see.

We stood so strange and awkward in the parlor while the sun poured in the windows off Fifth Avenue and shattered in the prisms of crystal dazzling above our heads. Patches of light dappled our faces. This could not be my sister, could it? She remained an eight year old girl in my mind's picture of her, and here was this lady twenty six years of age. Dutch pressed the palms of her hands together in front of her mouth and looked at me in disbelief. I stared, gulping down the vision of her.

—I am just back from two years in Paris, she said. —I'll be here a month before returning to Chicago. Mother's gone on ahead there without me, so

I took this chance to find you at last. The Childrens Aid Society gave me your new address.

—Oh my dear darling, sweet lovely Dutchie, I said, and embraced her again.

—My own sister. It's quite strange.

Anyone looking at our lace collars and elaborate skirts, our rings and bracelets and tortoiseshell combs, would never imagine how once we curled up like a litter of cats in the bed, how I pulled her hair and bit her, how she scratched when we argued so red stripes and claw marks crosshatched my cheeks. Long ago we two was wild savages crawling with dirt and holes in our shoes. Now you'd think the both of us was just Mrs. Fifth Avenue and Mrs. Park Avenue about to have tea and pastry, except for how fast our hearts beat, how tied our tongues.

Dutch gazed around her. I was proud for her to see what had become of me. The fireplace big enough to park a carriage, the marble of the mantel swirled and carved. She tipped her head back to the ceiling, with its panels of walnut and that chandelier sparkling, and I saw the approval in her eyes, how she smiled at me. Surely neither the Ambrose house, nor the VanDer-Weil one, was grand as this.

—Please forgive me for not warning you of my arrival, she said. —Eliot and I were staying at the Marble House, and since he has gone to London for several weeks . . .

—How many times I dreamed of this day.

—Strange, how your maid kept mistaking me for someone in the trades! As if I was a shopgirl delivering something. She insisted that I should go downstairs to the side entrance. Forgive me, but she said—

And here my sister leaned in to whisper, giggling —I could swear she said that *Madame DeBeausacq's* office was downstairs. I can't believe she would think I was looking for that horrible woman.

—Horrible woman?

—Surely you have heard of her wicked practice? Madame—ahem, is a foul murderess.

—Is that so?

—We have news of her even in Chicago. Even in Paris they call it . . . DeBeausacquisme. You must've heard?! Is she at work so nearby? She killed a poor cigar store girl and dumped her corpse in the river.

—Ha.

—She's quite the scandal. Thousands of innocents have died at her hands.

—That's just a pile of c**p, I said. Dutch winced, and I felt myself to be no more than a fishwife in her estimation, cursing and common.

—Would you care for coffee? I asked.

—Yes please. My sister nodded, quite cordial, but something was off. We stood about not knowing what was next or how to be. Our smiles were uneasy. Still, just to gaze at her was like a long draught of water to a fevered patient. As we sat by the window overlooking the gardens, we talked over each other, about Mam, and Mrs. Ambrose, and her husband Eliot, about my Charlie and Annabelle.

—Dutchie, wait till my little girl meets you, I said. —You'll be Auntie Dutch!

—Ann, said my sister, most uncomfortable, —just as I am sure you are no longer called by your childhood name Axie, I must tell you that nobody calls me Dutch or knows me by that name.

—Our mother named me Ann. I don't know who named you Lily.

My sister flinched. —I was only requesting that you—I have been Lily for so long now.

—If you would prefer that name, I'll call you it.

—Thank you.

Lily to me was the name of a funeral flower, and it sat alongside a thorn-bush of silence between us, for I found my sister to be a stranger in cobalt silk.

—I meant to come to Chicago to find you, I said. —I swore to Mam I would.

—It's good you didn't. It's a secret that I am . . . adopted. Even now . . . I must beg you not to reveal me.

—Your secrets are safe with me. I am quite practiced at keeping them.

—Please tell no one you ever saw me. Say I am a friend from your school days.

—Presenting Mrs. Lily Reardon, I said, —an old friend from my school days.

—Ha! Dutch laughed. —Mrs. Reardon! I remember you called her Mrs.—

—Mrs. Rump!

Dutch clapped her hand over her mouth. Mrs. Rump, Mrs. Rump. She was convulsed in giggles same as ever, but something came over her and she straightened herself back into a proper society madam as if she'd noticed all the low-class tics that remained in me, no matter how I strived to rid myself of the bad grammar I was born to. Perhaps Mrs. Lillian VanDerWeil would not care that I had Swarovski crystal and a bust of George Washington or that the pearls at my neck was genuine. The queerness between us was the wasted years we spent apart, and all the ways we didn't know each other like sisters should.

—Ann, she said, —where is our brother Joe?

—I thought you might have the answer to that question.

—I know nothing of him. His family—the Trows? Was that their name? Moved to Philadelphia, I think. I was discouraged from discussing him. Mother said he wouldn't come looking for me because he was too young to remember.

—He's twenty now. —Twenty one!

—He must be quite tall, she said. —His voice will have broken.

It was as if Joe stood there in the silence between us, a stranger with scraps of beard. I played with a fold of fabric in my skirt. Dutch gazed out the window, with elegant posture, and dabbed her rosette mouth with the corner of her napkin. She examined the backs of her fingernails. The ring on her left hand held diamonds and a pearl the size of a hailstone. She is a pearl herself, I thought, white and smooth and cultured.

—Your home is lovely, she said. —Your husband must be quite successful.

—He is a businessman.

—Ah. No longer a newspaperman? In what line of work is Charles now?

—Medicinals.

She nodded and raised her eyebrows. Her husband was also in business, she said. —He manages his family's finances. You know, they are the VanDerWeils of the Chicago Northern Railways.

—How nice. What a good match you have made.

—And you as well, she said, but now the smile had froze on her lips, and she pressed her fist to her mouth, her face crumpled into misery.

—Eliot and I . . . , she said, quite flustered. —Something is not right with me. I am unable . . . We have no children. She looked up at me like she was sure I'd be appalled. —Eliot says he must have heirs. He wants to know what is wrong with me.

—Och *mavourneen,* perhaps nothing is wrong.

—He will not speak to me during the day, and then at night— She looked away, scarlet with embarrassment. —Every night he goes to his gentlemen's clubs. He arrives home—

—Is he—? Intoxicated?

—It's because he can no longer bear the sight of me.

—But you're so beautiful. He could not find anyone prettier.

—My doctor in Chicago said that I have brought this state of affairs upon myself. The doctors in London and Paris cannot help me. It's my own fault.

—Malarkey.

—But it IS my fault! she cried. —I . . . attended college. If only I hadn't. It wasn't for long, really. It was only the study of musical annotation and theory, and a little bit of Latin and French. But Dr. Gundy says even that much is enough to drain the . . . to cause . . . My sister blushed and stammered. —He says those women who engage in taxing mental pursuits sap their generative functions.

—If French was bad for you, there wouldn't be no more Frenchmen. Did your fancy doctors tell you that spirits of alcohol in the male are an obstacle to generative function?

She blushed to the roots of her hair.

—Dutch—Lily, there are tablets you can take.

She stood up and went to the window. —I wouldn't know where to procure them.

—I can get them for you.

—You?

—Easily. They'll help you conceive a child in no time. Stay here and let me get the remedy for you. I'll only be a minute.

—Wait, she said, with a perplexed look gathering steam on her face.

—I'll just be a moment. I have them among my personal medicines.

She stared at me, her expression filled with a growing horror. —You're going to the office downstairs. That office *is* downstairs! Your maid told the truth!

—Maggie does not lie unless I ask her to.

—How could you? she cried. —How could you allow that woman, that Madame—to have an office here?

—Madame DeBeausacq is a fine lady, the most celebrated in New York. Just a bitty little thing. Quite wise and kind. She would not hurt a flea.

—She's a murderer! She's a felon! I've read how she—

—Mrs. DeBeausacq is only a midwife. She has delivered many ladies of healthy children and will never hesitate to help with any problems of female physiology or marriage questions or private matters of an intimate nature.

—She's a demon.

—She's an angel of mercy, I said.

My sister gaped at me.

—She would help you, too, I said, quietly, —if you let her.

Now she was alarmed, her eyes wide. —Is it you? Are you—?

I held her gaze.

—It's YOU, isn't it? YOU are Madame DeBeausacq herself!

—So what if I was?

—But that's ... inconceivable.

—Nothing's inconceivable if you can think of it, right? Not even a baby if you want one. A little VanDerWeil.

She hiccuped and covered her mouth.

—Dutchie, you was always a squeamish kit, I said, sighing mightily. —Madame DeBeausacq is a lovely person, if I do say so myself, whose vocation is to assist mothers to bring their sweet babies into the world and ease the afflictions of poor suppressed ladies with no other recourse. She's only a midwife, is all. The oldest profession, save one. And it's the other one, you know, the oldest trade, awaiting many a young girl with no other recourses. Unless I help her.

On my sister's face then was a look like old fish was rotting in the room. My own sister with her lip curled. She squared her shoulders, stood and gathered her hat.

—I must be going. I must get back to the hotel.

—Dutch, Lily. Please. Listen.

—Good afternoon.

—You can't leave now, Dutchie, after all this—

—Really, Ann. She stopped, trembling, in front of me, a terrible reproach cooking on her face. —What would Mam think of you?

When she said that a hot spike of anger provoked me and crossed my face when I spoke. —It was a puerperal hemorrhage that killed our Mam, a kind I prevent quite regular. If she had had a midwife she'd be alive in this room—

Dutch headed for the door, her face contorted.

—Dutchie, please, I've only just found you.

—I don't see how I can stay, she said, so agitated.

—What about those tablets? Wouldn't you—? Please. Dutch. They'll help you.

—No thank you, she said on the way out.

I caught her arm. —You don't have to stay with him, Dutchie. Your Eliot. If he's unkind to you. You could come here and live with me. You could have your own apartment here. It's all ready for you. And wouldn't the gentlemen line up then to come calling? Just leave him. You're a young beauty, Lily, you could—

—I could never, she said, her face pale as milk. —You have no idea. Never.

She veiled herself and fled past Maggie, out the door and into the street, where a beautiful green victoria waited. She climbed in it and drew the curtains. —Dutch! I cried. Nineteen years I had sought this day only to have her scared off by slander. —Dutchie! I called after her. But the traffic swept her away and I stood on the sidewalk, shivering, my hand raised in farewell.

I ran inside and found my coat, and then went down to the offices and took a package of Madame DeBeausacq's Natal Pills (black cohosh plus raspberry leaves and false unicorn root to enhance the fecundating properties). I went not to the stables for my own carriage, but to the street, where I hailed a regular hansom cab, so that I would not be recognized. We drove downtown and I paid the driver to wait outside the Marble House, where, breathless in the lobby, I asked for Mrs. Eliot VanDerWeil.

—Your name? asked the pickle-nosed clerk.

—Mrs. Ann Jones, I said.

—Mrs. VanDerWeil's no longer a guest here, he said, after a hesitation that revealed he was lying. Dutch was at the Marble House, but apparently had left instructions for this adenoidal larrikin to turn me away. I went back out to my cab and waited by the curb. Every twenty minutes I paid the driver to wait longer. Five dollars. Then thirty. I'd wait her out. She couldn't stay in there forever.

At last, toward evening, she emerged. My sister. Look at her. The graceful swan of her neck below her upswept hair. The cut of her gabardine dress. She clutched the arm of a gentleman. He was a fine swell type such as frequented Newport for the yacht races, with yellow hair and beard. He looked down into my sister's eyes and I saw how she gazed back up at him, like he was a life ring flung into harsh waters. So this was her husband, Mr. VanDerWeil.

—Dutch! I cried, and hastened out of the cab toward her.

She kept walking though it was clear in the stiffening of her shoulders that she heard me.

—Dutch! Still she did not acknowledge me.

So that's how it is with her then, I thought, the cat. She stabbed me to the core. I could not chase her. I had promised to keep her secret. Instead I went back in to talk to the desk boy.

—Mrs. VanDerWeil is a guest here after all, I said. —I just saw her leave.

—She left instructions that she will receive no visitors.

—It's very sad, I told him, and brought the tears to my eyes. —She's my long lost sister. Rummaging through my purse, I withdrew my handkerchief, and with it, the sum of fifty dollars. I dabbed at my eyes and wept a little and passed the money to the clerk. —Might you give her a package?

—I might, he said, smiling, and pocketed the bills.

—Thank you. Withdrawing to a bench in the lobby, I took a slip of paper and wrote:

> *Dear Dutchie,*
>
> *You know that blood is blood and we are sisters sure as daylight. When all is said and done what else do we have? (Each Other.) I will not tell your secrets nor make you fraternize with me, if you don't want. I am content to know you are well and happy (though I think you are not! my poor sister). Here in this package is the remedy. May it bring you the results you long for and don't be sad ~~no~~ any more.*

*That you turned your back on me just now in the street is a
cold fact I will always mourn. If ever you change your mind
you know my door is forever open to you. If you would try me
for a 2nd chance, meet me in the tea room at the Astor House
tomorrow at 3:00, no one will recognize me at all, I promise.
All's I want is to see you again.*
　　　Love, your sister Axie

I folded the note, attached it to the package, and addressed it *Mrs.
VanDerWeil.*

—Please pass this to her when her husband is not about, I says, handing
it over to the desk clerk.

—Never fear, says the clerk, —he is never about.

—I saw her with him just now. They made quite a pair.

—Oh, that was not—

—Not her husband? And who was it if I might trouble you to ask?
Along with the question I forked over another twenty dollars.

—A businessman named Pickering, says my new friend. —He owns a
fleet of merchant ships and has offices at Peck Slip.

—Thank you, I says, masking my astonishment, and left the premises.

My sister had a fellow on the side, it seemed.

Dutch did not meet me the next day at the Astor Hotel. She did not
respond to my note. Four days later, for twenty dollars, the desk clerk at the
Marble House reported that she had returned to Chicago.

Chapter Forty

A Change of Circumstances

The shock of my sister's appearance and disappearance caused a strange lethargy in me. I lost my appetite. My nights was restless and troubled. For the first time in many years I began again to nurse my knuckles in my sleep. Even awake I troubled them. Dutch had shunned me. I had lost her again, worse than before, and reviewed our brief meeting, over and over, for a clue to what I might have said, what I could've done to convince her to stay with me. If only I'd lied. *Madame DeBeausacq? Never heard of her.* All the money in the world, all the tessellated marble and Prussian fire screens was not impressive enough for my sister. Her loss preoccupied me above all else. When my work was done in the evening I wrote her letters disguised as Mrs. Reardon and sent them to the Marble House with a request for forwarding service to Chicago.

One morning at the breakfast table when I was thus preoccupied and Annabelle was humming over her toast, Charlie was as usual immersed in the headlines, and this day there was one that struck him.

—Postal Inspector Comstock assaulted in City Hall Park, he read aloud.

—He's that little round man, I said, —who crusades against smut peddlers and puts them in jail?

—Hmm, yes, said Charlie, reading with a worried expression.

—It wouldn't surprise me if one of them booksellers walloped him.

—No. Listen. It was a Dr. Selden. An abortionist, it says here. Comstock

the Vice Crusader had him arrested on obscenity charges. So the doctor
had a whack at him and Comstock was bloodied.

Charlie read out loud:

—"This is the first blood I have been called upon to shed for the
right," said Mr. Comstock. "My all if necessary, if only for my blessed
Redeemer."

—Mr. Comstock is a fox terrier of the Lord, I said.

Annabelle said,—Please can't we have a little terrier dog of our own, Papa?

—Do not interrupt, youngster, I said. —Mind your manners.

—Certainly, my kitten, we'll have a little dog, said her Papa, which sent
her skipping from the table without finishing her egg.

—I was suggesting, I said,—that Mr. Comstock is a rat terrier of Christ.
But Charlie's face was serious. —He says he is a weeder in God's Garden.

—More like a weed.

—Listen, Charlie said, and read on:

> Mr. Comstock has made the arrests of nine abortionists in
> New York City, and eight in Albany, but he has yet to capture
> the Great She-Villain DeBeausacq, who operates here with
> impunity. "Madame flaunts her nefarious avocation in the
> face of the world, and advertises openly," Mr. Comstock said.
> "Moreover it has been thrown in my teeth repeatedly that while
> I break up weak and inconspicuous abortionists, and send the
> devils to prison, I either dare not arrest the most notorious of
> them all, or else I have been bribed. This cannot be tolerated.

We sat at the table in alarmed silence. I took the paper from Charlie and
there was Comstock's threat like a bullet with my name on it. —We'll close
the office, I said.

—Well let's see if that's really necessary, Charlie said, and you could
knock me over with an ostrich plume so surprised was I at his tone. He
was back to his boostering fairweather self, smoothing my feathers with his
theories of the law and prognostications of my safety. —See? he said. —The
President himself—General Grant!—has pardoned the doctors who were
convicted, and all the others had their cases thrown out.

—The president?

—It seems Ulysses S. liked the argument of the defense, said Charlie, reading.

> The defense pointed out that there remains a legitimate use for the articles in question, the syringe and the curette, and unless INTENT to commit a crime can be proved, no conviction is possible.

—Moreover, Charlie said, —according to this account, these pardoned abortionists had not only a president, but a congressman, Mr. Tremain and a clergyman on their side. So. In my opinion—in light of Grant's pardon, these laws cannot prevail.

—Just so you know, Charlie, before I'd go back to jail, I'd kill myself.

—I hope you won't, he said, joking. —You know how I hate the sight of blood.

Then he grew serious. —You'll be careful, right? Morrill says it's prudent to keep certain medicines hidden in the wine cellar or somewheres unlikely. But I won't let any rat terriers nor hounds of hell get to you. And if they do? We know the right people. Don't we? We live on Fifth Avenue now. Mark my words. We'll live out our days here, with wee grandchildren running around the garden with Whiskers the mouse.

He ran an imaginary mouse down my back till I shrieked and swatted at him over the toast. I was happy to believe him. It was in my nature to put my head in the sand, believing that Yes, the worst was bound to happen but what could I do about it? I had my household and my ladies to worry about. I failed to be properly haunted by Comstock. Three years had passed since my time at the Tombs without the traps bothering me. Within days of the newspaper article, we again forgot to beware about postal inspectors. We believed the press was otherwise bored of me. The law would not bother now I was at my fancy address. Didn't I treat Fifth Avenue ladies every day? Comstock was a pompous tub of lard. I was protected by the List, by the Reticence and Decorum of my lady patients, and Comstock knew it. Despite all his brash talk, it seemed that the Vice Hunter was not much interested in medical practitioners such as myself. What really excited him, what really took up his attention in those years, was SMUT, and catching the peddlers of naughty postcards and dirty books. This he did with the zeal of a shoat-hog for a bucket of warm mash.

He went after Victoria Woodhull and her sister Tennessee Claflin, who wrote in their "Weekly" about Rev. Henry Ward Beecher's affair with a married woman. Comstock deemed this obscene (their writing, not the affair) and had the poor sisters arrested. Their bail was set so high, at $80,000, that the beleaguered ladies lingered many weeks in the Ludlow Street Jail and went bankrupt, forced to pay $20,000 in costs. He ruined them and they was paupers afterwards.

Also, he ruined some cove called George Train, whose offense was to publish certain passages from the BIBLE, including the story of Jehovah commanding Hosea to marry a hoor, the one about King David guilty of adultery, and the passages about Amnon raping his sister. For this Mr. Train was charged with obscenity and thrown in the Tombs, his reputation, health and finances destroyed, all for publishing Bible verses.

I did not think, *If Bible is smut then none of us is safe.* I carried on. I had to. My doorbell rang day and night. I was not a lady of leisure but a working midwife—worried about my sister who fled, our lost brother Joseph, the new mothers in confinement calling me at all hours, and my girl growing into a young lady. I went about managing the household, the gardens and the stable boys, the sodden hysterical Greta and her loutish husband Sprunt, my daughter's spelling tests and dancing lessons, our Saturday salons with the swells of New York Society, where Annabelle now sometimes performed so genteel on the Steinway, and Maggie served deviled eggs with caviar—while all that time Mr. Comstock was busy trampling out the vintage where the grapes of wrath are stored, like the song says.

What I did not bargain on was his terrible swift sword, the underhanded tactics of this Worst Enemy. He was a SNEAK. He assumed aliases. He used purloined stationery of the US Treasury for his schemes. He used false addresses. He lied. He made citizen's arrests whenever he felt like it. He sometimes pretended to be a woman! and wrote letters calling himself "Anna Ray," of Washington DC, and "Ella Bender," of Squan Village, New Jersey, and "Mrs. Semler," from Chicago, just to entrap his victims. He was a cheat and swindler more suited to be a poodle dog clipped in the lion fashion than a CRUSADER. I wonder did he picture himself in a flowered calico as he penned his lies? Did he flutter his eyelashes like Nanette as he wrote his flattering deceitful letters to his victims, poor Dr. E. B. Foote for example? This Foote was a respected Christian physician and author. Comstock, masquerading as Mrs. Semler, penned several notes to entrap him.

> *Dear Dr. Foote, I'm a steadfast admirer of your books, "Plain Home Talk," and "Medical Common Sense." Would you be so kind, dear sir, as to send them to me?*

Foote's books were only medical advice to families, on subjects such as Prevention of Conception. But for sending these works, under the Comstock Law, the good Doctor was arrested. Jailed. Fined. Shamed. Ruined to the tune of $25,000. His family lived after that impoverished.

Comstock was mean as any river thief or member of the Roach Guards, and it was rumored (with great interest to the Freudians now, as I write this in the new century) that he carried a rubber snake in his pocket which he used to scare children, but mostly it was his ceremonial Post Office badge and not the snake that he liked to whip from his trousers, shouting Arrest! His poor victims rotted months at a time behind bars, their health declining, their families falling apart, their reputations destroyed.

Over these years, ignoring me, Mr. Comstock seized THIRTY THOUSAND pounds of so-called obscene material. What did he do with so much lewdity? Me and Charlie began to joke that old Tony sat around the fire at night with dirty pictures tucked between the pages of his Bible, reading smut with his red flannel underdrawers aflame. We two had got very cavalier. —He'd rather ogle bare naked ladies, said Charlie, —than come after you, Axie. A raid on Madame doesn't come with a new set of naughty cards.

It seemed he was right. Despite his bragging Comstock did not come after me. Another year passed and there was not a word out of him.

Nor was there word from my sister. If I was haunted by anyone, it wasn't Comstock at all but Dutch. It had been thirteen months plus one week since she fled my parlor. Where was she? Wherever she was, she was ashamed of me. The luxuries of my home hadn't mattered a bit to her. For sure she thought I was beneath her. And yet, was she happy? She was not. It had showed on her like a fever. Her husband was cruel. She wanted a child. She had a lover. She had secrets she could never tell. I was one of them, a secret shame. If anyone knew the Evil Madame DeBeausacq was her sister, she'd die of disgrace. I believed with great grief that I'd seen the last of her.

But then, in the coldest week of February 1880, just after breakfast, I heard the bell ring, and Rebecca arguing downstairs. I dismissed the commotion as the usual dramatics from the household staff, till Maggie came to tell me that, waiting for me in the conservatory was a Mrs. Lillian Reardon. My sister.

I ran downstairs to her, flung open the door. —Dutch! I cried.

She stood very still, her eyes vague, and downcast.

—Sorry, so sorry, I meant Lily, I said, all in a fluster of emotion and correcting myself. —Oh I am so glad to see you, my darling sister—pardon me, I meant *friend* of my school days, you've come back.

Still she met me stiffly, could not meet my eye.

—I thought you'd never come here again, said I.

—Circumstances change, she said, stammering, —I—

—Are you all right?

She gave a panicked smile and twisted the diamond wedding ring she wore on her left hand, as if the finger itself had come unscrewed.

—You're shivering, I said.

—Am I?

In the parlor, Maggie brought us tea.

—Tell no one that I am here, Dutch whispered, when Maggie had gone. —Please, Ann. Do you trust your staff? Are they discreet?

—My staff is very good at keeping secrets. I pay them well for exactly that reason.

—Your housemaid—

—Maggie?

—She saw my calling card that day years ago. She knows the name VanDerWeil.

—She can't hardly read. Anyways, she's got secrets of her own she doesn't want spilled.

—What secrets?

—I'll never tell, I said. —But if her father ever finds her he is liable to scatter her brains around the scullery.

My sister sat clutching her cup, her eyes locked on the far distance. I felt sure she would now tell me her husband had discovered her affair with Mr. Pickering.

—What is it, dear Lily? I said. —What's wrong?

She shook her head in small rapid shakes.

—Are you hurt? I cried. —Has he thrown you out? Taken up with someone else? Is your foster mother Mrs. Ambrose angry? Has she discovered you know her secrets?

—No.

—What then?

The white of her throat pulsed as she swallowed. —I'm . . . Her gaze dropped to her lap and back again. Her meaning was plain.

—Oh Dutch! I cried. — Was it the tablets I sent?

—I did not take those tablets. My husband has been away on the Continent since the New Year.

—Perhaps when he hears the news he will come rushing back.

—You don't understand, she said, stricken.

And then I did understand.

—I have not seen Eliot, she said, white as powder, —in a year.

She stared out the window at the gray garden outside. The branches of the magnolia tree were dark claws against the white sky. Old snow dusted black with coal ash covered the grounds. She would not look at me. I came behind her chair and put my arms around her shoulders with my cheek resting on her hair, but she shrank into herself, her head down, the heels of her hands pressed to her eyes.

—I am lost, she said. —Utterly.

—No, you are found. I found you. We found each other.

—Mother thinks I am in Berlin with Eliot.

—And Eliot?

—He thinks I am here consulting Dr. Bedford for treatments of my malady.

—When does Eliot return?

—In April. April twenty first.

It was seven weeks away. —How many months gone?

—He left at New Year's I told you.

—I did not mean Eliot. I meant you.

She looked at me, blinking her scared eyes, and I asked her again about her turns. —When did you last . . . ?

—I don't know, she cried. —Three or four weeks?

—You are sure that Eliot is not—

—It's impossible, she said, and shuddered.

—You can tell me or not. His name don't matter.

She shook her head and wouldn't say.

—What do you want to do? Do you want to stay here? You can stay.

—I couldn't. She covered her mouth. —Not here. My mother—

—She's not your mother.

—For shame I can't stay here, she cried.

—I will take the child and raise it. Whatever you want. I will—

—No! I could never. Never. She shuddered.

—Then what? Is the father married?

In her silence I saw the answer was yes.

—I'm trapped, Dutch said. —I never thought . . . the doctors told me I was barren . . . that I'd never . . .

—You don't have to go through with it. I can help you.

—Shh. She put her fingers in her ears. —Don't speak of that. It's the murder of innocents.

—Phh. It isn't quite. But if you think so, why did you come here?

—You're my sister. I have no one else.

At last she lay her head on my shoulder and wept, and I felt so strangely happy. I was her sister, she said. She chose me. She was here.

I'd have given her anything, all of what I had. Ropes of pearls. A gala. A trip to Rome. For now I gave her the blue room. The drapes and bedspread in blue brocade satin, the bedstead in gold and ebony. She went under the covers scarcely to emerge for days. Tea cakes and bromides and possets would not comfort her. She was bereft and so alone. I coaxed the story out of her as I did with all of them, about how Mr. Pickering would have nothing to do with her now. That gold-bearded unicorn she pined for, who called himself a gentleman, had gone back to his wife in Newport and left my sister screwed to her predicament. Her husband Eliot was due to return from Berlin on April 21st—just six weeks now—and what would he discover when he arrived? His wife *enceinte*. Dutchie could not think past the twenty first of April. According to her she had no choice but to be soon showing and thus discovered and renounced and disgraced &c., no longer welcome as a VanDerWeil or an Ambrose.

So then what was she?

A Muldoon. Her only choices was with me. I had every possibility she needed. The medicine, or the operation, which could allow her to return to her old life, if she wanted it. Or, if she chose not to relieve herself of her obstruction, I had money, which would allow her to forsake her old life and start all over again, with or without a child. Whatever road she picked, she could stay here in the blue room with the carved medallions of bluebirds on the ceilings and the great windows looking out over Fifth Avenue, where the parade of carriages was a gorgeous circus, and the wide bluestone sidewalks were full of replacement husbands in tall hats.

—You could have yourself a new Mister in no time at all, I said. —Stay here and all society will know you as Lillian Reardon or Dutch Muldoon, or whatever other name you choose, new in town from Boston, and who will know the difference?

My sister shuddered in her misery and did not so much as glance at the bottle of Madame DeBeausacq's Lunar Pills for Female Complaint left by her bedside.

—If you are going to take them, I said, —please don't wait much longer. At a certain point it becomes too late. It will be the worse for you—

She put her fingers in her ears. She would not let me examine her. She would not tell me how far gone she was. Seven weeks, was my guess.

—You do not have long to make up your mind, I said. —Or rather, if you wait your mind will be made up for you.

—It's wrong. I do not wish to talk of it.

—Ignoring it? I have seen many who tried that method. It doesn't work. She flung her arm across her eyes.

—Tell me about your Mister Pickering, said I, soft to her.

—Gerald. He owns ships. He imports goods. What does it matter?

—Did you love him?

Tears welled and leaked from her eyes. —He said ... She paused to collect herself. —He said . . . I was the flower of the ages. He said I was like a dream. It was a dream, Ann, it was . . . you've no idea.

The dream she told me started not in a fairy bower but in the vertical railway at the Marble House Hotel. The dandy Gerald Pickering smiled at her quite boldly in that lift, my sister reported. When it stopped and the doors opened, he invited her to dinner.

—We went, Dutch said. —If only we hadn't.

As my sister told her story, her eyes were veined with red and her hair streamed black and wild around her shoulders. She was so white and delicate and sad. The terrible thing about Mr. Pickering was that he made her laugh. He paid attention. He listened to her prattle and told her such marvelous tales of adventure. He had seen the wild savages of the Congo and the snake charmers of Delhi, he had dined with the Ottoman dervishes and suffered through malaria and tempests and desert wastelands.

—He is the most remarkable storyteller, said my dupe of a sister.

—Always a dangerous trait in a man.

—No! Don't scoff at me. He was pressed into marriage by his family. As I was. He doesn't love his wife, any more than I love Eliot, or ever did. It was Mother's idea from the beginning, that I should marry Eliot.

—And Mr. Pickering? Whose idea was he?

—Mine! My sister blushed fiercely and stammered, —My own! I am not ashamed. Gerald said—he said he'd never known a lady as knowledgeable as I, and that it was so startling to him to hear such informed questions coming from . . .

—From?

—From such a pretty mouth. Dutch turned her face away, her shoulders shaking with misery.

—There now, *macushla,* I whispered to my Dutchie, so soft. —I can help you. You are not dependent on him or Mr. VanDerWeil, or the Ambroses neither. There's plenty of money here to answer your every need. Whatever you want is yours.

—Money can't buy what I want.

Listening to my sister as she cried, I was filled with a melancholy so dark it was like a blindness. I had found Dutch, but she was a stranger. When I sang to her, humming the old songs, she barely cracked a smile at all at all.

*　*　*

One morning, after she had been under my roof more than a week, she got up and went out in her heavy veils and arrived back before dark in a cab-for-hire, with her trunks and suitcases. She had been to her hotel, she said, where she had also retrieved her mail and posted letters on hotel stationery—one to her false mother Mrs. Ambrose, and the other to her husband Eliot, telling them she was indisposed, in treatment for her feminine ailment. She was weak, she told them, and doctors had advised her not to send or receive mail. Then she had checked out. They would be frantic, she said, but it was only for a few weeks, while she cleared her head. It seemed she was moving in with us. Was she? I did not dare ask for fear it would scare her away. I fed her rosewater and honey cakes and did not annoy her with questions. Little by little, hope like a weevil bored down in my heart and allowed me to think at long last that my dream of reunion lacked only our brother Joe to be real.

When Charlie was introduced to my sister he bowed low before her. —Dutch Muldoon! he said, and she flinched at the name.

—Lily, please. Mrs. Lillian Reardon, she said. —But you do look familiar, Mr. Jones. Have I made your acquaintance before? Perhaps in Boston? Chicago? Paris?

—Psst, it's me, he whispered, and winked. —Charlie off the orphan train. I remember when you were nothing but a squibben of a girl on your sister's hip. Do you recall when I showed you the cows outside the train window?

She blushed and shook her head, no, she did not remember any cows.

—It was me who taught you to moo! Charlie was a terrible tease.

—I can assure you, sir, Dutch said, —I never mooed.

—You did! I told her. —Charlie and some of the boys made a pet out of you.

—A pet? she said, with the back of her hand to her head. —Please. I am in no condition—

—Poor sister, I said, and shooed Charlie off to the stables.

That evening, when we had said good night to Dutch, he said, —Your sister is high and mighty, isn't she?

—She's miserable. And deserted by all her useless people.

—So, you'll just help her out and no one will be the wiser.

—She won't do it. She says it's wrong. Mrs. Ambrose has told her Madame DeBeausacq is an evil sorceress. Dutch said, "No matter how much I love you, Ann, as my sister, I could never bring myself to consent to such wickedness, and I pray you will come to your senses and cease your practices."

—So, you'll either bring her around or you won't.

—I told her I'd raise the child myself.

—Did you? he said, with keen interest. His eyes were lit with the idea of it.

—It won't never happen. No child of hers would be allowed to grow up here.

—Pffft, he said. —She puts on airs. Has her snout in the air. We'll bring her around, won't we?

Charlie was the only one who knew Dutch was my sister. Every one else in the household thought she was Mrs. Lillian Reardon, my patient, an acquaintance from my school days. Greta was suspicious to be sure. She told Rebecca she thought Dutch was some royalty, maybe a countess, because she got special treatment, poached eggs and finger sandwiches, served by myself on a tray with a greenhouse rose in a cutglass vase.

After another week of coddling, my sister cheered up nicely, riding out in the carriage with me, or sitting in a chair by the window where she wrote for hours in her diary. But the bottle of Madame DeBeausacq's lunar tablets on her side table had not been moved.

—If another week goes by, I told her, —and you do not swallow these, your decision is good as made for you.

—Don't remind me.

—Please Lily. Trust me. I'm professional in these matters.

She put her head under the pillow but when I tickled her in the ribs she removed it and laughed at me. —Oh Ann. Remember how we used to tickle our Joe?

I did remember. —Maybe we'll tickle him again some day.

—He's a *man*. Can you imagine?

We lay spooned together on the bed and imagined it. We loosed our hair and played with it, putting it up then putting it down. I took a piece of it under my nose for a mustache and she did the same while we examined ourselves in the mirror as men, laughing and mugging. She admired my figure and said, —Oh Ann you did turn into a fine good-looking lady!

—Not like you. With your eyes.

—No, no. Yours are . . . wise. They are Mam's eyes. Whereas mine—

—Never mind, never mind, hush, Dutchie. Oh I liked my sister so. She was an old familiar shoe to me, and while we passed the hours and shared our tea and traded stories, hope got up on its little new legs and began to toddle around in me, yes it did.

Annabelle approached my sister after school, without a clue that the beautiful pale-skinned lady before her was her own aunt. —Nice to meet you Mrs. Reardon.

—Please call me Lily, said Dutch.

—Lily was my best playmate when I was a girl your age, I told Annabelle.

—What did you play at with my Mama? asked Annabelle, and admired the bracelet of gold filigree on Dutch's wrist.

—We played at pitching pennies, Dutch said, and smiled.

—Only we used pebbles, I said, —since we didn't have no pennies.

—Axie, do you remember? Dutch asked.

—Why do you call my mother Axie? Annabelle asked.

—When we was your age, I said, —I was called Axie.

—And I was called Dutch. Immediately my sister looked sorry she had said it. —It was only a nickname.

—My mother had a sister called Dutch, said Annabelle, —that she cries over sometimes. She wishes she could find her, but Dutch is lost and Joe is lost and Mama cries when she speaks of it.

My sister flinched. —I am sorry your mama was sad.

—She is sad, Annabelle sighed. —Because her own Mam died, and her sister and brother were lost long ago. I don't know how. Annabelle turned to me. —How, Mother? How were they lost again?

—It's a long story. I'll tell you some other day, I said. —Now, what can we do for our friend Lily, to amuse her, and convince her to stay longer?

—We could have a recital, said my daughter, clapping her hands. —May I please?

—What kind of recital? Dutch asked.

—Annabelle's a musical child, I could not help bragging. —A young Jenny Lind, with the voice of a nightingale.

—What do you like to sing? Dutch asked her.

—Lieder songs and Irish songs and Mendelssohn, and whatever my teacher Miss Pearson brings me to learn.

—I like to sing all that too, said Dutch.

—So, we'll have a recital, Annabelle cried, and ran off to invite her audience of china dolls.

—You have a lovely daughter, said my sister.

—And so shall you have, some day, I feel sure.

She bit her lip, and her face was blanched with sorrow. As I left her room, I noticed that she lifted the bottle of tablets by the side of her bed and examined it. My heart stumbled then, and I did not know what to hope for. If she took the tablets, she would be free to return to her old life, with her husband none the wiser. But if she did not take them, perhaps she would remain here with me. For a moment, I considered replacing the tablets with sugar pills. Dutch would have her child then. And I might keep my sister.

Chapter Forty-One

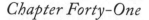

Take Your Seats Ladies
and Gentlemen

*I*n the morning Greta found me in my office brooding over Dutchie's predicament. Her knock on the door was strangely timid, for Greta was usually thundering and German, barging in.

—Axie? she said, entering in a cloud of misery.

—What's the matter? I cried, for her face was gray and drawn.

At my question, she began to cry. — It's my husband.

She shook her head and collapsed on the couch and I had to put my arms around my old friend and coax the story out of her but I was distracted and did not pay proper attention. Greta was wailing.

—My husband is *volltrunken,* a drinker and a lout und I hate him. He has broke us. He has drunk all of everything in the house und he is a cruel man mit a bad temper and he has hit me chust last night, Axie.

She showed me a welt by her ear that her hair had covered. Then out came a sorry tale about how Sprunt had drunk his own wares from the brewery and drunk his own salary plus all the great savings she had hoarded from her years of work. She related how he turned mean with a drink, how his nose got red and how he called her ugly and stupid and threatened to tell her secrets. —He says I need to get him one thousand dollars to pay off his debts. He says if I don't get more money he will . . .

—What?

—He will . . . tell Willi all of my past.

—You told Sprunt? Greta! You were never going to tell. Not anyone.

She put her face in her hands and wailed. —He made me tell. He . . . forced me. Don't ask me about it, please. She shuddered. —Now he says he will tell Willi that I was *eine Hure* and that his father was not a sailor who did not die at Cape Fear like I told him. Sprunt will say, Willi how does it feel to be the son of a hoor? And yourself a sin walking the street? So I must try to find the money somewhere. If I don't he'll tell.

—Are you asking me to give you a thousand dollars? I said, seething at how the evil troll Sprunt now had the baubles to try to extort money from me.

—Axie he has took all my savings! Greta wailed. —I'm no better off than the day you met me in the street.

I had to hold the bridge of my nose with two fingers. A headache was starting in the backs of my teeth, like ice applied to raw nerves. —Tell Mr. Sprunt to go to the devil, I said. —Tell him if he don't pay his rent and take care of his wife like a cove worth his onions then you'll move in here permanent.

—He won't pay. He hasn't the money.

My head throbbed. Pain was a long contraction in my skull. —Greta, don't you hear the doorbell ringing out front?

—Axie, but—

—We can talk about it later, I said, for I would at least be paid to discuss the troubles of the stranger knocking.

Greta got up to answer the door, her eyes still wet. —You will be sorry Madame High Attitude, she said, in a German Humph, and left. Then after a moment she came back and said, very clipped, —There's a gentleman here for your advice.

She ushered in a portly middle-aged article. He had ginger-colored side whiskers, with the chin clean-shaven. His black suit was rumpled but his white shirt was crisp with starch. A black bow tie gave him the air of a failed dandy.

—Madame DeBeausacq? he said, seeming nervous. Another poor fellow who'd got a lady in a jam. His small eyes glanced about the room with something like panic.

—Yes, come in, come in, I said, and smiled around my headache to make him comfortable. —Please have a seat, and I'll see what I can do for you.

—I am Mr. Cameron. He sat down, uncomfortable as they all were, and looked about the room, everywhere but at me.

—How can I help you?

He pulled the hairs of his mustache. He picked at his trousers and looked at the ceiling. —You see, me and the missus are in terrible debt, Madame. I have been unable to work because of a war injury. We have three children now, more than she can handle. And her health is not what it should be for . . . well, you know . . . ahem, a certain condition. I wonder do you by any chance sell articles to prevent, ahem . . . You understand, I'm sure, Madame, to prevent _____?

—Indeed.

—Another child would be . . . The poor fellow pulled at his top lip and fumbled in his pocket for a handkerchief. —So might you help me? Please?

He was just another sad sack with a mustard stain on his lapel. Anyone would feel sorry for a cove like that, what with the war injury, the sick wife, and the sweat of nerves that slicked his brow.

—I can provide you with several articles, I said. —The French have a device called a *baudruche,* for one thing. Do you know it?

He quirked his eyebrows in a question mark.

—It's for a gentleman's use.

He blushed quite profoundly. —I meant for a lady.

It always aggravated me to see how the men, most of them, did not want to be bothered for themselves. They wanted the lady to have all the bother.

—For a lady I have a preventative medicine. The instructions would be included in any packet you purchase.

—Is it reliable?

—It must not be used in . . . certain delicate female conditions, as it might have disastrous results, if you take my meaning.

—So, these articles will prevent, ahem . . .

—Conception, you mean?

He nodded, like the words pained him. —Is it sure?

—If you don't follow the instructions it's no more use than chalk. But it works most times, for prevention, with proper use.

—And if it doesn't do?

—If it doesn't, your lady can come to me for further treatment.

—And the price?

—Tablets are five dollars. Powders to unblock a suppression are ten dollars. The syringe apparatus to apply them is seven dollars. A procedure especially with overnight boarding is a considerable sight more.

—If I may purchase whatever you have, one of each.

—Certainly. Just a moment. I went to the back room and got him two bottles. One of powders, one of tablets. Also, a syringe. —She must apply a sea sponge prior, I explained, —soaked in honey. Following relations, she must remove it, then mix a paper of this powder with a cup of vinegar, fill the syringe with the solution and administer it to herself immediately. If she is obstructed, she will take these tablets as indicated.

The man winced and blushed and looked away as I spoke.

—Excuse me, sir, if I offend you, I said, mild as a librarian, —but the information must be conveyed accurately. If she uses this remedy precisely as instructed, a lady may operate with great confidence and will enjoy immunity from danger. It is, however, not fail safe. For that, you would need the *baudruche* as well. You will note that to protect privacy, the medicine is not labeled, and can be put away as tooth powders. The syringe is quite useful also to water the plants. The cost is fifteen dollars for the works.

My visitor got out his billfold blushing and cleared his throat with a great gargle of noise. He paid me and went away with his remedies. Our encounter was so ordinary as to be instantly forgotten.

Before dinner the next evening, Dutch dressed and came downstairs for Annabelle's recital. My daughter had spent the day charming my sister, and they'd passed the time practicing music. It appeared that Dutch was something of an accomplished pianist. Annabelle jumped about, arranging chairs around the piano, and handing out programs she had written in colored crayon for the audience—which was only me and Charlie, with Greta and her son Willi. Maggie was there, and her sweetheart Corrigan the policeman, and John Hatchet the coachman, who properly refused a seat despite Annabelle's begging. And Dutch, of course, the guest of honor.

—Take your chairs, ladies and gentlemen, Annabelle said.

—I am not a gentleman, said young Willi.

—No you are a stinkbug, said Annabelle. —But take your seat anyway.

He stuck out his tongue at her, and Greta scolded both of them, but when Willi sat in the chair next to his mother, she caressed his head and doted on him like he was a prize. He leaned toward her when she smoothed his hair and lifted his angelic face to gaze into her eyes. The son was as smitten with the mother as the mother was with him, and I was glad to see it, for Greta's troubles weighed on her. The lump on the side of her face had purpled and she fussed at her hair to cover it over, self-conscious and distracted. I had not given her any money and I wouldn't, not for that lout Sprunt.

Annabelle curtsied and announced, —I will play Prelude Number Fifteen, Opus Twenty eight, in D flat major, by Frédéric Chopin. When she sat down on the bench, her feet in their patent leather pumps only just reached the floor. My daughter was ten years of age, a pinkeen in skirts, except when she played. Then she became possessed of the music. Her eyes closed, and her little form moved into the keyboard as if the melody pulled and pushed her. The music was stormy, with the high notes very sharp and the low notes rumbling.

—She plays extremely well, Dutch whispered.

Annabelle finished with a flourish and took a bow. We all clapped and cheered, whistled and raised a racket that embarrassed me, because of how it disturbed my sister. She applauded quite proper, *clap clap clap,* her hands together like she was praying. She gave a sidelong glance at Charlie who drummed his feet and beat his hands on the back of the seat in front of him. Perhaps Dutch thought we should behave like our own parlor was the symphony hall, and applaud with white gloves on so as not to make too common a noise.

—Hooray, said young Willi, —it's over.

Annabelle stuck out her tongue at him again, and Dutch again looked affronted at the manners of my household.

—Willibald, now, behave yourself or Mr. Sprunt vill heff a word with you, said Greta to her son.

—Sprunt runt grunt, said Willi, and Annabelle snickered.

—We have a little surprise for you now, my daughter said, very theatrical, splaying her hands. —Me and Mrs. Lillian. We are going to sing the song *L'invitation au voyage,* by Mr. Charles Baudelaire.

Dutch and Annabelle smiled at each other like old conspirators, and the dark Irish resemblance between them warmed the cockles of my heart. It was a family scene such as I dreamt about long ago, peering through the windows of Washington Square.

—Ooh la la, I said, —French music.

—It's a poem by Baudelaire set to lieder music, Dutch said. —I learned it when I was a girl. This morning, Annabelle said she'd like to learn it too.

The two of them sat together and began to play and sing a melancholy little tune. Though the words in French was Greek to me, their voices were true and clear.

Mon enfant, ma soeur . . .

They played and sang while we listened, till my husband, who never did have no refinement, cried out, —Sing it in English, why don't you? so a fella can understand it.

Annabelle laughed at him, but not my sister. A stricken expression crossed Dutch's face. She whispered something in Annabelle's ear. It seemed Dutch did not wish to sing in English, but there was no stopping my showoff daughter when she had the stage. A born performer like her father, she was. Without waiting Annabelle began to sing the mournful song again in English. Dutch joined in, but reluctant. As I listened I knew why. They were singing a song about ourselves, me and Dutch, how we was parted.

My child, my sister, dream,
How sweet all things would seem
Were we in that kind land to live together . . .

When they were done it was very quiet until Charlie and young Willi broke the moment and resumed their boisterous cheering. I went to whisper in Dutchie's ear, the song haunting between us. —Dutchie, I didn't know you missed me at all.

—You'll never know how much.

—But you're here now, and we'll never be apart.

—If only it were that simple, my sister said.

* 　 * 　 *

At the supper table Dutch picked at the turbot en sauce blanc and took bird bites of the poppyseed roll. She smiled at Annabelle, who adored her quite plainly, and who would not leave her side.

—Is it true? my daughter asked Dutch. —Papa told me when you and Mamma were at school long ago, he taught you to moo. Is it true? Did he?

Dutch blinked. —Pardon me?

—Remember when you were a schoolgirl? Charlie said, very quick, guilty at the evidence he had talked perhaps too much to Annabelle about our guest. —I taught you to moo, and I could teach you to bark, too, couldn't I? I could teach you to speak dog.

—Oh do it, Papa! Please Papa, teach Mrs. Lillian. He's very clever at barking, Annabelle said to Dutch. —He can make real dogs answer to him. He does it in the park, whether it's a terrier or a hound, and they speak right back at him. Please Papa, teach her.

—Not at the table, I said, nervous of my sister's disapproval.

But Charlie barked, exactly like a Labrador. It was true that real dogs had been known to answer him, he was so authentic in his mimicry.

Annabelle laughed, and Dutch suppressed the smile on her rosebud mouth.

—Charles, please, I said, embarrassed. —You are scaring our guest.

—Like to try it, Lillian? Charlie said. —It's a simple skill.

—Charles!

—I'm offering lessons.

Dutch grinned, a flash of imp in her eyes. —Woof, she said, very proper.

Annabelle laughed out of control and I was filled with happiness.

—No, no, not like that at all, Charlie said, and demonstrated again. My sister answered him once—Woof!—convulsed with laughter all of a sudden, her cheeks pink, so that Annabelle got up unexcused from her chair and ran around the table to sit on her aunt's lap.

—Oh, Missus Lillian, I do wish you would stay here with us, she said, almost like I had coached her.

And my sister put her arms around the girl's neck and smiled at me over her dark head and said, —Oh Annabelle I wish I would, too.

With my hopes now high as a cathedral ceiling, we passed the rest of the supper without no more barnyard noises, thankfully. After dinner we went to the parlor, where Dutch lingered near the piano. —Dutch—Lily, I said, —I wanted you to know that I have hired a detective, to find our Joseph. I thought you'd be glad.

—Oh, Ann, yes, said she, mournfully. —But. I fear . . . disappointment. Mother explained to me long ago that it would be impossible to find him, since he was adopted so young, he won't remember us. Most likely the Trows don't wish him to know. Most families prefer the anonymity.

—Not our family, I said. A shadow crossed her face, and I saw the subject was closed off now. —I'm sorry, I said, —perhaps you would like to rest in the conservatory, or play for a while, to relieve your thoughts?

—Thank you. She smiled. —I'd like that very much.

I left her at the piano, but for a long time I stood outside the door as she played and sang. Her songs were melancholy. Despite our reunion, Dutch plainly felt herself to be all alone. She missed her friends and her so-called parents, the life of a Chicago society lady. She was heartbroken over her faithless Pickering, that bunger. Listening, I knew somehow that she would ask for my assistance after all, despite her reservations. She'd take the pills or go through with the procedure, and then go back to Chicago. I wouldn't see her again. The Palace of Jones, no matter its fine appointments, was not to her taste. We were all common bogtrotters to her, barking at the supper table. So it was not a surprise, after the household had gone to bed, when she came to find me in the library, where I sat brooding and reading.

—Tomorrow, Axie, I will come to your offices.

—All right. For what reason?

—I am feeling unwell, she said, but wouldn't say more. We sat for a moment in uncomfortable silence, before she made her excuses and went upstairs to sleep.

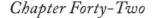

Chapter Forty-Two

A House Tour

*A*t nine a.m., there my sister was at the office door in a beautiful green dress, heavily veiled.

—Lily, please come in. Let me take your hat.

—I don't wish anyone to see me.

—There's nobody here. Greta is out with her son to take him to school.

Dutch sat on the sofa cushions, silent behind her veil. She reached her handkerchief beneath it to dab at her eyes.

—Dear Lily, I said, and sat next to her. —Please let me help you.

—I cannot go through with it.

—With which?

She lifted the veil off her face. The blue of her eyes was shot through with red lines, but she looked at me very clear and steady. —I do not love Eliot. But I cannot leave him. Mr. Pickering is . . . I cannot have him. And I . . . I cannot have . . . She swallowed and struggled to continue, but before any words came from her, somebody rang the front bell.

—Oh, mercy, said Dutch, and lowered her veil in haste.

—Shh now, no one will see you. Sit tight while I answer the door.

When I opened it there was the same gent as had been there some days before, with his rumpled coat and his gingery whiskers. Mr. Cameron.

—Why hello there, sir, I said, quite friendly. —You were here several days ago, weren't you?

—Yes. And now I have brought my friend.

—Please bring her in with you if she doesn't mind, I said, very mild, for often the ladies are frightened. —There's no need to be afraid, I called softly, to the lady outside.

My visitor stepped back, but with his handkerchief in hand, he did something with it beyond the door, flapping it briskly, as if signaling his lady it was safe to enter. Then, to my shock, in stepped not a lady, but a large hairy policeman, his mustaches waxed and his nightstick at the ready.

—Well I see you have quite a friend with you, indeed, I said.

Five more men entered. Two officers in uniform, and then still two more, in plain clothes, carrying notebooks. They stared at me frankly, scribbling all the while.

—Ho, it's quite a party, I said. —Why don't we get out the spirits?

—I am Anthony Comstock, declared my whiskery Enemy, brandishing a badge, —Special Agent of the Post Office and the Society for the Suppression of Vice.

—I've heard about you. You like to collect naughty pictures, isn't that right?

One of the traps covered a snicker.

—You won't find any smut here, I said.

—I have a warrant to search the premises, said my Enemy.

—For what purpose?

—You know yourself, he said, puffing up his chest.

—I'm not a clairvoyant. Pray enlighten me.

Then in his voice full of mucus and sanctimony, Mr. Comstock read me the warrant for search and seizure. —I will confiscate any articles designed for the prevention of conception, or any obscene material, or any instruments for the purpose of causing an abortion.

—There are no such articles in the house.

—We'll be the judge of that, madam, said one of the traps.

My sister had quietly stood up and was edging toward the door when one of the policemen politely stopped her exit. —Not so fast.

—Oh have mercy, she cried, from under her trembling veil.

The men with notebooks now appraised her, scribbling, recording what we said and did. They even scrutinized the titles of the books on my shelves, some which they removed and opened as if they might reveal the dark spells of witches.

—Who are these fellows? I demanded to know. —What are they writing?

—They are Mr. Sinclair of the *World* and Mr. Tibbetts of the *Tribune,* said Mr. Comstock of the Bungstarter News.

—The nerve! I said. —To bring the press along when you bust down a door.

My sister made a sharp gasping noise under her veil.

—Allow me to interview your caller, Comstock said, with interest.

—Please, said Dutch, tearfully. —I have nothing to say. I am only here on behalf of a friend. I am a married lady. My husband is a prominent merchant in another city. I cannot—

And here she broke down completely.

Mr. Comstock put the steak of his hand on my sister's shoulder. —There, there, dear. We are not monsters. There is the monster. He pointed at me.

—Please, do not take me to the police court, I beg you, Dutch said to him. —The mere mention of my name in conjunction with— She turned her head in my direction and cut me with her judgment. —The shame is too awful. I couldn't bear it.

—All right, now, dear, my Enemy said, pulling his whiskers. — But we must take down your name as we will require your testimony later.

—No, no, no, no, Dutch cried. —Please don't ask my name.

—Otherwise, he said, —we'll have to take you in.

There was a loaded silence while Dutch considered his lowdown threat, and then in a voice barely audible and filled with dread, my sister said, —I am Lillian VanDerWeil.

The fool. Ever obedient, she spelled out VanDerWeil for him, helpfully, thus spelling her own fate. As she did, she could see me behind Mr. Comstock's back, shaking my head. *No,* I said, silent, just moving my lips. Perhaps it was this signal that cued her to lie when the Crusader asked, —And where do you live?

—The Astor House, Dutch replied, and never mentioned anything about Chicago, or her extended stay at One East Fifty Second Street.

—Write the address here, he said, and gave her a notebook.

As she wrote, her pen was shaky. —I am so nervous, sir. So nervous, please understand.

—Go, then, said Comstock just like he was Jesus himself. —Go and sin no more.

—I beg you do not break faith with me, she said. —Please kind sir. It will kill me to be exposed.

My sister hastened out the front door, gone in a swish of velvet. She would be lost in the city, I thought. She would perish. But more immediate concerns distracted me. The police were now lifting the papers on my desk, reading them, while the reporters peered over their shoulders.

—Search this room, first, said Mr. Comstock to his henchmen.

—You can't, I cried. —I ain't done anything. You can't force your way in here like a troop of goats and do as you please.

—We have a warrant and must perform our duty, the Vice Hunter said. —It's God's work. He headed sniffing toward the back hallways that led into my very house.

—Let me go ahead of you, I pleaded. —Let me go straight to my little daughter so she will not be frightened by you.

But the terrible officials did not care about little girls. Or respectable female physicians. Or society ladies living on Fifth Avenue. Only their own brimstone and fire and righteousness. They began Comstocking around the office, opening drawers, pulling up the sofa cushions, looking under the furniture, ransacking cabinets. They was nothing but a parcel of armed curs operating under the guise of Justice.

—Don't neglect the waste bins, Mr. Comstock cried.

They smelt blood but so far they had only found little china figurines, and the spare lace doilies and antimacassars that kept the sofa back clean of hair oil. —Mind you check for hidden compartments and false bottoms, said the Grand Inquisitor.

There was nothing false about his bottom, I can attest to that. The man had appetites which was apparent in his waistline. In the heat of the chase he removed his coat, sweating like a beast, and before he tucked his shirt into his pants you could see a flash of red flannel above the top of his trousers. I suppressed a smirk. So! The Vice-hunter wore long scarlet underdrawers beneath his rumpled suit. What his other secrets were I could only guess. I must remember to tell this detail to Charlie, I said to myself. He and his philosopher friends would say the man had tastes more common to the bordello than the courthouse.

—Ahem! Sir! Come take a look at this, said one of the traps. From a sideboard he withdrew several bottles of medicines and held them aloft like trophies. Comstock in great pomposity of excitement inspected the labels. Removed a stopper. Sniffed.

It was all I could do to stifle a laugh. —What you've found is nothing. Gripe water for infants. Those are only such nostrums as you can find in any chemists. Go to my druggist Hegemann at the corner of Broadway and Walker Street and he'll tell you what they are. Woman's things, is all.

My Enemy's face was cold. His expression dismissed me. To him I was no more than a housefly buzzing about his balding pate. Him and his bloodhounds now went along out of the office into the back passage to the kitchen, where they surprised Cook and Maggie and the houseboy Robert having lunch. My own staff was then prevented from leaving the premises as the intruders went from storeroom to larder, looking for evidence. They did not find anything but sacks of flour and the apple barrel. But then at last they came to the wine cellar, where beyond the bottles of Haut Médoc, behind the port and sherry, the mongrels found boxes stacked full of pills and powders, medicines, a package of female syringes, several dozen French Letters, and many copies of Charlie's circulars. We'd done a bad job hiding them, not believing this day would come.

—Confiscate it all, men, said my wheezing Enemy. He was a bagpipe on legs.

One of the traps began to pile the swag into a sack. Mr. Comstock crossed his arms over his chest and ordered me, —You'll bring us to see the rest of the house.

—Certainly, I said. —I do so enjoy showing guests around in a tour. Wait until you see the *abattoir*.

My tormentor raised the pale slugs of his eyebrows in question marks.

—It is a French word for slaughterhouse, I said, —so my husband tells me.

Comstock flinched like he expected to find carcasses around the next bend.

—Oh dear, I said, —it's only a joke.

—This is no laughing matter.

—Well, I don't know what else to do besides laugh when a so-called GENTLEMAN pretending to be Mr. Cameron deceives me and barges into my house like a kangaroo, seizing personal articles.

—After you, he said, holding the door of my own dining room.

—Mother! said the little voice of my Annabelle, running fresh from her luncheon, arms wide. —Mama, she cried, and stopped short in puzzlement when she saw the policemen's mitts on me. The traps loosed their hold and shifted uneasy to be holding a mother hostage in front of her own innocent child. It must be said in their defense they smiled in spite of themselves at the darling manners of my Annabelle.

—Who are all these policeman friends of yours, Mama?

—Why, sweetheart, they are here to see our beautiful home.

—Should I show them my room? They will like to see my dollhouse.

—I think they will like the busts of Washington and Franklin best. I think just like Papa and me, they will like the American flag.

—Oh silly Mother, she laughed. —No, they won't.

Annabelle took my hand and we continued upstairs, much to the consternation of the Comstockian hanging party, who looked between her and me with bewilderment, surprised that the Witch of their imagination was a mother with such a charming child, who held my hand with affection and skipped and sang little snatches of a song in French, about sisters. *Mon enfant, ma soeur.* She had been teaching it to me.

—Brace yourselves, gentlemen, said Mr. C. from under his muttonchops. —This inspection could prove to be most unpleasant.

—What about the child? one of the traps inquired quietly.

—Unfortunately, said Comstock, —the poor innocent must be accustomed to all kinds of unseemly horrors and indecent sights and sounds, even in her own home.

The traps shuddered manfully. The two hacks scribbled in their notebooks.

Tibbetts from the *Tribune* fingered the panels of woodwork in the billiard room. —Excuse me, ma'am, is that black walnut?

—Indeed it is, I said. —From the forests of Borneo, or somewheres like that.

—What is that exotic fragrance?

—The smell of success, said I, —earned by a midwife's dedication to the nursing of society's finest young ladies, who come to me when they are nearing their delicate hour. Your own sisters and wives would be lucky to be in my care, to deliver your own children in luxury at my lying-in facilities. Surely, you must agree, there ain't nothing illegal in helping a woman in the hour of her greatest glory. Or, perhaps you're referring to the fragrance of the frangipani flowers specially imported by me from Mexico and fresh cut from my greenhouse.

To dispel my nerves I showed off the fine points of the décor, while Mr. Comstock went truffling in the closets, rummaging through dresser drawers. He seemed most disappointed not to find the buckets of blood and baby skulls he expected. Instead, he came upon only shawls and dresses, hats and hairbrushes and underthings. He stood in my bedroom pulling the whiskers at his chops, gazing grimly at the walls and carpets like a revelation would show up in the patterns of wallpaper and carpet fiber.

—Mama, what is he looking for? asked Annabelle.

—Oh, he thinks he might have lost something.

—What has he lost?

—His sense of decency, I whispered. —Perhaps his mind.

—His mind, Mama?

—Now run along to your music lesson, ya wee larrikin.

I kissed her sweet face, and she embraced me with elaborate passion, as if I was going off on a long journey. Perhaps I was. —I'll see you this evening at supper, I said.

—You will not see her at supper, said Comstock, when she was gone. —You are under arrest, Madame.

—For what, pray tell?

—For possession of illegal articles. We will leave at once for Jefferson Market Courthouse.

—Well, I don't like your underhanded tactics, coming here under false pretenses. You should be ashamed of yourselves.

—You'll come with us, said the trap.

—I'll go in my own carriage, thank you. At least I am entitled to that courtesy. And you'll allow me to take some oysters. I haven't had no lunch.

They allowed me to go to the kitchen, where I sent Robert out to find Charlie, who was downtown at Liberty Street where we still maintained offices. What would happen? I did my best to eat a bowl of stew, as I knew from sad experience it might be a long while before another meal would come my way. The beardless Officer guarded me. —Take your time, Madame, he said, so polite, the skin of his cheeks pink and smooth. —What's in the stew?

—The hearts of my enemies. Their tasty livers.

The poor lad looked terrified, till I put my hand on his arm, gave him a wink.

—A good-looking young man like you ought to know, this is all c**p, this dirty snooping business of Mr. Comstock's, I said. —Surely you can take one look at me and realize I'd never hurt a lady or any innocent, a gentlewoman and a mother such as I am.

He blushed to the roots of his baby teeth.

—How about you let me give you a good bottle of whiskey, I said, —and you'll let me just slip upstairs and out the front door.

—I would ma'am, he said, scarlet, —but Mr. Comstock, he's . . . phew. The officer wiped his brow and shook his head. —The man's a terrier.

—He's a regular bungstarter he is.

The whelp laughed but he would not let me go even for the whopping sum of money I offered. Comstock had the nerve to station him outside my dressing room while I changed to traveling clothes. Mr. Comstock would have to confiscate HIM for harboring sinful thoughts which was plain on the young trap's face when I emerged dressed up in black silk and velvet. I was thirty three years old, but looked not a day over twenty five. —Would you help me on with this then? I asked the poor stammering red fellow. He assisted me with my sealskin cape, and I smiled full at him before I lowered my veil.

Outside, there was my beautiful carriage waiting, the horses sleek in the noonday light, the silver of their harnesses glinting. Behind was a police wagon lurking to follow it. John, my dear driver, handed me up to the seat and helped adjust the lap robes against the cold but gave not a crumb of assistance to the slab of bacon who trailed me out of the house and trundled down the steps and now stood pulling his whiskers and tapping his foot on the sidewalk. With great effort, he climbed up beside me, wheezing.

—The Tombs, John, I said, with grandeur, —and hurry. Mr. Comstock is eager to show off his trophy.

BOOK SEVEN

The Hydra-Headed Monster

Chapter Forty-Three

A Weeder in God's Garden

*A*nd so we rode downtown together, me and My Enemy. He sat with both feet flat on the floor, his hands atop his knees, and looked straight ahead, barely disguising the smile on his lips. He was a tomcat, licking his chops, and yet strangely uneasy.

—You must be cold, I said, pleasantly, and attempted to spread the lap robe over his knees. —This is ermine from Russia, you know.

He blustered and refused it. —Never mind about that.

Oh brave and manly Comstock, refusing the ermine of a she-devil.

—Pray tell me, I asked, —do you enjoy your work? (It is always charming to ask a man questions about himself, says Advice to a Wife, by Mr. Chevasse.)

—Someone must rid society of its ills.

I laughed. He wheezed next to me and we rode along without speaking for a while.

—Did you have a mother? I asked.

—She died when I was ten. A sainted woman.

—I was twelve when I lost mine. She died in childbirth.

—As did mine, having her tenth child. God rest her immortal soul.

—We have much in common, then. Did yours ever sing to you?

—Yes, he said, very clipped.

—What songs did she sing? I persisted despite his evident annoyance.

—We sang Oh What a Blessing Is the Lord and other hymns. Many hymns.

—Ah. Well, mine sang Who Put the Overalls in Mrs. Murphy's Chowder. She sang Toora Loora Loo and Kathleen Mavourneen and too many others. She had a fine voice, my Mam.

—Your point, Madame?

—No point, sir. Just an attempt at polite conversation. I sighed. —But you can be assured that, had a skilled midwife such as myself been present at labor, our mothers would be alive today.

He flared his nostrils. —I will battle the hydra-headed monster of obscenity and sin wherever I shall find it.

It is you who are the hydra-headed monster I wished to say. But instead I asked, —Would thirty thousand dollars make a difference to you?

He smirked and stroked down the flanges of his mustache with his thumb and forefinger. —I have vowed, Madame, that every day I will do a good work for Jesus. Arresting you is my good work for today.

—Think of what good work you could do with thirty thousand dollars.

He did not laugh. He was a smug pudding of righteousness, and for my benefit, long-winded as a bellows, he recited me from memory what he called the COMSTOCK LAW. —Statute number 598 of the US Gov't amendment to the Post Office Act is as follows, he said, and reached into his pocket handing me a paper he found there, upon which were printed the very words he said to me that day:

No obscene, lewd, or lascivious book, pamphlet, picture, paper, or other publication of indecent character, or any article or thing designed or intended for the prevention of conception or procuring of abortion, nor any written or printed matter giving such information shall be carried in the mail. Any person who shall knowingly deposit, for mailing or delivery, any of the herein before-mentioned articles shall, for every offense, be fined not less than one hundred dollars, nor more than five thousand dollars, or imprisoned at hard labor not less than one year, nor more than ten years, or both.

He recited the His Law aloud, with his Connecticut vowels all plum in his mouth, his pride wide as his midriff. You could see the boy in him and how this moment arresting me was revenge for some injustice he felt himself to have suffered. With barely a pause he carried on by heart, the hot wind of his breath steaming the February air:

> Section 5389. Every person who has in his possession any drug or medicine, or any article whatever, for the prevention of conception, or for causing unlawful . . . a******* . . . or who advertises the same for sale, or writes or prints, any materials of any kind, stating when, where, how, or of whom, or by what means, any of the articles in this section herein before-mentioned can be procured, shall be imprisoned at hard labor in the penitentiary for not less than six months, nor more than five years for each offense, or fined not less than one hundred dollars, nor more than two thousand dollars, with costs of court.

—How about I give you fifty thousand and save all the trouble? I said, when he was done at last, but the beast only snorted.

At the courthouse men with notebooks pressed against the door of the carriage.

—What? Have you gone and alerted every newspaper in the country? for the purpose of furthering your own fame? I asked My Enemy, but he ignored me, adjusted the sleeves of his coat, and lumbered out ahead of me. John did not help him down, but gave me his hand, bowing. Immediately I was set upon by the jackals of the press and even John could not help as they jostled me and shouted questions.

—Do you repent your sins now, Madame?

—Where do you hide the bodies?

The pack pushed and shoved to get next to me, while Comstock preened his whiskers, oblivious of my terror.

—What's the charge against her? a reporter shouted.

—Possession of instruments for the purpose of malpractice, and possession of obscene materials, said my Accuser, who posed very grandiose and spoke indirect of himself as if he weren't a worm, but a hero. —They said Anthony Comstock only pursued the small fry. They said Anthony Comstock did not have the mettle to go after this harridan. Well, today, gentlemen, you can see the truth: Madame is not small fry, but the wickedest woman in New York, and today Anthony Comstock has brought her to justice.

They slavered and ogled me. They wrote in their notebooks and buzzed around so that it was all a lady could do to walk a straight line. The papers next day said Madame DeBeausacq walked into the courthouse Calm and Mild as a Morning in June. But in truth I was a dark February tangle of fear as they hustled me along. Inside the halls of so-called justice, Judge James Kilbreth waited for me in his black habit, a hairy spider. At the witness table I sat under my veil, awaiting proceedings, awaiting my lawyer, awaiting my husband.

I didn't see Morrill nor anyone who might stand for my lawyer. At last to my great relief, Charlie arrived with a grim look on his face, which further chilled my blood. He came to sit behind me. We spoke in whispers, our heads bent together so the lace of my veil fell forward and hid both our faces from the terrible gaze of the gallery, which overflowed with zealots.

—My darling, he said through his teeth.

—H***, I said, —where is Morrill?

—He's on his way.

—And my sister? She has fled. I am afraid for her—

—She's under the covers in the blue room. Having hysterics.

This news was a relief to me. She had not run off. I might still keep her.

—Of course she's having hysterics, I said. —They barged in and ransacked the place without so much as a by your leave, questioned her, wrote down her name. And the poor girl so delicate. And what they done in front of our Annabelle! It's an outrage, Charlie.

—I'd like to gut them with a fish knife, he said darkly, but his attempt to play the tough cove did not hide the fear darting in his eyes, like eels. —If you're lucky it'll come to nothing. You'll fight them very fierce. We'll bail you out of here faster than blinking. You'll be home for dinner.

But Judge Kilbreth had other ideas.

—Have you no attorney? he asked, peering over his spectacles.

I rose with my backbone straight, so ladylike-seeming you would think I was teaching Sunday school. Hearing how I talked to him, all sugar and cream and teardrops, you would never know the quagmire of rage that animated my spirit.

—Your Honor, kind sir, said I, —I ask to be released on my own good word. Haven't I come here, willingly, in my own carriage? You must understand that I have several ladies from distinguished families under my care, who are approaching confinement and require my attention urgently. Not to mention that I am the mother of a young child, who depends on me. (And here my voice trembled out of control.) —Think only of how upset and fearful she will be if kept apart from me, her only mother. Especially under such frightful circumstances as these.

Kilbreth peered at me coldly. He was a young unicorn, ugly enough to lift the turf off a bog hole as my Mam used to say. Without a blink, he pronounced bail. —In the amount of ten thousand dollars, he said. The look on his face said it was a sport to him, to pick this number from the air and wave it about like a pistol. Ten thousand dollars.

—Here, I said. From my purse I removed a packet, and held it up to show. —I have government bonds in that amount. These will act as surety.

—Security is required in the form of real estate only, Kilbreth said.

—Your Honor, said Charlie, —Our home at One East Fifty Second Street is valued at over two hundred thousand dollars—

A gasp came from the courthouse throng, flabbergasted at such wealth. You could hear the pencils of the press gnomes scratching at their notepads to get the figure down correct.

—No properties in your name will suffice, said Judge Kilbreth. —You must have local property owners to stand bail for you.

So they would again play these games, just to keep me in their cage.

—I can produce surety by six o'clock this evening, my husband said. —Please allow her to leave in the meantime.

—Bring her to the sergeant's room, said the judge. The bailiff escorted me to a crowded smoky nook in the back of the courthouse with several cells smelling of excrement and worse: despair. I waited while Charlie went off scrambling for money, sending telegrams to every man he knew who owned property. But at six o'clock he returned exhausted with Morrill.

—No luck, he said. —People are reluctant, they're afraid—

—THEY're afraid?! It's MY neck on the chopping block.

—The good news according to Morrill is that Kilbreth's more sympathetic than you might think. We'll have to see.

But it was too late to get me out before nightfall. The court adjourned for the evening and the judge went home to his sausage. The bailiff handed me over to a matron with stains on her apron. I would spend the night in jail. As she dragged me off Charlie touched my hand. The matron allowed him to embrace me and again I saw how he swallowed and shifted his gaze. He would not look at me. Nor I at him. I didn't want to see the cornered fury in his eyes or all I stood to lose now. The matron led me away to the paddy wagon, and as we went I sang Whiskey in the Jar to steel my nerves.

Whack for the daddy-oh, there's whiskey in the jar.

Singing, I was rolled over the paving stones to the Tombs and the paddy wagon's wheels was a doom rattle for me same as it always was for all the brave Fenians before me who came to these shores only wanting some turf to call their own.

In the lockup no joy was to be had in reunions with Mrs. Maltby the head matron who welcomed me back with her death's head grin. I was shown to my cage. No sooner had I retired to my hard cot when a terrible crawling was felt in the mattress. So with my purse for a pillow I lay down on the floor and slept not one cold minute. All told I rotted there in the Tombs five days between appearances at the courthouse, while the lawyers muttered about *res ipsa loquitur* and *habeas corpus*. It was Chinese to me. But what I understood too well was that this time they was out to put me away and ruin me for good. Comstock was known for it. He'd have my life and all my savings if he could. At last Charlie and Morrill paid a ratty pair of bondsmen to put up their property as surety. Both of them would only give their name as Anonymous. They wanted no part of my notoriety. Nameless, they was saints to me, and true to Morrill's prediction, Kilbreth at least allowed bail for me. Perhaps at last I had a judge on my side. I was released.

—Madame! called the newsmen as I left the courthouse, —Your comment on today's proceedings?

—Just a lot of little lawyers, I said. —They buzzed about me like flies.

Upon my return home I went immediately to my sister. She sat so pale in the wing chair, blue veins in the white of her temples.

—Dutchie, I cried, kneeling at her knees. —I'm so relieved to find you here. I worried you'd run off.

—Where would I run? I am trapped here.

—I'm sorry, Dutchie, I didn't know there'd be a raid on me. They'd no right to bust in like that.

—How could you expose me to such shame? she whispered.

—I'm the one who is exposed, not you.

—I gave my name. The police have my name. Oh why did I do that? Why? If only I hadn't! She fretted and bit her lips.

—You're safe here.

—Safe? she cried, so miserable. —Oh no. Not here. Not anywhere. This house is known. It's watched. The paper this morning called it a maelstrom of hell.

—Is that how you have found it to be, in your time here? A maelstrom of hell?

She pressed the heels of her hands to her eyes and shook her head. —No, she said, in her small voice. —No.

—Then stay here with me. This is your family.

—Don't you know? Didn't you hear? The papers said the government would call as witness a certain lady who was in the offices at the time of the arrest. It's only a matter of time before they publish my name! And if I testify . . . ? they will drag it into the mud.

—They don't know where you are.

—They'll find me! Word will get back to my husband. To my mother.

—That pretty crook you call mother need never know, if you let me help you.

My sister sighed so miserable and brushed the flat of her palm against her slender waist, resting it just below, as if to cover the state she was in.

—Lily, I said, gently, —tell me what you had decided, when you came to see me? You said you could not go through with it. With which? What did you mean by that? Have you taken those pills?

She began to gnaw at her fingernails. —Don't ask me that. Don't ask.

—There is still time.

By her lack of reply I hoped that my sister had decided to undergo her confinement and stay with me. I counted on my fingers and wondered if by October I would be an auntie. It was a secret guilty wish for me, as much as it pained her.

—This is my punishment, she said. —My trial. I see that now. And I must bear it.

Our separate trials hurtled toward us, mine the First of April, and her husband Eliot due to land the twenty first. Her predicament weighed on me as much as my own. If she testified, it would be against me. She knew my work, for I had explained it. And if I went to jail who would deliver her when her time came? How would she manage? Her husband Eliot would soon be on a ship, heading toward the Port of New York. He'd arrive in three weeks time. The month of March wore away in an agony of questions, of waiting. All signs were ominous. On Wednesday the eleventh, a magpie sang on the doorstep.

—Mam said a magpie was a sign death would come to a house, I told Charlie.

—We've had magpies before, he said, with false cheer, —and everyone lived.

His manner was unconvincing. He attempted to jolly me along in the usual fashion, finding coins behind my ears and roses under the pillow, but it was false cheer and it failed to lift me from my gloom. By the distracted pity in his eyes, and the set of his bulldog's jaw, I saw the truth: he believed I was doomed. He had already said goodbye. Had he?

Then on Friday the thirteenth, Charlie put his shoes on the bed. —How many times have I told you it's unlucky? I cried. He scoffed at me, and so I stood up from my chair too rapidly and it fell over backwards, which is unlucky too, and I told him so, and then we were shouting at each other.

—It's cr*p, he said. —Chairs and magpies and thirteens—it's hooey.

—Worse than putting out a light when people are at supper, I said, miserable.

—There's no science in your backward Irish thinking and less logic.

—Neither logic nor science ever convinced Comstock. He's the Holy Roller, I said, —it's all God with him. And his God would send me to prison.

—If God exists he would not have you in jail. We'll not allow it.

—How would you have me avoid it? kill myself?

—No need, he said. —The charge won't stick. You'll walk away.

—Why don't I just walk away now? Before any of it starts. I'll get on a boat. I'll go to California.

This idea got his attention. —California?

—Let's leave. We'll take Belle and go. Chicago. Boston. No one will find us, no one will know. We'll go in the dark, we'll take what we can carry. I'd rather kill myself than go across the river to the Pen.

He looked at me and half a smile spread over his face. —You'd never do it, would you? Run just like that? He snapped his fingers. —You wouldn't dare.

—I'd leave a note.

—What would it say?

—That I'd went to jump off the bridge.

—Ah, and instead of jumping off the bridge you'd go to Paris.

—And after a suitable time you would come and bring Belle to me.

A smile played around his lips, crinkled the corners of his eyes. —How long is suitable? Six months?

—Six months might do the trick.

Now the cockeyed plan sat there like a plump baby thinking about taking a few steps, and the both of us, me and Charlie, smiled at it.

—Who'd believe it? I said. —They'd catch us. We'd live like rats on the run.

—Paris. Think about it. Or London, if you prefer.

—You wouldn't come. You'd never show. You'd send me off and be shed of me. While I fled across the ocean you'd act the part of the Aggrieved Man. I could just hear you now, Charlie, wailing, Oh the Tragedy of my wife's death. Oh Poor Widower Jones. You'll walk the riverbank for show, pretending to search for my corpse. Suicide is a Mortal Sin, you'll say, and Mrs. Jones was Guilty of it and so much else. So sad, so very sad. Meanwhile, you've got the bank accounts, the house and the stables with your beloved horses. And you'll find some pretty cooze to raise our daughter, the poor motherless thing. Oh yes, you can bet all the ladies of Fifth Avenue would be after you and your fortune, thinking me dead. And where would I be? Conveniently supposed to be in a grave! Secretly abroad, no way to come home without facing manacles.

He was regarding me now without mercy. He liked this scenario too much for my comfort. —You'd have to trust me, wouldn't you? It's a good idea. Just up and leave. Fake your death. Oh ho, he cried, —you'd have to trust me now at last.

The tick of his pocket watch was loud as my heart as he sat there so handsome in his shirtsleeves. But I wouldn't buy it, what he was selling. Never trust a man who says trust me. He was trying to shed his wife, that was it. Was it? I didn't know.

—I'll take my chances with Mr. Comstock, I said, miserable.

—Suit yourself. If I was you, I'd pack a bag and have it ready.

—If you was me I'd be stupid as you think I am.

—It was your own idea, darling. I'm just saying I'll back you. If you're game.

He didn't say Chickenheart but that was always it for him. Was I game? Was I chicken? Would I dare?

Friday afternoon, Annabelle invited her little school friends over to our house to play. They would have a concert, she announced, so busy and excited. The poor nightingale had no inkling of her mother's impending doom just weeks away. She set out the chairs in rows and placed her dolls in the empty ones and invited me and Charlie and Dutch as audience. But the afternoon wore away and her little friends did not come. Not Sylvia or

Daisy or Marguerite. Their mothers had kept them home. Annabelle sat by the window looking at the carriages passing on the avenue. Not one of them stopped.

—I don't care, she said at last. —I hate them. She sat at the piano and began to play anyway. The sound of her fingers on the keyboard in the parlor were a torture, for when they took me to jail I would never hear their sweet sound, nor gaze at her little head bent over the white notes. I left my seat as dark emotions overtook me and fled down the back stairs toward the office.

—Mother! my girl called after me. —I'm playing, Mam. I'm not finished. I'm playing. You can't leave. You may not leave!

But she was forced to carry on without her mother, the fate I always feared. I went weeping down the corridor, hoping to find a telegram from Morrill on my desk. Maybe he had got the charges dropped. Maybe it was all put right. Perhaps by some divine intervention Judge Kilbreth had agreed to our demands, had thrown the case out on grounds it was a farce. I hoped for miracles. Perhaps Comstock had exploded from eating too much plum duff. Perhaps his red drawers had burst into flame.

But no luck. No telegram. No word. I would be in court in a week.

Chapter Forty-Four

Cordelia

*T*hat last week before the trial, it did not rain but it must pour, for here on the Thursday was somebody at the office door very early, knocking and beseeching Greta please to let her in. —Oh please Christ Dear God open the door, the woman cried.

It was none other than that young bucket of trouble, Cordelia Shackford or Mrs. Purdy, who was supposed to be living in Philadelphia as Cordelia Munson. Four years past my first trial, here she was again just days before my second, her laces tight and her clothes in an uproar. Greta came in to me while I read some legal papers from Morrill.

—I could not dissuade her, says Greta, whispering. —She said she had to see you. Only you. No matter what. And also I need to see you MYSELF please in private—

Poor Greta looked distraught but before she could finish, in came my undoing.

Cordelia. A madwoman now, the face gaunt and splotched red in the cheeks. Her pretty eyes were sunk in, the blue all spoked with red lines, and she cried and paced and chewed her lips from the moment she walked in. I wished she would walk out again, but despite the trouble she had caused me I pitied her.

—Mrs. Purdy, I says.

—You forget I am not Missus anybody. He never married me. No one ever did.

—What gives you the nerve to walk in here after you had me arrested and shamed and dragged to prison?

—They FORCED me, she cried. —I didn't mean to accuse you. It was that Dr. Gunning that forced me. The police laid me down and he examined me against my will. He said he knew what I'd been up to. They forced me to give your name up and go to court against you. And I felt so bad about it, Madame, what with yourself like a mother to me and your husband so kind. I only wish I could say the same of Fortune, for here I am again in trouble.

She stopped, and her eyes dropped downwards quick and back up so she was perfectly understood. She didn't need to say the word. Indeed she couldn't, for she was choking and snuffling.

—Please, she said, —I've nobody else at all and never forgot what you said to me, that should I be in need I could turn to you.

—That was before you testified against me before the gallery in Jefferson Market Court. That was before you had me sent away from my child, to the Tombs.

These words provoked fresh sobs from my visitor, which issued from her in a great herking mess. —I'm sorry, I'm sorry, she cried. —There was no chance to explain.

I tried to harden my heart, but something dark and terrible was bottled up behind her orphan eyes. —I don't have time for you now. It's a risk for you even coming here. Surely you know I have troubles of my own.

—Yes, I read the papers, but I had to see you before they lock you away. Please ma'am, if only you can help this time, before you're taken off—

—The nerve of you. You've come for a quick fix? Is that it?

—A man chased me on the street, Cordelia managed to say, but stopped in a red boil of misery. —He—

—Did he interfere with you?

She nodded, the whites of her eyes stark.

—He's a madman, she said, heaving sobs. —He came after me two times, the first time six weeks ago. Then again, Saturday, he . . . threw me to the ground and _____.

Her hysterics and the horror of her story was such that I relented. I went around to where she sat, stroked her hair, so black like my own and unkempt. The girl did not know a hairbrush from a saucepan handle. She

leaned her head against my hip as I stood there and clamped her arms
around my legs and held on. The flesh of her wrists was yellow with old
bruises. I unglued her arms from around me and sat beside her the better
to examine them. Turning her palms over and rolling up her sleeves I drew
in my breath: There was terrible cuts scabbed over. Long cuts on the soft
underside of the forearm, red in the white along the blue piping of vein.
She turned her head away as I looked.

—Sweetheart, I said, —have you tried to hurt yourself?

She shuddered and did not answer. The sight of her, the whimpering
and madness and misery, provoked a terrible rage in me. I didn't want to
help her. Why should it always be me? Wasn't there no one else? I wanted
her to go away and not return. It wasn't fair that she should be here, now,
on top of all my troubles. She'd only make things the worse for me as she'd
done before and why must I take a risk for her?

—I can't fix you up, I said, my heart a snail in its hard shell. —I got
problems of my own. I got a family. A little girl. They're going to send me
to prison.

—Please. I'm sorry Missus. But it wasn't my fault. I didn't do anything
wrong.

—I know the feeling. I didn't do anything wrong neither.

—I was going about my business, walking to the market. I had my room
in the boardinghouse and a nice lithographer fellow courting me named
Hatcher, Jimmy Hatcher. But this other man Hines was after me and I told
him to leave me alone but he watched me and hid himself in the alley and
I was coming along with a basket in my arms and—twice! It was not just
the once and—

—Ah sweetheart.

—He'll come after me again. I traveled two days to get here. To get away
from him. Besides, who will have me now in Philadelphia? I'm scared. I'm
very frightened, Madame. My fellow Jimmy doesn't believe my story. Says
I brought it all on myself. Says it was my fault, and why was I walking out
alone with a basket of washing? He says probably Hines is my lover, can
you figure? when Hines is only a deranged man. How I hate him. He is no
more my lover than a frog, yet how can I prove it? Hatcher won't marry me
now, he says I'm spoiled for him. And I can't go back there. I won't.

I knew that feeling too.

—I'd kill myself before I would, she said. —I'd jump from a window.

—No, now, you won't hurt yourself again. Don't even think it.

—You said to come here, she cried. —You told me to. If I ever needed a place. You promised.

And it was that promise I regretted now. Shouldn't it be moot? Yet even with the vultures of the law circling again she was back to haunt me. Why was it some people had one trouble after another? It was as if for Cordelia the one trouble of her mother dying gave birth to another trouble and so on into forever. If only she would stop her sobs. The noise was freakish, broken like something from an asylum. You would do anything to make it stop.

—I wish I was dead, she said.

—All right, I said, very angry. —Never mind. I'll fix you up tonight, fast.

—Thank you, she said, and fell on me again with elaborate gratitude.

—But you can't stay, is that clear? They can't find you here. My trial starts Monday upcoming. Four days from now. You must leave right away.

She nodded. —I'm sorry, Madame. I'm sorry. Forgive me.

I scuttled her up the back stairs and settled her down in one of the rooms. She was our only patient.

—Greta, I said, back in the office. —I'll need your help.

—No, Axie, she said, her voice despondent, —I vill need YOUR help.

In the press of events I had neglected the troubles of my friend, and now I saw the damage they had done her. Greta sat at the front desk staring sadly out the window at the glimpse of sidewalk, her black hair tight in its pins. Her gaze was vacant. Her demeanor shaky with drink. She bent her head and pressed the heels of her hands into her eyes, crying. I made noises of sympathy and stroked her dark head. —What happened to you?

—Mr. Sprunt has told Willi. He told my son I was a _____.

—He didn't! Oh Greta.

—I didn't give him the money, so he said, 'Willi your mother is a hoor and you're the b*****d son of a hoor.' He said to Willi, 'Your father was never no sea captain.'

—The scut, he didn't.

—He did. Und Willi came to me asking . . . why did I lie to him? My son only twelve years of age said he will be ashamed all his life to heff me as his mother.

—Nonsense, he won't believe a word Sprunt says.

—But he does! Already he won't look at me. He stays by der window and only spins his tops and plays mit his marbles and chalk.

Greta cried and cried, her eyes swollen. No matter how I tried to embrace her she was unbending. —I told you, she wailed, —I told you if I didn't heff the money what he would do! We heff notting! Sprunt has drunken every nickel.

—I'm sorry. I should've given it to you. I've been distracted.

—Oh the trial, the trial, is all you talk about, it is only you and your trials, YOUR trouble and *Kümmerniss,* your patient Mrs. Lillian, chust because she is the railroad princess, you spend all your days mit her, you bring her the custard and the caviar, and the rest of us, you don't care you don't listen you don't ask what about Greta? What about Greta who works for you all these days?

—You're my friend. Haven't I paid you? Haven't you had enough to buy a little house and raise your son alone and find yourself a husband?

—Husband! A *Schwein.* A dog. He has ruint me. He told my son the thing he promised he never would tell and my son now will not speak to me! I am ruint forever.

—Nonsense. Leave Sprunt. You will tell Willi that every word from that bullfrog's mouth is a poison lie. You will bring your boy here and move in with us.

As I said this the idea comforted me. Greta would live here with us, as she did in the old days. If they threw me in jail then Greta would be here, at least, with Annabelle and Willi. She could oversee the household. She knew the works of it.

But she looked at me now with dismay in her face like milk clouding a cup of tea. —If they will lock you up, Axie, Willi will never speak to me again. Already he snubs me.

—It will be all right. Willi is your son. Sprunt can't take him.

—I am so shamed. He won't forgive me.

—He will forgive you. I bent my knees and got down low so I could look her in the eyes. —I need your help tonight. There's a patient.

—You said no more patients.

—Just this one.

—Always the patients, the house, the trial. I am tired. I'm dead. Maybe I might as well be.

—I am tired, too. But this girl has been r***d.

At the sound of that word, Greta put her face in her hands and cried harder.

—You'll help me tonight?

—All right, she said, after a long sour moment, but she was not happy about it.

And neither was Charlie, who said, —Why you'd help that sorry sad piece of string Cordelia I don't know. Have you lost your mind?

He went off in disgust with his crony Will Sacks and I did not expect to see him till daylight. After Belle had gone to sleep, after I'd told her a story and sung her *shoul aroun,* tucked her in and blew out the lamp on her nightstand, I went heavyhearted upstairs to Cordelia Purdy or Shackford or whatever it was she called herself now. Her hair was brushed and she had had a bath in my very own tub. It was an indulgence I offered only her among my patients, and it made me happy to see the pleasure the motherless Cordelia took in the luxury of that room, the mirrors and the marble. She wore one of my dressing gowns and smelled of lilac water, but her eyes was dead and spooked. I am proud to say I did soften to her then and remembered her motherlessness and her ordeal at the hands of a R*p*st. I gave her a bottle of whiskey and said, —Come along now love. We made our way down the back stairs to the office. There was Greta with a peevish face.

—Now Greta, I said, —you remember Cordelia.

Greta nodded and gave a watery smile to our patient. She could not manage more than that, however, and was cold and distant as she moved about, laying out the syringe and the curette, the bowl and a roll of bandages.

Cordelia cried quietly while I began.

—Don't cry now, Greta said, sharply, —Madame is going to fix you up.

I did my best. It was rough again. The poor girl's parts was damaged and scarred worse even than before and there was marks of yellow bruises on the soft inside of the limbs and what seemed to be the burns of matches. Greta and me looked at each other and was wordless about the horrors we imagined. I sweated, sick with how I hurt her. Cordelia cried and thrashed.

—Hold still, I said through my gritted teeth.

Greta crouched down right by Cordelia's head, whispering, —Don't move, please, *Liebchen,* you're doing good.

But Greta was a distracted assistant. Twice I called her out of a trance to hand me the gauze or the dilators. The scraping took a long time. It hurt Cordelia very bad. —I'm sorry, I said. —Sorry, love. Sweat poured off me. My patient bit down on a cloth and thrashed with her eyes shut.

At last I asked Greta for the ergot solution of vinegar but she had not prepared any. I waited while she mixed it, and she handed it to me absently and said, —If I may go now, Axie, I am tired.

—You know it's not through, I said, quite angry. —You'll stay till it's finished.

Her eyes filled with tears. Greta did not like that I spoke to her sharply but for once I did not care. SHE was not the one going to court on April First. I administered the solution while Greta held Cordelia's hand, streams of water running down both their faces, and me a welter of nerves and pity and fury at all of them, the mess of it all, that it came to this.

—There now, I said, —all finished.

The patient whimpered then sat up and vomited. —The pail, Greta, I said, but my friend took her time getting it and cleaned the mess up in a huff. I lay the patient down again. —There's a good girl, I told her, with as much tenderness as I could muster. Which was not much. It was nine in the evening on one of my last nights of freedom and I was not in my bed beside my husband with a glass of brandy.

—Don't leave me, Cordelia said, very weak.

—Nobody will leave you, I said.

—I am alone. Mortally alone.

—I'll stay with her tonight, Greta said, grudgingly.

—I thought you wanted to leave, I said.

—Truth is I don't want to go home. Willi will not speak to me. And Mr. Sprunt *ist ein Knilch und ich hasse ihn so viel.*

—Oh Greta, I said, —I don't know what you said but the two of us is in a fine f*****g mess.

—What will happen to us? my friend said, and rested against me. —What will happen to any of us?

—We'll carry on best as we can.

—YOU will, maybe. Your husband is a good man.

This stopped me. Greta always said Charlie was a dangler. She was the one who said he had *Ein kleines Schmuckstück,* a piece of trade on the side. Now she said I was lucky. He was a good man.

—Always he is devoted, said she. —You have the luck while I have a lout.

I mused on this idea of luck, for it had never seemed to apply to me. —You'll be fine without Sprunt. You'll live here. Bring Willi over in the morning and you two can have both rooms upstairs after Cordelia is gone.

Cordelia stirred in her bed when she heard me. —But I can't leave, the poor patient murmured, weeping and still drunk. —I've nowhere to go. Not back to Philly there's men in the hedges. I've no one. I've only cabbages. I will be your housemaid. Please.

—Hush, I said. —We'll talk about it in the morning. Rest now.

We helped her muttering and bleeding up three long sets of the back-stairs and settled her, with Greta bunking next door. I crept down the hall-ways past my sister's room and seen her light was off. I went and washed myself and climbed into bed next to Charlie. He snored so loud it was a comfort, and I fell asleep.

Around three o'clock a.m., Greta came into my room, whispering, —The *Fräulein* wants you. No matter what I say it does no good. She says you must come.

Charlie cursed at being woken up but I put on my wrapper and went down the corridor with Greta to see the patient. In the lamplight Cordelia looked fevered, her eyes bright in their dark sockets. She clutched my hand and thanked me for saving her life, all the while showing no signs of want-ing it, curled up under her covers, a ball of misery. —You won't send me away, now, will you Madame? Please don't. I'm afraid. Hines will come after me again. He will, Missus. I've no one. Nowhere to go.

It was late. I was exhausted. My weakness and her pleading undid what was left of my good judgment and so again I failed to turn away from risk because it wore the face of a crying woman. I said Cordelia could stay another few nights. —But you will be out by Monday morning, the first of the month, before daylight. I could not have her in my house while I was at trial. —Monday morning not later. Sunday would be better.

—Please, Missus, I am—

—By Monday morning. That's the last day.

Chapter Forty-Five

The Hounds of Hell

*W*e was now a house of desperate women. My sister, trapped. Cordelia broken. Greta despairing. Me accused. And Charlie, pacing and scribbling on scraps, scheming with Morrill. All of us sleepless. Outside on the Avenue the lawmen paced up and down at their appointed stations, spying out of their maggoty eyes, assigned by my enemies to watch over us, to mark the comings and goings of the house. What a boresome show it must have been, for by day it was only lawyers, Mr. Morrill and Mr. Stewart, my defenders arriving with their papers for me to read, their strategies. Or it was Annabelle returning from school, where again my poor angel suffered the taunts of her schoolmates, little cats in ruffly pinafores calling her Daughter of a Witch, etc. Afternoons, I went riding out as usual in the park, alone, and returned to supper. The house retired early. But in the dark, the stairways was haunted by white nightgowns. We women roamed with our hair loose, or long in a plait hanging down the back, soundless in our stocking feet. Greta and me went back and forth to our poor patient, who sweated and moaned. Dutch wandered the halls. The piano played late at night. The stairs creaked. A door latch groaned. There was whispers of crying.

Sunday, March 31st, was the day before I was to face my Accusers. That morning I encountered Greta on the stairs, fretting and biting her lips. She had been home to see Willi but found him with Sprunt, learning to play gin rummy. —My son don't speak to me, Greta said, her eyes full of terror and her breath full of gin. —He is gambling already. He calls me *eine dumme Frau* like Sprunt calls me, und—

—He should be spanked, I said. —And no dinner.

But Willi would not leave Sprunt to stay here with her, she said. —He calls him Papa! And scorns me, his own mama.

—Now listen you silly kraut, I said to her, —the boy has always wanted a father and Sprunt has temporarily distracted him. You tell Willi to come here to me and Uncle Charlie.

—The truth is, said Greta, crumpled, —my husband is through with me.

It was a good thing, to be shed of Sprunt, but Greta would not be convinced today. She had her black moods and the many tumblers of spirits she emptied didn't help. She was so sad and I should've paid attention to her but I didn't. I left her to her troubles. It was the last day before my ordeal and I would spend it with my Annabelle. We drove out with Charlie to the park, where the cold snapped at our faces but our hands was warm with the fingers laced under the ermine lap robe, so soft I could think only how I wished to transport it and my little family with me to prison, all of us together there, a thought so backwards it shows how desperate are the bargains of the cornered.

—Your mama might have to go away, Charlie said to Annabelle as we wheeled around the Meer in Harlem. We had agreed to prepare her a little, in case the worst happened. —But she'll only be gone a little while.

—Why? Annabelle cried. —Where? Where will she go?

—She might go to a hospital, to help some ladies who need her, Charlie lied, while I looked at him over the top of her head, my eyes raw as peeled fruits. His were skittish with anger and sorrow.

—I don't want you to go, Mam. Not ever again. You promised.

—Well maybe I won't have to go at all, I told her, as brave as possible. —But if I do, you'll be a good girl and write letters to me, and I'll be home before your next tooth is out, so I will.

Now Charlie explained more of his lie to her, about the ladies in a hospital, and how they needed my expertise, and how when it was done I'd come home.

But my angel cried, —Mam, I don't want you to go, and held on to me, and I thought if the sky would only open and swallow me it would be a welcome punishment for the torment of motherlessness I'd soon inflict on my innocent girl, only ten years old. Even younger than I was when I was took from my Mam. I should've quit my profession four years before, when I had the chance, when I gave my word. Recriminations fed off me till they grew fat.

In the evening after supper I went to Cordelia in her bed and explained to her again in the strongest terms that by morning she must leave. —I will be in the midst of a trial and can't manage you and won't risk having them discover you. You must be away before daylight.

—I have a pain here, she said, weakly.

—Perhaps this will calm it. I gave her five hundred dollars and instructions to leave when there was no police about.

—But I am Miss Munson, she said, off her head. —And I am Mrs. Purdy. And Mrs. Nobody.

—Where will you go?

—Not Philadelphia. The bushes are full of bad men. There's hair on the backs of their hands. If you eat onion you can scare a man away. But onion left out on the sideboard takes the poison from the air, and I am an onion. I will die of it. My eyes have seen the glory of the coming of the Lord.

She was out of her head singing and rambling. Or, she was faking. Was she? Her fingers was bitten raw, the nails gone down to the half-moon nearly. One of the long scabs on her wrist had opened and bled onto the sheet and I was put in mind of my Mam and the red swollen wreck of her arm. She would die, I thought. I always believed it likely that one of my ladies would die. Just my luck, it would happen now. I felt Cordelia's head. I checked her belly. She did not have fever.

—You're fine, I said, when it was plain she was not. —I've done all I can for you.

—You have not anointed me Missus nothing, nor have you rinsed the underthings.

—Pardon? She was acting. She was malingering.

—You're a mercy, she said with her eyes rolling. —A cabbage of mercy.

And she was a faker. If she was going to die or be out of her mind I preferred her to do it elsewhere. It was my own hide now I needed to save. I couldn't care about her.

—You must leave tomorrow. Take the money and go. Good luck to you, love, I said, and kissed her goodbye.

—Oh Madame, please don't make me leave. I'll have to swallow spirits of turpentine. I'll have to leap off the windowsill. I will jump in the river.

—I trust you will find the strength, please, to move on, I said, and fled.

When I went in to see my sister, she stared into the fire, drinking a glass of claret, and did not look up.

—Dutchie, I mean Lily, pardon—

—Call me whatever you like. She shrugged, smiling. —It doesn't matter now anyway.

—Before the week is out they could take me to jail.

She closed her eyes and put her hand low on her waist again, resting it there. —What if they call me as a witness?

—If they haven't by now they will not, I told her again. —The lawyer assures me they will not likely. They've no evidence against you, and the case will come to nothing.

—Already there is such a scandal, she cried. —I am sorry for you. Sorry for all of us. Your name is more tainted than my own.

—What is a name? It's nothing. I'm not ashamed. You shouldn't be, neither.

—Shame is all I know. Shame and regret.

—What I'm trying to say, Dutchie, is that it would seem you might still have some days to . . . to change your mind, if you require my assistance. Even if they do find me guilty—which I am not—they might not pronounce a sentence on me for days or even weeks after a judgment is made. I'll come home here tomorrow evening and every night of the trial. And Mr. Morrill appears quite sure that the charges will be dismissed.

—I hope so. For your sake.

—And yours? Eliot returns in three weeks.

She shrugged. —The Lord will guide me and show me the way.

So it seemed she had decided. She would leave. Would she? She was wavering.

—I wish you'd stay here. Oh Dutchie, if they take me away to prison who will stay with my daughter? It would relieve me to think of you here with her. Promise me you won't go away. Greta and Charlie will help you. And then when I am free again—

She closed her eyes, smiling. —I would like that. To stay with Annabelle. You have a lovely family.

—So will you consider it?

She smiled again and nodded and promised me, —Yes, Ann, I will consider it.

I kissed her good night with a melancholy deep in my bones, and to my surprise, for a moment she clung to my shoulders like the Dutchie I knew from her days as a winkle attached to me.

—Good night, Axie. I am sorry for all the trouble I've caused you.

—You are never no trouble to me. —You're my sister.

Just before daylight on the morning of April First, I woke, listening. Someone was afoot, drawing a bath. I heard water running in the mysterious pipes of the house and was relieved. It would be Cordelia, preparing for her journey to Trenton. So she had been faking, as I suspected. The money had convinced her and now she was leaving in darkness, as I asked, before the traps could accost her. With a sudden clamp of fear, the thought of the trial that awaited me later that day at Jefferson Market Court made me cringe under the covers, and for a while I drifted in and out of troubled dreams.

It could not have been longer than an hour that I dozed this way, fitful and tormented. At last, unable to tolerate my nightmares any longer, I rose with stiff limbs and went quietly to my dressing room to start my toilette, determined to arrive in the courtroom so finely attired they would write me down for the ages as a queen.

In the dressing room, finding my robe and slippers in the lamplight, I felt a prickle at the back of my neck, as though someone watched me even now. The gallery of the court. The newsmen puffing their cigars. For them I selected my black silks, my diamond earrings, my lace veil. Who could say I wasn't a lady? I ran my hand along the rack of dresses. Silk and crepe. Fur and velvet. The feel of the fabric sent a shudder through me like desire. Ahead perhaps was only the scratch of prison woolies, moth holes in the sleeves. Standing there in my closet, lost in dread, my nerves was further disturbed by a sound out of place. Short. Repeating. Something sickening

in it. Liquid. I listened at the bathroom door and heard it then, the plink
of water landing on water. Someone was in the bath. The master bathroom
had two entrances, one through my dressing room, and the other leading
onto the passageway. Well, I would not begrudge poor Cordelia a bath,
after her violation and ordeal, as long as she left as promised.

—Cordelia? I said, softly.

There was no answer. No sound but a hollow drip.

I turned the knob but the room was locked. The nerve of her, I thought,
to lock me out. —Excuse me, I said, in a flash of annoyance, and retrieved
the key from the closet. It made an important click in the lock as it released,
and I opened the door, knocking.

—Cordelia?

Her back was turned to me.

—Cordelia.

She had fallen asleep. I went to touch her shoulder and sprang back with
a grim small cry, the world upended in a wash of blood. She was dead in
the water. The bath was red and her black hair a weedy dark tangle floating.
Her right arm fell just outside the rim of the tub, and her hand lay dangling
where she had dropped a kitchen knife, bone-handled. It lay on the white
tile, clotted with gore from a red stripe cut across the neck, from the left ear
across to the notch between her clavicles.

A terrible noise came from me. A lowing. Sucked out from the pit of
my heart so hard it did not stop even as I turned my eyes from the sight.
My sister. My sister.

—Oh Dutchie, I said, and sat down in convulsion before the dressing
table shaking so the jars of perfume rattled on the marble surface. Double
fists pressed to my mouth to stop the sounds, but the noise came out of me
harsh as metal on stone. —Dutchie, I cried.

If only it was me there bled out in the water.

It might as well have been. It felt so. All was lost now. They would say
I'd killed her. The wardens would hang me from the gallows on the Bridge
of Sighs. My daughter would grow up without her mother, same as I done.
Even in the welter of grief my mind raced fast like a cornered rabbit, darting for the exits wherever I might find one. Think, Axie, I says to myself.
Save your tears for later. I forced myself quiet. Stilled myself down, then
lifted my eyes to the mirror. There she was, so ghastly. Our Dutchie. In the

reflection I seen how she was still a Muldoon, how she looked like me and how we was twinned as ever, one dead, the other quick, and all our dreams in matched shambles around us.

That reflection, so uncanny in our likeness, showed me what to do. The plan was far-fetched, a wing and a prayer. It couldn't work. It had to work. There was not no other way now.

I turned to face the form suspended in the water. The water dripped, such a loud sound. Approaching her, I took the ring off my wedding finger. Oh *macushla,* I said, *aroon machree.* When I lifted her hand the cold of it sickened me, and yet I did not flinch, only removed the ring on her finger put there by the useless VanDerWeil. Next, I twisted my own rings onto her watery knuckles, diamonds and gold on her cold hand. I kissed her fingers and curled them around the kiss, so that she might hold it, my Dutchie, in her grave. *Oh Mam I am sorry.* Oh Dutch. Weeping with my lips bit down to blood, I removed my diamond earrings, little tears like flowers they were, of brilliant ice set in silver, beautiful as she was. I brushed aside the dark seawrack strands of her hair and clasped them to the collops of her lobes. Oh my Dutchie. She was only sleeping, that hair tangled in my fingers. I kissed her and my tears fell into the water where they turned red with her own. —Sleep with angels, I whispered, my voice broke. I kissed her again.

In great haste now, I left the room and went to shake my husband awake.

—What? He sat up in alarm, so you could see his heart pounding in the veins of his neck. —What is it?

I told him. I said knife and neck and cut and throat, the words so awful and bloody. I was half insane in the murky dark. He shook himself awake, gasping.

—I put my rings on her, I said, trembling. —All my jewelry.

—Why? What are you talking about? He took the rounds of my shoulders in his hands and held me at arm's length and shook me. —Your jewelry? What for?

—Listen, I'm leaving. You'll say it's me. She is me. Will you do it? You'll tell them I was distraught. You'll say it's me there in the tub.

He digested this idea for the barest of minutes, then rousted himself from the bed and ran into the bathroom to see the gruesome scene for himself. He was gone a while, too long, and when he returned, he had

Dutchie's trunk with him. He began stuffing her clothes into my closets, frantic.

—There's no evidence left she was ever here. He was pale and serious and in great haste. —You must clear out now. There's no time to waste.

I dressed in a panic and packed a bag, heedlessly throwing in dresses and shoes and jewelry. I took as much money as we had in the safe at the back of the armoire and stuffed it into the roll of my spare stockings.

My husband asked me questions. —Where will you go?

—Boston first.

—Good. And then?

—I don't know. Canada? London.

—What name will you go by?

—I don't know. My hands flapped. Keening noises escaped me.

—You are Mrs. McGinty, do you hear? You're an Irish nursemaid.

—I've no papers.

—You'll get some. Leave now.

—First I must write a note. I have to leave a note.

He handed me pen and paper. —Say they drove you to do it, those hounds of hell.

I wrote with shaking hand.

> *It was the hounds of hell drove me to it. Mr. Comstock with his underhanded sneakery and Mr. Greeley and Mr. Matsell with their lies, and Dr. Gunning that sanctimonious snake. You never NONE of you did care about a WOMAN, no matter how misfortunate, and all of society shall think on its uncharitableness toward the fair sex when they think about me, who only tried to give sanctuary and comfort to your poor afflicted daughters and sisters, your mothers and discarded sweethearts. I can't no more face the canker of your laws or waste away in your Tombs. So thus I choose to spare my family the pain of the trial about to start at Jefferson Market Court. It's nothing but a charade. Farewell, and may my death be on the conscience of my false accusers for the rest of their days.*
> *Signed,*
> *Mrs. Ann M. Jones, April 1, 1880*

—Hurry, hurry, said Charlie.

I handed him the note but had lost my nerve. —I can't go. They'll never believe it's me in there. They'll arrest you. How will you—

—Greta and me will swear it's you that's dead. We'll say you've been despondent and threatening to jump off a bridge.

—You'll pay her?

—I'll pay her and I'll pay the coroner and I'll pay whoever needs paying you can be sure. Now get. Out the basement door.

—When will you bring my girl to me? When will you come?

Charlie looked me hard in the eyes. —When I've finished mourning my dead wife.

My knees buckled, listening to him.

—I'll come, he said, hustling me to the back stairs, —when I've attended to our poor innocent child, now left motherless because of Comstock and his dogs, who hounded my sweetheart to death.

Sweetheart, he said. It was a word like a chloroform rag over my face.

—What will you tell her?

—I haven't thought that far ahead.

—You'll never come, I said.

—I will, why won't you believe me? Six months at least. He pressed my face between his two hands. —Now go. Hurry.

—But her grave.

—Ah, I nearly forgot. He pulled from the pocket of his robe a letter addressed to me in Dutch's writing. —It was left on her bed. But you haven't time to read it now. You must leave. Go. Read it later.

—Promise me on her grave, on Dutchie's grave, you'll come. Promise me.

—You have my word. Go.

—Charlie? I was weeping.

—Axie, go now. The house is about to wake. You haven't a minute to lose. Then he pulled me to his chest and clamped me there. —Trust me, love. Trust.

Chapter Forty-Six

Mrs. McGinty

*T*he dark was thicker than the crepe that hid my face but even still I felt exposed, as bone in a fracture. Old snow scabbed the sidewalks, and I picked my way along as fast as my boots would go. Maggie's woolen shawls snatched off the hook in the backstairs on my way out the door were warm around me, but already I missed my sealskin cape, left behind. I was not a lady no more, but a servant girl hustling on an errand. The wind witched at my neck and the handles of my heavy carpetbag bit through the kid of my gloves, but worse was the grief that had me by the entrails. I ran and stumbled. My sister's bloody death followed after me. Clumps of woe and panic massed in my throat. I hurried along. The streets was empty except for the dog carts and wagons of the early tradesmen stirring to life, their lanterns wagging. At every sound I expected the hot hands of the law to snatch my elbow. I'd be mistaken for a streetwalker, or worse, recognized. Where was a hansom cab? At this hour not one wheel on the cobbles was for hire. When at last I reached Lexington Avenue, my breath in an uproar, there was the omnibus, and I clambered up the steps and paid the fare. On the hard bench, between a drunken butcher and a snaggletooth flower seller in faded gingham, the loud pounding of my blood made me reel. I was stunned and nauseous all the way to the Grand Central station. All the way to Boston. And for a long time after that.

The train lurched north through Harlem and carried me in a terrible state across the river into the marshlands of Pelham. The weak early sun lit the blond cattails, and flocks of black birds flew up scattershot like a handful of tacks thrown against the blue sky. My sister was winging up through the ether now with them, I imagined, and tried to see her flying in white radiance like an angel. But every time I closed my eyes all I seen was the bloody gore of her death in a tableau before me. At last I opened the letter she left for me, and as the train hurtled onward like the long ago train that carried us to our separate fates, I read her words with raw wet eyes.

> *Dearest Axie,*
>
> *Do not be sad when you find me. I am happy now, in God's arms. In life I could not find peace any longer, as I have been a shameful disappointment to all of Chicago, to Mother, to my husband, and to you, I am afraid, for I realize that under the circumstances it would be impossible for me to go ahead and live together as sisters as you and I both always dreamed. It is quite plain that I would not be a fit mother. Certainly the weeks ahead would only have brought more shame and infamy upon me, in light of your own trials. I do not wish to be a burden to you or testify against you or choose any of the other sad paths open to me. It is right that I should be punished for my wickedness. I am a terrible sinner. I have nowhere to turn. Please do not reproach yourself, thinking you could have prevented me. I long to close my eyes and find a welcome oblivion. I wish you well and hope that all your trials are resolved, and that God willing, you will someday find our brother. Remember me, and pray we'll find each other in heaven.*
>
> *Love,*
> *Dutch*

The letter left me sad and hollow as a marrow bone gnawed by dogs. The train barreled on in its urgent clattering, and I saw now I was orphaned all over again.

After two days, I arrived at Boston's Park Place Station. I disembarked and made my way to a travelers' hotel across the street. I paid in cash for a room and signed my name as Mrs. McGinty, of New Haven. In my terrible lodging, the smell of tobacco filtered under the doorjamb, and the sound of trains rattled the windows. I barely slept. Then in the morning I made my way back to the station and paid a passenger arriving from New York for his copy of the *Times,* dated April 3rd. It featured—on Page One—a full accounting. I read it with shaky indignant hands.

END OF A CRIMINAL LIFE; "MME. DEBEAUSACQ" COMMITS SUICIDE; SHE CUTS HER THROAT WITH A CARVING KNIFE, AND IS FOUND DEAD IN A BATHTUB—THE BODY DISCOVERED BY A HORRIFIED SERVANT—A VERDICT OF SUICIDE BY THE CORONER'S JURY.

The notorious Mme. DeBeausacq is dead. Having for nearly fifteen years been before the public as a woman who was growing rich by the practice of a nefarious business; having once served an imprisonment for criminal malpractice; having ostentatiously flaunted her wealth before the community and made an attractive part of the finest avenue in the City odious by her constant presence, she yesterday, driven to desperation by the public opinion she had so long denied, came to a violent end by cutting her throat from ear to ear. The news startled the whole city. At first the announcement was looked upon as a hoax, but when it became known that her death had been officially communicated to the court in which she was about to be tried on an indictment . . . doubt was removed and the ghastly story of the suicide became the talk of everybody.

The talk of everybody. I did not care. It didn't matter. The coroner's jury had pronounced the death a suicide. *My* death. Madame was dead and so was Mrs. Jones. "The wages of sin is death," said the *Times* editorial. Mr. Comstock's only comment was "A bloody end to a bloody life." He bragged that mine was the fifteenth suicide he had inspired.

I was bereft.

* * *

Under her alias, the Widow McGinty moved shortly into a room overlooking the Charles River. She sent word to Mr. Jones with the address. After that she kept quiet. Six months, he had said. She walked the streets of the Back Bay in her black mourning. She sat on the benches of the Common on brisk spring evenings, afraid and hunted, sure someone would recognize her and shout her old name. If she saw a policeman, she crossed the street. She did not speak to a soul. She read the New York papers. Among them, only the *Sun* had a whack at her tormentor Comstock and spoke the truth about him and Madame DeBeausacq:

> Whatever she was Madame had her rights, and the man
> who cunningly led her into the commission of a misdemeanor
> acted an unmanly and ignoble part.

According to the *Times,* another of Madame's defenders was a clergyman named Reverend Charles McCarthy, who preached a sermon that made Mrs. McGinty proud. She wished she'd have been there to hear it herself. She would've kissed him.

> Madame was hunted down by miserable subterfuge, by
> cunning and heartless fabrications, by open and mean lying. Her
> so-called crime is one shared by many respectable physicians,
> even abetted by a Christian minister, who has defended his own
> conduct with sound moral reasoning, before the trustees of this
> church.

But such crumbs of understanding was small comfort, for Madame DeBeausacq had not been dead two weeks before rumors began to circulate that she was alive and well. Mrs. McGinty read the New York papers and saw a letter to the *Tribune* from a Mr. J. H. Jordan, who styled himself a carpenter, in which he claimed he had delivered a coffin to Madame's house, for a patient who had died, and that it was this patient who was dead in the tub—while Madame lived on. And another letter writer, to the

Times, said he'd seen Madame in her carriage, riding around the streets of Philadelphia.

Mrs. McGinty had no carriage, but the idea that Madame had been seen alive made her so frightened of detection she traveled nowhere without a veil. She wrote letters and mailed none of them. If she sent word to anyone she was sure it would be intercepted. A servant would discover the secret and betray her. She must wait. At night she took to her bed and gnawed the raw knuckles on the backs of her hands. Terrible recriminations plagued her dreams. She had broken the promise to her Mam. She had failed her sister. She had doubted her husband always, and despite his promises she doubted him now. Would he come, or would he not? He had said once he would not forgive her. He had said Trust Me. He was a good time Charlie and in bad times he shouted and drank whiskey and hated her. Sure he hated her now in the tempest she'd left behind. He would not come. He was not by her side to seduce her out of her fears with his winks and his trick of finding a sweet behind her ear. In his absence, Mrs. McGinty was left to banish the demons of suspicion and mistrust by herself. He will come, she muttered, he must. And as she repeated this idea to herself, she made a choice to believe it, for such hope was all she had now, buried like a talisman in the folds of her widow's weeds.

It would take six months, wouldn't it? That was the number he mentioned. Six months. In the light of day, it seemed a reasonable number. After all, to flee too fast would arouse suspicion. And her husband had at least six months of affairs to settle. He was talking to the police. He was organizing a funeral. He was burying her sister in a cold grave, ordering the headstone, having it carved with his wife's name.

He was burying his wife.

He was lying to the servants. He was enlisting Greta to lie.

He was handling the coroner's inquest. He was talking to lawyers.

He was lying to their daughter. Drying her tears. Burying his child's mother.

He was selling the house. Organizing the accounts. Packing away the furniture.

Six months at least. But for Mrs. McGinty in the dark, six months was just the same as NEVER. How could Charlie forgive her? He had buried his wife. At night, she pictured her husband as the Merry Widower, laughing into the eyes of Gigi, Lila, Sally, Joan. She imagined her daughter calling one of these frippettes Mother, bringing her violets on a spring day, and Mrs. McGinty's heart lurched for all she had given up. She grew gray and quiet with grief and recriminations.

In May, after many weeks of lonely obscurity, the date of her birthday arrived. Didn't she deserve a present? She did. So Mrs. McGinty took herself to dine at the Hotel Vendome in the Back Bay. She ordered coffee and cake and took a seat along the red velvet banquette in the tearoom. It was a shock when she caught a glimpse of herself in the mirrored wall. She was a black blot in widow's weeds amidst the reds and gilt of the décor. A milkskin of sadness filmed her blue eyes. She was no longer young, but a dame of thirty three. Her figure had got thick through the waistline since her arrival in Boston, for she was fond of the city's famous cream pie, and liked extra molasses with her baked beans. What did it matter? She was alone. Her sister was dead. Her brother nowhere. Her husband and daughter gone from her. In the tearoom of the Ritz, she ordered another slice of cake.

In the Boston papers over the next weeks and months she read new headlines about Crusader Comstock busting booksellers as smut peddlers, jailing doctors and pharmacists. Why? just for writing instructions on how a woman might use certain medicines. It was now illegal to use the mails to send an anatomy textbook to a medical student. Miss Ida Craddock killed herself after Comstock caught her mailing a pamphlet.

At last, in late July, when the money she had raised from the sale of her jewelry had nearly run out, Mrs. McGinty dared to address another envelope to Mr. Charles G. Jones, at One East Fifty Second Street, New York City.

> *Dear Mr. Jones,*
> *Greetings from Boston. Since I last seen you all is as can be expected with me. My recent loss plagues me with sorrow every*

day, and my sleep is troubled. The doctor says this malady will
be relieved whenever I am reunited with my loved ones, but as
I do not know WHEN that will be, I am sorely TROUBLED.
The money I have made from selling salt water taffy is nearly
exhausted. Here in Boston the summer is mild and the Public
Gardens are blooming. You would love to see the swan boats
on the lagoon. They are paddlewheel contraptions shaped like
white birds and a person can ride across the water on their backs.
Perhaps one day soon you and your little daughter could visit.
Tell her we will ride the swan boats and have cotton candy. Kiss
her for me and give my best to your wife. It is my fervent wish to
see you and your family very soon.
        —Mrs. P. McGinty

Not two weeks later came a reply, a letter containing five hundred dollars in cash.

Dear Mrs. McGinty,
    Thank you for your letter. Enclosed is the money you are owed.
Thank you for sending the boxes of salt water taffy. Certainly
we will visit when our affairs here are more settled, and we have
completed the sale of our house, sometime after the summer.
        Sincerely, Mr. Charles Jones

Mrs. McGinty, laboring under her alias, read the letter and hung on to the phrase "Certainly we will visit." It was hardly an endearment. She knew Charles Jones was afraid to write down anything that might reveal her identity, or that the Notorious Madame X was yet alive. He did not want to betray her whereabouts. Still, poor Mrs. McG. feared he was rid of her, buying her off for $500. She wished for some little word that he loved her. That her daughter missed her. She was tormented by grief.

Still, alone in the wilderness of Boston, Mrs. McGinty came to see from a distance what Mrs. Jones could not see close up.

WITH him, she had thought he only cared for her because of money. WITHOUT him, she seen that it was the both of them together who made Madame DeBeausacq so rich and so Notorious.

It must be admitted that Madame had quite enjoyed being Notorious. RESPLENDENT, they said she was. HANDSOME.

Now nobody noticed Mrs. McGinty wore little pearl-gray boots of kid-skin or wrote down the details of her hat with its Spanish lace. It was not written anywhere that she took her cake at the Hotel Vendome. Nobody cared. She was not useful. Nobody knocked in the middle of the night to say Come Madame Quick Please Oh Hurry Please.

In my exile and loneliness, I saw that perhaps I had mistook Charlie Jones. All the years I had been longing for my family of Muldoons, searching for my brother and sister, listening to tales of dastardly double-dealing men, I thought Charlie dangerous, of the type Mrs. Dix and other women had warned me against. He could be furious, yes. He had hit me once. Yelled often. His whereabouts frequently was a mystery. But he came home eventually, didn't he? So far he did. It seems I had forgot he was just a plain orphan all along like myself, and orphans only ever want the one thing which is Home. Now I saw. He was Home to me. If only I was Home to him. Was I?

For six months Mr. Jones and Mrs. McGinty corresponded occasionally in a strictly businesslike manner, till at last, in September, came a letter about a "visit," and Mrs. McGinty took the streetcar along Commonwealth Avenue to Park Place Station to meet the train arriving from New York. The wind whipped bits of paper into eddies at the corners of buildings and it was not the *sheehogues* at play, not at all, she thought, but trouble stirred up. The sky was like porridge, lumpen and dull, with a yellow tinge that said a storm was coming. Mrs. McGinty carried an umbrella, which served to give her anxious hands something to hold.

The New York train arrived clanging in a hiss and shower of soot. Mrs. McGinty trembled, all nerves. The squeal of iron was so sharp it hurt her teeth. Crowds of people began to spill out of the passenger cars and onto the platform. In their dark suits and long dark traveling dresses, they streamed toward the little island of Mrs. McGinty in her cap, her common cloak.

And then there they were, her family, Charlie with his shifty dark eyes and his bent smile, his arms soon around her, right out in public, and Annabelle, taller and a little gawkish now, with her face contorted in disbelief. She had only just been told, on the train ride North, the surprise person she would find on the platform.

—Mrs. McGinty, said Charlie.

—Mama? said Annabelle with the color drained from her face. —Is it you?

So lost was I in their long embrace so intoxicated with the smell of my daughter's hair and the stab of longing caused by the softness of my husband's whiskers against my cheek that I didn't notice a pale young man standing behind Charlie, holding his hat, smoothing the wiry tufts of his red hair.

—Ann, said Charlie, after a long moment, —I have brought someone else for you.

The stranger stepped forward, a queer look on his face, shy and hopeful. He held out his hand. —I'm Joseph. Joseph Trow.

How d'ye do? I began to say, when all of a sudden I known who it was.

—Our Joe, I said, faint. —Is it?

Chapter Forty-Seven

Mother ____

My brother is not a tall man. He is unlike me and Dutch, with his bricky hair and the sand of freckles across his nose. He is narrow in the shoulders and waist, and when he smiles, a small fat boy so familiar comes toddling out from the corners of his eyes to greet you, a devil of mischief already loose, even before he says, —So this is my sister with the Ax in her name.

And he holds his arms out like he's known you all his life.

But he didn't remember any of it. Not the train. Not how he slept on me like I was his own personal mattress. Not the smell of horehound on Mrs. Trow's breath, or how she lured him with her brown candies. Not how he once called us AxieDutch or held his fat arms out for us or wailed for us when we were out of sight and wouldn't tolerate anyone but me to sing him to sleep or how I loved him. He did not remember the song Kathleen Mavourneen. He did not remember Mam.

It would've broke my heart that he forgot but now I seen it was a blessing. No memories like mine to gnaw his knuckles at night with sharp teeth. No secret like Dutch had had to conceal under the stockings in her dresser. Life for Joe Trow was clover, a credit to Mr. C. L. Brace and his theory of fresh air. Joe grew up strong in a pretty town called Brandywine, Pennsylvania, after Mr. and Mrs. Trow left the settler's life in Illinois and returned back East to run the family dairy. Joe was—they told him—their natural son, and they fed him milk and molasses. They taught him to play a fiddle and how to birth a calf. He had a coonhound named Nuisance and that was as close as trouble ever got to Joe. He'd been to school through the twelfth grade, knew geography and the names of all the Kings of Europe, if not the Kings of Lurg. He had woke up one morning and announced he would go to New York to seek his fortune, when Mr. and Mrs. Trow made a surprise announcement of their own:

—You were born in New York, said Mrs. T. —And so were your two sisters.

And that's how it was that Joe was twenty years of age when he set out to find me, and two years later, he did.

—I always felt there was a secret, he said. —At last I know it.

A secret is a dangerous article. While I have kept many for others, I mistakenly believed I did not have a secret of my own. A secret is what will make you exposed to ruin and perhaps for that reason I did not excavate what was buried so deep amongst the shells and husks and peelings of my constitution. Hid like that, an old onion sprouting and decaying in the cellar, my secret threatened to rot me from the inside. I did not confess it even to myself, how I loved him. Yet when at last after so long apart my husband Charlie greeted me at the Park Place Station, his face puckered and a tear in his eye, my secret flowered up. To my own shock out it came.

—I do love you, I blurted very soft. But I might as well have said to him, *You do love me.* Because at last through my own mistrusting orphan eyes I seen that he did. It was there in his face and it was there in the fact of him standing on the platform. He did not let me down. After all these years, I seen love was not only a poem of wild red sparkles. It was Charlie in his rumpled suit, his hair gone salty at the sides, holding the hand of our girl, and bringing my lost brother to me.

—What do you think I have in here? he whispered in my ear, patting his trouser pocket rather suggestive as our little family proceeded from the train station.

—Mr. Jones! I said, pretending shock, and he stopped my mouth with his own.

—It's not Mr. Jones it's Mr. _____ now, says he, and then from beneath my shawl with a flourish he withdrew a pamphlet about a White Star sailing steamer, bound for Liverpool, three days hence. —We'll have ourselves a stateroom, Missus. He winked, waving a fan of tickets at me.

—Liverpool? I said, counting six tickets altogether.

—Then on from there to London.

—Who's the other three tickets for besides us?

—Joe's coming with us, for starters. And Greta's invited, with her son.

The news was a poultice to heal my scarry heart. We were off all together. Me and Charlie with our girl, and our longlost Joe who stood with me now, and Greta who stood with me for years and had stood up for me at the coroner's inquest, Charlie said.

—You should've seen our Greta, he told me. —She wept up and down at those inspectors and carried on over her dear employer, Mrs. Jones, dead of suicide, and telling all the assembled how Mr. Comstock drove you to it with his sneakery, how you talked of suicide for he filled you with such despair you wished to die.

—He did fill me with despair. He still does.

That terrible morning, Charlie said, Greta had scuttled Cordelia Purdy down the backstairs and off to Trenton with a purse of gold and promise of more, to buy her silence. Dear Greta the companion of my youth had stood at the grave in Sleepy Hollow weeping my name and come home to Annabelle to comfort our girl these long months, telling her *Liebchen* you will see your mother again, your father promised and would not deceive you.

Within twenty four hours, Greta my true friend and her boy Willi also arrived in Boston, and while we waited for our departure we all stayed several nights in the bosom of luxury at the Hotel Vendome in the Back Bay. The place was lit through with electric lamps, and Charlie and me flicked the lights off and on like we were puppeteers over a troop of fireflies. Greta said she had never slept on such linens, and Willi and Annabelle ran along the hallways and went up and down the vertical railway lift between the floors. Joe went out exploring Boston, for he announced it was full of history, and he had a passion for all things historical. —I'm going out to see the town they call the Cradle of Liberty, he said, heading for the door.

—If you find it, bring it back here, for perhaps we'll need it. A midwife is always needing a cradle.

But Joe came back from exploring and declared Boston was only half a city. —It doesn't even have an elevated railway, he said, —and New York has more than one. He couldn't wait to get to London to see the Paddington Station and the London underground. My brother, it seemed, had a tedious fondness for trains that I did not share (between him and me, that much hadn't changed), but I smiled at his excitement as he discussed the wonders of steam locomotives and subway tunnels. He was our same Joe, wasn't he? And wouldn't he have had a great deal to discuss with our sister Dutch? seeing as how she'd lived so long with railroad magnates. But they wouldn't have that talk, now, or any.

On September 19th, our little troop of emigrants went down to the Mystic Wharves of Boston and presented our papers under the name Mr. & Mrs. _____ which was imprinted on the passenger lists, along with the names of my brother Joseph Trow, and Greta _____ and her son Willi. Our collected trunks and luggage was only clothing, and a few selected books and curios. On the morning of the following day, we sailed for Liverpool, England, in three separate staterooms, with stewardesses to attend us and music in the dining room nightly.

Out on the deck, after we had our sea legs, Belle flew a little kite off the side of the ship, her hair a flag in the wind. —Come here, you wee nelligan, I told her, —and let me comb your raggedy urchin hair.

—I am not a nurchin! she cried, and flung her arms around my neck and kissed me and declared for the hundredth time that she would never let me go away again ever, and I promised I would not, nor even let her out of my sight, and I did not for a long time after that. As the ship forged and steamed ahead over the waves, fire in its belly and wind in its sails, the family of us, mother and daughter, father and uncle, Greta and Willi, strolled up and down, fed crumbs to seabirds, breathed the salt air like it was a cure we were taking. We sat in the deck chairs wrapped in blankets, we played Whist and Charades and Twenty Questions with the other passengers. We were missing only our sister, our Dutchess. Eleven days after we left her sad lonely bones back in the United States of America we landed in Liverpool, and from there we made our way to London in a couple of hired carriages.

Money was not an object, Charlie had explained. He sold our house for three hundred fifty thousand dollars, and liquidated the assets of Madame

DeBeausacq, valued at one MILLION dollars, such that when we got to London we was able to set up housekeeping in fancy St. _____ and later stake Joe to his own place and set him up in business as manufacturers of patent medicines, and send Belle to the Girls Academy where she quickly learned to speak very British, and to wear tortoiseshell combs in her hair. She went to symphonies with her friend Clarissa and to see Gilbert & Sullivan's performance of *H.M.S. Pinafore* on the London stage, and dance the waltz. Altogether she was not a nurchin at all, as she used to say so charmingly, not a nurchin like her father and mother was, called Street Arab and Guttersnipe and Little Wanderer. She was a lady, pure and refined, with a grand piano in her parlor and a closet full of silks.

These days, years into the new century, Joe has become an expert at pharmaceuticals, and the business of mixing various remedies provides him and his family a good living. He lives not two doors away from me and Charlie here in London, on an excellent street which cannot be named. My enemies would hunt me down and smite me if they knew that I'm not dead under the pines in Sleepy Hollow. My hope is to torment them with these memoirs of my notorious life to let them know I have lived refined and happy across the sea. While the English law similarly claims certain of my ministrations is a CRIME, there's no shortage of English ladies who need my assistance, of the highest class. But I don't make the mistake of treating the fancy ones and worry instead over the poor, preventing orphans where I might, and tending the mothers. The *Times* of London has put the number of "public women" as they are called here at eight thousand six hundred, and the number of brothels at two thousand three hundred. I move quietly among them in my woolen cloak, my clean apron, undetected. I do not advertise and invite no patients to my home. Despite my experience as a hunted woman, I operate without fear of discovery, for the authorities seem as indifferent to the wretched of London as they was to the wretched of New York. For a small fee, or none, I treat the females' disease and obstructions. I give them pills and preventatives and procedures and never fail to give thanks for the new mercy of ETHER, which is freely available in these modern times. I have a traveling ether apparatus and mask to fit over my ladies' faces. It's a lullaby. It's a marvel. It's a blessing. They call me Mother _____.

Whenever I am out on such an errand, my carriage waits anonymous on a nearby corner. When I return, the footman dismounts to hold the door, assists me up the step. Inside, I draw the carriage curtains and while we trot away from the East End or Piccadilly, I exchange my plain garments for finer ones. A shirtwaist of velvet with lace at the collar, skirts of watered silk. I arrive home at _____ Street perfumed and bedecked with pearls, no different than if I'd gone for tea at Buckingham Palace. The parlormaid in her black uniform takes my cape at the door. If it is after lunch, the butler brings me tea in the drawing room, where I look out over the park and wait to spot my little nephew and niece, Nicholas and Eugenia Trow. They are often out with their governess, or their silly mother Winifred, the English girl from Gloucester my brother married some years ago. Winifred knows everything about roses and peonies, and we both enjoy discussing the protocols of the Royal Family, the line of succession to the throne, and which Earl is the b*****d child of which Duke.

Just this morning, Charlie brought me a collection of newspapers he'd gotten from a seller in the Strand, the *Herald* and the *Times* of New York, where Comstockery flourishes like an infection of yeasts. The Roundsman of the Lord has been busy smiting vice wherever he sees it. His list of victims is long. Poor Margaret Sanger arrested for the crime of printing an article called "What Every Girl Should Know"; the Colgate company persecuted for its advertisement of the Preventative Powers of Vaseline; two thousand pounds of so-called smut confiscated and burned; the production of Mr. George Bernard Shaw's *Mrs. Warren's Profession* on Broadway nearly shut down for being a dirty play. The very silliest news is the story of how Mr. Comstock got his red-flanneled underdrawers in a twist over the Art Students League. It seems the artists' brochure featured charcoal studies of nudes—an offense to our Anthony's prudish sensibilities. The *Herald* reported that Comstock had arrested the League's desk clerk, a Miss Robinson, age nineteen, for distributing this OBSCENE material. So hysterical did poor Miss Robinson become at her court appearance, so faint with palpitations, that a doctor had to be summoned.

How exciting it must be for our Tony, arresting delicate young female clerks. How proudly he must puff his feathers, boasting of such conquests.

By way of retort, one of the clever art students published cartoons of Mr. Comstock modeling naked for a drawing class, wearing only a top hat above ample hams. Another young genius wrote a sonnet about him, calling him "a sexless clown." Still another, my favorite, suggested that he be boiled in oil. Where they would find a pot big enough, I do not know.

I am even more uncharitable than those students. For me, fate would be sweetest if My Enemy found himself penniless and pregnant, made to endure a confinement and bear his child, and bring it out in the world in suffering agony just as ladies do. Perhaps it would not be too much to ask that he could have a fistula. But as this is but a pipe dream, I take my revenge where I find it, out in my carriage, driving through the park in the sunlight, in my new diamond earrings, in front of all London society. From time to time, in the New York papers, they print another rumor that I've been spotted in Boston or Paris, and that it wasn't me dead in the tub that April morning. April fool, you might say.

But it is no joke at all. Not when I think of who she was, and how I did not get to know her, and I curse the forces that made her life so intolerable she had to end it.

I am at wits' end, she wrote in her diary. *I'd rather die.*

Please God take my soul and forgive me my sins.

She wrote that, but I might have written it too, for the sin of not saving her.

In the afternoon, I sip my glass of tea, or take a little bit of sherry with my pound cake, and hope that today my friend Greta will take herself away from minding her grandsons, Willi's two *bratwursts,* as we call them, and come for a game of whist, or that I will see my darling darling Annabelle driving up in her equipage, to bring her children for a visit. There are four of them, all delivered by me their Gran. I spoil them with sugar lumps, like they were ponies. The littlest sits on my lap and calls me Grandmother. If they are very good I let them try on my jewelry and give them the clear glass marbles in the china bowl to play with. Annabelle chastises me, for she thinks the baby will choke on one. —You swallowed a penny when you were that size, I tell her, —and it turned out eventually, in the _____.

Annabelle does not like me to refer to such coarse matters. She is a proper English Rose, married to Henry Summers, a handsome barrister. While he looks like a prancing nincompoop in his long white wig, and it surprises me to have a member of that high class profession in my own family, it is certainly convenient. Besides being an excellent lawyer, Henry is a good papa to young Joseph, Cecilia, Andrew, and little Lillian, who everybody calls Dutchess, or Dutchie sometimes.

—Dutchie come and sit on your Grandmother's lap, there's a good girl, I say, and she clambers up and puts her arms around my neck, or takes my two cheeks between her miniature paws and says, —Ooh Grandmother you are a beautiful granny.

—Oh Dutchie, I tell her, —you are a beautiful Dutch, so you are.

It gives me a pang to hear the name, to say it. Even at five years of age, the child is the copy of my departed sister. When she sings at the piano in her sweet voice, I am reminded of what I lost, and how it was kept from us, and I dwell upon the promise I made to Mam, and the men who thwarted it with their laws and intrusions and bearded certainties. I brood over every one of my enemies. I do not forgive them. I don't forget. I write this now for Dutchie cold under the ground, no tombstone in her name, her child unborn. If she had not been trapped by secrets, so conflicted by shame, she might be here in this room with us, where I scribble peacefully in a corner, where our brother Joseph tosses cards at the table with my husband Charlie (who has got fat off English cream), where the sweet lovely children play on the Brussels carpet, happy cousins, pretending the flowery patterns are their gardens. Sunlight crashes through the windows, fracturing off the droplets of crystal in the chandelier above their heads, so that the sparkles look to be sylphs and *sheehogues* flitting among the paisleys, having a bon-fire. I must remember to leave out a saucer of milk for them on the win-dowsill, to ward off mischief.

THE END

Author's Note

My Notorious Life is a work of fiction. It is based partly on the life and death of Ann Trow Lohman (1811–78), also known as Madame Restell, who practiced as a "female physician" in New York City for roughly forty years. For the purposes of this story, I have appropriated from Lohman's life and times some facts, dialogue, trial transcripts, newspaper accounts, advertisements, and events, but have otherwise invented the life of the novel's protagonist. While I have attempted to maintain accuracy in terms of the general history and customs of the period, and while real historical texts and figures such as C. L. Brace and Anthony Comstock do appear here, I have invented scenes, dialogue, and circumstance and have also reconfigured events and changed some chronology, when such changes suited the story.

Acknowledgments

I am indebted to dear and expert friends Roberta Baker, Amy Wilentz, and Nick Goldberg for their multiple close readings, editorial wisdom, encouragement, and jokes in the margins.

For support in perseverance, great thanks are due to the late Wendy Weil, and to Anne Edelstein, Diane McWhorter, Carroll Bogert, Tia Powell, Barbara Jones, Robert Lipsyte, Alexander Papachristou, Anne Detjen, Sally Cook, Anthony Weller, Erica Schultz, Susan Lehman, Bobbie Smith, Teresa Mason Corrigan, and Rita Grant Buckley.

Thanks also to the English Department and administration at Bard High School Early College, and to my extraordinary students there, for all they've taught me.

For technical expertise and inspiration by example, I am grateful to Dr. Joan Berman and Dr. Jean Chin, obstetrician-gynecologists of courage, warmth, and integrity.

I owe a great debt of gratitude to Sarah Burnes, and her colleagues at the Gernert Company, especially Logan Garrison and Rebecca Gardner.

Heartfelt thanks to my excellent editor, Alexis Gargagliano, for her expertise, enthusiasm, wisdom, and support. Great helpings of appreciation to Nan Graham, and also Kara Watson, Kelsey Smith, Dan Cuddy, David TerAvanesyan, Tal Goretsky, Katie Monaghan, Sophie Vershbow, and the entire marvelous team at Scribner.

Thanks, too, to Helen Garnons-Williams, and Bloomsbury, UK.

I could not have written *My Notorious Life* without the information, images, maps, recipes, advertisements, and ideas I found in newspaper archives and many books, especially a biography of Ann Trow Lohman, *The Wickedest Woman in New York*, by Clifford Browder (1988), and *The Wonderful Trial of Caroline Lohman*, a pamphlet published by the *Police Gazette* in 1847, which sold for six cents a copy. Other invaluable works include *Orphan Trains: The Story of Charles Loring Brace and the Children He Saved and Failed*, by Stephen O'Conner (2001), *The Dangerous Classes of New York*, by Charles Loring Brace (1880), *How the Other Half Lives*, by Jacob Riis (1890), *Lights and Shadows of New York Life*, by James McCabe (1872), *Anthony Comstock, Roundsman of the Lord*, by Heywood Broun and Margaret Leech (1927), and *Clinical Lectures on the Diseases of Women and Children*, by Gunning S. Bedford, M.D. (1856). Thanks to the Cushing/Whitney Medical Library at Yale University for a copy of *A Female Physician to the Ladies of the United States: Being a Familiar and Practical Treatise of Matters of Utmost Importance Peculiar to Women*, by Mrs. W. H. Maxwell (1860). Thanks to Jim Logan at Sleepy Hollow Cemetery in Tarrytown, New York, for attempts to read the weathered inscription on Ann Lohman's grave.

My family sustains me, and I am overwhelmingly grateful to my beloved parents: my mother, Joan Manning, an artist who made me a writer; and my father, Jim Manning, who taught me not to quit. Thanks to Richard Dunne and Patricia Dunne, for encouragement and inspired knowledge of the Irish diaspora. To Rob Manning, Jim Manning, Kim Crowther Manning, Wendy Dunne DiChristina, Mike DiChristina, and Robert R. Morris—thanks, thanks, thanks. And thanks to Gertie M. Dunne and Moon E. Dunne, who walked me regularly.

And to my three miraculous children, Carey, Oliver, and Eliza Dunne, and to my adored husband, Carey Dunne, all my love.

About the Author

Kate Manning is the author of *Whitegirl,* a novel (2002). She is an adjunct faculty member of the English Department at Bard High School Early College in Manhattan, where she teaches creative writing. A former documentary producer for public television, she has won two local Emmy Awards. She has written for the *New York Times* and the *Los Angeles Times Book Review,* among others. She lives in New York City with her family.